Slave
for revenge

Ann Owen

DEDICATION

To my father
I miss you so much

CONTENTS

PROLOGUE

London, 7 Courtnell Street, 24th December 1847.

It was Christmas Eve night, and Jane Hartwell couldn't find anything better to do than toss and turn beneath her blankets. Lying face down in bed, she pressed her forehead into the pillow. Oh, dear! Why was she so restless?

But she knew the reason. She knew the reason, all right.

The next day... the damn next day!

She groaned in the darkness of the room. Outside, the wind was beating against the windows, disturbing the silence of the night.

Tomorrow. Tomorrow would be Christmas Day. And for Christmas lunch, there would be no one but herself, her father, Rona and...

Oh, damn. Throwing off the blanket, Jane sat up and set her bare feet on the carpet.

And that odious, odious man. Guy Spencer. Rona's son, also known as 'the Evilest Evil Villain in Villain City'. Oh very well, only Jane called him that, and only in her thoughts. His real, noble title was Earl of Ashbourne. Yes, among his pompous characteristics, he was also a very wealthy peer of England. Jane had known him for eleven years, and she could definitely claim that the title of 'Evilest Evil Villain' suited him much better.

She shivered in the cold room, listening for any noise. Was that noise the ground-floor door shutting?

No, that was impossible. The Evilest Villain wouldn't deign to return home before dawn. Pretty funny, wasn't it? Guy had accepted the Hartwells' invitation for Christmas Eve dinner... just to leave immediately after eating! Some would say he had been inconceivably rude. Mind you, Jane hadn't wanted to spend the evening with him. He was her stepbrother, that was true, but she had stopped looking for his company since she was thirteen. No, she sure didn't want him at home. If she was upset, it was just because the front door hadn't been barred because of him.

1

He had gone out to see a woman, probably. Or to engage in some sordid boxing match. What a way to celebrate Christmas Eve...

Jane bit her lip. She wondered how he behaved toward his mistresses. Could any of them wipe that stupid grin off his face?

Oh, Jane was so annoyed with him. She reached out to touch the candle on the bedside table. The darkness was almost total. In the hearth in front of her, there were the remains of a fire. The embers, with a few heatless sparks, barely illuminated the room. Jane lit the candle with a match. Everything was white and pink around her. Her bedroom was small; it was a garret, actually. It had been repapered with delicate colors a month before, to make it cozier. The ceiling sloped down toward the window, forming an intimate niche. Jane often sat in that niche, among the softness of the cushions she had filled it with. The attic room was tiny, yet Jane wouldn't change it even for a royal palace.

And speaking about royal palaces... oh, damn. Guy Spencer, the 4th Earl of Ashbourne. He lived in a sprawling palace, didn't he?

Yes, he did, of course.

And of course, with this rhetorical question, she was thinking of him again.

Oh for pity's sake!

Because the Evilest Villain hadn't stayed at his great palace in St James's Place for Christmas, damn it. He had joined the Hartwells at Courtnell Street—and just to ruin their Christmas, Jane suspected. This could be the only reason. Certainly, he hadn't missed any of them. Since he had moved to Ashbourne House, he'd never visited them. Not once in two months! This was the way it worked for him. On his twenty-first birthday, about two months ago, he had inherited the fortune of the Spencers. He had been behaving like a scoundrel since then. A week ago, his name had appeared in a gossip newspaper, next to a married woman's name. It seemed there had even been a duel! He was a libertine and a rake. Of course he was. He was the spitting image of his father, the infamous third Earl of Ashbourne whose name, when pronounced, still scared Rona to death.

With a sigh, Jane put on her fur slippers and stood up, courageously abandoning the warmth under the blanket. She took her woolen dressing gown from a chair and hurriedly put it over her nightgown, shivering with cold. Maybe it was the beginning of a fever, she wondered hopefully. A pretext, any kind of pretext, to avoid Guy tomorrow! The evening they'd just passed had been agony. Eating had been impossible for her. Her stepbrother, with a wry smile, had called her "little sister" whenever he had talked to her. He had never stopped looking at her, and she hadn't been able to swallow anything. As a matter of fact, even Rona had seemed agitated... and she was *his mother*, for heaven's sake!

Not surprisingly, they had almost exclusively spoken about food.

"Would you like some more consommé?"

"Would you please pass me some salt?"

Only Jane's father had really tried to talk with Guy. Ah, dearest Papa... he was always willing to see the good in each person. Even in that stepson of his. But Guy, predictably, had fulfilled all the bad expectations everyone had ever had of him since he was a child.

Jane sighed. She walked on the soft carpet that covered the center of the room. She wanted to calm down and sleep. Some warm milk would be helpful. And no, she wasn't going downstairs to see if Guy had come home. She wouldn't even approach the front door. What did she care if the door barrier was in the right place or not?

But again, who knew? Maybe he wouldn't even come back to Courtnell Street. Maybe he regretted the luxury of Ashbourne House. Oh, he was so full of himself. An earl, of course! His Majesty, The Emperor Guy.

If only Jane's father hadn't asked him to sleep at Courtnell Street that night! Jane let an exasperated sigh escape her lips. But her father *had asked* him to stay. It had been because of a family tradition: on Christmas morning, they were used to opening the presents together. This was the first Christmas since Guy had moved away, after all.

"It would be sad without you," Jane's father had told him.

Ha!

As if that scoundrel cared about family traditions.

Jane reached the bedroom door. She opened it slowly to avoid any noise. Just one day, she reminded herself. No, just half a day. Half a day with Guy. With his smiles and his harmless sentences, uttered in a voice that didn't sound at all harmless to her. Why did he always seem to laugh at her when he talked to her? Why did he always seem to tell her more things with his eyes than with his words?

The candle trembled in her grip. She took a breath and stepped out into the dark hallway, walking among the shadows of the ceiling joists. Jane's bedroom was the only one up there. Her father's bedroom was on the first floor, Rona's was near his, and the rooms belonging to the servants—an elderly maid and a cook—were located on the ground floor. Jane had moved to the small attic room in early December, after a long argument with her father and Rona. She didn't regret that choice. She liked the view from up there, she liked the pitched roof and the romantic window seat. Now, though, her heart took a strange beat as she walked into the hallway before the staircase. Everything was so dark... and the wind was making such a heartbreaking wail against the windows. She had been too busy sleeping, during that month, to realize how the attic looked frightening at three in the morning, with its narrow corridor, ceiling beams, and sharp shadows. Jane was tempted to go back to her room, bar the door, and hide under the blankets. She swallowed and called herself silly. She was sixteen, damn it, sixteen and a half years old! Stupid creaks couldn't scare her. If she had still been the frightened little girl of years before, when she climbed up to the attic holding her breath, she would have thought every noise was the howl of a monster; but she was no longer the frightened little child she used to be.

Right?

Squaring her shoulders in a naive challenge, she walked firmly and passed the corner to reach the staircase.

And then she gave a choked cry.

There was a man on the stairs, almost at the top. Jane didn't breathe and didn't move. Her heart was in her throat.

The man on the stairs was bent with his weight resting on the handrail. He raised his head abruptly when he heard her scared voice. He stared at her for a moment, then blinked. "Jane," he murmured, and half a smile came to his lips. He straightened. At twenty-one years old, he was tall and strong, and, to her, he had never looked as tall and strong as he did now, in the darkness of the night.

"G-Guy..." she stammered, feeling suddenly naked in the nightgown which left her ankles exposed. "What... what are you doing here? I mean, you know... Rona has made up the guest room for you. It's... it's downstairs."

He went up a step. "Oh, I... I made a mistake, I guess," he said with a hoarse, thick voice. He wore an open black cloak and an elegant dark suit under it. "Because of the habit, I suppose. After all, you know, my..." He stopped speaking, then smiled as if to himself. "My bedchamber was up here, when I lived here, wasn't it?"

Jane swallowed. Yes. Yes, it was. Until two months ago, the little attic room was Guy's bedroom, at least nominally. He had never stayed in Courtnell Street for long, even before his moving. He had always spent most of the year at the university or traveling abroad with his friends. So, basically, he had never stayed with the Hartwells for more than three weeks a year.

"Now it's mine," she murmured.

"Really?" Guy raised his eyebrows. He had dark hair and dark eyes. His irises had the peculiar trait of shining even in low light. "And what did an angel like you ever do to deserve this? Why have you been exiled up here like a criminal?" He smiled. "Or should I say... why have you been exiled like *me?*"

Jane's heart was recovering from the jolt of a moment ago; but if the surprise was over, the panic was not. Without realizing it, she stepped back, leaning against the corner. She hadn't been speaking tête-à-tête with her stepbrother for a long time: for three years and eight months, to be exact. She remembered perfectly when and why she had started to avoid him like the plague.

Her hands began to sweat. "N-no, I..." she stammered, suppressing the urge to flee. "I moved into your room because, you know... I like the... the view from up there."

"You like the view. What a surprise. I had something you wanted, then." Guy went up another step. "And don't you ever feel alone up here, Jane? Don't you ever wonder if maybe your family is trying to forget your very existence?" His voice was slurred but perfectly understandable. He climbed the last step.

Jane retreated beyond the corner.

"Guy," she murmured, feeling very small next to him. He was more than a head taller than her. Her bladder pushed against her lower abdomen, and that was ridiculous. Come on, was she so scared she got the urge to pee, seriously? "Guy, maybe it's time for you to go to bed."

"I have just rolled out of bed. Well, it wasn't my bed, exactly." He passed the corner and rested his left hand on the wall for support... and in this manner, blocked her way. "And you?" he asked, and Jane smelled a sharp odor of whiskey, and something else... a heavy, sophisticated scent, probably of the mistress he had been with. A too-pungent scent... certainly not a perfume produced by Hartwell's Perfumery, nor of the highest quality.

"What are you doing up at this hour, little sister?" Guy looked to the short, dark hallway under the bare ceiling. "And in this creepy place. Don't you remember what my mother used to tell you when you were a child?" He took another step toward her. *"Don't go up to the attic, Jane, darling,"* he mimicked. *"There are monsters up there."* He stepped forward as she backed away. "You should listen to her, Jane. It's dangerous to go out alone at night."

I am not out alone at night, I am in my home! She held back these silly words. Guy was just joking, and she didn't want to show him how afraid she was. "I couldn't sleep," she whispered. "I thought some warm milk might help."

"And why are you going back, then?" He gestured beside him, stepping aside to make way for her. Just ten inches of space to get by. "Go right ahead, little sister."

But she wasn't his sister, she had never been, and Guy definitely was not her brother. His irises shone strangely, and his strange words frightened her even more. The bedroom was just behind her back, but she couldn't possibly turn and go into it, running away from him for no reason at all. It would be absurd. Embarrassing. Probably, it would even offend him: Guy had always been formally polite to her... well, in recent years, at least.

"Why are you just standing there, little Jane?"

Guy's tone dropped, becoming husky. His narrowed eyes, dulled by alcohol, sparkled with a dangerous light.

"No glass will come to you, if you don't go and get it."

He moved forward. Jane was against the door, and she wanted to open it and race into her room, even though it was childish, even though...

As Guy lifted his hand to her face, finally her instinct prevailed. Jane turned and grabbed the door handle. The candle slipped from her hands and went out.

At that moment, a strong arm gripped her waist.

Get off me! she tried to scream, but a heavy hand came over her lips, shutting her up, and all that she could say was a useless "G—!"

They remained in the dark, with the sound of the wind slamming against the shutters. Guy leaned against her back and, in the cold night, Jane felt his warmth over her, over her robe and nightgown. She tried to scream again, but his big, strong hand made it impossible. It was taking her breath away. She put her hand over Guy's, but she couldn't remove it. Her head spun; the air was too thin. And she was so scared of fainting—no, God no, that couldn't happen, it shouldn't happen!

"Are you thirsty, Jane, little angel?" Guy's words brushed her cheek with his hot, insinuating breath. "Would you like a warm drink?"

Terrified, she felt pulled against his muscled body. He smelled male beneath the scent of whiskey, beneath the perfume of his mistress. It was a dangerous scent, like smoke and sweat. She could feel the heat of his mouth near her ear. God, he was so big, a giant to her, and, with that arm, he could easily...

"My sweet, shy little sister," Guy murmured, and his voice, suddenly chilly, froze her. "As pure as a lily, and... and so God-fearing." He put his left hand between her legs, under her robe.

Jane struggled and tried to stop him. With dismay, she realized he was touching her in her most intimate place. His fingers rubbed on her nightgown's fabric, sliding in the folds of her forbidden lady parts.

"Mmmmm!" She wailed against his palm, bringing a hand to his to stop him. *Don't! Don't!*

Guy chuckled against her ear, moving his fingers between her thighs in a shameful way. "Don't you want me to touch you, Jane, angel?" he asked, cold and hoarse at the same time. "That's too bad... too bad indeed. Because do you know what I think, when I look at you? I think how I'd like to fuck you, little Jane... I'd like to put you on all fours and fuck you like a bitch in heat. Because prudes like you," he pressed behind her, and his groin was hard and threatening against her butt, "are the best in bed. The horniest."

Hit by these words, terrified by what they meant, she wriggled against his palm. Perhaps because he was drunk and off-balance, perhaps because he let her go, finally Jane, with a sharp flick of her body, managed to get free from his grip. She didn't think. She just moved instinctively, only to get away. She opened the door, slammed it behind her, and lowered the little bar lock.

God... God!

She stood behind the door, with her hands against it, as though she could prevent Guy from demolishing it if he wished to. After a moment, she heard a soft knock on the wood. She jumped away as if it were on fire. She stared wide-eyed at the door with one hand on her heart. She felt her bladder aching with terror, the urge to relieve herself was becoming more and more intense.

"Go away, Guy!" she sobbed. "Go away or I'll scream, and I'll wake up the whole house, I swear!"

She heard him laugh on the other side of the door. "Oh, poor little girl..." he said with terrible sweetness. "I've scared you, haven't I? I'm such a bad, bad boy. No, don't you cry, angel... I'm not going to break down this door. I'm leaving now. I just want to tell you one last thing: you better watch out, Jane." His voice turned serious, no longer with any sign of drunkenness. Serious... like a promise. "You better watch out, because the monster around the corner will get you, sooner or later."

1.

Four years later.

Guy Spencer, the 4th Earl of Ashbourne, didn't get immediately out of the carriage. With one boot on the footplate, he looked at the house in front of him. Courtnell Street, Number 7. The three floors of the house were as basic as ever. There were five steps at the entrance, with two white columns on either side. The walls were white too. On the first floor, the windowpanes were hidden behind purple wooden shutters, a little splintered in the corners. Closed shutters covered the attic window as well. The roof, seen from below, looked like a red mouth above a white smile. Guy smiled as if in response, and touched the edge of his top hat in a sort of greeting.

He descended slowly from the carriage. The sidewalk ice didn't allow him any abrupt movement, but it wasn't for that reason that he restrained himself. No, it was for a fierce emotion, which swelled his guts and his chest; a violent, satisfying feeling, pushing against his breastbone, making his breathing faster. He wanted to hide this feeling, because today everything had to be perfect, everything had to be memorable.

The footman closed the carriage door behind him.

"Thank you, George," said Guy, and his breath condensed into little clouds before of him. He turned to the driver. "It'll take an hour or so, Lewin," he informed him. "You and George may wait for me in a warm tavern."

The driver smiled gratefully at him. "Thank you, my lord."

Guy nodded and turned toward the house. He gripped the golden knob of his walking stick and beat it on the sidewalk. He was elegantly dressed, way too much elegant for an afternoon at Courtnell Street, even though it was Christmas Eve. Against the white snow, his figure stood out with violence. He was dressed in black. His suit was black, his overcoat was black. Only the scarf around his neck was white, and the tie underneath that, and his shirt.

The heels of his shiny boots made a resolute noise on the sidewalk as he went toward the staircase. He climbed the stairs without holding the wrought-iron handrail. On the landing, he stopped to contemplate the purple door and its rectangular decorations. He inhaled a breath. The air filled his lungs with sharp frost. He raised his hand toward the door. Two brusque knocks. Then he waited. He didn't mind the bitter cold; he didn't even notice it today.

After a moment, he heard some noise beyond the door.

He smiled, straightening his posture and squaring his broad shoulders. The door opened, and the delicate, timid figure of a blonde girl, wearing a modest gray dress, appeared in the doorway.

"Jane," he murmured with a smile. "It has been a long time, little sister."

2.

On the house's threshold, Jane swallowed. "Guy," she murmured with difficulty. "Thank you for coming."

"Whenever my little sister needs me, I will always be there."

Guy's half-smile underlined the irony of his words. The last time Jane had seen him had been ten months ago, at Rona's funeral. And now that Jane was in front of him, she felt lost. All the words she had prepared for him went out of her head.

Why was Guy supposed to help her?

But he *had* to help her. He had to.

She lifted her gaze to look at him, or at least she tried to. Guy was still a head taller than her, as if his strong will and his iron strength weren't enough to put him in an unfair position of advantage. As always, Jane was nailed by his dark, almost black, irises. She felt weighed up and evaluated, like a fat, well-browned leg of lamb, ready to be eaten. She swallowed hard and, with the courage of despair, smiled and stepped aside.

"Please, come in."

He nodded and followed her into the hall. The window curtains, as well as the ropes around them, were black. The mourning for Rona, in the sudden impoverishment of the Hartwells, stood out sadly in the naked hall. The house was big, suited for respectable members of the bourgeoisie, but there were no carpets on the floor, and only five of fourteen rooms were still in use. Jane herself had opened the door: there were no longer servants at home.

"If you give me your overcoat... and your hat," she murmured.

Guy agreed with a nod. In his right hand, he was holding a black walking stick with a golden knob: he gave it to her and she took it, blushing. It was silly of her to feel humiliated in serving him, especially because she was about to ask for his help. She put his stick in the umbrella stand and opened the wardrobe. It was no longer the shiny mahogany wardrobe, with the mirror on its right side and bright hooks for hats; it had been replaced with a wardrobe of worn light wood.

If Guy happened to notice the change, he didn't mention it. He removed his top hat and Jane placed it on a shelf.

She turned toward him. Guy had unbuttoned his overcoat, but he was still wearing it. Gritting her teeth imperceptibly, she moved behind his shoulders and pulled it off him gently.

"Thank you, Jane." Guy's voice was hoarse and, she was certain of this, amused. "It's embarrassing that I can't take off a coat by myself, isn't it?"

No, that's not the embarrassing part, Guy, and you know it very well. You can take it off by yourself, your beautiful coat. You're simply clarifying the power hierarchy here, "big brother", but I assure you—and bitterness mingled with despair in her thoughts—*that isn't necessary.*

Her heart beat in panic and pain. No, Guy wouldn't help her. Maybe he no longer hated her, not like he used to do when they were children, but he wasn't a soft-hearted man. No, definitely not. Maybe he had forgotten envy and jealousy, and now he felt only indifference toward her; but why on earth would he help her? The 4th Earl of Ashbourne didn't help anyone. And certainly not his detested stepsister.

Jane smiled sadly. Trying wouldn't make things worse. Oh, surely not worse. Clenching her fists to work up the courage, she led him in the living room. It was a bare room, and it had never seemed so miserable to her, not even when they had sold much of the furniture four months ago.

"Sit down, please," she said, pointing to the old sofa that had replaced the large one that he perhaps remembered. "Would you like... may I offer you some tea?"

Guy lifted a corner of his mouth. It was a weird thing, this one of his: his smile didn't soften his features, it made them somehow more dangerous. His face wasn't irregular, except for the nose, broken two years ago in a boxing match, that was slightly crooked in the middle. His lips were soft, and his thick, dark lashes framed his singularly beautiful eyes—long-shaped, seductive eyes. But his forehead, framed with a V-shaped hairline, furrowed mockingly, and the almost black of his irises always seemed to imply something... strange? Threatening? Insinuating... this was the word that came in Jane's mind, a word she didn't even want to acknowledge.

"Some tea... yes, thank you," replied Guy in a low voice. "It's exactly what I'd like, little Jane."

She blushed at the endearment. Well, of course, they had grown up together—as far as you could grow along with a scoundrel like Guy, aggressive during his childhood, sarcastic during his adolescence—but now he stared at her, and she knew that there was no fraternal tenderness in his words. She tried not to think that once, four years ago...

She took a deep breath. He was drunk that night. He didn't know what he was doing. "I'll make it right away," she said with some difficulty. She walked quickly to the kitchen.

Don't run away from him, Jane, for heaven's sake. You need to talk to him. You can't run away like a rabbit.

Running away? Who, she? Jane "Lionheart" Hartwell? Never ever. Well... perhaps a little bit. She sighed and entered the kitchen. The teapot was on the stove. She picked it up by the handle and placed it on the tray. She was trying, not too unconsciously, to postpone the moment she would go back in the living room. She had already prepared two cups, one with a broken handle. Lemon. Milk. She took the cake she had made a few hours ago. She had gone on a spending spree to buy the ingredients: white flour, eggs, red apples. She had considered it necessary—but surely not sufficient—to feed the pride of a man whose clothes cost more than all the remaining furniture of Courtnell Street, Number 7.

She gazed at the porcelain tray. Unhappily. It was so cheap, like the tableware on it. She cast a glance at the centerpiece, the only Christmas decoration in the house: an arrangement of mistletoe and red berries. She reached out to pluck a sprig to decorate the tray, but she stopped herself halfway.

You kiss under the mistletoe.

She blushed at the stupidity of her thought, but let her hand fall anyway. Lifting the tray, she walked to the living room.

Why are you slowing down? Come on, Jane. Grit your teeth, take a breath. And talk to him.

Guy was sitting where she had left him on the shabby sofa. The morning light came through the window and struck him on the right side, emphasizing his muscular figure. He rested his elbow on the sofa arm in a relaxed pose. Yet, to her, he looked like a leopard about to jump. Perhaps because of his dark, formal clothes, or perhaps because he was so big, on that sofa. He occupied half of it. He had always been strong, now more than ever. Like many aristocrats, Guy liked boxing, but unlike the other aristocrats, boxing wasn't just a pastime for him. He had been favored by nature with above-average height and a strong constitution, and had sculpted his body as a piece of art. Without an ounce of fat, his bulging biceps pushed under his tailored suit, his massive chest filled the jacket, and, under the dark trousers, his legs were long and muscular. His weight was, in a rough guess, more than fourteen stone. If he had worn torn trousers and a work shirt, he would have looked in every way like the longshoremen who unloaded crates at the London Docks. Even for his behavior, Jane suspected: the name of the 4th Earl of Ashbourne often appeared in gossip newspapers, both for his scandalous love life and for the disreputable boxing matches he joined in the slums.

Approaching him, Jane was surprised yet again by how different he was from Rona, the fragile woman who had acted as a mother to her too, for fifteen years.

"You made my favorite cake, little sister."

Jane forced a smile, putting down the tray on the little table in front of the sofa. She was far too aware of his eyes that were following her as she bent down. She wore a dress too light for the harsh winter and, now, she regretted wearing it. It was one of her few dresses still presentable, but she would give anything to have chosen the everyday one, with a simpler cut, made of black wool that fell baggy—and much more reassuring!—on her body.

You're as pure as a lily, little sister...

She shook her head to banish the memory of the words that Guy had whispered to her four years ago.

...and those like you are the best in bed.

Oh, for heaven's sake! Nothing had happened that night, had it? He had seized her, yes, but she had wriggled free and run away. And it hadn't been Guy's fault, anyway. He had simply drunk too much. Probably, he didn't even remember that he had assaulted her. Jane had said nothing to no one, least of all to him; she had just started to avoid him even more, after that unfortunate Christmas.

Chewing nervously the inside of her cheek, she put the cup of tea in front of him. Guy didn't offer to help her, but that, of course, was predictable.

"You still blush," Guy said.

"B... beg your pardon?"

"When you talk with someone. With a man." He smiled. "With me."

Jane opened her mouth to say something, then closed it. She didn't know how to answer, and she felt awfully uncomfortable. Everything was always so difficult with Guy. His gaze made her shake as though she were on hot coals. *Some men, my darling,* Rona had once told her, *wear lambskins over a wolf's heart.*

That, at least, was not Guy's case. He was like a wolf, yes, but he had never pretended to be otherwise.

"My mother," said Guy, like he was reading her mind, "must have scared you with her stories about how wicked men are, mustn't she?"

At this, saliva choked her, and she started to cough. It took her a few moments to regain her composure.

Guy laughed, amused by her efforts to control embarrassment. "All right, all right," he said as she cleared her throat and managed to get back her color, "resume breathing, angel, I'll change the subject." He nodded toward the door. "Isn't your father joining us?" he asked taking the milk jug and pouring it in his tea.

"No, he is... is at the factory."

13

"Oh." Without waiting for Jane to serve herself, Guy lifted the cup to his lips, taking a sip. "What a pity."

Jane hesitated, then decided to speak plainly. "It's not a coincidence, Guy, I... I need to talk to you alone."

She handed him a plate with a slice of cake and sat down next to him, at the distance the length of the sofa allowed her.

"I guessed so." Guy broke a piece of cake with his hand and put it in his mouth, chewing it slowly. "Exquisite," he murmured after a moment. "You truly are a lily, Jane."

And those like you are the best in bed, aren't they?

"So, angel."

She blushed. She met his black eyes and her heart began to pound hard in her chest. She looked away.

"Your father's situation, I understand, is a little... difficult." Guy took another piece of cake with his hands, ignoring the little metal fork beside the plate. "Your accountant, Stokes, sent me a disturbing dossier." He put the cake in his mouth and savored it slowly. He licked his thumb, then took the towel beside his plate. He wiped his fingers with maddening meticulousness and then, opening his jacket, pulled out some typed papers.

Jane took a deep breath. Why did Guy seem to have fun as he studied the alarming documents about the Hartwells?

"This house, practically, doesn't belong to your father anymore." He glanced her sideways, not raising his face from the papers.

Trying to hide her dismay at his tone so openly pleased, Jane cleared her throat. "Mr. Green said we can stay here until the situation improves."

"Oh, but the situation will *not* improve." Guy ran his finger over a sheet, checking the accounts payable. "Your father signed promissory notes for a sum exceeding, let me see... heck, whenever I think about it, it seems bigger. Three thousand five hundred pounds. He owes this money to a certain Mr. Owen. One of the notes will mature next Monday, so if this Owen wanted," he leaned back on the sofa, relaxed, "he could have your father arrested."

I know. Of course I know. "I... I tried to contact Mr. Owen. But he didn't respond to my letters or visits. He's an elusive man: he seems to conduct his business through intermediaries. Now he is out of town, and I... Guy, my father..." She closed her eyes, and despair overtook her. "Everything went wrong, everything! If the cargo hadn't been lost, we would have made it. We would have paid our debts on time."

But their cargo had been shipwrecked in a storm three days ago.

And Jane's hopes had been shipwrecked too.

"You're making it sound like a matter of bad luck," said Guy with a sarcastic smile, "but as far as I know your problems didn't start today. Your father's mismanagement of his business has resulted in steadily growing losses. It was inevitable to get to this point." Guy put the documents on the table, tilting his head an inch to the side. "I guess Mr. Hartwell doesn't know yet that he has lost everything."

Guy was intuitive. Maybe cruel, maybe insensitive... but he had always been able to understand things quickly.

"I can't tell him," Jane whispered. "I told him about some delay of the cargo, because..." She put her cup on the saucer, making it turn slowly. "Because after what happened..." She hesitated. *After your mother's death.* But how much would these words hurt Guy? To her, Rona's death was still an open wound. "After the tragedy," she murmured at last, "nothing is left for him but the Perfume Shop. If he knew that it is failing..."

"If he knew, he might kill himself. Am I right?"

Jane winced. Hearing Guy say these words was terrible, especially with such careless levity. "He has nothing else left," she said with a shaking voice. "Only his business, only the workers he pays every week. If he loses that too, only guilt will be left for him. He already doesn't care about his health. After the... the accident..." she paused, then went on with an effort. "After the accident, his right leg got damaged, but he refuses to follow any therapy for his limp. Guy, it almost seems..." She swallowed, and her shoulders drooped with pain. "It almost seems he regrets not dying that night."

"So, you're asking me for help, aren't you? Help from *me,* no less. Your evil stepbrother."

Jane bit her lip. Yes, she was asking for his help. She had waited as much as possible, until Mr. Stokes had plainly explained to her the desperate situation of her father's business. Mr. Stokes had *strongly* advised her to find a solution as soon as possible. Of course, what he had really meant was: "Go ask your rich stepbrother for money."

So, she had had to give up her pride. Whom else did she know rich enough to help her father? Though nothing bonded Guy to the Hartwells after Rona's death, he was their only hope. Because if Jane's father went to debtors' prison... her father, for whom every sunrise looked like a punishment...

"But there's one thing I don't understand, little Jane. I've always been a bit thick-headed, you know." Guy smiled wryly. He put his thumb and forefinger to his forehead, near his dark hairline, and rubbed his skin lightly. "The fact is, it escapes me why I should help you, precisely. In memory of my mother, perhaps? In memory of the love she always gave *you?*"

The love she always gave you. These words struck Jane like a whip.

She didn't answer.

"I'm sure you understand," Guy continued with a distant voice. "We are not talking about a few hundred pounds. Should I give lots of money to a family that, after all, has no longer any link with me?"

"Just... it would just be a loan, Guy. And... and five hundred pounds would be enough, you know... to pay Mr. Owen next Monday."

"What would you solve with five hundred pounds? You'll have to pay the same amount next month. And the month after that, and so on."

"But Mr. Stokes... he told me you offered to help my father, some time ago."

"That's right. It was two years ago." Guy brought his shoulders back, giving a smile that didn't touch his eyes. "Some of your father's creditors came to me and I offered to refund them. But your father said *no*. Or rather, to be crystal clear, it wasn't your father who refused my money. It was *my mother*. She wrote ordering me neither to pay off Mr. Hartwell's debts nor to interfere in his financial situation. Did Mr. Stokes tell you that?" He crossed his legs with a calm, measured movement. "My mother didn't want to have anything to do with me and my money. Probably it was she who suggested to your father to turn to the moneylenders. This," he picked up the papers from the table, "is the result. So, Jane, I'm asking you again. Why on earth should I help you? Not in loving memory of Rona Spencer, Lady Ashbourne... I mean, Rona Hartwell. As a matter of fact, if I had to respect her wishes, I shouldn't give you a penny."

"Do it for my father, Guy." Jane clutched her hands together to make them stop trembling. "He's... he's a good man."

Guy laughed. "*A good man*... God, Jane, I've seen you grow and blossom... but you are like a child when it comes to dealing with reality." He ran his thumb over the corner of his mouth, curved in a mocking smile. "Come on, don't make that mortified face. I'll give you that, you are right in this. Mr. Hartwell is a dear, kind man. He even cared about me when I was a little boy. He actually tried to be my friend." With the little fork, he broke a piece of cake, but he didn't eat it. He merely played with it on his plate. "Sometimes he drove me mad. One day, he took me hunting with him. He had half a mind to have a little chat with me, a father-son kind of chat. He wanted to create a special bond between us, something like, you know, 'Even though I'm not your real father, I'll always be there for you' or nonsense like that. He annoyed me so much that, instead of shooting the quail he pointed, I took a shot at him. From that day on, he didn't try anything like that again." With the fork, he broke the piece of cake, then looked up at Jane. "No," he raised his hands in amusement, "please don't look at me with those distraught eyes, my little Jane. I didn't hit him, unfortunately. I didn't have a good aim, at that time."

"Why?"

"Why what?"

"Why did you shoot him?"

Guy stared at her for a moment. His face became serious for the first time since his arrival. "Because I'm my father's son," he answered finally.

He lifted his hand toward her, touching her cheek. Jane jerked and pulled back.

"You wouldn't have heard much of the third Earl of Ashbourne," continued Guy, letting his hand drop. "I should have hardly any memories of him, for he died when I was eight. Yet I remember everything. I remember the bruises on my mother's face. The way she wept desperately when she lived at Ashbourne House with my father."

Street noises came from outside. Something fell with a crash, perhaps a fruit box from a wagon. A driver stopped his horse with an angry voice.

Guy seemed to notice none of this. He went on with a serious, emotionless face. "After my father's death, my mother tried to erase his memory from her mind. She refused to stay at Ashbourne House and moved to Axbridge with her parents. She didn't bring any portraits or miniatures with her; she wanted to forget everything about the third Earl of Ashbourne. She could never forget his face though, for I was his spitting image. She never forgave me for that."

Jane put her hand on her neck, feeling uncomfortable. "Please don't say that, Guy. You know that's not true." As the words came from her lips, she felt like a hypocrite. And she felt guilty toward her stepbrother. That was strange, since he, for her, was still the one and only holder of the less-than-flattering title of 'the Evilest Evil Villain."

"Oh, come on, angel." Guy laughed, shaking his head in disbelief. "My mother would have much preferred to never see me again after my father's death. Unfortunately, my father's last will imposed me on her, so she had to take me living with her when she left Ashbourne House." He made a faint smile. "No, that's unfair. I think she would have taken me with her anyway, even if her income hadn't depended on it. My legal guardian was a man of very ill repute, and my mother's heart was in the right place. But she shuddered every time she looked at me, and her disgust has been perfectly justified over the years, hasn't it? My scandals. My mistresses. Oh, but you're blushing again," he sneered, resting his hand on his cheek and looking sideways at her. "I guess I shouldn't talk to you like that. After all, you have always been so... *innocent*. My mother loved that about you." He appraised her with half-closed eyes. "You were a comfort to her, probably more than your father. You could be spiteful at times... but she was blind to your faults, wasn't she, little Jane?" Guy took a sip of tea. His eyes moved to the table and he smiled strangely. It was a thoughtful, remote smile. "One day... God, I remember it like it was yesterday. One day you took all my school notebooks and threw them into the fire. You didn't save one, little witch. Months of schoolwork to ashes."

"Guy, I..."

"You were mad at me for I don't know what reason," he continued. "Perhaps I had broken a doll of yours or perhaps I had told you to go to hell, because you really were annoying when you followed me all over the house. Anyway, at some point you started calling my name desperately. I thought that maybe someone was cutting your throat and I ran to your room, and you..." Guy chuckled, almost impressed. "You were standing near the fireplace, with all my notebooks in your hands. You were holding them above the fire, and, when I got to the door, you let them fall. I don't know why you looked so calm while you were doing it. Maybe you were planning to run away while I was busy plucking the notebooks out of the flames. But you were wrong, I didn't give a damn about my notebooks. I much preferred to teach you a lesson you wouldn't forget. So I jumped on you. I threw you to the ground, but you were a small, weak thing, and I'd always found it boring to beat up the weak. So I merely gripped your wrists and shouted at you. I just wanted to scare you, I wanted you to wet yourself with fear and soil your flowery dress—you know, that stupid pink dress you had, which made you look like a lace doll. But at that moment, my mother entered the room." Guy looked up and stared at her with narrowed eyes. "And guess what happened next, Jane?"

"Guy, I was just a child!" she protested, wounded by his unfair words, "and you always rejected me, and you broke all my..."

"She sent me back to boarding school." Guy smiled with a hard look in his eyes. "I had to spend a long, lonely summer at the boarding school. All my schoolmates were at home for the holidays, and I don't think you can imagine how hot, and empty, a school can be in the summertime."

Jane took a breath. "That's why you're here, then." The despair in her throat almost prevented her from speaking. "You're saying that you won't help us, because once I burned your notebooks."

"No, not exactly. I am here today to tell you why I think I shouldn't help you, but also to ask *you* why *you* think I should do it."

The angry voices from outside had gone. Behind the closed window, the clapping of the horses' hooves came muffled, along with a few words, loud enough to be heard through the thick glass.

"So, angel?"

The winter-morning light, with its snowy glow, emphasized Guy's dark, imposing figure. His black eyes shone with quizzical amusement.

Why should he help them?

"I know that nothing forces you," Jane murmured, looking down. "We are not even blood relatives."

"No, we are not." He picked up the papers from the table. "But we grew up together, didn't we, Jane? It's a bond we cannot ignore. Maybe it isn't affection, no," he coldly smiled, "we sure can't call it affection. But I may decide to pay off your father's debts, after all."

Jane raised her head. "Will you do this?"

"I said I might."

"Guy, please, don't play with me. If you want to say no, say it clearly."

He lifted the left corner of his mouth. "Do you remember that summer I was talking about? When my mother sent me back to boarding school?"

"Guy..."

"Just answer, will you?"

She gritted her teeth. "Yes. Yes, I do remember."

"It was kind of an unpleasant business, do you remember it, Jane? You cried your eyes out for days. You couldn't understand why my mother was punishing me so severely, and I couldn't, either. But I figured it out a few years later. See, the fact is that she saw me lying on you, Jane. And guess what she thought."

He looked at her in silence, waiting for an answer. But Jane wouldn't answer. She didn't want to know what Guy was implying.

"She thought that I was going to rape you, Jane," he said. "She thought that I was going to rape an *eight-year-old* girl."

Jane shook her head in nauseated denial. "What are you saying, Guy? Are you crazy?"

"She screamed hysterically, perhaps you don't remember it, but she completely lost her self-control. She wouldn't listen to any reason. She didn't even listen to *you,* when you told her it had been your fault. You told her you had started the quarrel, you told her about my burned notebooks. And she ignored you. She had *never* ignored your tears before. Rona had always listened to you, she had always realized your every wish, but not that time. That time she sent me away. Simple as that. And when I came back at Christmas, the crappy attic room had become *my* bedchamber. Have you ever wondered why I was sent away for so little, Jane? Have you ever wondered why my mother, from that day on, kept me away from you?"

Jane tried to swallow. It was like swallowing sand. "Guy, you can't truly believe this!"

"I believe this all right."

"You weren't even thirteen... you would never have done something like that!"

Guy's laugh was tired. "No, of course I wouldn't have. But you see, my mother realized something." He lengthened his arm on the back of the sofa, with his fingers an inch from her face. "The fact is, Jane, that someone like you is an ongoing challenge for someone like me. My mother had to send me away, don't you see that? She realized that I would have tried to ruin you, if I had had the chance." His fingers reached out to touch her cheek, very lightly on her skin. "And you know what? I have the chance, now."

Jane jumped up and stepped away. "Guy, what... what are you saying?"

He got up slowly. "How much I used to hate you, Jane. I hated everything about you. I hated it when you ran to your father as he returned from a trip. When you sang with my mother with the happiest look on your face... when I heard them talking about your sweetness, your beauty, your revolting compassion toward the orphaned and the sick."

He took a step toward her. He was absolutely serious, his face no longer holding the sardonic, relaxed expression of a few minutes ago. His narrowed eyes shone fiercely.

"Please, Guy, stop it! You're scaring me!"

"I want you to be scared, Jane. More than this."

Terror, pure terror, exploded inside her, blurring her vision. This was no joke. Guy was there for one reason, and for one reason only.

Somewhere, in her heart, she had always known it.

He took another step, and she backed away. She hit the wall behind her, a few feet from the fireplace. On the mantelpiece, there were small miniature paintings of the Hartwells: Charles, Jane, Rona; and Guy Spencer, too, the 4th Earl of Ashbourne. When Rona was alive, Guy's painting was kept hidden behind the other frames: but now it was close to the other ones... like a family member.

"Do you want my money, Jane?"

With wide eyes, she watched him approach until his body was a few inches from hers. Guy leaned down to whisper in her ear. His breath was warm, his voice soft.

"So, what's your answer, angel?"

He kissed her lobe, and Jane, with a sob, bowed her head and asked the question she feared most.

"What are you asking me, Guy? What do you want from me?"

He put both his hands on the wall, imprisoning her, and, bending his arms, leaned his body into hers. "You know what I want," he murmured with a sort of sorry tenderness. "Don't you, little one?"

3.

Jane was trembling. Powerless, she leaned against the wall. Putting his hands on her hips, Guy kissed her right cheek, which was wet with tears. Her flavor... God, how he had waited for it. Dreamed of it... been obsessed by it. Now it was under his mouth, under his tongue—she was soft and sweet, and smelled of candy and hawthorn. For a moment, her scent overwhelmed him, taking away his words. His cock pressed against his trousers. He should have been ashamed of himself, but God forgive him, shame was the least of his emotions now.

"Why are you crying, Jane, angel?" he murmured against her skin. "You should be happy. You can save your father... that's what you wanted, isn't it?"

He put his hand to her face, on her left cheek, and lifted her head. She was... dazzling, yes, this was the word. Her cheeks were as pink as those of a baby girl, and her eyes were of such unusual color. A color that had haunted him over the years, hazelnut brown mixed with gold, full of sparks. The light in her eyes... drew him inexorably, as the flame draws the moth. Lying naked on a bed, her light had to be blinding.

"I'll take care of your father, little one..." he said. "If you'll take care of *me.*"

He stroked her mouth with his thumb. Her lips were full, their color like dawn when it fills the sky.

Jane's eyes were wide with panic, totally shocked. "We grew up together, Guy... my God, how can you? You are... a horrible man, a..." Her mouth twisted into a pained grimace, devouring the last epithet. "Villain," perhaps, or "monster," the words that she used to call him most often in her childhood. Now she was twenty, almost a spinster by society's parameters... but, to him, she didn't seem very different from then.

"Oh, come now," he said in a low and ironic voice. "Don't tell me you didn't expect it. Don't play naive with me, Jane... I'm not my mother."

A very blonde curl had escaped from Jane's simple bun. It had fallen on her face, and Guy moved it behind her ear. Jane bit her lip, barely breathing, as he touched the shell of her ear. Seeing her white teeth against her pink lips almost made him groan with desire.

"Why are you looking at me with such scared eyes?" he asked quietly.

21

"You should be thanking me, you know. I mean, my offer is very generous. I usually pay my whores a few pennies, but you..." he smiled, caressing the silk of her cheeks, "you will cost me much more. A promissory note every month, for six months. That's what you want, isn't it? You can have it, Jane. You can have the note expiring next Monday as well, of course." His voice grew husky as her scent filled his chest. "Under one condition, angel. You will have to do everything I tell you, with total dedication... and total submission."

Her eyes were like great, wonderful wells of innocence. They filled with terror at his clear, unambiguous words.

That's right, little one, Guy thought with a sort of bittersweet emotion. *You got it right.*

He didn't want just sex from Jane. Oh, no. He could have sex anywhere. Sinking his penis between warm female thighs was something he could get on any street corner. From Jane, he wanted so much more. He wanted to control her in every aspect of her life, he wanted to have her completely under his power.

He wanted her to be his slave.

He bent down to kiss her neck. Wild excitement kept him from listening to other, contradictory feelings inside him. For someone like Guy, blackmailing a young woman into sex was absurd, even unthinkable. He was a member of the Gang of Knives, for God's sake. If the other members of the K-Gang knew what he was doing to Jane, they would call him a pig, a hypocritical son of a bitch... they would beat him with kicks and punches... perhaps they would also give him a couple of stabs below his waist.

But here, the matter was entirely different.

Jane had to refund his entire life, by God.

"So..." he muttered in an unsteady voice, "what's your answer, angel?"

He savored her neck, as white as alabaster. Jane stood motionless, swallowing desperately against his tongue.

"You... you don't even like me, do you?" she whispered, and her words vibrated against Guy's lips. "You can have all the women you want, but you want me just... just for revenge, for... for the love your mother gave me."

"Revenge?" Guy stood up and, putting his hand over his heart, raised his lips in a cynical smile. "You're wrong, little one. Mine is an act of pure kindness. If it were revenge, I'd just watch while your father gets arrested and you get thrown into the street." He leaned forward, bringing his mouth to her ear once more. "By the way, what do you think you could do for a living, at that point? Your only option would be to become a whore, my angel. A common, cheap whore. And I'd come in your brothel, and I'd screw you for the price of a loaf of bread. So you see, I'm only going to lose out on this deal. But I have a good heart, so..." he managed not to smile as he said that, "so I have chosen to do you this favor. Tell me now, then... what's your answer, angel?"

The fire crackled in the fireplace with less force. It was about to go out with dark smoke, since no one was stoking it, and its wood was low-cost and damp. The light from the window bathed Jane and Guy with the glory that only a snowy morning has, and the noises from outside were sporadic. The cold weather was keeping people home.

The clock next to the fireplace was ticking the seconds passing without Jane's response.

Guy puffed out his chest with impatience. God, how much time would it take, having her damn, inevitable answer? He was about to burst with arousal.

"Well, I'll take it as a no," he finally said with feigned indifference, stepping back a step. "So that's it. But you know, I didn't think you were so selfish, little Jane... letting your poor father down in this way."

He turned, with the flies of his trousers embarrassingly swollen. Oh, very well. Some parts of his body weren't really able to pretend indifference, were they?

"Guy."

He smiled, letting the air out slowly through his closed teeth. Oh, Jane, Jane... He turned toward her. "Tell me, angel."

"All right," she murmured without looking at him. Her face was emotionless, almost as if she weren't there.

But you are here, little one. And I'll make you sense all the shame and all the humiliation I'll be able to inflict on you.

"All right what?" he asked, coming back.

"All right, I accept your... your conditions."

Guy stopped in front of her. "Are you serious?" He lifted his hand to her wet cheek, and Jane shuddered. Her disgust made him meaner, and aroused him at the same time. His cock was having the most powerful, painful erection of his life. "You don't even know what you're talking about." He took her chin between his fingers, forcing her to look at him. "Do you understand what I want from you? I'll be your master, Jane. You'll have to do everything you're told, without any objections. What I tell you, when I tell you. Are you sure you can do it?"

"I... I..." she stammered. Oh, she was there, she was there all right.

He weighed her up with cynicism, then let go of her chin, pretending to be bored. *"I... I,"* he mimicked. "What should I do with this babbling, precisely? Let me speak clearly, Jane. Do you think I give a damn about your father? Or about you? If I am willing to pay so much for you, it is to see you jumping at my every order, as obedient and submissive as a slave."

Jane winced, and shock blanched her cheeks. Guy was afraid to see her fall to the ground, but he remained apart from her, staring at her cruelly.

"Well, little one, I'm asking you again. Are you sure you can be my slave?"

"The fact is... I... I never..." Jane shook terribly and bowed her head. "I don't know if I... I will be capable of..." She bit her lower lip, sucking it between her teeth in distress. She couldn't finish.

"If you'll be capable of pleasing me?" Placing his hands on her hips, he pulled her against his erection. Jane's body was soft and graceful; five feet and a half of pure delight. Her breasts were as soft as rosebuds and she had the sweet, fresh scent of spring. "Don't worry, I'll explain everything to you. I'll be a patient teacher... and you'll be my willing pupil, won't you?"

She didn't answer, overwhelmed by panic. Her body was burning in his hands, like a hot ember.

Ah, little Jane... I got you at last. I promised you, remember?

"Won't you, Jane?" he repeated.

She put her hands on his shoulders, to support herself, and bowed her head. She nodded. Yes, Guy seemed to hear her say. Her trembling answer wasn't acceptable. And she should have answered immediately. But Jane was facing a... hard time, undeniably, and Guy decided to turn a blind eye to her mistake. It was honorable of him, wasn't it? Especially because it was dictated by Guy's rush to get to the next step with her. His cock pressed against her body. Jane probably knew the meaning of his erection—she was a volunteer nurse at the hospital, after all. The functioning of the human body was supposed to be well-known by her, at least in theory.

Guy brought his hand to her blonde, shiny hair, caressing it. "All right, angel." He moved a step back and she withdrew her hands, raising her head in alarm. "But you have to prove to me that you're actually willing to please me in every way," he said, and his body became tense with anticipation. "I want you to kneel in front of me, Jane. Right here. Right now."

She opened her mouth in mute dismay. In the hearth, the fire crackled with its last signs of life; everything else in the bare living room was silent.

"Kneel, Jane," repeated Guy. "Kneel down at my feet, and thank me for the help I'm giving you."

"Are... are you serious?"

"I'm dead serious. Do it, Jane. Show me your gratitude... and your submission."

Her eyes filled with anxiety. "Guy, please... my father will return in minutes!"

"Then you'd better do it now."

As if it had been invoked, the clock struck eleven in the morning. Jane turned toward it frantically. Her eyes were wide open in alarm. Guy admired her delicate profile, her body wrapped with a dress of the past season. No mercy peeked out from his excitement. His, she was *his;* a spasm of wild desire flooded his testicles as he studied every detail of her, like the avaricious enjoys the sight of his treasure. Yes, her body belonged to him. All her breaths, actions, words, belonged to him. Jane looked back at him in silent prayer.

In vain. "Do you want me to go away?" Guy asked coldly.

Jane swallowed, shaking her head. She closed her eyes, poor little girl, and stood still in the middle of the room. But then, finally, her knees started to bend. Guy held his breath, shamelessly happy, aroused... and victorious. He watched her lower herself until her knees touched the floor. And she was there, kneeling at his feet, with her back straight, her arms at the sides, her very blonde head at the height of his swollen groin.

It was happening. The fantasy that had been filling his every day and night was about to come true. The sight of this young woman—whom he hated so much, since forever—this woman at his feet, was likely to make him come in his trousers if he didn't control himself.

So perfect.

So fair.

It had to go that very way. He took a deep breath. Calm. He needed to stay calm. Because revenge is something that demands perfection. And what was going to happen would be perfect.

"Good girl," he murmured gruffly. "Now thank me, Jane. I want you to thank me."

Jane kept her eyes lowered. "Th... thank you, Guy."

"You're welcome, angel." He caressed her face with his fingertips, then put them in front of her mouth. "But I also want you to kiss my hand."

Maybe these words didn't reach her immediately, because she remained motionless. Guy had expected a protest, but Jane made none, too scared by her father's return. After a few moments, without looking at him, she brought her lips to his hand and kissed his knuckles. She was sweet and gentle, just as he had imagined. Excitement shook his voice, as he ordered her: "Look at me while you do it."

And this was a dangerous request... dangerous for *him*. He shouldn't look at her, especially not her lips, because he was as horny as a teenager.

Jane looked up. Her eyes were stunned; she wasn't crying, overwhelmed by the inconceivable situation she was in. She put her mouth on his knuckles, and Guy admired the difference between his olive skin and her pink lips. The warmth of her mouth. And the whiteness of her face...

He placed his other hand on her silky hair. "Good girl," he murmured, caressing it. He brought his thumb to her lips. They were soft and full. He pushed his thumb between them, separating them. Jane's eyes widened in terror. She didn't know what he had in mind... and how could she, that little girl?

Somewhere in his mind, a voice yelled, *Stop, Guy. Don't do it.* But his cock stood erect, his breathing was fast and hard. Stop? And why, pray tell? He wasn't stealing anything. Jane was selling herself, and he was buying her, simple as that.

He moved his palm over her mouth. "Lick me," he said, and his longing prevented him from speaking in a firm voice.

"Guy...?"

"Shhh." He stroked her head. "Just do it, angel. Lick my hand like... like an affectionate puppy, Jane, show me how much you want me to help your father. You... want me to help him, don't you?"

Jane took some deep breaths. Her exhalations caressed Guy's palm, open in front of her face. After a few moments, she stuck out her tongue. With its tip, she touched the lines of Guy's palm, tickling him delicately.

"Good girl... but don't be shy, do it with your whole tongue. I... I want to feel it well... yes... oh, yes, like this..."

Jane's eyes were wide open, but they didn't meet Guy's. Her gaze was fixed and almost blind, and Guy stared at her mesmerized. This was true prostration, so different from the kind some of his mistresses liked to play at.

But this was not a game.

And for the first time in his life, he was about to use a woman who didn't want him. Yet—she wasn't just any woman. She was *Jane Hartwell,* and may God strike him dead if he would stop now. It wasn't remorse that prevented him from breathing, but a powerful, intense triumph. Jane was moving her tongue up and down his hand, wetting it with her saliva, and Guy wondered if it was possible to ejaculate without even touching himself. He hoped not, because his penis quivered in his pants, blowing the fly in an exaggerated way. A more experienced woman than Jane would have been worried at seeing such a powerful demonstration of his desire. But the innocent girl at his feet, well... she sure was about to be *surprised.*

"Oh... yes, like... like this," he murmured, "it's awesome, little one..."

He closed his eyes, panting, enjoying her sweetness. He felt the dampness of her saliva and, under his fingers, the wet of the tears that had begun to fall from her eyes silently, almost unconsciously.

"My fingers now," he muttered with difficulty, opening his eyelids. "Lick my fingers." He brought them in front of her mouth. "From base to tip... bring out your little tongue, Jane, and lick them well... here, like this... good girl..."

She didn't protest. Her nose was red, the expression in her eyes shaken, her face feverish. From her open mouth, she stuck her tongue and licked first one of his fingers, then another.

"For their whole length, move... move your head, angel..."

She obeyed, following the length of his forefinger, from its base to its tip. He raised her face pulling her bun back, to make her look up at him. He wanted eye contact from her. She, taken aback, remained with her tongue out, too humiliated to think.

"You like licking me, don't you, Jane?"

She blinked, then understanding filled her eyes. "Please, Guy, my father is coming back. Please..." She swallowed desperately. "Please, let me get up!"

"Say it, angel. Say you like licking me. I want to hear it."

"I... I like it," she sobbed, twisting her mouth.

Guy smiled. "I know you do. Go on, then." Stretching his index and middle fingers out, Guy slid them between her lips. The cavity of her mouth was hot, delightfully hot and humid, and the moment was coming. Guy wondered if he would climax as soon as he put his hands to his breeches. God, he hoped not. He didn't want to come on her face. No—not on her face.

He started to push his fingers between her lips, back and forth.

"Suck my fingers, let me... let me see how much you like it..."

His erection stood between them, hiding her partially from his view. Gripping her hair, he pulled her face back and guided her into the movement, giving her the right rhythm. Her lips tightened timidly on his fingers. She was too humiliated, too shocked to realize what she was doing. She moved her head meekly, and her breathing was irregular, convulsive against his hand.

"Yes... suck them... with your lips and tongue, not your teeth," he smiled with a cruel enjoyment, "never your teeth, remember."

He held her head firmly by the hair. He didn't want her to shrink away... but God, he couldn't wait a minute longer. It wasn't the most delicate way to make her meet his penis, but she should familiarize herself with it quickly, and what better way to break the ice? He withdrew his hand from her mouth and brought it to the fly of his trousers.

"Now I'll give you something else to suck..." he murmured, suffocated, "something you will love."

He undid the two rows of buttons that fastened his trousers and lowered them along with his breeches. His aggressive cock stood in front of her face, aching and throbbing with a massive erection.

Jane put her hand on her mouth, stepping back with her knees. "No..." she closed her eyes not to see it, to deny it, to run away from it, "Guy... God, no! Please!"

"No?"

He pulled her toward his cock, crushing her face on his balls. Jane put her hands on his legs, resisting.

"No! No!" she sobbed.

Guy rubbed her face on his dick and balls. He felt the pulses that were bringing him near to orgasm and closed his eyes, breathing deeply to regain control. It was kind of hard with her face on his scrotum, her warmth, her skin... God!

"You're my slave," he gasped, "is that clear? You must do everything I tell you, *everything*, or our deal is off. And I want you to lick my cock *right now*. Pull out your tongue as I have taught you and lick it, Jane. Lick it all over."

Pressed against his groin, Jane moaned desperately. Guy pushed her head back, allowing her to breathe.

"Lick it, Jane... please me with your velvet tongue, and I'll pay that note off tomorrow." Guy pulled her toward his cock without banging her face on it, leaving an inch or less between her and his rod. He wanted her to submit voluntarily to him. From the window, the light came violent and bright, hitting Jane and the big, hard, erect cock in front of her. It looked like a living, pulsating shaft, red with excitement and craving for her wonderful mouth.

"If you don't do it..." threatened Guy, with a ragged breath, "your father will go to prison... to prison, understand...?"

"God..." she sobbed. "God."

Yes, God. She shuddered, twisted her mouth; but the invocation made the miracle. After a moment, she stuck out her tongue. And she... oh, *God*.

"Oh yes, *yes*..."

Jane... Jane was *really*...

"Yes, like that, angel, just like... oh, *yes*..."

Guy felt risky dizziness as she touched him, as she moved her tongue up and down on his cock. He was enraptured, fascinated by this scene. What was happening was unbelievable, crazy... shocking. Her tongue was on his penis, and Jane—the pure, innocent Jane—was moving it all over.

"Jane... open... open your eyes, I want you... to enjoy the view..."

And it was a great view, no doubt about it. His cock was fully engorged, swollen with veins and excitement, the corona of his glans red and pulsing. Jane's small tongue went on and on, naïve and sweet, wetting it all around.

"Do you like it, angel?..." He pulled her head back. Her eyes were full of tears. "Do you like the taste of my cock?"

"Guy, please... oh, please, let me stop...!"

He smiled, using his erect dick to caress her face. He did it gently, first caressing her left cheek, then the right one, his penis's damp knob already dripping a few drops of pre-come. He would have wanted to force her to answer "yes" to his question, but he knew he didn't have the time. He couldn't wait any longer, he really couldn't. He directed the head of his penis between her lips. Her eyes widened, but she made no resistance. She let him in.

"No teeth..." he reminded her hoarsely, "it's... it's the only rule..."

He smiled and drove her head a little forward, making her swallow his big glans, then pulled her back.

"Oh, yes... yes, suck it... taste it well..."

He was shamefully taking advantage of her, but remorse was a distant voice, buried in a double-locked room of his mind. Inside him, there was only space for one emotion: exaltation. He wanted to enjoy everything of this triumphant moment: Jane kneeling at his feet with a mouthful of his cock, her bright bun of light blonde hair, her face reddened by tears.

"You're so pure..." he murmured while her lips were moving, humid and hot, on his penis. "So God-fearing, aren't you? But look at you now, my angel... look how much you have fallen down."

With her mouth wide open in the attempt to accommodate the size of his cock, Jane moaned desperately. Against any decency or morality, Guy pushed his crotch against her, keeping her head still and making her swallow half of his rod, hitting her palate once, twice, three times.

"Yes, like that... good... good girl..."

Watching her was... God... too much. It was a heavenly retreat, wet and soft, her mouth. The head of his penis slammed in her throat, and Guy, hearing her moaning distraughtly, realized he had to stop. He didn't want her to feel sick. With difficulty, he brought her head back. He pushed his cock to the side of her mouth, and the swelling that distorted her profile made him moan with excitement.

"Oh, you naughty, naughty girl," he panted. He moved forward and back, deforming her features with each thrust, mesmerized. "You... you were born to suck me..."

Delaying his orgasm was unimaginable. He would have wanted to last longer, but the matter was beyond his control. Stopping, he brought her mouth back up to the tip of his penis. Jane let him guide her back and forth on the plump head of his erection, her eyes shocked and disbelieving. She scratched him from time to time with her teeth, and she didn't move her tongue the way he liked, but he would teach her how to perform the perfect blowjob.

Another time.

Now he had to come.

He put a hand on his cock, stroking its base. He would teach her that, too. God, it was the first blowjob Jane had done, and she sucked in the worst possible way, but to Guy, it seemed the best ever.

"I want to give you a... a gift now," he gasped. "I want you to swallow the juice of my balls. Don't spit it out, Jane... don't... oh, God, *yes*... I'm coming, little one... I'm coming..."

He threw his head back, holding her still by her hair as violent spurts of semen flooded her throat. With effort, he managed to lower his gaze and admire her while the orgasm shook him and seemed to never end.

He was coming in her mouth. It was really happening.

Desperate, Jane moaned for the quantity of sperm that was pouring into her. Guy held her head still, keeping her from retreating.

"No, swallow... swallow my cum... all of it, Jane... every *drop* of it..."

With her eyes closed and her body tense, she obeyed, drinking convulsively. Her lips twitched on his penis at every sip. Her bun, gripped in Guy's hands, was undone for the most part, many locks escaping from hairpins. A bit of cum came out of the corner of her mouth, mixing with the tears that covered her face, and Guy knew that he would never forget that glorious image.

He emptied himself completely inside her. Without mercy. Without remorse. And without strength, in the end, from this magnificent, devastating orgasm. Exhausted, he leaned against the wall. Then he gently pulled her back, because she, naively, was still sucking his cock. Her lips were swollen and reddened. In silence, Guy passed his forefinger through the come at the corner of her mouth and, without a word, put it in her mouth.

Jane closed her eyes and sucked his finger.

A few minutes ticked by before Guy could speak. He just kept her head against his left leg, stroking her hair. Jane held her face down, and he could see only the top of her head. From the street, he heard the barking of a dog, and a breathless voice that called out: "Come back here, Poppy!"

Guy blinked to focus on the young woman at his feet. "You're good at it, angel," he murmured, satisfied. "You showed me heaven today."

She remained still. Her knees, probably, hurt. Guy took her hair and lifted her head. Jane submissively let him handle her. Her eyes were open. Open and... absent.

Fully prostrated.

"You liked sucking my cock, didn't you?"

There was only one possible answer, and Guy wondered if she could give it to him. Jane swallowed hard, and her eyes seemed to ask him when all of this would end.

"Just say yes," he suggested gently. "Make me happy, angel, and I'll go away."

"Yes," she whispered, closing her eyes.

With a smug smile, Guy put his thumb on her lips. "I could have bet on it. And tell me... did you like the consistency of my, er... cream?"

His cock wasn't tired yet—if he stayed here a minute longer, he would certainly use her lavish mouth again. *I'll have fun with you, my little Jane... oh yes, I'll have a lot of fun with you.*

"Y... yes," said Jane, and unconsciously she swallowed again.

Guy laughed, genuinely amused. He released her and stepped back, pulling up his trousers.

"Good," he replied, looking at her from above as he buttoned his fly. "Then tomorrow I'll give you more. Happy?"

4.

Guy wasn't moving fast enough, and the punch hit him in the chin.

The right hook was one of the most treacherous moves in boxing, and it had caught him off guard. His head turned too fast. He couldn't maintain his balance and found himself on the floor before he could say "fuck you."

Standing above him, Stephen Weymouth laughed. "Today you're a useless prick, Guy."

Guy looked up at his friend. "Yeah," he muttered, touching his sore chin with his hand. He sat up, staying still for a moment to regain balance. He knew how to fall, so he almost didn't feel the pain from the impact with the floor.

He and his friend were in the gym of Ashbourne House. The room was large, and the French windows let the winter daylight in. The light would not last long. It was already half past three in the afternoon.

The boxing ring was right in the middle of the gym. It was a square twenty feet per side, with a post at each corner. Thick, red ropes were attached to the posts, delineating the fighting area. The ring was set on a raised platform; Guy liked the idea of being separated from the rest of the world when he boxed.

Stephen went toward his corner of the ring. "You are as strong as a bull, Guy, I'll give you that," he said, removing the protective bandages wrapping his hands. When he had put them on, before their training match, they had been immaculate white. Now they were dirty with stains of blood, sweat and dust. "But strength is not enough to be a good boxer, old bean. I told you a million times, you need to learn to move more quickly."

Guy got up without clinging to the ropes. "You will never see me fighting like you," he replied. "You make my head spin with your idiotic jumps." He moved to his corner, opposite Stephen's, and removed the bandages from his hands. To be honest, Guy moved quite well in the ring. Not to mention that his right jab was kind of a lethal weapon, if he put all

31

his strength in it. Yet Stephen's boxing technique was faster, and, not rarely, effective. That bothered Guy a lot. "I have to tell you this, man," Guy continued. "You look like a chicken with its ass on fire when you jump around me like that. Sometimes, I don't understand whether you're going to hit me or ask me for a dance. Maybe you fear you'll get fucked in your ass if you stay still for more than a second. In that case, no, you won't. I promise you."

Stephen laughed and picked up a white cotton towel hanging on the corner post. He wiped his face and his light brown hair, then drew the towel across his bare chest. He had hardly any chest hair at all; he was as smooth as a baby's butt. The good thing about it was that he sweated less than Guy when they fought.

Guy looked down at his dark chest hair and shrugged. It was a sign of virility, wasn't it? Anyway, he would take a bath later. He threw the bandages on the floor. There was a clean towel hanging on the post by his side. He took it and wiped his face, his hair and his powerful body.

Guy's massive strength was the result of years of training. Since he was a little boy, he had spent a lot of time engaging in intense physical activity. He had pushed himself beyond his limits of fatigue and pain, for no longer being afraid of anything or anyone. He had spent endless hours pulling himself up with one arm, hanging on a bar, once, twice, a hundred times; a lot of hours of sit-ups until his abs burned. He had made his body stronger, day by day, hard with steel muscles. He had challenged and beaten up everyone that crossed his path, first at Eton, then at Oxford. He looked at the opposite corner of the ring. Stephen Weymouth included.

"You know, Ash," Stephen said, raising his right hand to show him his grazed knuckles, "we should begin to consider the use of boxing gloves in our training matches."

"Boxing gloves are for pansy-asses."

There was a bottle of water on the floor, near the post. Guy picked it up and, lifting it to his lips, drank deeply.

"You are so bloody stubborn, Ash. I don't want to get every bone in my hands broken because of you."

"Well, I don't want you to be a huge pain in the ass, and yet you are."

"You have no idea how huge, old bean." Stephen grinned and took a sip of water from his bottle. Although he had just fought, he sipped his water with aristocratic grace. His body was lean, not at all as massive as Guy's, and Guy was taller than him. Yet, sometimes Stephen could show anger enough to be a challenging opponent. "What about your stepfather, Ash?" he asked. "How's your *glorious* revenge against him going?" Stephen's words were filled with heavy irony.

Revenge against *his stepfather.* Guy held back a smile. *My friend, you are so naive sometimes.*

"So, Ash?" insisted Stephen. He spoke with a light tone, but his eyes were attentive. "Have you thrown your money in his face this morning? Judging by how distracted you are today, I would say you are still thinking about it."

Stephen wouldn't stop asking until he got an answer. Guy had planned to hurt his friend a little during their boxing match, just to postpone Stephen's questions about the Hartwells. Alas, it had been Guy who had finished on his back after a seven minutes' fight. Instead of putting his every effort in winning, he had been thinking of Jane even during the match.

And speaking of Jane... oh, God. His treacherous cock shuddered with lust. The glorious memory of Jane sucking him flashed in his mind. Her mouth was so soft, and warm, and...

He felt observed and took a breath before returning his gaze to Stephen. Sooner or later his friend would find out what was really going on, but, if God wanted, he wouldn't find it out today.

"It was... interesting," Guy finally answered in a voice devoid of inflection. Interesting, indeed. A breathtaking blowjob usually is.

"I can't understand you, Guy, really I can't. What sort of fun do you have in bullying Charles Hartwell? He doesn't deserve this. He is a decent man."

Except for the fact that, of course, Guy wasn't bullying *Charles* Hartwell, exactly. "A decent man indeed," he replied with a wry smile. "Pretty damn decent. That's more than enough to entice me in kicking his ass. Wouldn't you agree?"

Stephen smiled in spite of himself. "You say so much bullshit, Ashbourne." He took his shirt hanging on the post. "But it's over now, isn't it?" he asked, putting his shirt on. "Your revenge is finally over."

My revenge is just begun. "More or less."

Stephen straightened his shoulders. "Ash, for fuck's sake. Did you pay off his debts or not? Holy shit, you won't really have him in debtors' prison, will you?"

"Whoa, calm down. I'll pay off one of his notes tomorrow, as a Christmas present."

"One note? What about the other ones?"

"Don't worry, I'll pay off all his debts... eventually."

"Eventually? Why not now? What is this, Ashbourne, some sort of a stupid cat-mouse game? Bloody hell. You've already forced him to ask for your help. It shouldn't have been easy for a proud man like Charles Hartwell. Isn't it enough? Come on, I told you from the start. Revenge against your stepfather doesn't make any fucking sense."

Secrets, secrets. It wasn't the first time Guy had kept a secret from his friend, and it wouldn't be the last.

"Let me understand, W." Guy threw the towel on the floor and straightened his shoulders. Attacking, always attacking, is the first rule of any victory. "Who bribed the captain of the cargo ship in feigning shipwreck? You. Who bribed Stokes? Also you. Who sent the lawyer to Charles Hartwell, to get him to sign those fucking promissory notes? Let me think... yes, it was you again. And now you dare to preach against me?"

"I don't believe it, are you actually saying I'm the one to blame for this shit?" Stephen shook his head in amused bewilderment. "God, what a shameless butt-face you are. I helped you, yes, but only until your mother's death. I mean, I have always thought you had every right to demand an apology from her. Yes, I admit it, you had the actual right to force *her* to ask for your help. But afterward, your revenge stopped making any sense to me. Ash." He gave him a pained look. "Now she is dead. She is out of your reach. I'm sorry that it happened, but it *did* happen. So, what's the point in getting revenge on your stepfather? You're acting like a total moron."

Guy shrugged. "I spent too much time and effort to let him alone so easily. It would be an unforgivable waste." A waste indeed. He closed his eyes, overwhelmed by the memory of Jane knelt before him; her fair hair shone as she moved her head gently, back and forth... back and forth.

"And your stepsister?"

Guy opened his eyes suddenly. "My stepsister what?" He turned to the ropes, his back to Stephen. He felt the truth printed on his face, the orgasm of a few hours ago written all over his features.

"Don't pretend you don't understand what I mean. Jane Hartwell. You usually forget about her, but you shouldn't. She is just a young woman without any faults, and I bet she's very worried for this difficult situation."

Actually, no, Guy didn't *at all* forget about Jane. He counted to ten, regained control of himself, and turned to face Stephen.

"Don't worry," he said with an irony that his friend could not grasp, "I'll take care of Jane. In fact, you know what? Maybe I'll give her a good dowry, when all of this will be over."

"Why don't you put an end to it now? Leave the past behind you, Ashbourne. Aren't you tired of begging for a bit of attention in Courtnell Street?"

Guy was reaching for his shirt. At those words, he turned. "I'm not the one who begs, I assure you."

"And how can that make you feel good? You're humiliating a crippled man... a man twice your age."

Guy put on his shirt. "Do you really want to know what makes me feel good?" he asked, jumping down from the boxing ring. "Get my revenge, W. It's..." he recalled Jane with a mouthful of his cock, "...ah... it's a wonderful sensation."

Stephen went down with a jump, and he was behind him before he got to the door. He put his hand on Guy's left shoulder, stopping him and making him turn around.

"Revenge? Against whom? Charles Hartwell's only crime was to love your mother. He even cares for *you*, for fuck's sake!"

"Weymouth, listen. You helped me to get him broke, and I thank you for that. But now stay out of it. Don't tell me what to do with my life, because I never tell you what the fuck you should do with yours."

"Yes you do, you asshole. You do tell me how to live my life, every fucking day. You're my bloody guardian angel, Ashbourne, the biggest pain in my ass. If tonight, say, I went to the den of St Giles, you would get me immediately, and you would beat me so hard I would hear the angels sing. You don't allow me to smoke my sweet opium pipe since when, a year, you son of a bitch?"

There was embarrassed, angry affection in Stephen's words. He never talked about his addiction to opium. It was an uncomfortable topic between them. Guy shrugged. Stephen's gratitude toward him, though never spoken aloud, embarrassed him. Guy was a man of action, what the hell, he didn't talk about emotions or shit like that. Yes, he was sort of Stephen's guardian angel, so what? He wouldn't allow Stephen to get addicted to opium again, and that was all. After all, they had known each other for so many years. He and Stephen had met at Eton when they both were students. At first, they had hated each other. Well, of course, because Stephen used to be the peacemaker in every fight, and Guy used to beat him up to teach him to mind his own business. And then, almost without realizing it, they had become like brothers. It may happen, when you get to know the vomit smell of another man, the strangled cry that comes from his throat when you kick him in his balls.

"Just because I need you sober," Guy replied drily. "Anyway, I don't piss you off talking about the revolting relationship you have with your family."

He started to turn away from him, but Stephen hit his shoulder with his closed fist. Stephen could dare to hit him like that, while every other man would lose his hand.

"Oh, the Hartwells are *your* family, are they?" Stephen smiled mockingly, and Guy felt the desire to stick his friend's head in a latrine full of piss, as he used to do at Eton. "I thought they were just a useless stepfather always traveling and an insignificant stepsister you never speak of."

"You know nothing about my business with the Hartwells," Guy said. He went toward the door, leaving the gym without looking back.

5.

"You shouldn't have sent us your servants, Guy. And definitely, you shouldn't have sent us all this stuff!" Charles Hartwell looked at the table laden with delicious food and shook his head. "God in heaven, Jane and I will eat leftovers until next Christmas."

Jane didn't lift her gaze from her plate. She played with the food on it, soaking a little piece of meat in the green sauce aside. She wasn't eating. She wore an ordinary gray turtleneck dress, and her hair was tied in a simple bun on her nape. Her mouth was contracted with tension, her eyes were swollen, red, surrounded by deep dark circles.

Uh-oh, Guy thought with cynical amusement. Jane must have spent the night thinking about him. Or rather, thinking about a *part* of him... "I have the honor to be with you this holy day," he answered in a perfectly polite voice. "The very least I can do is keep you from any extra cost."

He wiped his mouth with a napkin. With a sort of pleased astonishment, he thought about the absurd, amazing flaws in the world's mechanism. For example, despite the discomfort Jane was obviously feeling, and despite her tired look, her cheeks were rosy, glowing with delicate complexion. How could it even be possible? She sure hadn't worn any makeup; she had never worn makeup in her entire life. Yet she was shining, as fair as the dawn that Guy had seen that very morning, from the window of his bedroom at Ashbourne House, after giving up on falling asleep.

He, too, had had an agitated night.

"Jane," he said mellifluously. "I think you don't like Rose's cooking."

Jane's fork froze on her plate. Charles's presence forced her to behave normally, and Guy was very much enjoying her hopeless efforts to appear relaxed. Really, the girl wasn't that good at feigning. She wasn't looking at Guy, of course. She was as tight as a violin string, but, after all, she had never been comfortable in his presence. All in all, given what she had gone through yesterday—or rather, what she had *sucked* yesterday—she was doing quite well. Guy couldn't even imagine what shame she felt, remembering his taste, his pleasure, his words... and reliving the abuse she had surrendered to.

"It's v... very good," she stammered.

"I'm pleased to hear that," Guy said. "So please, eat a little more, angel. Just to make me happy."

To make me happy. Yesterday, he had said the same words, and today, like yesterday, he was giving her an order, a humiliating order. Jane swallowed. In the dining room, the table was laden with all the colors of the rainbow. There were different kinds of meat, a lot of sauces, vegetable purees, roasts, in a stunning cacophony of combinations. That superfine food was served in cheap, everyday plates, because there was no longer good china at 7 Courtnell Street. That stinging contrast just underlined Guy's arrogance. Guy Spencer had invaded their home. It wasn't just his presence: he had wanted to occupy any space. He had planned it to be precisely like this. Yesterday, after his meeting with Jane—a memorable meeting indeed—he had sent a letter to his stepfather. He had written that he would be more than happy to *accept the honor* to have Christmas lunch with the Hartwells. He would have invited them to Ashbourne House—he had written—but he was sure they wouldn't have appreciated it, so he would take advantage of their hospitality. The letter had been sent along with Rose the cook and two other servants. Guy had imposed their presence on his stepfather, making clear that by refusing them, Charles Hartwell would have refused him too. He didn't want "to cause any trouble to him and Jane," Guy had written. But it had been just hubris, masked by politeness. Guy's show of power had come under the aspect of Christmas presents, processions of butchers, deliveries of fruits and sweets. He had sent flowers, too, a lot of flowers. There were flowers everywhere. In the middle of the dinner table, there was a delicious composition of peach roses that caught the light from the windows. On the other side of the composition, in front of him, was Jane. She, too, had the innocent beauty of a flower.

I hope you like my gifts, you velvet tongue. "Then, angel?" he urged. "Would you eat a little more for me?"

She bowed her head. After a moment, she lifted her fork to her lips. The fork was trembling in her hand.

A wave of dangerous exaltation spread in Guy's chest, filling him with fierce contentment—a burst of contentment so powerful, it almost scared him.

"What about you, Guy?"

Charles's voice was low and calm, and Guy strongly hoped his own face didn't let show any lascivious intent. He had masturbated twice before leaving Ashbourne House, to avoid looking at Jane with crushing lust. But he wanted her, he wanted her desperately. She was his. That shy girl over there, dressed in gray, who was eating with difficulty, was *his*. She was sweet, she smelled so good. Yesterday, when he had held her in his arms, he had realized how welcoming her body was, and damn it, he had to stop thinking about yesterday *right now*. And definitely, he had to stop thinking about what he was going do to her later this afternoon.

"How have you been lately?" Charles asked. His stepfather had grown emaciated since the last time Guy had seen him. Charles had something scruffy on his face. His sideburns were long and uncared-for, and his grayer-than-blond hair was a bit messy. More than that, the light in his eyes was faint, as if missing. "We haven't seen you in a while."

You haven't seen me since my mother's funeral, but you won't say it aloud, will you, Charles? "Oh, you know, Mr. Hartwell," he said lightly. "I like having fun and shocking the *ton*."

And shedding a lot of blood from the ton's guys, by the way, Guy thought. Some blood would be shed this very night, if everything went according to his gang's plan. This year, Christmas had happened on a Night of Knives and, despite the holiness of today, Guy and the other members of the K-Gang wouldn't give up their mission until they achieved their appointed target.

Thinking of the incoming K-Night made Guy stiffen. Even if he had joined the Gang of Knives more than three years ago, he hadn't got used to their missions yet. He let out his breath slowly to calm down. Fortunately, he would be in Jane's company soon, and he'd have some relaxation with her...

Well, maybe relaxation wasn't the word, exactly.

"The papers speak of you very often, my boy." The grief had aged Charles Hartwell ten years in ten months, yet his stepfather was the same caring person he had always been. Caring even with Guy. He was really interested in his stepson's life, he wished him every good.

Wasn't that paradoxical?

"Newspapers exaggerate as usual, Mr. Hartwell. I'm a good boy, really." From the corner of his eye, Guy saw Jane's face twitching. Somehow, she lifted another morsel to her trembling lips.

"Not that good, I daresay, Guy. You got your nose twisted in some fight of yours, didn't you?"

"That happened years ago, sir. I'm much better at dodging punches now."

His stepfather cocked his head. The wrinkles on his face were becoming evident, yet he had still the charm which had always characterized him. His dark green eyes, despite the sclera becoming a bit yellowed by tobacco, were intense and acute. "Sure you are," he replied with an ironic smile, "except for the fact, of course, that you have rainbow bruises all over your face."

Guy suppressed a gesture of annoyance. "Hardly any bruise at all." He had just a big purple contusion on his left cheekbone and another on his chin. He hadn't hidden his face under a slight beard, because one wasn't supposed to wear a beard on Christmas Day. Well, his face could have been worse, anyway. He had joined two fights yesterday. The first one with Stephen, the training match Guy had lost almost immediately; the second had happened later, in Soho, during the night. Guy had spent Christmas midnight that way: poorly dressed, at the Red Fox Tavern, thrashing one of the customers. Specifically, beating up a brute who had knocked over the tray of a serving girl. The reason had been a mere pretext, anyway. Guy had crushed him savagely, leaving him injured on the floor, just to release himself. Or at least, he had hoped to vent his tension. In fact, this physical outlet had proven to be ineffective. Once home, he had tossed and turned in his bed, feeling restless, impatient... and exalted.

He looked at Jane; she had had a complicated night too, hadn't she? And he could imagine why. His penis shuddered, his body felt no guilt at all. He couldn't wait for...

"Guy?"

His stepfather's voice called him back to his good sense. Guy blinked and cursed himself. Even though Charles was slow-minded—all the dully good men are slow-minded, aren't they?—his paternal instinct could make him notice that, alas, Guy wasn't looking at Jane the way a brother should look at his sister.

Definitely not.

"Mr. Hartwell," Guy said with a smooth voice, pulling back his shoulders. "I must confess something to you. I haven't come here just to celebrate Christmas with you and your lovely daughter. Actually, I'd like to talk to you in private"—Jane raised up her head suddenly—"about a delicate matter."

He felt Jane's frightened gaze upon him, he felt her eyes on his face, in his soul. Poor little girl, he thought with derision. It was so easy to keep her on tenterhooks. It was so easy to have her completely in his power.

* * *

After lunch, Jane watched her father and Guy as they got up and went to Charles's studio. Her heart began pounding uncontrollably. Her father walked leaning on his cane, trying to hide the pain of his damaged leg. At his side, Guy looked more impressive and stronger than ever. He gave her a look. It was like hot iron burning her skin. She flattened against the couch, clutching her workbasket like a pathetic handhold.

Her father's cane beat rhythmically in the hallway, and Guy's resolute steps followed him. The old man and the young. The sick man and the healthy. It was strange how nature had sorted things, Jane thought. The cruelest soul was hidden right in the most beautiful body—Guy's perfect, magnificent body.

The study door shut with a bang. Surely, Guy had pulled the door with determination. Jane stood up. Her movements were mechanical. She was trying to not think about what had happened to her yesterday. Thinking of that would immobilize her. She needed to move. To act.

She reached the door, looking in the hallway. The servants sent by Guy would see her eavesdrop, but what did that matter, anyway? They wouldn't tell Charles Hartwell, they would tell their real master, Guy Spencer, the 4th Earl of Ashbourne. And Guy already knew how much Jane was worried about this whole situation.

Her chest hurt with heavy oppression. She hated Guy, oh, she hated him so much. What was that devil telling her father? Was it possible that, yesterday, he had fooled her? Maybe he had never wanted to help her father. Maybe he was going to reveal to him his real financial situation. But Guy couldn't be so cruel. He could not!

Lick it, Jane.

Could he? Yesterday, he had smiled and, standing over her, had forced her to do that... that *thing*.

And he had kept on smiling while...

Oh, Guy, how could you? You were my hero when we were kids.

The thought was painful and struck her without warning. She felt ashamed for the affection she had given to him as a child. He was a... a monster, a devil.

With her breath held and her throat tight, she walked toward the study door. She stopped outside and put her ear over the door. She hoped she could overhear every word of the dialogue between Guy the Devil and her father.

* * *

"Mr. Hartwell, your financial situation is problematic."

Charles Hartwell was sitting behind his desk. He put a cigar to his lips; he had offered one to Guy, who had refused. Heavy smoke odor surrounded them by a light blue color.

"Tell me something I don't know, will you?" Charles smiled sadly. "It will be a boring conversation otherwise."

Guy restrained his impatience. He was sitting on a hard wooden chair that would have been more suited to a schoolroom than to a house. But of course, Charles was not a teacher, and Guy, definitely, was not a schoolboy held after class for punishment—even though he was sitting in front of the desk with a respectful expression on his face.

Oh, screw all of this. He relaxed his posture, leaning on the back of the chair. The cigar smell did not cover the smell of the old books stacked on the floor. There were a hundred volumes in the room, if Guy had to guess. A lot of books, one might say. But they were few considering that, until a few months ago, there had been two or three thousand books in the now-closed library on the other side of the house. They had been sold for the most part, Guy supposed, sliding his eyes over the piles against the wall. The remaining books were cheap, worn... like everything else in this house.

"You can't pay off your mortgage."

Guy spoke without inflection. He was merely pointing out a fact, like a simple chronicler. But as he said these words, he leaned forward, propping his elbows on the desk. He wanted to violate the older man's authority, his space. "I know you well, Mr. Hartwell," he continued quietly. "You won't ask Mr. Green to let you stay here."

Charles blew out the smoke, and his green eyes followed the spirals. "Has Stokes contacted you?"

"I have contacted him." Guy put his hand to his pocket. He pulled out a yellowed sheet of paper. "This is the result of the meeting I have had with him." He threw the sheet on the desk. Charles looked at him questioningly.

"I redeemed this promissory note yesterday," Guy said. "It's yours."

The smoke of the cigar rose in complete silence. Charles's hand was still. Perfectly still. There were no tremors in his fingers. Pain, both moral and physical, had scarred his soul and sucked his will to live, but he still had the courage to face his financial difficulties. Slowly, he put down his cigar in the ashtray on the desk. He neither touched nor opened the note. He did not need to read the signature at the bottom, or the amount, or the maturity date.

"I would have redeemed it by myself," he said finally. Resting his elbows on the desk, he folded his hands together and bowed his head, supporting his forehead with his thumbs. "The cargo is arriving in port soon. A matter of a few days." He straightened his head with a resolute light in his eyes. "You shouldn't have paid it off, Guy."

Shouldn't he have? As a matter of fact, yes, he should have indeed. Because the cargo in port, the lie that Jane had told Charles, ironically wasn't a lie at all. The cargo ship had arrived in port one week ago. It was still there, just waiting to be unloaded.

"Yes," Guy replied, shrugging his shoulders. "But I much preferred not to wait for the maturity date, sir. It's best not to mess with moneylenders."

Charles picked up the note from the desk. He toyed with it without opening it. "I'll pay you back in a few days. I need just a little time to sell some of the cargo."

"Mr. Hart—"

"I won't accept your money," he interrupted coldly, letting the note fall down on the desk again. "Do not even try this, Guy Spencer, 4th Earl of Ashbourne."

"On the contrary, you'll take it. I do not want to hear one more bloody word, Mr. Hartwell, you'll take my fucking money, and that's it."

Charles raised his eyebrows. Of course, he hadn't expected a gut reaction from Guy. Charles had never seen a gut reaction from Guy before. Guy was aware of his stepfather's opinion about him. Charles thought Guy was a sardonic, detached, emotionless man. And yes, Guy was. He was just

41

like that. Even at this moment. What he had just said, his visceral reaction, wasn't visceral at all. He had planned every word. He had planned everything for days... for months, actually. But things are never as one expects, are they? And Guy, more surprised than his stepfather, realized that a fit of inexplicable anger swelled his chest. A fit of remote, useless, *ridiculous* anger.

Why the hell was that?

It couldn't be because of this damn house. It couldn't be for the hidden memories between these damned walls. No, he was sure not. Maybe it was because of the incoming Night of Knives. K-Nights always filled him with logical tension—understandable, acceptable tension. Anyway, he wanted to quell it. He opened and closed his fist, breathing deeply. "I'm sorry," he said. He was just playing a part, wasn't he? Yet his heart pounded uncomfortably in his chest. "I'm sorry. Let me explain, all right? Jesus Christ, Hartwell. I have been living with this curse all my life."

"Guy..."

"No. No, it's my turn to talk. Don't you like my money? You'll take it just the same. I don't give a shit about what you want. No, let me finish. I have to tell you this, once and for all: I am fucking tired of all this bullshit."

Surprisingly, Charles laughed. "Yeah, I see." He ran a hand over his forehead, smoothing his wrinkles out. "But tell me, sonny boy, because I'm curious. What do you think you'll solve by giving me your money?" He was smiling, but his eyes weren't. His eyes had an expression of heartfelt detachment that only laudanum could extinguish. "No," he lifted his hand to stop Guy from speaking, "I'm not talking about me. I'm talking about you. Why do you think you'll feel better if I accept your help? You know me, Guy. I lost everything"—his chest rose in tough emotion—"I lost everything ten months ago. Only one thing is left for me, and it's a bit of useless pride. And now, you are telling me I must give up my pride, too." He pulled back, resting his shoulders against the high chair back. "Don't act as if you don't understand what this means, Guy Spencer, 4th Earl of Ashbourne. You are the proudest man in all England, so please, don't bullshit me. Stop dancing around that, and start talking straight. Tell me why you want me to accept your money."

Guy held the older man's gaze. Charles had aged weakly, while he, Guy, had become stronger. What was in his stepfather's irises, what emptiness filled them? The duel with their eyes had just begun. Yet Guy's aggressive behavior wasn't the best way to convince Charles to give in. It was a pity, since it would be much easier that way. Aggression had always come easy to Guy.

Guy placed his right fist into his opposite hand, creating a ridiculous support for his forehead.

He bowed his head. So what? What was the problem? It was just an act,

42

he thought, and his chest tightened, and a sudden bitterness took his breath away.

What was the *fucking* problem?

The fire crackled in the fireplace. It wasn't cold. Guy had sent a lot of wood to Courtnell Street. There was wood enough for a month, at the very least. The study they were in was about two hundred square feet. This small room, Guy remembered, was used by servants a few years ago.

It was cozy, though, wasn't it? Outside, it was a cold but serene Christmas Day, and the clear afternoon light illuminated the white walls and the floor and the books. This small room, barely livable and almost empty of furniture, had a warmth that, in the immense rooms of Ashbourne House, was completely missing.

Guy cleared his throat. "Mr. Hartwell," he said as breath returned to his lungs. "You are a proud man, I'll give you that. I know you could get out of this shit by yourself. In four, maybe five years, you could do it. But here's the problem. Jane. Jane would grow old while waiting for this situation to change. She would live in a flea-bag room in a boarding house, that's what you could afford out of here. She would have no marriage prospects." Guy straightened slowly, leaning his back to the backrest. "But if I help you through this hard time, with an interest-free loan to be repaid at leisure, things will get better soon. You have to allow me to help you, sir. You have to allow me for Jane's sake. You know, I'd like to provide a good dowry for her. And... and I'd also like to bring both of you to live with me at Ashbourne House. This way, she can really aspire to a good marriage."

"You want us at Ashbourne House, no less." Charles shook his head, twisting his mouth. "And I should do it, you say, for Jane. That's a very well-done moral blackmail, Guy, you're good at it. You still haven't answered my question, though. And I can be a bigger asshole than you if I put my mind to it. So I'm sorry, but I really want to know. I want to know how helping us would make you feel better."

Well, for one thing, I'll fuck your daughter every day. I'll fuck her so hard she will forget her own name. "Why are you asking, if you already know?" Guy blurted out. "My mother loved Jane very much. Are you satisfied now? I said it. I just want to do something that would have made my mother happy. I had always tried to disappoint my mother, and you know it. I did things she didn't approve of. Hell, sometimes I even managed to spread false rumors about myself, just to hurt her."

Charles reached for his cigar, which in the meantime had died. He retrieved a match that, maybe because it was damp by the cold, or maybe because it was cheap, didn't catch. He struck it again, and finally the flame arose with acrid dark smoke. Charles lifted the match to his cigar and took a drag. A sliver of smoke rose from its red tip.

"Son," he said after blowing out the smoke. "I loved your mother, but I was never blind to her faults. You tried to deserve her reproaches, and you did it well, I must say. But I told you when you were a child, and I'm telling you now: you weren't the one to blame."

You weren't the one to blame. Guy wondered how long he could continue his deception. *Wake up, Mr. You-Weren't-the-One-to-Blame. I'm going to fuck your daughter, I'm going to bang her in any position. Deserving a reproach, indeed.*

"Yes," he replied impassively. "I remember when you told me. And I," he smiled with awareness, "shot you in response."

A slight smile painted his stepfather's face. "As proud as the devil, even as a kid."

"I was, yes. But my mother is dead now, and I can never make things right with her again." And he wouldn't have even tried, anyway. Rona had never wanted or loved him, so what? Guy had learned to live with that, since he was a kid. He had understood his mother. In fact, he had fully agreed with her. But Jane... Jane was another matter entirely; and if he was bringing up this "sad and lonely little boy" shit, it was, cynically, to make Charles feel guilty. His stepfather had been driving the carriage that killed Rona, ten months ago. The carriage had gone off the road because of the snow.

"But really, it doesn't make sense to dwell on the past," Guy continued softly. "It happened. We can't change the past. Mr. Hartwell, I can see you're not convinced yet. I understand your situation, but you have to try to understand mine. Let me do this. Let me help you to restart your business. Listen, you refused my money two years ago. You have to take it now. You don't have the strength to get back on your feet all by yourself. The pain debilitates you, it's obvious. The drugs you're taking... they are necessary, of course, but don't you deny it: they keep you from thinking clearly. Let me help you. I'll work alongside Stokes. I know all of your moral qualms. I won't fire anybody, I give you my word. I'll hire no child under age 12. And... and I want you and Jane to come with me to Ashbourne House. You're the only family I have left."

Charles remained silent. He was no longer smoking the dark, thin cigar between his fingers. He was just looking at it blankly. "Jane at Ashbourne House..." he murmured.

"It doesn't have to be forever, if you don't want," Guy added, conciliatory. "Soon, you will have enough money to buy a house on your own. I myself would buy one for you, if I didn't know you're too proud to accept my offer."

"All your friends are marquises and dukes, Guy. What do Jane and I have in common with aristocrats?"

Guy waved his hand before his face, the way you might try to get a pesky fly away from you. "I wipe my ass with my friends. Pardon my bluntness."

"Oh, your bluntness is just fine with me, son. But the fact is, I can't imagine Jane among people like them."

Then you'll have to use your imagination better, because I'll have Jane with me at Ashbourne House. "You can't imagine her living closely with me, that's what you really mean." It was better to bring the subject up now. His stepfather should have noticed Jane's tension with Guy, and Guy couldn't keep on pretending ignorance. "Come on, do not deny it. My mother must have told her dreadful things about me. Things like how wicked and dangerous I am. Is that right? Jane is afraid of me, I guess, just the way she used to as a child."

"As a child?" Charles shook his head, and a loving smile appeared between his gaunt cheeks. "No, you're remembering wrong, Guy. She adored you as a child. It was pretty baffling, actually. She was such a shy little girl. She used to avoid everyone... but you. I could never understand why she was always following you around, why she was looking for you all the time. After all, you were a boy who could hardly be called friendly."

Guy looked down to the floor and raised the left corner of his mouth. *You're remembering wrong.* The truth was that Guy remembered very well those first years with Jane. He remembered how she used to be his shadow. How shy and petite she was, always watching him from afar... He also remembered how long he had tried to get rid of her. Innumerable times he had told her to leave him alone. He had treated her badly, he had broken all her toys... just to be left alone.

It had been useless.

Jane had kept on shadowing him, and every time, when he happened to lift his eyes, she would be there, maybe hidden around a corner, staring at him with her huge golden eyes.

But she had grown up at last, hadn't she? And it had happened: she had stopped following him, running after him, looking at him.

"Maybe," Guy murmured, rousing himself from his thoughts. "But you're right, I don't really remember." He looked up, banishing the image of a loving blonde little girl in a corner of his mind. "But now, I want to make things right. Let me make things right."

Charles put down his cigar in the ashtray. "She's still an introvert," he said hesitantly, watching the cigar smoke getting thin. "Rona kept her in a bubble her entire life, and I... maybe I should have intervened."

"You can do the right thing now. Come with me to Ashbourne House."

Charles rubbed his forehead, furrowed with worried uncertainty. "Let me think about it a few days, Guy. I know you think I'm selfish—" he cocked his mouth into something that looked like a smile "—but I'm worried about Jane, not me. There's no more happiness for me in this house: don't you think I'd like to see her settled... and happy?"

And then you could shoot yourself in the head, couldn't you, Charles?

"Jane has always lived here," his stepfather continued. "But she doesn't really have many friends. The girls she knows are not even worthy of that name, actually, since they stopped showing up as soon as we began to have financial trouble. She hasn't even seemed to notice, and after all, she is very different from those silly girls she met at the music school. She is interested only in teaching the little orphans of St Mary Orphan Refuge, you know. And nursing the sick at the Christian Hospital. So you see... I don't think she can fit into your rich palace or among your aristocratic friends."

Guy smiled. Jane would do anything he wanted her to do, *anything,* and this knowledge puffed his chest with... with what, exactly? Pride, exultation, power?

"Why don't you let her decide?" Guy said with affected calm. "Let me talk to her." He paused to clear his voice of any husky inflection. "Let me talk to her *alone.*"

Charles hesitated. "All right, then," he muttered after a long silence. "I owe you this, after all." He pulled a bell rope. After a moment, there came a slight knock on the door.

Jane, you're here, Guy thought, and wild anticipation accelerated his heart. *Now you and I are going to celebrate Christmas Day, little one.*

6.

Jane was climbing the stairs silently. Guy had said, "Please, lead the way, Jane", and she was escorting him upstairs, in this house that didn't belong to her anymore. She tightened her hand on the rail, feeling colder at every step. Guy was quiet, he didn't urge her to go faster. She couldn't tell what he wanted her to do. His silence was oppressive. She almost couldn't bend her knees, cold sweat was wetting her temples.

Going with him. Going with him up to the attic room.

Guy had asked her father if he could see his old bedroom, and what was her unsuspecting father supposed to answer? "Of course." He had answered an appalling "of course." And he had stabbed her with a few terrible words. "Jane, darling, would you accompany him?"

Now she was a few steps from the first-floor landing. Down the hallway, on the left, there was another staircase. It was a smaller, grayer staircase, leading to the attic. Jane closed her eyes. That was an unwise move from her since she, already confused, stumbled on the last step. She opened her eyes to find a handhold, but it was too late. She fell forward, and she would have hit the floor if Guy's strong arm, from behind, hadn't grabbed her around her waist. She straightened herself up, but Guy didn't let her go. He held her. He was strong, his scent was smoked musk. He was like a rock, he was supporting her, but he was bringing no relief to her. Because something pressed against her buttocks. Something that Jane had already met; something of which she had tasted every inch.

"Be careful, little Jane," Guy whispered in her ear, and she closed her eyes from his warm, tickling breath. He was holding her only with his arm, but it was like a cage, his arm. "I don't want you to get hurt."

"Don't you?" The words came out from her mouth without thought. She couldn't possibly think, close to him that way, terrified by his muscular chest pressed against her back. "Won't you hurt me, then?"

Guy smiled against her cheek. "Let's go upstairs," he murmured. He pushed her forward with his body, making her climb the last step. On the landing, he let her go slowly as if he knew that her legs were shaky. "Come here." He moved to her side and took her hand. Jane raised her head and tried not to cry in meeting his eyes sparkling with dark desire. "Now I'll lead you, angel."

* * *

47

With a trembling hand, Jane opened the door of the bedroom which had been first Guy's, then hers. She moved stiffly. Behind her, Guy couldn't see her face, but he knew she was terrified. While they were climbing the stairs, he had wondered if he should pick her up. Like a newlywed, he thought now, and smiled, seeing her walking to the most distant wall, as if to escape from him.

He appreciated the graceful contour of her body and slid his eyes to her inviting buttocks. Jane was slim, but she had curves where he liked them. The curves of her hips, in particular. Her high and round bottom. Her nape, visible under the bun, was in a V-shape; small curls had escaped from the bun and now were decorating her neck, up to where her dress allowed a glimpse. She was wearing a high-necked dress like a schoolgirl. Soon, she should change her way of dressing. Guy would remake her wardrobe, from bonnets to boots. She would be his in every fold of her body, of her clothing... of her breathing.

Across the room, Jane turned. Her golden irises widened and pierced him. Guy's heart, stupidly, missed a beat. Closing the door behind him, he followed her into the room. He couldn't believe that his mother had sent him up there when he was thirteen; surely he wasn't tall and wide like now, but holy shit, it wasn't even a three hundred square feet room. Only the servants' rooms were that small at Ashbourne House.

He noticed a fragrance in the room. It was subtle but present in the air, fixed over the years on the walls and wallpaper. It was like the fragrance of some simple flowers, forget-me-nots, whitethorn, violets with their soft, delicate petals. It was Jane's scent. Sweeter than sugar, more delicious than honey, it was still here, as if an industrious bee had mistaken this miserable attic room for a garden, sucking nectar from flower to flower, alighting on pistils and, with its little paws, spreading pollen through the air.

When Guy had been living up here, this room had had modest furnishings: a bed with a wooden headboard, a desk, a bookcase on the left wall. Now, there was nothing at all, not even the carpets. Everything had been sold, Guy supposed. Only some boxes were piled in a corner.

He walked toward the right wall. He reached out, touching the pastel wallpaper. It was very pale pink, almost white, with patterns of flowers with cherry pink petals.

Ah, little Jane...

He turned toward her. She was on the left of the window niche, leaning against the wall. She clasped her hands before her belly.

"You changed the wallpaper," Guy murmured. "Now it's pink. Just perfect for you. But tell me, Jane... where was your bed?"

Was she breathing? She opened her mouth and no sound came out. She was supposed to answer if she remembered the rules of their deal: obedience, submission, complete solicitude in pleasing her master. Guy had no doubt she remembered. Yesterday he had laid the foundation of their relationship in a... well. Unforgettable way. In his trousers, his groin, defying the law of gravity, was the conclusive proof of that. His powerful erection was hardly unforeseen, of course, because he had thought of her delicious blowjob. Guy took a breath that puffed out his chest. *But buddy,* he thought looking at the bulging fly of his pants, *you must have a little patience today.*

"Th...there," stammered Jane, pointing to the middle of the room.

Guy followed the direction of her forefinger. It was in the same position as his bed had been when the attic room belonged to him.

"How was it?" he asked softly. "Was it white? A white... canopy bed?"

She nodded, and her golden eyes looked immense with terror.

"It suited you," he approved, turning back to the wallpaper. It was the very same room in which he had been living for years. What color were the walls when it was *his* bedroom? What fucking color? He couldn't answer, not even if he thought about it for a hundred years.

* * *

In the small room, behind the closed door, Guy's movements were calm and measured. He was looking around, perhaps remembering the time spent there, when he was a boy. He showed no visible emotion. No sweetness, no sadness, no anger.

"Pink," he repeated. He put his hands in his pockets and turned, walking slowly toward her. When he was in front of her, he lifted his hand to her cheek.

Jane stopped breathing.

I don't want I don't want I don't I don't...

Guy's palm was warm, and his thumb brushed her lips. Jane squeezed them together, but he didn't do what she was expecting. He didn't dip his thumb into her mouth. He put his left elbow on the wall, bending over her and touching her chest with his, and kept on caressing her mouth with his finger. The room was cold, but Jane's chills came from his hot, insolent hand.

Shaded by long lashes, Guy's eyes peered at her. His gaze was clouded with something that even Jane could understand. Lust. He wasn't smiling, his clean-shaven face was utterly serious. It was Christmas Day, but Guy wasn't a good boy, and his facial imperfections stood out like inkblots on paper: the huge contusion under his left eye and another, smaller, on his chin. He let his hand come down on her neck, touching the shell of her ear with his thumb. His fingers were light and gentle, and caused her shivers for the cruelly pleasant sensation. "Go to the window," Guy murmured.

Jane blinked.

"To the window," repeated Guy. He withdrew his hand and stepped back, pointing toward the hollow space before the window, on his left. It was the window seat that Jane had always adored; from up there, she had loved the world... and Guy had hated it.

Jane could barely sense her legs. Panic, and Guy's fingers, had reduced her to a jelly of dismay and anguish. Her heart... she was only heart; it was flapping in her chest, deafening her with its roaring beat. But her father was waiting for them on the ground floor; and whatever Guy wanted to do to her, or wanted her to do, it had better happen as soon as possible. *You'll get used to this,* she thought as her feet led her to the window. *You'll get used to being this man's slave.*

But he wasn't just any man. He was Guy. In her memories, sometimes she could still see him as the tough, fearless child who once threw himself into the River Mole just to save her.

And now, what was she supposed to do? Just open her mouth and let him in.

As she got to the window, she took a breath and looked back at him.

Guy was smiling as he approached her. Jane couldn't back away; the niche, about one and a half feet deep, prevented her.

"Look out of the window," he said when he was in front of her.

Her heart sank. Having him behind her shoulders alarmed her more than having him in front of her, but she obeyed. Outside, the world was just the same. The road, from up there, looked smaller. There were some children and nannies taking a walk for Christmas along the snowy sidewalk, and their colorful overcoats brightened up the place. On the right side of Courtnell Street, there was an old house, closed behind an iron gate and a wall seven feet high. From over the wall, some branches of the house's tallest trees came out. The old house wasn't abandoned but was very neglected, and when Jane was a child, she used to be frightened by the elderly lady who lived there. Maybe that same lady still frightened the children of Courtnell Street.

"Do you like it, Jane?"

She jerked and started to turn. Guy put his hands on her shoulders, stopping her, and moved closer to touch her back with his chest. And further down, his hard, ravenous virility pushed against her derrière.

"The view," he explained, his voice smiling. "Do you like the view, Jane?" He moved his hand forward and put it on Jane's breast, touching her from behind with his palm. She stiffened. Was he going to... *take* her, she wondered? Was he going to take her right now, in the attic room, while her father was waiting for them?

"Please, Guy," she whispered in anguish. "Please, not now!"

From behind, he leaned down his face to brush the right side of her face. He chuckled against her cheek. "I do love it when you beg me, Jane." He lifted a hand to her nape and pushed her forward.

"Guy!"

"Shhh." He pushed her with more energy. "Bend forward, angel... put your hands on the windowsill."

"Guy, no..."

But his hand was pressing, commanding... dominating; and she surrendered. Bowing at ninety degrees, with her vision blurred by unbearable shame, her bottom protruded obscenely toward him in a scandalous invitation.

Guy's voice sounded hoarse and sensual. "You told me you moved up here because of the beautiful view, is that right, Jane?"

God, what... what a despicable man. Jane felt angry tears pushing against her eyes. Four years ago, on Christmas Eve, he hadn't been drunk at all. He remembered everything.

"Is that right?" he repeated.

"Y... yes, it... it is."

"So, angel," he placed his hands on her buttocks and everything around her began to spin, "since you love this view that much, look outside... and enjoy yourself."

* * *

With her back to him, bending over like that, Jane was a gorgeous sight. She was keeping her head up, looking outside as she had been told, and the curve of her spine was sinuous and feminine. Guy's cock, still caged inside his clothes, pressed against the fabric of his trousers in a painful complaint. His arousal was aching.

Have a little patience, my friend. Soon you'll have a lot of fun.

With both hands, he lifted Jane's skirt. Her bottom, covered by a white petticoat, looked like a fruit ready to be eaten. The petticoat wasn't as voluminous as the ones Guy's mistresses wore; Jane's was modest and simple, devoid of lace and colorful ribbons.

He folded her skirt over her back and placed his hands on her buttocks, enjoying their awesome mass.

What a glorious moment, what a glorious *ass*...

He heard her sniffling. Was she already crying? Merciless, he slid his hands under the hem of her petticoat and lifted it up. He touched the lower edge of her long knickers, then slid his hands higher, to her buttocks, squeezing them in his palms, massaging them... claiming possession of them.

His. His his his...

"What a view, angel..." he gasped. "It's a delightful view indeed..."

He pressed his groin against her. Her heavy knickers likely made it impossible for her to feel his cock in all its huge eagerness, and Guy himself had his own trousers on; but her body was soft and full, and underneath her dress... oh, what was under her dress would take him to heaven.

So close to him, Jane's fragrance went down into his lungs. It gave him the same pleasure as the first sip of hot chocolate on a snowy day.

He brought his hand forward and touched her mound of Venus through the fabric of her underwear. Her breath was hard and fast; perhaps she was weeping. Moving his palm up and down, he stroked her vulva gently.

There was no fire lit. Jane stayed still, and her position seemed to offer her butt to him; only her long knickers and her socks protected her legs from the cold. Poor little thing, Guy thought with cynical derision. While looking at her simple lingerie, he decided he would buy her new underwear: whorish, red underwear—something meant to embarrass her. Something that would put her in her place. He would make her understand that she had no innocence left. She was just his slave; except that, at this moment, her simplicity was mesmerizing him—her pink socks, her modest garters, a few inches of her white skin above, and then again white fabric, her knickers this time, devoid of ornaments.

Muffled sounds came from the closed window. Guy and Jane were on a too-high floor; it wasn't close enough to the road to be reached by the world outside's noise. Jane, just her, was breathing hard; hers was a breathing wet with tears, flushed with shock.

Guy brought his hands to the ribbons holding her knickers in place and pulled them loose.

They slid to the ground.

A strangled cry came out of her mouth. She hadn't been able to hold it in, but Guy didn't turn his attention to her. He didn't scold her for having bowed her face. He didn't even check if she had closed her eyes. There were only her buttocks in the world, now, to him. Oh, they were white, soft, delicious buttocks. He had wondered a thousand times how Jane would look without clothes.

He stepped back to admire her better.

She was beyond imagination.

Her exposed, innocent ass had a perfect heart shape, and her legs, shapely and straight, were so tense that if she kneeled, they would break. The crevice separating her buttocks was contracted, but this forward-bending position didn't allow her to hide the exciting rear view of her cunt, even if she was desperately tightening her thighs. She wanted not to disclose the treasure between her legs, but it was useless, he could see it, he could enjoy the blonde flower he had dreamed of so badly. Her intimate hair was as fair and delicate as everything about her.

Guy remained silent, but not to torture her, not this time. He wanted to get a good look at her. Every detail, God, he wanted to see *everything*. He would never forget the picture before his eyes: her dress and petticoat, her pink socks, her white smooth skin. And her pussy so shy, so coy, and the perfect shape that, in that temptress position, her buttocks showed him with round generosity.

What a beautiful, magnificent heart.

Jane's terror was rising from her body in an almost physical way. Guy's penis swelled inside his trousers; his throat was dry. With a finger, he touched her cunt lightly, pushing forward between her thighs. Jane clutched her legs together with a start. Uselessly. It didn't work, it *couldn't* work. Ah, that was a perfect position. Divine position. If God fucked, he did it that way.

He brushed her cunt with caution. Jane was dry, and he had expected nothing different. He went up with his finger to fondle her anus and kept doing so, going up and down, slowly.

"I like the view, too..." he murmured huskily. "So very much, my little one."

* * *

His finger, please God, no... not there, in the folds of her sex! "Please, Guy," she sobbed, hating the desperation in her voice, "please, don't..."

"Shhh, angel... enjoy... enjoy the view..."

That... monster. Cruel, yes... God, his hand! Wide-eyed, Jane was seeing nothing of what was laid before her. His finger touched her where she was most obscene, and she could feel his eyes behind her as if they were burning her skin. He was looking at her, and her position could conceal nothing, nothing of her body...

In front of her, the daylight was blinding. Only white. She had always liked the world seen from up here; being as shy as she was, and uncomfortable in any place, she often felt lost, or weak, or at the mercy of events. When she felt so powerless, she ran up to the attic. Even this morning, at dawn, she had run to this comforting little place of hers... this very morning's dawn.

Guy's finger separated her intimate lips and caressed a sensitive spot at the beginning of her vulva.

"Oh, God, no..." Jane closed her eyes, feeling her legs bend. His hand was moving on her gently, and the sensation it was causing was scandalous—the *sound* of it was scandalous.

She clung to the memory of a few hours ago, when a bright pink had painted the snowdrifts on the road: she had wrapped up in a blanket, and, sitting in the window seat, had blown out the candle, filling her eyes with the beautiful sight. But now—now here she was with her butt protruding in the air as if she were asking Guy to touch her; and she was letting Guy handle her as he pleased. She was trying, oh, she was *so* trying—but she couldn't succeed. She couldn't ignore his finger, no matter how much she attempted to; it was delicate, caught between her pursed secret lips; it went up and down, up and down, in an indecent caress, and rhythmic, and... and...

It can't be, it mustn't be...

But it was; it was a scary, tormenting... *pleasant* sensation.

Oh, no—anything but this. She couldn't debase herself to the point of... Oh, *God...*

She moaned as he touched the little pearl between her intimate lips. Did he know? Did he know how she felt when he touched her pussy?

But yes, of course he knew... he *wanted* her to experience these wicked sensations, he wanted her to enjoy her abasement. She couldn't let him degrade her in this manner, she needed to hate his diabolically tender, seductive touch.

She needed to hate *all* of this...

Jane's legs became liquid.

Oh, why was he doing this to her?

She stiffened her hands on the niche and raised her head, forcing herself to look at the houses on the road, at the flowers in the window across Courtnell Street; hellebore and holly, red berries and green spots in the snow, and no, she thought, God, no... don't let him do *this* to me...

She sobbed, feeling defeated, while his finger kept on rubbing her. It was delicate and unrelenting and was generating a strange heat, a sloppy and melted heat, not only in her privates, but in her lower abdomen as well; she didn't want that warmth bathing her with dense and hot oil, she didn't want this sinful, squashy dissolution in her legs. Overwhelmed by powerless guilt, she breathed open-mouthed, panting with inexcusable need; oh God, she hated Guy; she differed from Guy and his animalistic lust. She wanted to be different from him, she couldn't...

Guy stopped his fingers. He withdrew his hand, and Jane blinked with a feeling of absurd disappointment. She cast it away; her prayer had been heard, hadn't it?

It was over, she thought with agitation, while her legs were still shaking from the waves of wet heat Guy's hand had caused through her loins.

But Guy put his hands on her buttocks, and Jane lowered her head; no, it wasn't over... it had just begun.

"Keep looking outside," he ordered her, "enjoy what you wanted so badly..."

"Why are you so mean, Guy?" she heard herself ask. "What did I ever do to you?"

"Mean, am I?" His voice sounded amused, and with his fingertip he began to slide up and down between her buttocks, brushing the entrance of her vagina. "That hurts me, angel..."

He touched her inner thigh, lifting her leg and freeing her right ankle from the knickers, then opened her legs a few inches apart. He withdrew his hands and, moving languidly, went forward to her side. Alarmed, Jane turned to face him.

"No," he said, "keep looking in front of you, angel. But..." he brought his right hand before her face, "but while you're doing it, lick my fingers wet."

She had known he would tell her to do so. While her gaping eyes fixed outside, she stuck out her tongue. She licked his fingers, crosswise, little, ring, middle, and index fingers.

"Do it with your whole tongue, Jane... yes, like that... just like a lapdog."

Her taste was there, on his fingers—it was a shocking, immoral taste.

"You have such a velvety tongue, Jane... as soft... as silk..."

Jane looked at the monochrome white sky, and the snow on the roofs and the trees, while Guy, standing at her side, stared at her face, at her mouth... enjoying every moment of her submission.

"Do it faster, Jane... lick me faster..."

And Jane did it. She moved her head quickly up and down, savoring his palm with no pride left. The slurping noise she was making was overly degrading; she was lowering herself for him to the point of no return. Slavishly, she licked him as she had been told: with her whole tongue, like a lapdog, no, like a... a *bitch,* and she knew it, oh, how well she knew it, she was aware of it at every moment, as her tongue lapped against his skin without stopping, in that fast, mortifying rhythm he had imposed on her— that rhythm that made her look like an animal. As he put his index and middle fingers in her mouth, she sucked them, following his movements with her head: forward, backward, the way he had taught her yesterday. Forward, backward... had she already learned to humiliate herself so much?

Oh God, yes, she had. She had lost every shred of her dignity.

"More saliva," Guy ordered with an uneven voice, "wet me more, angel, I need... here, yes... oh, yes, soak my hand like that... good girl..."

Jane kept on staring in front of herself, but her eyes betrayed her, and she couldn't help but notice the bulge in the trousers of the devil at her side. She knew what would happen now. Guy would drop his trousers; he would put his... his thing... in her mouth... yes, he would make her suck his... his member... right now, right here, in front of the window, with her naked bottom in mid-air, while she would shiver with cold and shame.

Tomorrow I will give you more.

"Good..." Guy muttered. She had completely wet his fingers, his hand; even she had saliva dripping down her chin, and this made him smile smugly. "You are an obedient slave, Jane..."

Contrary to what she expected, he didn't drop his trousers; he went behind her again. Jane didn't have the time to breathe a sigh of relief, because his hand, moistened with her saliva, touched her between her inner thighs and then slipped to her pussy. He gently stroked her vulva, resting on the soft golden hair that covered it. In the small room, it was cold, but a wave of heat shocked her body, melting her inside. Up and down, up and down... and she was completely opened to his hand, completely exposed to his eyes. She was indecent. What remained of her modesty?

"Guy... Guy, don't..."

"Shhh..."

Lubricated by her generous licking, his fingers slid easily between the lips of her womanhood. He parted them, slipping into her folds with gentle rubbing. A thick juice, under his soaked fingertips, gushed out from her because of these continuous, experienced caresses; it happened naturally... and terribly. He teased the entrance of her pussy; appalled, Jane felt a finger come inside her, greeted by her tight, sopping orifice.

"You told me you love this view, Jane..." Guy murmured with a not very firm voice, "tell me, how do you love it now?"

When would this obscenity end? The cold in the room did not exist anymore; there was only Guy's plunging, his fingers playing between her legs. His hand was through her fleshy intimate lips, and a squishy oil flooded her lady parts. It had been his touch's fault, that damn, wicked touch of his, and she found herself sloppy from his relentless, arrogant rhythm that melted her; and farther back, a finger entered her, a phalanx, perhaps two, into her, oh God...

"Is it good, Jane?... the view?..."

In front of her, drops of water were falling from the icicles hanging down from the upper window frame; and the glass, just a few inches from her face, was misted with her warm, hard breathing, forming a wet veil of fog.

"Please stop," she murmured, forgetting that the word "no" was forbidden with him. "Guy, *please...*"

Guy laughed softly. He did *not* stop. His fingers kept on playing among her silky, prohibited curls. He was having fun, he was laughing at her and at the physical sensations she couldn't hide from him. Oh God—he knew. He knew what she was feeling, he was mocking her for that. Yet, Jane could not control herself, cruelly not, while she was being touched with this arrogance, with this pitiless mastery. It was startling and disconcerting, but in her belly something loosened, overpowered by a wave of liquid emotion—as the water of a river slips among smooth, shiny rocks along its path, exploding in a hundred crystal drops.

"You do really like... this view, my angel..."

Guy's voice was hoarse as if he were feeling the same pleasure he was giving her.

Pleasure?

Had she just thought *pleasure?*

It couldn't be; it *shouldn't* be, and Jane gasped for air. Her pussy opened to accommodate Guy's finger more deeply into her drenched heat. Jane arched with a moan. Her belly was hot, like flames inside her, despite the cold room. Was it the humiliation she felt that made her moan like this? Below her navel, there was a tension she had never experienced before. It was pulling in her loins with fierce, involuntary need. She closed her eyes, and her mind forgot everything: her father, the debts, the blackmail...

She threw her head back, breathing with her mouth open, and Guy, that perfidious, that vile, that cruel devil, brushed the little button at the beginning of her swollen lips, titillating her, and his touch was making an immoral sound against her wet flesh, like the sound of the gentle rains of April, or the damp splash of childish jumps in the puddles after a storm.

"Oh, yes, Jane... this view is... breathtaking..."

Jane's legs widened, liquefied and trembling, to be touched more, to make Guy get deeper. With twinges of wet arousal in her belly, her vaginal entrance was offering itself to him, *Guy get inside me, oh please, Guy, please,* but he didn't plunge his finger all the way—his fingers were moving back and forth, back and forth just an inch or so, while his fingertip circled on her little knob so wisely, so perfectly. Oh, Guy was the devil, he was the damned devil...

"Jane..." he called huskily, but she couldn't answer, lost in these sensations, with her eyes closed. "Jane," he repeated, stopping his hands. She groaned in frustration... in what? Frustration? Did she want him to continue, really, did she want this devil to continue touching her?

She opened her eyes and managed to get them fixed out of the window, breathing heavily, her heart beating savagely. Her inner thighs were damp, she was moist, swollen... a liquid fire was flowing over her, enslaving her with vicious waves of heat. What was happening to her? Guy's hands, hot and wet from her secretions, were motionless on her vulva. How did his hands make her forget herself?

"Jane..." Guy paused, taking a deep breath. His voice was rough, rasping, as it had been yesterday, when he had told her, *lick it, Jane... suck it all.* "Now I want you..." he continued softly, "I want you to describe the street to me."

Describe what?

"Tell me what you see..." repeated Guy, and slapped her on her left buttock, making her jump. Was he... *spanking* her? "Tell me before I get angry... you don't want me to get angry, do you..."

"No, I..." she murmured. "I see a... a..." She moaned as he started to move his fingers again, slowly, smoothly. Guy was cruel, but his hands weren't, his hands were gentle and tender, *don't stop, Guy... please don't stop...* "A house... the house where Mrs... ahhhhh..." Jane looked down. Guy slapped her buttocks again, and she straightened her head with a difficult effort. "Mrs. M... Marks..." she managed to say. Between her legs, she was dribbling, and it wasn't the saliva she had wet Guy's hands with, no, it was a denser liquid than that, it was a warm, voluptuous oil...

God, it was *herself.*

She got her head precariously up, with sudden snaps when he touched the swollen little pearl at the top of her sex, and inside her pussy, his finger violated her, pitiless and insistent, with a dishonorable noise... *shlick;* shamelessly, *shlick;* wonderfully, *shlick, shlick, shlick.*

"Mrs. Marks..." Guy's voice sounded different from how she had ever heard it, full of desire and smiling at the same time. "And you were scared of her, weren't you, Jane?... of that woman..."

Did he remember? Did he remember the secret she had confided to him as a child? He was touching her, he was shaming her, but Jane's heart trembled and she thought she could cry, cry with joy, just because of this tiny, silly memory she shared with him, only with him in the entire world.

"How... how can you r... remember... how... oh, Guy... Guy..."

"I remember, yes," he murmured suffocated. "I remember very well, my angel."

* * *

He did remember. His heart swelled; Jane was in his hands, a wet, trembling angel, beside herself with arousal; and it was about to happen, she was going to climax. Guy dropped his pants and took his hard erection in his hand. He began to stroke his dick while looking at her. She was helpless in front of him, and he didn't stop caressing her cunt, so wet and warm, a melting lake of passion.

She was excited, eager.

She was *his.*

"What's... what's happening, Guy, what's..."

Jane's voice was choked with unknown sensations. She was scared, for she didn't know what was going on, she didn't have a clue. Innocent little girl, this would be her first orgasm, and pride almost caused Guy to lose his self-control. But today wasn't meant for him, not for him, and he didn't give her any breaks, and he touched her without pauses, without pity, where she was swollen and flushed and pleading for more.

Come between my hands, my angel... come, come for me... "Tell me what you see..." he said again as he touched both himself and her. "Tell me, angel..."

"The snow... the snow is white... and everything is so..." she groaned, arching her back, without looking outside anymore, but it was fine, he wouldn't scold her, he wouldn't scold her, his Jane, his hot, sensual angel; "so beautiful, Guy, so... *ohhhh!*"

She was his, only his, and as the orgasm shook her, Guy felt her contractions under his fingers, and felt her pleasure, and heard her guttural moan of wild delight.

It was the shameless moan of a woman gasping through her first, shocking orgasm.

"You're right, Jane..." he murmured as he let himself come, spattering her buttocks with thick streams of his sperm, "it's beautiful... it's so beautiful."

7.

The gas lamps lit Brushfield Street with a monochrome glow. It was the night of December 25, yet there were whores hidden in the shadows, working as always. Some of them took a step forward as Guy passed them. Their clothes were low-cut and colorful, but while they could look vivid in the sun, they almost faded out in the damp light of the lamps, among the dirty-white snowdrifts.

"Looking for company, handsome?"

Their voices, whispered and croaky, remained behind him. Their rouged faces and crimson lips disappeared in the shadows again.

The comings and goings on the sidewalk prevented the ice from forming. Thin streams of dirty, muddy water flowed on the road and muffled the footsteps of the passersby hanging around so late at night. Ahead of Guy, a man, walking briskly, suddenly swore and began to jump on one foot. Since no street-sweepers ever shoveled up the horse manure in that part of town, the man over there had just stepped over a steaming pile of shit. That was a typical problem of inattentive persons. Guy passed by him as the man, uttering slurred imprecations, uselessly kicked the wall to clean his ruined shoe. There wasn't enough illumination on the street. The high houses beside the road prevented the light from penetrating the darkest corners, and the narrow blind alleys were perfect hiding places for thieves.

Guy didn't care. He wasn't the prime target for criminals. He was dressed poorly, he was six feet one inch tall, and his imposing physique was an effective deterrent for any scumbag hunting for victims. Offenders prefer frail, drunken, wealthy fellows.

He passed by a whore who, with her coat open, was showing her few beauties.

"Hello, tough guy... do you want to have fun?" the whore shouted behind him.

Guy didn't stop walking. He strode to the appointed place for the meeting of the Gang of Knives.

The place where he was, the stink all over the street, everything around him was in absurd contrast to the afternoon he had just spent with Jane.

Guy couldn't think about Jane now.

He had to focus on the mission waiting for him. He couldn't indulge in any distractions, not now. He couldn't think of the way Jane had reached her first climax between his hands. He needed to wait for this night to end. Soon the K-mission would be over, and he would be home; he would wash the blood off his hands, he'd wash away the smell of slaughtered meat from his body. And only then, finally, would he allow himself to think about what had happened in the small attic of Courtnell Street, Number 7.

He knew he was about to undertake a difficult task. The details were still to be planned and he needed to meet the other members of the Gang. He already knew something about this mission though. In the morning, he had received a message informing him of the time and place of the meeting. The message also said: "K-Level One." In the language of the Gang, the K-Level One was the worst. It involved shedding of a lot of blood, splattered bowels and other various organic matter.

Guy was wearing a long black cloak, a miserable old hat and a scarf that covered his face. He hoped he wouldn't meet any acquaintances, for he would be recognized despite his disguise. His height and physique were difficult to conceal, even though he was walking slightly bent, like an actor performing in The Hunchback of Notre-Dame.

A little-talented actor.

He shrugged. Few aristocrats would be surprised to see him in the East End of London. It was hardly a secret that the 4th Earl of Ashbourne was used to mixing with common people. Every newspaper wrote about it. What a total waste of ink, Guy thought. They reported about how often the 4th Earl of Ashbourne took part in drunken brawls at the most infamous taverns of London. At the aristocratic clubs, there were other rumors. Some claimed (often with hidden admiration) that the poorest areas of the city were a sort of hunting zone for Ashbourne. In the suburbs, some said, Guy Spencer would look for women to bend to his wicked desires. Poor women were the best victims, for they couldn't afford to seek justice.

What a son of a bitch, that scoundrel Ashbourne!...

Guy's lips lifted in a smile both sarcastic and disgusted. He leaned against the wall to let two drunken men by. They were holding each other because of their unsteady balance. Guy didn't meet their gaze. He needed not to draw attention to himself. It was the first rule: Never attract attention during the K-Nights. The two drunken men, however, didn't seem to look for company or trouble. They were happy in their drunkenness; they were singing a dirty song with slurred voices.

Oh pretty, pretty, pretty Mary
Open your pretty, pretty legs for me...

Guy kept on walking. After a few minutes, he arrived at 2 Brushfield Street. It was a decrepit, abandoned three-story building. By some miracle, it was still standing. Its bricks were cracked and there were big holes in its rotten wooden shutters.

It was simply perfect. The place was supposed to be exactly like this.

On the right side of the building, there was a stairway leading to the basement. Guy walked down the frozen steps, holding onto the wall for support. If he broke his leg, it would be regarded as some kind of battlefield wound, but not one of the most honorable kind. There were definitely greater dangers during a K-Night.

In his right boot, Guy could feel the weight of the hidden, sharp dagger he would be using soon. The mission was about to begin, and he was ready. And maybe, if he were lucky enough, it wouldn't be his turn to throw the Last Knife.

8.

Jane was walking slowly on the street, keeping her face down. She was careful to avoid the puddles and the snow on the sidewalk. It was the last day of the year, and the last day she would live in Courtnell Street. She was holding a heavy wicker basket, and her hands tightened on it as she faced a large and disturbing ice sheet. The basket was full of sweets for the children of St Mary Orphan Refuge. It was weighty, but somehow it was helping her to maintain her stability.

Her head was bowed, so she almost collided with a pram. She looked up and, with some effort, smiled at the young woman who was pushing the pram. The baby boy in it was covered with blankets and pillows, and Jane could see only his little nose and his eyes closed in serene sleep.

The young woman smiled back, stepped aside and kept going. Jane looked straight ahead. The orphanage was down Moorhouse Road. It was a walk she was used to doing every morning, but today that half a mile seemed long, almost endless.

Would Guy allow her to continue going to her orphans?

Guy.

The thought of him immobilized her. For a moment, her right foot remained suspended in mid-air over the gray sidewalk.

She hadn't seen Guy since Christmas Day. Since when...

Blushing violently, she took a deep breath and let her foot go down, resuming walking.

She was about to move to Ashbourne House. With *him*. Her father had agreed to go. Charles hadn't even been too surprised, to tell the truth, when Jane had ardently assured him that yes, she *did* want to go living with her stepbrother, "like a real family."

Her father had probably thought that Guy had talked her into moving to his palace by using some kind, affectionate words. Dear Papa, he couldn't even imagine what Guy was doing to her... On Christmas Day, when Charles had seen Jane's misty eyes as she had come back from the attic, he must have believed that Jane's tears were due to some touching feeling. He couldn't suspect how Guy had ignobly caressed her. Guy... Guy had ejaculated on her skin, he had enjoyed every moment of her degradation. And afterward, he had looked at her from above and had just said: "You must be at Ashbourne House within a week, Jane. Convince your father, or our deal is off." Then, he had turned his back on her and had got out of the room, leaving her crouched on the floor. She had stayed there for many minutes, disheveled and exhausted, feeling his semen sliding down her legs. As her confused mind had finally cleared out, a devastating wave of shame had washed over her. She had remembered Guy's dissolute hands, and how his touch had made her shake with demeaning, outrageous pleasure...

The cold air made white clouds in front of her face, but Jane didn't feel cold. Her cheeks were on fire.

Guy hadn't been nice. He had told her no sweet words. He had given her orders, and she had meekly obeyed. He had touched her in any way he'd wanted, and had put her in front of the attic's window because he wanted to punish her. He wanted to take her childhood memories away from her.

Tears stung her eyes. She held them back.

She shouldn't have felt such inexcusable pleasure... she should have hated Guy's touch, his hands, and...

She swallowed. No, she shouldn't think of him. She shouldn't.

She shook her head and looked up. The great, austere church of St Mary the Virgin was before her.

It was a tall, dark building, with three rows of mullioned windows. Climbing plants grew over the lower right corner of the church, attenuating the gray of its walls. Despite the severity of its design, Jane's heart relieved in looking at it.

Her pupils were inside. They are waiting impatiently for her. It was a joy for Jane. It was her last joy of 1851, and probably her last joy for a long time to come.

Beside the main entrance, there was a small door, which passed unnoticed by most visitors of the church. The door led directly to the orphanage. There were sixteen little orphans inside. Sixteen sweet little souls.

Today, Jane would make them happy. Today, she could give them more than a few apples and a lot of smiles. The wicker basket was bulky in her hands. Inside, there were sweets and candy and a cake—a real cake, filled with chocolate and nut cream. She had sent them many presents the previous days: Guy had supplied the Hartwells with food, clothes, and wood, so why not share all of this with those in need? Why not use all that abundance for something good, something that, even though it couldn't diminish Jane's humiliation, would not, however, increase it?

Because some of Guy's presents did increase her humiliation. Just that morning, a seamstress named Mrs. Boswell had brought her new dresses and *colorful* undergarments.

Colorful!

The dresses were bright. Their colors were light. The seamstress had said that the 4th Earl of Ashbourne wished his stepsister to stop mourning Rona's death. The large petticoats were full of ruffles and lace. And they were stiff, please don't forget their stiffness. Some of them positively creaked when Jane moved. Jane wasn't used to having her skirts inflated like that... how could she possibly move with ease, with all that crinoline?

It will be the least of your problems, angel, a mocking voice whispered in her ear—a male, bullying voice, a voice which, since Christmas Eve, kept on talking in her mind, laughing at her from morning till night, without rest.

Her least problem... right. The first one would be...

Shaking her head to get rid of that fixed idea, Jane opened the door of the orphanage. She wasn't wearing a new dress. She had put on her old overcoat. *My old overcoat, Guy.* She had put the new clothes away in a wooden chest. From tomorrow, she would become a property of Guy Spencer, 4th Earl of Ashbourne. Today, she could still be herself. Maybe, to others, being Jane Hartwell wasn't that great. She was just a young woman with little responsibilities: teaching orphans in the morning, nursing at the hospital in the afternoon. To her, it had always been enough. To tell the truth, at the hospital she often felt inadequate, but that never happened with the orphans of St Mary—*her* kids, as she thought of them. She understood them. She understood their way of speaking, their fears, their dreams. While teaching them, she never bent her gaze. She was rarely that confident with adults, maybe because she, too, had been a child without parents, at least for the first years of her life. Her mother had died in giving her birth, and her father, busy with his perfume business and his own pain, had entrusted her to her maternal aunt and uncle's care.

Sometimes, Jane thought that perhaps her father had abandoned her when she was newborn because he couldn't bear to see her. She was the cause of her mother's death, after all. Yes, Jane thought—maybe her father had hated her at first. This consideration was painful, even now.

She had spent the first years of her life in Somerset, with the Gardiners, some relatives of her mother. She didn't remember them much, they were just quick flashes in her mind. There was Uncle George, always serious with his black outfit. He was the pastor of the small town of Axbridge. Aunt Emily, his wife, had always dressed in black, too.

And there was something else Jane remembered. Miniature paintings. Miniature paintings of a baby boy. These small paintings were everywhere: on the mantelpiece, on the walls, on the shelves. This baby boy's name had been Edward, but he had died three years before Jane's arrival. He had been the first and only son of the Gardiners. Edward wasn't among them, not in person, yet he *was* among them. So, you weren't allowed to laugh in their house, because Edward was dead. You had to walk slowly. You couldn't make any noise. Above all, you shouldn't bother Uncle George and Aunt Emily.

Her aunt had fed Jane, though. She had washed her, she had looked after her. But Emily Gardiner, with her gray hair and tired eyes, would never risk loving a child again, and Jane had quickly realized that nobody cared for her. Not in that house. Maybe nowhere. Not that Charles had abandoned her *literally*. He used to visit her at the Gardiners' three or four times a year. During his visits, Jane never complained or cried. At four years old, she barely spoke: she said hardly any words at all, as if learning difficulties prevented her from speaking. Jane had never asked Charles to take her away from that place, but, luckily, someone else had: Rona Spencer. Yes, Rona. She had noticed the little, invisible Jane Hartwell. She had noticed the way Jane avoided everyone, her speech impediment, her loneliness. So, Rona, the widow of the 3rd Earl of Ashbourne, the most important woman of Axbridge, had memorably faced Charles Hartwell. Showing a personality no one could imagine from her, Rona had yelled at him...

And that was how it all had started. Rona had loved Jane first, and only later her father.

And then, Jane had met Guy...

Don't think of Guy.

Don't.

Jane swallowed and roused herself from these memories. She closed the door and prepared her sunniest smile. She expected to see Thomasina, the cook, in the doorway. Instead, she saw Mrs. Barnaby, the orphanage director. Jane's smile froze on her lips. There was an inexplicable difference between a smile of joy and one of circumstance.

No, Mrs. Barnaby was not a bad person. She just had very strict rules about some things.

Mrs. Barnaby didn't smile. She never smiled. "Oh, Miss Hartwell," she greeted her, as practical as the dress she was wearing. "You have arrived early."

Yes, because I hoped I could give the cake to the kids before your arrival. Jane sighed and tried to hide her disappointment. "Yes, I'd like to see the children with no rush," she murmured. "To express to all of them my good wishes for the new year."

"Give it to me," said Mrs. Barnaby, holding out her hands toward Jane's basket. Her hands were greedy, and she looked like a hawk. Hawk-Barnaby.

"Actually," Jane pulled back the basket, shrinking back a bit, "I would like to eat this little cake with the children."

"They have already eaten their pudding," Mrs. Barnaby muttered, moving aside and letting Jane into the narrow hallway.

Classic Hawk-Barnaby objection. "But it's the last day of the year..." Jane tried to soften her. The problem was, Mrs. Barnaby was used to doing what was right, nothing more. The kids had already had their breakfast, so the cake was one cake too many.

Hawk-Barnaby looked at Jane sideways. "You looked a little dejected," she said, and, much to Jane's surprise, she gave a slight smile. "Is it because of my refusal?"

Not just for that. Jane's mouth twitched, and she opted for a half-truth. "A bit. Might you turn a blind eye this once?"

The older woman merely shrugged. It wasn't a refusal, was it? Perhaps, with the arrival of the new year, Mrs. Barnaby had softened a bit. Jane clung to this hopeful sign and followed her to the common room.

The room was small, providentially small, otherwise it would have been too cold in winter. Not today: the fire was crackling happily, thanks to the wood Jane had sent to the orphanage on Christmas.

On the sofa, there were two sleepy children; three of them were sitting at the table. They were writing, and, Jane noticed with a flicker of joy, they were using the notebooks she had sent yesterday. On the floor, a little girl was cradling a piece of wood covered with a cloth. Other heads stuck out behind the chairs and other furniture.

"Good morning," she said with a vivacious tone. A tone she never used when she talked with the butcher or the baker or the shoemaker. This confidence appeared just for the kids and for her father. For Rona, before her death. And for Guy, when they were children.

Guy... no. Oh no.

She swallowed and went on: "Won't you say hello to me today?"

The children saw her. An immediate noise of chairs followed, along with exclamations of joy. They ran to the door and surrounded her. Richard, Arthur, Elizabeth... little Joanna with her lovely freckles and short red hair, and Claire, Robert, so frail he disappeared in the old shirt he had on. The children were of different heights and ages, from five years old to nine, but they all dressed similarly: brown and threadbare trousers for the boys and brown and threadbare skirts for the girls. Very practical dresses indeed... in the genuine Hawk-Barnaby style.

"Hey," Jane laughed. "Let me in. How about eating something nice this morning?"

"J... Jane," said Michael, a little boy with a bulbous nose, "is it true you'll b... b... become a co... countess?"

Jane sighed, slowly undoing the ribbon of her bonnet. "I'm going to live for a while with an earl," she murmured in response. "But I won't become a countess." She would become the slave of an earl... his plaything.

His doll.

Don't.

Don't think about him now.

She put the basket on the table and took off her overcoat. She turned around to place it on a chair, but Mrs. Barnaby prevented her from doing so and picked it up, making for the door. "I'll take it to the main entrance. I need Thomasina for the tablecloth and the plates, anyway."

"What have you b... b... brought us, J... Jane? A c... cake?"

Michael stuttered painfully today, but Jane wouldn't lose hope. Maybe it was worse than usual because he was so excited about the surprise. Lately, Michael had been speaking almost fluently. Jane had taught him the same nursery rhymes that, years before, Rona had taught her to push *her* to speak. These rhymes had worked with Michael too, improving his speech. Maybe he had been abandoned because of his stammer. He wasn't born an orphan; he had been accepted in St Mary at four years old. He was eight now.

"Pralines?" Robert ventured.

There were both pralines and cake, and Jane laughed cheerfully, forgetting Guy's blackmail for a moment.

"Come on, show us!"

The kids were looking at the closed basket as it were a treasure. She looked down at Joanna and ruffled her hair. "Let's wait for Mrs. Barnaby. It'll be a wonderful party." *And let's hope 1852 will be a great year,* she added silently. *Oh, how I hope the next six months will pass quickly!*

Quickly, my God.

Quickly.

She took a breath and counted the kids around the table. One, two, three... fifteen. Where was Henry? Jane went to the fireplace looking behind the sofa. He was certainly in the kitchen, or hidden, or...

Then she saw him. A blond boy with his face bent down, sitting on the floor. He was behind the sofa and was looking into a white square box, four inches per side, twelve inches tall. The box was open at the top. Henry didn't seem to have noticed the noisy, happy confusion in the room.

"Hey, little man. Aren't you going to greet me?" Smiling, Jane approached him. "Look, there's something you'll like."

Henry didn't look up. "I don't want anything."

"Oh, come on," she murmured, brushing his shoulder with her hand. She knelt beside him and peered into the box. The contents made her shiver. "Oh, Henry!" she exclaimed. "Why have you captured that poor cockroach?"

Her voice trembled as she said it. She was awfully afraid of cockroaches. That one in particular: it was Mr. Cockroach, the Cockroach King, if cockroaches ever decided to have a king. It was large, shiny and horrible, with fast little legs. Its black armor stood out against the white box. The hideous insect tried to climb the walls to escape from its prison, but

Henry's hand sent it back down.

"I told you not to harm insects, Henry. They suffer too, you know."

Keeping his head lowered, Henry shrugged. The purple burn on the left side of his face was visible just at the bottom, on his chin and neck. What had scarred him? Boiling water? Acid? No one knew. He had been in custody of St Mary for five years, and his face had always had that terrible mark. If you looked at him from the right side, his beauty was startling; when he turned, it was a blow to your heart, every time, for the ache and the impotence you would feel.

"Cockroaches," the boy said, backing up a few inches and taking the box, "are disgusting to everyone, even to you. Why are you pretending that you even care?"

"But Henry..."

"Mrs. Barnaby said you have become rich," he interrupted, closing the top of the box with his right hand.

Jane blushed to the roots of her hair. "My stepbrother is rich. Not me."

"He could buy the orphanage, then."

Yes, he could. How can I explain this to you, little man? Not only isn't he going to buy this orphanage, but he probably won't allow me to come here to see you again. She would spend the next six months with Guy; but what would he permit her to do? She had to tell him that teaching at the orphanage was important for her. *Guy, these kids... please don't take them away from me.*

"It's... complicated, Henry."

He grimaced, and the defect of his cheek looked worse. His skin irregularities stood out in small purple bumps. "It's always complicated for the rich, isn't it." He looked up, and as always the miracle happened: the deep blue irises erased the burn, the scar, the asymmetry of his face. "You've brought sweets and candy... is it because you won't come here anymore, now that you're a countess?"

Jane opened her mouth. *Of course. Of course I'll come here again,* she wanted to answer, but she couldn't. She couldn't! "I'm not a countess," she murmured finally.

It was impossible fooling Henry with a non-answer. His thoughts were as fast as him. He stood up and, turning the box toward her, threw the cockroach in her direction. The black insect hit her on the chest. Jane jerked in surprise and terror, giving a little cry. Off balance, she thumped her bottom on the floor, frantically shaking off the cockroach from her.

"Henry!" she called him back as the insect fell down and ran toward the wall. She got up, but Henry had already made for the door. He didn't give her time to stop him, to tell him goodbye, to tell him, "I hope to see you soon, little man, I do really hope so." Jane watched Henry's blond head disappear as Mrs. Barnaby and Thomasina came in with the plates and spoons.

9.

What the hell am I doing?

Charles looked at Jane and, for the umpteenth time, asked himself the same question.

What the hell am I doing?

His daughter was sitting on the sofa, wearing a green overcoat. She had a parasol of the same color over her lap, and she was clutching it with both hands. Actually, she was clutching it so hard, she probably would break it in a minute. Gosh, Jane had sounded sincere when she'd told him that she did *really* want to move to Ashbourne House. Yet Charles couldn't quite suppress a "something-is-wrong" feeling. For example, the stretched expression on Jane's face was *definitely* wrong.

But maybe, Charles was just being overprotective. He wasn't used to seeing her like that. Jane was very elegant today. Her winter overcoat was of exquisite cut and excellent quality. It was a present from Guy, of course, and it was a really nice, expensive coat. But somehow it looked strange on her. It was not because elegant clothes didn't suit Jane, but because... oh, come on! She didn't need fancy clothes, as a white daisy doesn't need colorful petals to be beautiful. How could Guy not understand, for God's sake?

Charles, what the hell are you doing? "Honey, if you've changed your mind..."

Jane winced. Deeply immersed in her thoughts, she hadn't noticed she was being carefully observed. She shook her head quickly. "No, Papa, I'm happy. I'm very, very happy. I'm just... a little scared, that's it."

"Scared of what, my child? Of Guy's aristocratic friends?"

Jane bit her lower lip and nodded. She had become beautiful, Charles realized with a kind of bittersweet amazement. She had high cheekbones, rosy cheeks, and full, naturally red lips. And there were her big, beautiful eyes. Her irises were neither brown nor hazel, but a mixture of gold and amber. It was an unusual eye color, inherited from her mother, Mary Jane Gardiner. It had been Mary Jane's only good feature; and Mary Jane's eyes still lived on in her daughter.

Oh, Mary Jane...

I know you're marrying me for my money, Mr. Hartwell. I'm ugly, not stupid.

Charles smiled at this twenty-two-year-old memory. Mary Jane had been ugly indeed... ugly to others. And opinionated, daring, quarrelsome. She had lacked the sweetness so typical of Jane. Nobody had ever thought Mary Jane lovely... except Charles. Charles had known Mary Jane's sweetness at night, in her generous arms. Like her beauty, his first wife had shown him and him alone her inner tenderness. He had felt privileged with Mary Jane; and he really had been.

Jane, on the other hand, was beautiful beyond all expectations. Somehow, she reminded Charles of her mother: he saw Mary Jane in Jane's expressions, in her forehead shape and in her strange eye color. But what had been excessive or unsymmetrical in Mary Jane was smooth, delicate and attractive in Jane.

Unlike her mother, she was also naive and timid to excess. It was a longstanding, deep-rooted problem. It had never been solved, not even when Charles had finally taken her away from her aunt and uncle's house and their less-than-good care. She was a little girl of five back then; Rona had become her stepmother and had taken Jane under her wing. Rona had taught her to speak. She had helped her to get rid of her major stammering, and above all, she had given her the affection Jane had never received before. Yet, Jane's character hadn't strengthened. Probably, it was inevitable. Charles's frail second wife wasn't the best person to teach a little girl how to be more confident. Anyway, Rona had loved her like a daughter, and her affection had seemed a godsend to Charles.

He shifted in his seat, trying to ease the ache in his right hip. The forced immobility made his pain worse.

The fact still remained that Guy's friends were aristocrats, rakes and expert seducers. And Jane was so innocent. Charles couldn't help but fear that, among such men, she...

No, no. He shook his head. Guy would protect her. At least, Charles wanted to believe so. Guy cared for her, didn't he? Sometimes Charles even wondered if his stepson was *in love* with her. Charles had given up finding the answer. It had always been impossible for him to understand Guy Spencer.

"Jane."

"Yes, Papa?"

"We are entering a new world. A world more... unconventional than ours. At first you will be dazzled, but..."

"I won't be dazzled, Papa."

Why did her voice sound that forced to him? "Do you happen to remember what Rona used to tell you, child? Men sometimes..."

Jane blushed to the roots of her hair. "...are wolves wearing lambskins,

70

yes," she muttered with a hint of sadness. "I know."

You know nothing, my child. "Guy has promised to protect you, Jane. He'll keep you away from... unworthy persons. So please, give me a smile, my dear. You're not afraid of some foppish marquess, are you?"

Jane smiled rigidly. As a matter of fact, she seemed about to literally break her parasol in half.

"God, I think I'm making a huge mistake, my child." Charles rubbed his forehead with his thumb and forefinger. "I hope I won't regret it."

"It's just a matter of a few months, Papa. Just a few months," she repeated, as if she were trying to convince herself. "Until we can afford our own house. This very house, maybe."

"No, not this one," said Charles in a whisper, looking around the living room. It was almost empty of furniture, but, at the same time, it was full of invisible presences. There was Rona, silently embroidering by the fire. A five-year-old Jane was playing with her dolls on the floor. Guy was nine or ten years old. He was frowning as usual, while peeking at Jane over the top of the book he was pretending to read.

There were way too many memories there. Bittersweet, haunting memories.

A carriage stopped outside the door. Jane's knuckles grew whiter.

Rona had always tried to keep Jane away from Guy. Charles was bringing them together. Was it the right thing to do?

Outside, the carriage was waiting to pick them up.

Charles took a deep breath.

It was time to say farewell to Courtnell Street, Number 7.

* * *

The 1st of January 1852 was a cold, snowy day. Yet inside the rich carriage which was bringing Jane and her father to Ashbourne House, it was nicely warm. There were two warming-pans filled with hot water at their feet. The carriage was big, and its interior was covered with burgundy padded fabric. The seats were soft and comfortable. The street's potholes were barely felt inside and didn't bother the passengers.

Or, maybe, Jane noticed no discomfort because she couldn't. She wasn't noticing anything at all. She was tense to the point of feeling sick. Over her lap, she had a heavy blanket, available to the carriage's passengers; she was clutching it with her fingers.

The carriage was drawn by two bright black horses. The livery of the footmen was dark blue and gold, shining with the traditional colors of the Spencer family. Everything looked like it was straight out of a fairy tale. It didn't even seem real.

But it was real.

Everything was real.

Jane forgot to breathe. Her chest compressed with anxiety.

Ashbourne House.

She would soon be at Ashbourne House.

She had seen Guy's magnificent palace only from the outside. She had never gone inside. Ashbourne House was built in the middle of the most aristocratic part of London. The palace had been passed down from generation to generation. With the whiteness of its stones, the romantic climbing roses on its west side and its rows and rows of glossy windows, it looked like a princess's castle. Rona had been banned from Ashbourne House after marrying Charles Hartwell in 1841. She had been banned by Mr. Blackwood, Guy's legal guardian, who, as executor of Guy's father's will, had managed the Earl's properties until Guy came of age at twenty-one.

So, paradoxically, Ashbourne House, which like most great houses was partially open to the public, had been forbidden only to the Earl's widow and her new family. None of them would have gone there, however, and Rona least of all. She had hated Ashbourne House, and Guy had never tried to invite her to the palace after taking possession of it. Even Guy, after all, hadn't set foot there until he turned twenty-one.

Guy. Guy Guy Guy...

His name echoed loudly in her head. She wondered how her father, sitting silently in front of her, could not hear it.

Guy, please, don't hurt me.

Guy, please, don't take everything away from me.

Guy...

The carriage passed through an imposing iron gate and climbed an uphill driveway. It stopped, finally, in front of a huge mansion.

Ashbourne House.

The facade was marble, and a large garden separated the house from the prosaic gray buildings of London. The garden would be a perfect picture in spring; now it was covered by white snow, and the classical round fountain in the middle was turned off because of the freezing temperatures.

A footman opened the carriage door, and Jane looked up at the staircase to the entrance.

It was like a blow to her heart.

The 4th Earl of Ashbourne, Guy Spencer, was standing at the top of the staircase. He was wearing a black cloak, and his imposing, dark figure stood out against the white marble columns at the sides of the massive wooden front door. He straightened his shoulders and, watching them from above, he said with a lazy smile, "Welcome to Ashbourne House."

10.

I'm such a good boy, aren't I? Guy thought, observing the cup between his fingers. He was sitting in the smallest drawing room in Ashbourne House. It was the smallest but, of course, it was as big as the whole house at 7 Courtnell Street.

It was teatime. How long had it been since he'd had proper tea at Ashbourne House? Yet here he was, with an appropriate cup in his hands, cake, and sweets on the table.

And bread and butter—fuckin' real bread and butter.

He smiled and looked at Jane from above his cup. She had arrived at Ashbourne House less than three hours ago. She was slowly sipping her tea, and she seemed so small on the large blue velvet sofa. Her high-necked dress was pale yellow and stood out against the elegant fabric. It was a new dress, she had not challenged him by wearing something threadbare at Ashbourne House; nevertheless Guy had to explain to her that her style of clothing was wrong. Quite wrong. *You won't need these high-necked dresses, little Jane,* he thought with a slight tremor in his lower abdomen. *You will get hot in here, trust me.*

He was feeling almost drunk with her a few feet away from him. It was a sensation of burning comfort, and it had started as Jane had crossed the entrance of Ashbourne House.

Oh, that moment...

Guy closed his eyes, reliving the scene. It had been as exciting as an orgasm: she had frozen in the immense entrance hall, among the bright gold and purple walls, and the light from the large windows had hit her violently, and Guy's aristocratic power had poured on her. The hall ceiling was as high as the palace, and a profusion of paintings, frescoes, statues, and carpets had imposed itself on her eyes. And there were flowers, flowers everywhere, on the polished corner tables, by the side of the curtains, everywhere. The big windows illuminated the space, carrying the eye up to two majestic twin stairways that led to the upper floors, and downstairs a small Jane Hartwell had seemed unable to move and breathe. This entrance hall was telling her a simple, unequivocal thing: *you are a little nobody, Jane*

Hartwell, and Guy Spencer, the 4th Earl of Ashbourne, can crush you under his heel whenever he wants.

Charles Hartwell put his cup into the saucer with a bang. He was sitting in an armchair to the right of the sofa, watching his daughter with a frown. Guy was sitting on the opposite side, in the twin armchair to the left. He was restless against its high back. The style of the furniture was neoclassical, and its structure was balanced between light cherry and dark walnut. Greek and Roman shapes were supposed to be useful for achieving mental calm... too bad they were totally wasted on Guy's present mood.

All he wanted was to have Jane naked in his bed.

The fire crackled in the large marble hearth, and Guy noticed that Charles, looking away from Jane, was watching him.

This was a big problem indeed. Hiding his desire was no small thing.

"How do you like your room, Jane?" Guy asked mildly, breaking the silence.

She didn't lift her eyes. She was clutching her teacup between her white and delicate fingers. Her hands contrasted faintly with the porcelain; they were small and graceful against the decorations of leaves and petals on the cup.

Guy stared at her bowed head in fascination. He was afraid to show his impure thoughts, but really, he couldn't help but watch her. Jane had her hair in a bun, with a middle parting, and a few silky curls had escaped from it. Thank God he wasn't near her. He wouldn't have been able to resist the urge to reach out and touch her ringlets.

It was only four in the afternoon, but it was a gray first of January. The drawing room was well lit by many large silver chandeliers, or maybe it was Jane who was shining.

Guy thought so.

"It's... it's a lovely room, thank you," she stammered in response.

Lovely... yes, Guy had thought she would like it. Her suite must have looked immense to her. It was divided into a living room, a bedroom, and a nice dressing room full of mirrors, clothing, and perfumes. Guy had had it refurbished just for her, in shades of pink and white. Guy had gone in just yesterday. He had fantasized about every piece of furniture. It had been childish of him, perhaps, but also drop-dead satisfying. While looking at the Rococo sofa, flashy with its pillows full of ruffles and lace, he had imagined Jane standing before it, with her petticoat lifted to her waist, her hands on the back of the sofa, and him behind her... *inside* her. He would possess her everywhere, on every piece of furniture. Jane wouldn't see anything in the room without thinking of him.

He observed her with half-closed eyes. Next to her, there was a small table with a vase of white roses; and roses were throughout the room, but it was Jane, and Jane alone, who stood out in that garden.

"Did you mind that I set you up on the second floor?" he asked hoarsely.

Guy's bedroom was on the second floor as well. It was located in another wing, of course, and he hoped that would be enough to reassure Charles Hartwell.

"From up there, you could enjoy the best view," he explained, trying to cover the irony in his voice. "But maybe you would prefer an easier floor to get to, Jane? The ground floor, like your father?"

His interest was affable. It was a pity that she could not dare to ask for a room change.

"No. No, it's fine," she murmured, tightening her grip on the handle of her cup.

He couldn't add the question he wanted so badly to ask her. If she liked *this* view, too. Guy took a sip of tea, trying not to think about the attic room at Courtnell Street.

With a scowl, Charles put his cup on the table. He rested his forearms on the finely carved armrests and, finally, spat out the frustration he was holding in his throat.

"Everything is so damn huge here, Guy. I feel like half a man."

Guy lifted a corner of his mouth. *If everything were damn "small" you would feel exactly the same, Charles. You're no longer your own master, and this is the price to pay, didn't you know that?*

"Half a man, sir? You seem just the same to me. A very whole nuisance, as always."

"So, what did you expect, I'd be over the moon for joy?"

"I have that effect on people, usually."

"Yeah, sure," muttered Charles. "Well, here we are. The Lord of the Castle has ordered, and we have obeyed. Explain to us how this thing is supposed to work, big boy."

Big Boy. Guy smiled at his stepfather's patronizing words. *Ah, Charles, you can treat me like a child all you like.* "You should explain it to me, sir," he said with derision, derision that Jane alone could grasp. "You are my stepfather, after all."

Charles looked at him with "bullshit" written all over his face. He was dissatisfied with this answer, was he? Very well, Guy could go on with even bigger bullshit.

"What do you mean, how does this work?" he asked with a bored voice. "What are you talking about, your everyday life? Well, then. You will have a carriage at your disposal. Jane as well. I don't know if your daughter is a horsewoman. She wishes to become one, maybe?"

He looked at her, but she bowed her head over her porcelain cup more deeply. She did not answer.

Guy shrugged and went on. "If she wants to go horseback riding, the head groom—or I, if she will wish so—will take her to Hyde Park. There's no need to be formal, Mr. Hartwell. For all your requests, you can ask the butler, Stevens, you have already met him. He knows he must obey you as he does me. If you want to come. To go. Ashbourne House is all for you. Explore it as you see fit. There is the garden and, if that's not enough, there is the bordering park. You won't lack space." He took a sip of tea. "But if you ask me, I have a secret hope. I would like Jane to oversee the household. The housekeeper, that grim-faced Mrs. Robinson I introduced you to a few minutes ago, pesters me with her trouble about domestic stuff... who to hire, who to fire, what to eat for lunch. Things like these are vital to her. I give her no satisfaction, and I am worried that she will resign sooner or later. Jane—" he turned to her, pushing a bit against the back of his armchair "—this house urgently needs to be overseen by a woman. Would you do me this honor?"

"Honor," he had called it. And it certainly was... but for Jane, for Jane alone. Guy was asking Jane to manage Ashbourne House as only a woman of the family would have the right to do. A sister. A mother.

A wife.

Charles noticed this courtesy. "It's kind of you, Guy," he said, softening his tone. He loved his shy daughter, and pride shone in his green eyes as he looked at her. "Jane, darling? What do you think about it?"

"I..." Jane murmured, raising her eyes for a moment. A moment that Guy felt in his gut. "I'll be happy to help, Papa."

Charles looked doubtful. Her response lacked enthusiasm, and Jane's tension was palpable. Certainly, time would smother her discomfort. You get used to, like, everything. But now, how could a little virgin like her stay calm? Jane knew that soon the big bad wolf would eat her. She couldn't help but be frightened.

"So, Mr. Hartwell," Guy said, turning toward him with difficulty. He had to deflect attention from Jane, since pretending wasn't precisely her forte. "I hope I have reassured you. This is your home, and you can do whatever..." *the fuck* "...you want."

Charles smiled wryly. They both knew Ashbourne House was not his home. "And what about the perfume factory?"

Guy dismissed him with a wave of his hand. "I'll take care of that for you, Mr. Hartwell."

"Oh, really?"

Yes, really. "We've already talked about this."

"You talked, not me. And I'm not an invalid, Guy."

"Actually, you are."

These words were *not* wrong, exactly, but sure they had come out at the wrong time. Guy hadn't intended to start such a discussion with Jane in the room, but the surrounding tension was working against him. He had to play the good-brother role, and the only thing he could think about was Jane supine and naked on the floor, covered with his own body.

Hell no, it was not easy at all.

She raised her head in astonishment and shock. "Guy..." A weak whisper, a sweet supplication in her golden eyes. Just her eyes, fixed on his.

Do not humiliate my father, please...

But he didn't intend to humiliate him. And since the discussion had begun, he had to take it further. "You are an invalid," he repeated quietly, turning away from Jane's gold with a hard effort. "Climbing the stairs out here, a little while ago, was agony for you. Do you think I didn't notice? Or your daughter didn't notice?" He looked at her, and Jane seemed to become tinier, sinking her head into her shoulders. "Am I saying something new, something you don't know, Jane?"

She did not answer, and Guy turned to Charles. He couldn't look at Jane. She stirred him too much, especially in his lower parts.

"Sir, you're asking me what will happen and all right, I'll tell you. First, I'll buy you a wheelchair. So at least you'll be able to get around Ashbourne House, if nothing else. I didn't suggest a tour of the house, and it was unbelievably rude of me—but then again, how could I suggest it? You cannot take a step without squirming. And so here we are, the three of us, having tea like old ladies. Maybe you're happy with that, but Jane would much prefer to explore the house, since she will spend a lot of time in here."

"No, I," said Jane quickly, "I'm fine, really."

Oh, I know, angel. I'm the one who can't wait anymore. "Sure you are," he said, placing his cup on the table. "You know what? I'll take you to tour the house right now. And your father will wait here alone, like a grandpa."

Jane opened her mouth. Silent panic filled her eyes.

"Your daughter needs to think about herself, Mr. Hartwell," continued Guy. "She has to learn not to be so damn altruistic."

The irony of these words was heavy. Shouldn't God strike him down for uttering them, or at least have him choking on his tea? But no, nothing happened; and Guy remained unpunished and very pleased with himself, silently approving the blissful injustice of the world.

"Guy..." Jane murmured again. Despite the chilling prospect she must fear a lot—a tour of Ashbourne House alone with *him*—she could not bear her father humiliated, and this gave her the strength to speak.

Don't worry, little girl. I know what I'm doing.

He thought he knew it, at least. He wanted to have Charles out of the house most of the day, and he had a strategy for achieving his goal.

First, Guy knew that everyone, sooner or later, gets to realize something: it's better to be attacked than to be pitied.

Second, Charles Hartwell was forty-eight years old: he must have found out, by now, how true the first point was.

"Your bad attitude has even got worse with age, son," his stepfather said flatly. "I would have never thought it possible."

"I'm stating the facts: you are a cripple, sir."

Guy hoped to have planned his words with discernment. If Charles felt affronted enough to send him and his *strategy* to the devil, it would be a problem.

"And you deserve no pity," he continued, "because it's your choice. You don't care about your health. You do no rehabilitation exercises. It doesn't really matter why you're conducting yourself in this way: it's time to give it a rest. Tomorrow morning, two doctors will come here, and they'll throw you out of your bed. I told them they can kick you if necessary." *More to the point, they'll keep you busy, while I please myself with your delectable daughter.* "I'm sure your condition is not permanent," he added, softening his tone. "Your leg can recover, you can stop feeling pain." *You have been punishing yourself for ten months, this is the truth. You still feel guilty for my mother's death.* He didn't say these words aloud. Judging from his stepfather's tense countenance, he got the bloody impression he had pulled the rope too much.

"And this, Guy," said Charles slowly, "is how I will be my own master here."

This was the decisive moment, and Guy hoped to get the answer right. Theoretically, he knew how his stepfather's stupid heart worked. In practice, even a stupid heart can have unexpected reactions. Especially a stupid heart.

"It's not about being your own master," he replied calmly. "I'm treating you the same way you would treat me if I were in your place. The way I *hope* you would treat me," he added softly.

Charles placed the cup on the saucer. He gave a slight sigh.

Victory.

"You know, Guy, I've always wanted you as a son—as a real son, I mean. Now you seem to agree with me, but damn it, I forgot how much of a..." he glanced at Jane, hesitating, then searched for a word that could clarify his thoughts without offending her. "How much of a plague you can be," he said, but this word didn't really seem to satisfy him, and he snorted. "Jane, what do you think, honey?" he asked her. Under the purposeful annoyance filling his voice, it was clear that Guy's words had hit Charles's heart in the right place and in the right way; his stepfather thought Guy cared about him and was moved by it. "Should I let this big boy control my life?"

Jane turned white. "I... I think you could use a little rest, Papa," she whispered, throwing a quick, pained look to Guy. What was the need for words, with eyes like hers?

Please, don't hurt my father.

78

Please, don't hurt ME.

"All right, then," Charles surrendered. "Two weeks of vacation," he told Guy, who managed, somehow, to turn his eyes away from Jane. God, he had to touch her. He had to touch her *now*.

"Two weeks of vacation," repeated Charles. "But tomorrow, I'll go with you to the perfume factory. I have to explain a few things to you. And regarding the wheelchair you were babbling about, you can shove it up your..."

"Where, sir?"

Charles smiled. "Use your imagination." He leaned back in the armchair. "As for the rest, all right. For a while, it will be up to you to decide my life."

"These are the worst words to tell him, sir. If you don't mind me saying so."

Everyone turned toward the voice coming from the doorway. Guy first of all. Stephen Weymouth stood in the doorway.

Uninvited.

"Hey, old bean," he said to Guy.

Hey old bean, my ass. What was he doing there? "Weymouth, what..." *the fuck* "...are you doing here?"

Stephen shrugged. "Happy New Year to you, too." Without waiting for an invitation—that would not have come, anyway—he entered the room. "Aren't you going to introduce me to your relatives?" He looked at them with a smile. And his smile became enchantment as his eyes rested on Jane.

Guy felt his knuckles itch. That was something he was accustomed to. He was used to feeling that way when some man showed interest toward Jane. But Stephen was just watching her, by God, and Jane was Guy's property now.

For six months, she was *his*.

He stood up. Charles leaned on his cane to do the same, but Guy stopped him with one hand. "No, please, don't encourage him."

His stepfather didn't listen to him. Using his cane as leverage, he pulled himself up from his chair with a palpable effort. Guy sighed and Weymouth approached the sofa.

"This is Charles Hartwell, my stepfather," he resigned himself to say. "And Mr. Hartwell... this is Stephen Weymouth, one of Baron Weymouth's sons. The stupidest one, to be precise."

Stephen reached for Charles. "Ash's stepfather, at last," he said, shaking his hand. "I have been longing to talk with you for some time, sir. See, there's something I need to ask you. Something I don't understand, really. Why on earth didn't you drown him as a child? You should have done that when you had the chance."

Charles smiled. "Once he nearly drowned, actually. But it wasn't my fault... at least not completely."

"Drowned? Seriously?" Weymouth gave Guy a surprised look. "Where... when?"

"In the Mole River, sixteen years ago. But the river spat him out. He was hardly digestible, I guess."

Weymouth laughed. "You definitely have to tell me what happened. But first..." He turned to Jane and lowered his voice; he himself seemed to become smaller. He always knew how to put others at ease, but with Jane, he couldn't succeed: she seemed to sink into the sofa. "First, I would be honored if I could be introduced to this charming flower."

Guy clenched his fists, but it was his stepfather who answered. "This is Jane," he said. "My daughter."

Jane started to get up, but Weymouth didn't allow her. He knelt at her feet like a ridiculous cavalier. Jane blushed, and he took her trembling hand. "Enchanted, miss," he said, kissing her hand gently.

Enough. That was enough. "Weymouth, spare us your mawkish ways. Get" *the hell* "out of here."

Stephen looked up at Guy, raising his eyebrows. "Uh, now I see. You are of the kind of possessive brothers. He says so, miss," he turned to Jane, and lowered his voice as if to share a secret, "but he likes me a lot, you know."

Guy didn't agree with him, especially now. He reached out to his friend's tie and pulled him up by it.

"Get out, W. This is family time."

He let go of Stephen's tie and pushed him toward the door.

Stephen planted his feet and refused to move further. "Oh, come on!" he protested with an indolent voice. "You can't really expect me to be alone on New Year's Day. Besides," he added, sitting down on the sofa with a fast and unexpected movement, "I definitely want to hear of that time you almost drowned. This tough guy is still afraid to swim, you know," he added, turning to Charles.

Guy made a gesture of annoyance. Not to mention, of course, the annoyance he was experiencing in seeing his friend sitting next to Jane. He had to restrain himself not to grasp his neck and lift him from the sofa.

"I'm afraid of *nothing,*" he pointed out in a warning tone.

Stephen raised his hands in ironic surrender. He was truly risking a couple of teeth, didn't he realize that? That would be a pity, Guy thought, it was the very New Year's Day.

"Sure you are," Stephen replied with a mocking smile. "I almost forgot how manly you are. But Mr. Hartwell, please—do tell. Did this giant slide into the river because of his clay feet?"

Charles sat in the armchair and gave a distant smile. "No, not exactly. Guy, do you remember what happened?"

Just like it was yesterday. "Not at all," he replied. And, as expected, his skin began to itch and his hands to sweat. No, by God, he didn't want to listen to childhood memories. He went to the window, turning his back on the others. It was approaching five in the afternoon; outside the daylight was gone. "I guess it was too tedious to remember," he continued with an annoyed edge in his voice. "So please," he said, turning to his stepfather, "could we move on to something else?"

"Don't count on it, big boy. When you asked me to come here, you were supposed to know that old men like me live in the past. We like talking about the jolly old days."

"And I'd like to hear this story," said Stephen. "Big boy," he added teasingly.

Guy was not amused. His breathing became shallow and quick. Could he tell Charles "this is my house and you have to follow my rules"?

Could he stop him from speaking?

No, he fucking couldn't; but he couldn't relive that damn day either.

"We were in Painshill Park," his stepfather began, and Guy's heart suddenly beat with violent thuds against his sternum. It stirred him so powerfully, he heard Charles's words in a suffused way.

"By the riverbank. It was in 1836, on the 22nd of May. I remember the date perfectly, it was my daughter's fifth birthday. Guy's mother and I had been married for three months, and I had made up my mind to make our respective children friends." He twisted his mouth into a frowning grimace. "Not such a good idea, in hindsight."

"Make it brief, Hartwell," snapped Guy, then tried to lighten his tone. "I mean, there's no need to make this much fuss about it. Go along a little faster, will you? I want to throw this nuisance out—" he pointed Stephen with a nod "—but at this rate, we'll still be here at midnight."

Stephen shrugged, giving him a sly look. "Do not worry about me, Ash, I'll stay for dinner. What were you saying, Mr. Hartwell?"

Charles smiled, then placed both hands on the knob of his cane and leaned forward.

And Guy knew he was about to relive every moment, every fucking moment of that distant day.

"Well, we were sitting on the grass," his stepfather said with an absorbed expression, looking at a corner of the floor. "There was a tablecloth, a picnic basket, a lot of nice things to eat. The most important moment of the day had arrived: Jane was about to open her birthday presents. Except she didn't want to open them. Why? Well, Guy wasn't sitting near us, that was why. That scoundrel was on the riverbank, throwing stones into the water."

"He has always been as affable as he is now, I take it."

"Yes, you can bet on it. Well, I guess it was his right to be left alone, but my daughter didn't agree. Children are like that, you know. They want everyone to celebrate their birthday. So, at some point, she throws her gift boxes all over the place and runs to him, yelling at him that he is bad, and that she hates him and that she doesn't want him to sing her birthday song, anyway."

Charles didn't say that Jane's words had come out like small bursts, because at the time she couldn't speak well yet. Guy closed his eyes, and a little girl, knee-high to a grasshopper, reappeared before his eyes, with her rosy cheeks and her braids and her golden eyes full of tears.

I dunwan... your s... s...s...SON-GG!

"She didn't sound very convincing, did she?" Stephen said. He glanced to his right, where Jane, with her head down, was fiddling with the cup. Only the lower part of her face was visible: her mouth, pink and beautiful, was tight, and her cheeks were glowing with discomfort.

Charles nodded. "No, not really. In fact, as she said these words, she began to cry. That didn't impress Guy much, though. He wasn't even ten years old, but he was an irritating little rascal, I mean, pretty much as now. He snorted and stood up, looking straight in front of him. In that area, the river narrowed, becoming a stream with a fast and violent current. The rocks in the river protruded from the water's surface in a way that, before the accident, had looked poetic to me. There was this splashing foam against the sun of that spring day... it was picturesque, really. But if you have a kid like Guy along with you, you'd better not think about how picturesque the place is. So, Guy was standing, and he had this impassive face on, I mean, how could I understand what he had in mind? After a moment, it was clear. Without warning or any hesitation whatsoever, Guy jumped into the middle of the river, landing on a boulder which showed only its tip."

Stephen whistled. "Whoa," he said softly. "Typical of him, to risk his life rather than say a gentle word to his little sister."

"Yeah, let's say he always wanted to have his way. Anyway, I ran to the riverside and ordered him to come back, but he—" Charles shook his head and pursed his lips "—he stuck out his tongue and jumped on another rock, where the river was deeper."

"And he fell into the water."

"No. See," Charles said, putting his hand on his forehead, "the fact is that at that point I was seriously scared. I started to scream and curse. In short, I behaved like a fool. I was in panic. And Jane must have believed her stepbrother's life was in danger, so she decided to go and save him. And she, too, jumped into the river."

Stephen's smile faded. An astonished understanding rose in his eyes, and he turned to Jane, redder than ever. Then he looked at Guy.

And so, you and she were like strangers, huh?

Guy held his friend's gaze. *Stay out of this, W.*

Charles shifted in his seat. Even the armchairs with the softest pillows are uncomfortable when you have to look death in the face one more time. "Jane, as small as she was, missed the boulder. Obviously. She hit her head on it and ended up underwater."

"And Ashbourne dived to save her." Stephen anticipated Charles with a low tone.

Damn, it had to happen. Guy took a breath and turned his back on them. Outside, the fountain in the garden was off, and the lawn, covered with snow, gave the day a motionless aspect, as if timeless.

So different from May 1836.

Behind him, Charles replied with a strange sweetness in his voice. "Yes, he did. He himself, who had said maybe ten words to Jane during the previous three months, had dived into the tumultuous river, even before I could take my boots off. And he was fully clothed, he didn't even stop a moment to remove his boots, the fool." He cleared his throat. The hardest moment of that awful day had arrived. "But somehow, he managed to catch Jane and resurface with her. The current was strong, it had already dragged them some feet away, and Guy clung to a rock with one arm. With the other, he was holding my daughter. I took off my boots and jacket and threw myself into the river to rescue them. Sixteen years ago, I had strength and endurance, but Mole water was fast, freezing, you could neither breathe nor move in there. I was moving my arms, but I seemed to remain still... it's a nightmare I've had a hundred times since then.

" 'Grab Jane,' Guy shouted when I finally reached him. 'Drag her to the riverbank!'

"Jane had fainted. She was like a dead weight in my arms, and I did as he said. But trust me... if I had had a hard time reaching them, getting back with her in my arms seemed impossible. After several minutes, I found myself on the riverbank again. Rona grabbed my daughter, and I turned to go and retrieve the wretched boy who had caused all that trouble. But he wasn't there. He wasn't in the middle of the river anymore. The current had carried him away, and I... I just stood there, like an idiot, staring at the empty rock, refusing to accept what I was seeing. With his heavy clothes, and the boots on his feet, he could not survive, it was just impossible."

"He did survive, though."

"What perception, man," Guy snapped without turning around. "I am still here, aren't I?"

Charles smiled. "Yes, he did survive. I found him after twenty minutes—the longest twenty minutes of my life. He was almost one mile away, unconscious on the grass, but he was alive. He had swallowed a lot of water. I massaged his chest, I turned him to one side—and thank God, he began to cough. And then, as he was spitting water, he murmured a few words, just a few words, mind you—but they were so peculiar, Mr.

Weymouth, I will never forget them."

Guy held his breath. *No, don't say it, Charles.*

"What do you mean, 'peculiar'?" asked Stephen.

"Hartwell." Guy turned to stare at his stepfather sternly. "Hartwell, that's enough."

"What's the matter, big boy?"

"Papa," said Jane in a whisper. She clutched her cup tensely. "Papa, if this story embarrasses Guy, maybe... maybe you shouldn't tell it?"

"He needs to be embarrassed, darling."

"Yes, I agree," said Stephen. "And then," he spoke in a hurry, "what did Ashbourne say that was so terrible, Mr. Hartwell?"

Charles nodded his head. "Something terrible indeed, Mr. Weymouth. Guy said," Charles's voice grew croaky, "he said, 'Wake up, Jane.' " Charles smiled and a heartbreaking glint flashed in his green eyes. "He said: 'I'll sing your birthday song, I'll sing anything you want, but please open your eyes.' "

Weakness.

Cursed weakness.

After many years, the memory of his stupid vulnerability hit Guy again, and it could still take his breath away.

The fire crackled in the hearth. In the silence that followed, Charles gave his stepson a look both moved and daring. "Here, son," he said softly. "Was it that terrible?"

"I was just a child, Mr. Hartwell," said Guy, concealing his agitation under an annoyed tone. "And let me give you a piece of advice. You have to remember that people change. They outweigh their limitations." He gave him a hard smile. "And they take their revenge." He looked at Jane who, with her head down, was wiping her eyes furtively. Treacherous tears had fallen down her cheeks as she had remembered how a fearless hero had once saved her life. Little Jane... she was no longer that child. No one would save her now.

Stephen looked at him and a new, disturbing awareness shone in his eyes.

"Revenge, huh?" muttered Charles. "If you intend to retaliate against me, big boy, you're wasting your time. I just revealed that a long time ago you had a heart under your overdeveloped chest. You can dig into my past all you want, you'll never find out a secret as shameful as this one."

Stephen did not smile at Charles's joke. "And then," he said slowly, "then your plan worked, Mr. Hartwell. Guy and Jane became friends that afternoon."

"Actually, everything went on more or less as before," he said with a sigh, "Jane always chasing Guy and Guy always fleeing from Jane. But my stupid stepson stopped jumping into rivers, if nothing else."

All right, that was enough. Even the most accurate strategies have their flaws, and Guy realized that it would not be easy to behave kindly toward his condescending, annoying, paternalistic stepfather.

"Have you finished yet, Mr. Hartwell? If there are other anecdotes you want to tell, I'd rather go up on the roof and throw myself off."

"You really are a jewel of politeness, Ash," said Stephen curtly. "And you, Miss Hartwell, please." He looked at her. "Could you explain to me something? I see you don't lift your eyes... and I cannot blame you, I wouldn't look at me either. Please, just tell me this: why did you seek the company of an abominable human being like him?"

Jane's eyes were veiled with sheer emotion. "We were kids," she whispered. "He was my stepbrother... wasn't it natural I cared about him?"

"If you say so." Stephen rubbed his forehead and remained silent a moment, lost in his thoughts. "You know, Miss Hartwell, when Guy and I were at Eton, somebody used to write to him often," he finally said in a pensive voice. "I used to wonder who could write to such a waste of air and space like him, but the curious thing was, Ashbourne never wanted to tell me from whom these letters came. That was a big mistake on his part, because I never leave a mystery unsolved. Please, do tell me, Miss Hartwell. Those letters... were yours, weren't they?"

Guy leaned back against the cold glass of the window, folding his arms across his belly. Stephen was putting the pieces together, and that was inevitable. His friend had always had a way with numbers and puzzles.

"Oh, I..." Jane bit her lip, hesitating. "I was very young, I... I don't remember well."

"No?" Stephen asked doubtfully. "Well, it was a long time ago, I suppose that's understandable. Any clue why he didn't tell me it was you?"

It was a trap, of course, and Jane fell straight into it. "Maybe he was embarrassed," she said, shifting uncomfortably under his attentive gaze. "I was just an... an annoying little girl, and he..." she lowered her voice, with sad emotion, "he didn't even answer me."

"Is that why you stopped writing to him, at some point?"

"All right, that's enough." Guy pulled away from the window and walked toward them. "I will count to three, W. You're still here when I finish, I kick you out."

"But here's the problem, Guy. You're not able to count to three."

Guy took him by the collar of his jacket with both hands.

Stephen made no resistance and let Guy pull him up. "Hey, you are creasing my coat," he protested, but his tone was devoid of real fun.

Guy put his mouth near his ear, dropping his voice so that only Stephen could hear him. "How many balls do you like in your scrotum?"

"Two, I guess?"

"Fine. Shut up and get out, then."

"Forget it. Today I'll have dinner with you." He nodded toward Jane.

"And with your lovely sister."

"I'm sure," Guy closed his right fist and planted it in Stephen's gut, causing him to blow out his breath at once, "that you have other things to do this evening."

Jane let out a muffled scream. Unfortunately, there was no actual need to be worried about Stephen. The blow hadn't hurt him that much and, when he straightened, he had a strange, tense smile on his face.

"You've just made a big mistake, Ashbourne."

Oh sure. How could Stephen truly think his maneuver would go unnoticed? Deluded wanker. He had brought his left fist near Guy's side, but Stephen wouldn't have him fall over in front of Jane, not by some stupid blow to his liver.

Guy stopped Stephen's fist with his right hand.

Stephen's smile widened with unusual ferocity. Then he hit Guy in the gut with his other hand. Strong and unexpected, the punch took Guy's breath away.

"Well, old bean," Stephen whispered, stepping back as Guy bent. "You started it, didn't you?"

Guy did not ask himself what Jane and Charles would think of his behavior. He straightened up, took a breath, and rushed at Stephen.

"Guy!"

Jane's voice held him with his fist in mid-air.

Stephen raised his guard, but didn't take advantage of Guy's indecision; he just shrugged. "It's, uh... just boxing training, Miss Hartwell," he explained with the kind of sweetness one would use to calm a puppy.

Charles stood up slowly. He had a slight smile on his face. "Guy, big boy," he said, "maybe you and your friend should train in another room."

Guy lowered his fists and straightened his immaculate tie. Yes, it would be better. A boxing session was the only thing he could do at this point, actually. Stephen wouldn't go away, Guy couldn't hope for it Therefore he had to tell him clearly to mind his own business for his own good. He cast a quick glance at Jane. She was staring at them with her mouth agape. She was shocked but also oblivious, for the moment, that Guy would soon have her in his hands.

If only he could feel the same. If only he could forget the desire he had for her for just a minute. But jolts of need didn't stop running through his belly, making him behave imprudently.

"You want us to move to another room, sir?" asked Stephen, adjusting the ponytail that held his ridiculously long hair back. "Aren't you a fight fan?"

With a grimace of poorly concealed pain, Charles put his weight on the walking cane. "In fact, I am. But I don't think my daughter will appreciate seeing two big guys like you boxing. Boxing is a man's sport, isn't it? It's not lady stuff."

"May I dare to disagree, Mr. Hartwell? Many women enjoy watching boxing. Some of them dress as men just to attend the matches." Stephen turned to Jane, who drew back a little. "Would you like to watch while I destroy this giant?" he asked her softly. The tone of his voice worked. Jane looked up and stared at him for longer than Guy could bear. The itch in his hands became more and more intense.

"Oh, I know he is bigger than me," Stephen continued when Jane mumbled something unintelligible. "But there is one thing you need to know, Miss Hartwell. In boxing, it isn't the strongest one who wins, but the most stubborn. Like in life."

* * *

Guy was getting ready in his corner of the ring. Stephen looked at him from the opposite corner. "Do you still have them, Ash?"

Guy had his back turned to him but, judging from the way he stiffened, Stephen realized he had understood.

"Have what?"

Guy was shirtless, ready to fight. On his left shoulder, there was a cross-shaped scar, four inches long, which stood out against his olive skin. He had got it in some fight outside a tavern, years ago, or so he had told Stephen. That scar revealed a lot about him, as did his powerful muscles and broad shoulders. Guy Spencer, these things were saying, is not the sort of man who keeps letters, he isn't a sentimental person.

Or at least, he wasn't supposed to be. "Don't pretend you don't understand, Ashbourne. Jane Hartwell's letters. The letters you used to grasp and read in secret at Eton."

Stephen looked at his own hands wrapped in the protective bandages, but he wasn't really seeing them. His mind wandered back to Eton; once a week, in the college's refectory, the Eton students received their mail. "Your eyes shone brightly when a letter arrived for you. You feigned indifference, but you couldn't fool me. You were never happier than on Tuesday mornings, when Mrs. Woodhouse used to pass among us with her basket full of letters to deliver."

He stared at him, but Guy didn't turn to him.

"You say so much bullshit, W."

"Why did Jane Hartwell stop writing to you?"

Guy turned around, shirtless, with his bandaged hands clenched into fists. "Are you ready to fight, or do you want to have a chat while knitting, like old ladies?"

"Answer me. Suddenly she ceased to write to you, why?"

"W., see this square surrounded by ropes? It's called a 'ring.' One usually fights up here, they definitely don't talk about crap."

"Do you remember the first Tuesday no letter arrived for you? You beat

87

half the school that day. And during the rest of the week, you beat the other half. How old were you? Sixteen, seventeen?"

Guy smiled derisively. "If you believe I can remember stuff like that, you're a simpleton."

The lightness of his tone didn't fool Stephen. It couldn't; he had known Guy since they were both thirteen years old. Stephen felt his heart race. While he had been listening to Charles Hartwell, a worrying suspicion had been born in his mind. Now, that suspicion became a certainty. A sudden weakness came over him as he grasped the meaning of what he had just found out.

It was like a kick in the face.

"So that's it," he whispered, clinging to the ropes of the ring. "You've never wanted to take revenge on your stepfather. Christ, not even on your mother." He squeezed the ropes between his hands. "Jane Hartwell, she's the one you wanted."

11.

Over the last two and a half years, Stephen Weymouth had helped Guy Spencer wear down, impoverish, and finally ruin the Hartwells. Meanwhile, he had been wondering why his friend had decided to take such useless revenge. Guy had lived without his mother's love all his life, so why on earth would he want Rona Hartwell to ask him for help? What satisfaction would Guy hope to get, after all those years of rejection and coldness?

It didn't make any sense.

But now, everything made sense.

Stephen felt the ground giving way under his feet. He looked at Guy's strong body in the opposite corner of the ring.

It made perfectly good sense why Guy hadn't abandoned his plan after Rona's refusal to ask him for money. And he hadn't abandoned it even after her death. His professed aim had always been to get an apology from his mother, yet he had started to put his plan in practice only two years ago, on Jane Hartwell's eighteenth birthday.

And yes, this made fucking sense too.

"You never wanted revenge on your mother, did you?" said Stephen with a dry throat. "This whole thing meant only one thing to you. You wanted to get back into Jane Hartwell's life."

"Are you ready to train?"

"So, you're not even going to deny it?"

"Deny what?"

Stephen felt terrible nausea. God, he thought he knew him. Guy was his best friend. Stephen had spent a great deal of time with him over the years, he had even wept in Guy's arms...

But Guy had never wept in his.

This conclusion struck him painfully. Guy had told Stephen nothing about himself. Nothing about Jane. Nothing *real*. Stephen had always suspected his friend kept secrets from him; dark secrets, wounds on his body he had never explained, money he had taken from his bank without giving Stephen, his accountant, any further details for his ledger.

Stephen had thought it could be something about extreme sex. Or perhaps, who knows, Guy enjoyed facing some deadly challenges, like fighting against circus lions. Guy loved rough stuff like that... or rather, Stephen *thought* Guy loved stuff like that.

But Jane Hartwell...

A dreadful doubt arose in his mind and if it was true, Stephen couldn't deal with it, he just couldn't. It shed new light on Guy's unspoken words, it went against all principles and morals.

"Your mother refused your help two years ago, Ashbourne," he said with an effort. "Why didn't she trust you? I want the truth this time. Did she know what your sister meant to you?"

Guy was standing straight in the middle of the boxing ring. His posture was rigid, but he showed no shame. "Jane is not my sister."

No, she wasn't his sister, painfully not, and Stephen felt his gut tighten. Jane Hartwell was under Guy's thumb, and now her shy, beautiful face struck Stephen's heart. Like a cold, sharp dagger, the shocking truth stabbed him in the chest. Jane had looked uncomfortable—no, *scared*—a little ago. She almost couldn't speak, as if...

"Answer me, you son of a bitch!"

He lunged at Guy, pummeling his face with a sudden fist that made him turn to one side and move back a step.

"Why did your mother refuse your help? Did she want to keep you away from Jane?"

Guy swerved to avoid being hit by his jab, and tried to crush his left side, but Stephen jumped away.

"I don't know, all right?" Guy replied, parrying a punch to his body. "My mother..."

He received a powerful punch to his face, which stunned him for a moment. He defended himself by attacking Stephen with a one-two combination, then he moved away towards the ropes.

"I don't know," he repeated, wiping a trickle of blood at the corner of his mouth. The bandage on his hand got stained with bright red. "But yes, I think so."

He returned to the center of the ring, and Stephen threw a blow at his face. He wanted to ruin his features; Guy's face was perfect, too perfect, he didn't deserve it.

"Why that? What did you do to Jane? She stopped writing to you, Guy... why? Tell me why!"

"Whoa, why all this fuss, W.? Do you think I did something horrible to her? She was a thirteen-year-old girl, for fuck's sake!"

Stephen threw a combo of two straights and a hook. Guy blocked it and replied with a hard punch to his chin, then moved back.

"Thirteen, huh?" Stephen said, out of breath, shaking his head to clear his stunned vision. "How do you happen to know that she was thirteen? You just said you didn't remember, you asshole!" He hit him with anger and then jumped away. "Why have you taken her into your house?"

Guy pushed him against the ropes and began to launch quick blows to his stomach, until Stephen fell to his knees. Then he stepped away. "I have a score to settle with that girl," he replied heavily, "and if you're smart, you'll stay out of it."

"A score to settle? God, do you want to force her to... *fuck* you?" Stephen got up holding onto the ropes, but nausea prevented him from moving. "Jesus Christ, Guy... have you already done it? God, no. Tell me you haven't."

"Bloody hell, W.," Guy snapped, clenching his fists. "What's so terrible if I use her to have a bit of fun?"

Stephen couldn't answer.

God, it was true. It was true.

It was revenge, Guy called it that, and Stephen had helped him. To Stephen, it had looked like some stupid way of Guy's to gain his mother's attention, only that. But now, he realized he was an accomplice in the abuse of a girl. An innocent, sweet girl. And beautiful. Stephen had seen her before, but never up close. Up close, she was dazzling, with a scent of vanilla and delicate flowers. Lily of the valley, perhaps, or hawthorn flowers. She was fair in complexion, and her cheeks suddenly blushed when she felt observed. Her lips were naturally pink, her hair was golden, and she had golden eyes.

She had the beauty of an angel.

And then there was the beauty of the devil. Guy's beauty. In the gym of Ashbourne House, shirtless, he was clenching his fists and stretching his arms. He attacked Stephen again, trying to hit him in the face. With his dark hair and olive skin, his strong features made him more threatening. His iron muscles, his crooked nose, and even the V-shaped hairline that framed his forehead were constant reminders of his violent nature; and his straight eyebrows hardened his long-shaped, almost black eyes. He had developed every muscle of his body, which was hard both inside and out. His arms were twice as wide as Stephen's; his mighty pecs were covered with a soft dark hair, hair that thinned into a line running from his navel to his groin; he had narrow hips, which were a counterpoint to his broad shoulders, and two bands of parallel muscles defined his abdomen. Where ordinary people were weak and flabby, Guy was arrogant armor against the world.

Stephen swerved, raising his arms to shield himself. "Tell me how this shit works, Ash," he swallowed, and painful impotence slammed into him. "Tell me, does she cry when you fuck her?" Stephen closed his eyes as he uttered these words. He knew what it meant when you can't say no. He'd discovered what it means at eight years of age, and now his face twitched as he remembered Uncle Hugo's sour smell and the barn where he used to take Stephen to "play." A wave of anger ran through his body. "When were you planning to tell me?" He dodged another blow. "When were you planning to tell me I'm an accomplice to this crap?"

"Never, as a matter of fact," said Guy, parrying a punch to his nose with his forearm.

Stephen saw red and, dodging a straight blow, struck Guy in the stomach.

Guy was expecting it and, tightening his belly, almost broke Stephen's metacarpals. The pain was huge, but not enough to cover his anger. "How can you feel good," Stephen murmured, nauseated, "in fucking a woman who doesn't want to have sex with you?"

"There is no woman who doesn't want me." He took a punch on his left shoulder, then returned a jab to Stephen's gut. Stephen hit him in the face, and Guy spat blood.

"Oh, am I to understand that Jane Hartwell is happy to open her legs for you? No, she doesn't want you, you disgust her, and it's the story of your life, disgusting the Hartwells!"

"Now," said Guy, slamming a fist into his stomach, "stop it at once, or I really will hurt you."

Stephen remained bent, then straightened with a wry, sickened smile on his face. "What's wrong, Ash, do my words sting you? Hasn't your little sister's pussy calmed you down yet?"

"I told you to stop. Right now." He raised his guard and watched him, determined to crush him.

"Oh, I see, you have some sense of honor, don't you? I mean, you're forcing your stepsister to have sex with you, but at least you are ashamed of yourself!"

"Fuck no, I'm not ashamed at all!" Guy unloaded a hard right to Stephen's jaw, and this movement left drops of shining sweat along the back of his arm, like broken glass. "And do you know why, you moralistic prig? Because I made a deal with her, that's why. She accepted my conditions. That's all. I'm paying her, I'm *handsomely* paying her. Don't you ever forget it. All she's doing, she's doing voluntarily."

"Voluntarily, my ass!" Hopping around him, Stephen tried to smash Guy in the mouth. He wanted to make him spit a couple of teeth, oh, yes, it seemed a good idea to him, the best he'd ever had. "You've ruined the Hartwells on purpose, you shithead! The freighter with their goods never wrecked, it's still in the harbor, it's just waiting for you to allow the unloading of the cargo—but you'll never allow it, will you!"

Despite his huge build, Guy had good footwork and he could move his mass of muscles with unexpected lightness. Stephen was faster than him, though. Furthermore, he was madly determined to hit him badly.

Are you ready to be knocked out, you piece of shit?

He avoided Guy's punch and emphasized his movements, well aware of how his hops bothered his friends. "Pansy-ass jumps," Guy called them. Well, Stephen would show to that bastard how much a pansy could hurt.

"Christ, Weymouth, just stay still for a moment, for fuck's..."

A powerful blow to Guy's right side interrupted his words. It was strong, precise, harmful. *And pansy-ass, Guy. Just remember this when I'll knock you down.*

And Guy was knocked down, inevitably. To his knees, like a penitent. But it wasn't enough yet. Today, it couldn't be enough. For the first time in his life, Stephen played dirty. He went behind Guy and, grabbing his right arm, twisted it up behind his back.

"Shit, Weym—"

Guy stopped speaking, but he didn't scream. He was a proud bastard. Stephen twisted his arm more, and that was no joke. "Did you make her cry her first time, Ashbourne? Did you feel good, when you took everything from her?"

Bastard. Lousy bastard. And the worst thing of all, which made Stephen jerk Guy's arm further up his back, was that he couldn't hate Guy, not even now.

"I haven't..." Guy stifled a shout as Stephen brought his wrist up higher, "...I haven't fucked her yet, but..."

He raised his right foot behind himself, between Stephen's slightly parted legs. He slammed it up.

"Shit!" Stephen shrieked.

It had been a low blow. Stephen let him go, doubling over. God, it hurt like hell. As he was holding his balls, Guy stood up and watched him with detachment. He didn't look angry with his friend's dirty play, and a sudden realization struck Stephen.

He could do nothing to change Guy's mind.

Nothing to at all.

To Guy, he was just a friend who needed to be protected from himself. Nothing else. Stephen's opinion never affected Guy. Whereas to Stephen, even now that he knew what a bastard his friend was, Guy's opinion meant everything.

"Stop your preaching right now, Weymouth, or next time I'll smash your balls."

Guy said it quietly. He didn't grab Stephen's arm, he didn't use the same unfair trick Stephen had used on him. He didn't take advantage of Stephen's weakness.

It was always like that. Guy the strong one, Stephen the defeated. Even now. Stephen had tried to explain his feelings to him in the only way Guy could understand—using hard, wild violence—but he had failed anyway. Guy was even happy with Stephen's anger. He had an opponent at his level for once. He liked to fight, he loved to match antagonists who gave him a hard time. Stephen had badly wanted to hurt him, and instead, he had done a favor for him.

As he realized that, he felt a desolate, ridiculous need to cry. "She's so sweet, Ash," he said with a choked voice, straightening and dropping his arms to his sides. "How can you do this to her? Leave her alone. You said you haven't fucked her yet, don't do it, in the name of God. Forget this crap." He looked at his friend, at his broad shoulders, at his narrow hips. At his statuesque insensitivity.

"I'm sorry, W." Guy went back to his corner. His face was bruised, and blood came out of the left side of his mouth. "Jane has to pay. And she will."

"Why do you hate her so much? What did she do to you?"

"Nothing you want to hear." He was standing turned from him, his back rippling with muscles, and the scar on his left shoulder stood out like an inverted cross—the mark of the Devil. "But she owes me, I assure you."

"To the point of ruining her? Do you want to use her and then throw her away like an old rag?"

Guy took the bandages from his hands and let them fall on the floor. "Is this the reason why you are so upset? Her future after I let her go?" He grabbed the towel from the post and wiped the blood from his face. "Then don't worry, W, I'll give her a lavish dowry when I'm done with her. She'll pay off her debt and then will be free to start a new life, as rich as a princess."

"Are you kidding me?"

"Why, what's the problem?"

Stephen felt very tired. "You'll screw her in every way you can think of, and then you'll give her a good dowry," he said flatly. *"This* is the fucking problem. Jane Hartwell is not a whore, one like her remains a virgin until marriage. Why do you want to ruin her life?"

"Ruin her life, my ass. A good dowry erases anyone's past."

"So what, will you pay some shitty aristocrat to make him marry her?"

"Shitty aristocrat? We are aristocrats too, or did you forget? Show a little respect for your own class."

"You know how these things work, Ash. You bribe a ruined aristocrat into marriage with Jane, and she will be sorry for the rest of her life. Do you want her to marry someone like your father?"

"Well, it would be a perfect conclusion, wouldn't it?"

"You're not being serious. God, she doesn't deserve it."

"You don't know what she deserves." Guy's eyes hardened. "You know nothing about Jane Hartwell."

"Fucking tell me, then!"

Guy jumped down out of the ring and, with his shirt in his hand, he went to the door. He left without replying, and at that exact moment, Stephen knew he needed to get himself high on opium. Right now, after more than a year of abstinence. It was the only way he knew to get through the night, since he knew with whom, and how, Guy would spend it.

12.

Why do you hate her so much? What did she do to you?

Eton refectory, 16th April 1844.

Mrs. Woodhouse was walking among the long tables of the refectory. Her long skirt brushed the floor, her bulky body barely slipping between the rows of chairs. The students were sitting around the tables, having their breakfast.

Mrs. Woodhouse had a big wicker basket between her hands. It was chock-full of letters, so it didn't make her movement any easier.

Guy looked down at his plate. The small white loaf of bread was untouched; the jam, on the side, was just a crimson stain against the white porcelain.

I don't care.

Beside him, Stephen Weymouth was eating in silence. They had returned to Eton on Thursday. Since then, they hadn't spoken much to each other, sullen and silent, both of them.

Guy had not asked Stephen how his Easter vacations had been; not well, judging by his friend's depressed look, but Guy neither said nor asked anything. All he could do was to brood about what had happened in Courtnell Street during his Easter stay.

Mrs. Woodhouse was approaching his chair. His head started to pound in anticipation.

I don't care whether or not she has written to me.

Around them, the students were chattering incessantly. The babble was constant, and loud laughter broke out from time to time, even if Eton regulations prohibited it. With their heads still on vacation, they all had something to say, some funny stories to tell. About the loss of their virginity, maybe. At eighteen years old, it was normal, wasn't it?

Guy clenched his fists. His palms were sweaty. Even he was no longer a virgin. Why wasn't he saying it? Why wasn't he bragging about it, as did the others?

Mrs. Woodhouse was two students away from him.

Guy's breath became shallow. He gave no time for the air to enter his lungs; he felt stifled.

You disgust me, Guy Spencer! I never want to see you again!

These words, shouted by Jane Hartwell one week ago, resounded in his mind, but he didn't care, he didn't care, he didn't care at all.

Not at all.

Mrs. Woodhouse took out three letters, and left them to the boy on Guy's right. She stepped forward and stopped, rummaging in her basket as always.

Hell, what did he care? He hoped Jane hadn't written to him. Her letters were so silly. 'I did this, I did that, it always rains here, I miss you.' Her stupid, and always very accurate, drawings, pictures of nightingales, of flowers... of Guy, sometimes, and he seemed almost good-looking in those portraits.

Mrs. Woodhouse frowned and dropped her empty hand. She made no comment and walked on.

Guy sat motionless, his eyes staring at the jam in his plate, his breath held, his heart pounding in his head.

At his side, Stephen Weymouth gave him a look. "Ash, what's wrong?"

It was a lot better this way, Guy thought. He was free of her, at last.

"Ashbourne?"

Guy got up at once. His chair fell to the ground with a thud.

How many times had he been punished because of her? Sweet, shy Jane Hartwell, *my ass!* She was just a liar, she just took advantage of Guy's kindness, that was it. She made it sound like she couldn't live without him, Guy, stand by me, Guy, I've missed you, and he had felt sorry for her, that was all, *sorry*, and that was why he had never told her to go to hell, only for that.

He was free at last. He was free and *happy*. He couldn't even stand Jane Hartwell, he had never been able to stand her, and had he known it was that easy to get rid of her, he would have done it before.

The classmate sitting to his right looked up and watched him questioningly. He was a frail, thin boy, with pimples on his face and kind eyes.

"What the fuck are you looking at?" Guy growled.

Luke Michigan was a victim of all the bullies at Eton, so he could recognize trouble when he saw it. He raised his hands with apprehension. "I don't want no problems, Ashbourne."

Guy grabbed him by his immaculate tie. The refectory fell silent. At Eton, nobody ever fought in the presence of the teachers. It was a stupid thing to do, and the 4th Earl of Ashbourne wasn't stupid. Even more, it was the first time he was picking on a weak guy.

"You already have problems, you bugger!"

"Ash," Stephen called to him, worried, reaching out to touch his forearm. "Ash, leave him alone."

Guy jerked his arm away. His fist shot out lightning fast and caught Luke Michigan in his face, sending him flying to the ground. His chair rolled over with a crash. Guy pounced on him, punching him over and over again.

In a moment, the refectory broke out in chaos.

The teachers rushed towards him, Stephen yelled: "Guy, what the hell are you doing?" and several hands held him. The French teacher, Monsieur Dutarque, and the music teacher, Mr. Mayfield—incidentally, the most muscular men of Eton—grabbed Guy and took him away by force, while he was still kicking at anyone in his path.

Monsieur Dutarque caned him. Hard. And he passed the following days in and out of the Repentance Room, the RR. It was a little chamber very similar to a prison cell, which had a small window too high to look out of. It was just a crack of light against the dark wall, with three iron bars that, in the afternoon, cast long shadows on the floor.

When they let him out of the RR, within a few days he was in there again, because some students crossing his path had ended up bleeding from their mouth and nose. When he broke the arm of a son of Viscount Wallingford, David "Lardass" Wallingford, the headmaster threatened him with expulsion.

There were limits even an earl couldn't cross.

Guy calmed down then. He learned to be careful, engaging in acts of violence only when there were no witnesses. He began to choose his opponents for their strength, especially the bullies, the ones who had no interest in complaining about his conduct because they were just like him.

He would not be expelled, he would not go back to Courtnell Street.

He would not see Jane Hartwell again.

So, he was disgusting to her, wasn't he?

Well, she was disgusting to him.

In fact, he hated her.

13.

Jane looked out of the window of her bedroom at Ashbourne House. The "room" Guy had set aside for her wasn't just one room. It was a suite, and it seemed like a house to her. Beside the actual bedroom, there was a dressing room on the left and, passing through an arch, you could enter a large, lovely boudoir, with a tea-table and chairs, and two corner tables with large bouquets of light flowers, and a sofa, and even a new, shiny piano.

Close to her large canopy bed, there was an armchair and a round footstool, and soft white carpets. And there were pink pillows... pillows everywhere. Everything smiled fluffily, everything was full of lace and embroidery.

Her suite had surprised Jane. She had thought brothel rooms were always in red tones. But somehow, the soft decorations around her humiliated her more. Guy was sending her a message by these fairytale-like things.

In the adjacent boudoir, along with the other furniture, there was a bookcase with romance novels and moral fables. Books she actually liked, because Guy flaunted his arrogance even this way.

A dark wooden door with a shiny silver knob connected the dressing room to the bedroom. Inside the dressing room, there were a lot of clothes, toilet mirrors, perfumes, and even cosmetics.

Why on earth had he bought her cosmetics for her? She wasn't used to wearing any makeup.

Jane wasn't sitting on the bed. It didn't belong to her. Nothing in this suite did. She wasn't looking around her. Her eyes were wandering over Ashbourne House's garden, towards Green Park.

It was a public park, so it was hers, somehow "hers."

It wasn't easy to ignore Guy's garden, though, because darkness didn't hide it completely. Bright lamps were shining among the trees and the flowers, like a show of stars between the snow and the shadows. Their light eclipsed the park, immersed in the dark.

Jane took a deep breath, trying to calm herself. Her heart was slamming inside her chest.

A few moments ago, a young, gentle maid had knocked on her door. The maid was supposed to help her to undress and comb her hair. Jane had smiled, but she had refused her help. She had done everything alone. As she had always done, *alone*. Even if her new clothes had needed ingenious changes for putting them on with no one's help.

It was just a garden, in the end, she thought as her eyes rested on the lamps swaying in the slight wind. It wasn't a world apart, even if it seemed so. When she had seen it for the first time, that afternoon, she had stared at the white snow. It covered the maples and the bushes of junipers. How beautiful the climbing clematis, in an arch of leaves, were. They led to a greenhouse—a greenhouse, there were flowers in the middle of London.

Snow...

Jane shook her head. She didn't want to think again about the attic of Courtnell Street, no, she wanted to forget what had happened there.

What Guy had done to her.

Shuddering, she wrapped herself in a woolen dressing gown. It was her old dressing gown. The one that belonged to her, and she needed to feel true to herself, she needed to wear her things.

Outside, a lamp swayed in a gust of more intense wind. Jane held her breath.

Don't go out.

Please don't go out.

It didn't go out. Its flare trembled, then resumed a homogeneous light.

Jane exhaled, resting her forehead against the cold glass. She didn't want to think about the day just passed. It was anguish to think about it. The discussion about Guy and her father had been agonizing. Oh, how cleverly Guy had put a Damocles' sword over Charles Hartwell's head! He had promised him to make him feel alive again, but Guy's words were false and cruel, as false and cruel as him.

After that, the day had slipped away like in a dream. Jane remembered almost nothing: neither the words of that young man, Weymouth, who at the end hadn't stayed with them for dinner, but had taken his leave right after the boxing training with Guy; nor her father's words.

She remembered Guy's words, though.

When he had asked her if she liked her room.

When he had told Charles that their presence thrilled him.

When he had advised her to go to bed. *I see you're tired, little Jane.*

She had done as he'd told her, and now she was trembling.

Behind her, there was the arch separating the bedroom from the boudoir, and Guy would come from that direction. She knew it, but she kept her eyes fixed on Ashbourne House's garden, and Green Park, with its blinding darkness.

Guy, I beg you, if you really want to do this to me, then do it soon.

She didn't allow herself to think about his caresses in the attic room of Courtnell Street. About Guy's whispers. He had made her lose control; and as Jane had bent her wet legs, dirty with his semen, overwhelmed by an ecstasy she she'd never expected the existence of, Guy had left her down there, leaving with no kind word. With no hug, with no gentle kiss... and... and Jane had wished for his kiss.

Now, this seemed the most atrocious thing of all to her.

Guy, don't make me forget who I am. She didn't want physical pleasure from him... she couldn't allow herself to feel pleasure with him again. *Hurt me if you want, but please, please Guy, don't make me feel like... like...*

She shook her head with shame. If only she could get away from him, if only...

But the Hartwells had nothing. And the next promissory note would expire in less than a month.

Her heart ached as she thought of the conversation between Guy and her father. Charles had looked happy, happy for the first time in ten months, when he had agreed to take a rest for a while.

He had watched his stepson with pride and affection. With such heartfelt affection.

Oh, Guy. You're so cruel. So false.

So wicked.

And she could never reveal Guy's deception to her father. That would be even more atrocious than telling him their real financial conditions. Jane couldn't...

A sudden noise made her jump. It was a noise of opening hinges, the kind of noise she feared most. It didn't come from the boudoir door, the one leading to the corridor. It came from the dressing room. The room behind the wooden door and its glossy silver knob.

The knob turned. The door opened.

Guy came in.

14.

"Boo."

Guy smiled, looking at Jane, and the color disappeared from her cheeks.

Surprise, little one.

For three generations, the Earls of Ashbourne had handed down to their descendants a yellowed sheet: the secret map of Ashbourne House. There were some hidden passages behind the walls, and one of them connected the master bedroom to Jane's dressing room. Guy didn't know if every previous Earl had used to give that room to their mistresses, this detail wasn't on the map, but Guy thought so. Maybe even his father had used the passage for that purpose.

He looked at Jane and her terrified eyes.

Maybe his father's lovers had had that expression, too.

Ah, inheritance...

He stepped into the room. "Hello, little one." He closed the door behind him. "Were you waiting for me?"

She did not answer. Guy shouldn't have gone to her room so early. He should have left her in an agonizing wait of an hour or two, but in the end, it had been he who hadn't been able to wait. He was craving to touch her. He knew his desire would calm down eventually, but now his cock couldn't wait anymore. It was pressing against his breeches. He was wearing them under his bare chest. And he was wearing his dressing robe. It was a way to wrap, so to speak, the gift.

Even Jane had wrapped herself in a dressing robe. In a *cheap* dressing robe. And underneath the robe, Guy was sure, she was wearing her old undergarment.

Jane was defying him.

Ah, little one. You shouldn't have.

A shiver of anticipation ran through his spine. "Come here, Jane."

She swallowed. She was looking at him in a panicked manner, but as if it was inevitable; when one is in danger, they don't close their eyes, they have to see what will crush them.

Jane's chest was rising and falling in deep breaths. With tentative steps, she walked towards him, stopping at over four feet away. Stepping forward, Guy raised his arm and slapped her face. The sound was sharp. Jane's face remained turned to the right for a few moments, her mouth slightly open in shock.

"The next one will be harder."

With two fingers, he straightened her face. Her irises were huge, golden with panic and pain. And the inevitable happened. Her mouth trembled. Her eyes filled with tears.

She started to cry.

It had been a mild slap, but she was like a child... a child nobody had ever slapped before.

"What..." she sobbed. "W...why?"

Guy gave her another slap. On her right cheek, this time. Like the other, it was mild but made an annoying prickly noise.

"Guy!" Putting her hand on her cheek, Jane took a step back. She twisted her face, her mouth shook violently. Had he continued, she wouldn't have just cried. She would have sobbed desperately, as she used to do as a child.

Guy came closer and, bringing his hand to her nape, pulled her towards him. "You know why," he said with a low voice.

Terror filled her eyes. No, she didn't know why. She didn't understand this anger.

Guy released her with a push and took the collar of her dressing robe between his fingers. "What's this stuff?"

"My... my robe?" she sobbed.

"Yes. Your robe." He exhaled loudly, pretending an annoyance he was far from feeling. The only thing he wanted was to undress her, toss her on the floor, and fill her with himself until she begged for mercy. "Tell me why you're here, Jane," he ordered in a tone of harsh irritation. "In this house. In this room."

She breathed quickly. Her delicate breasts rose under the cheap robe.

"Answer me, Jane." He raised his hand in an explicit threat. "Answer me, if you don't want me to leave visible marks on you. Your father could notice them tomorrow."

She cringed, sinking her head into her shoulders. Her ragged breath interrupted the silence in the room. The crackling fire in the hearth was still alive, and the bedside lamp illuminated the soft furnishings in every piece of furniture, in every blanket and pillow. Everything was white and pink, full of lace, full of bright ribbons.

It was a princess's room.

And in her old dressing gown, the princess was sobbing. "To..." she whispered. "To be your l...l...lover, Guy."

"No, that's wrong." He grabbed her nape and pulled her against his chest, so tight she could barely breathe. "You are here to be my slave. *Slave,* Jane. I get you new underwear, you put it on. Is that clear?"

"Yes," she sniffled, nodding her head. "Yes, Guy, I'm... I'm sorry."

He released her and stepped back. "Do you want me to send you and your father back to Courtnell Street?"

"No... no!"

"Oh. Because it sure looks like you do."

She tightened her robe around her body and bit her lip in distress. The tips of her white teeth glistened in her pink mouth. It was a bad idea on her part. Remarkably bad; Guy's cock stood up, if possible, even more. He came closer to her and placed his hands on her waist. The curve between her slim waist and her rounded hips was delectable.

"Are you ready for this, Jane?"

"Y...y...yes."

"Then stop whining. Keep on crying, and our deal is off."

Jane nodded, keeping her face down. If she had spoken, she would have cried more.

Guy pretended to reflect. "Maybe we should do a little test," he murmured. "You know... to see if this thing works or not. There's no point in wasting time, Jane, if you can't satisfy me."

She stiffened. His words made her golden eyes widen, freezing her. "A test?"

"Yes, angel. I want to try you. I bought you sight unseen, but in retrospect, you probably aren't what I'm looking for."

Oh, she was. She totally was. He struggled to control the smile that would give him away.

"If you pass your test," he continued lightly, "we will proceed with our agreement. Otherwise, you will return to your own home, with your debts and trouble. And your..." he smiled, mocking, "...virginity, of course. Agreed?"

Pale and distressed, she didn't even try to answer; and he... he just thought, *Now you're mine.* He caressed her cheek with his index finger and, moving it beneath her chin, lifted her face. *Mine in your every breath, Jane. In your every gesture.* "Do you know how a cattle sale works?" he asked softly.

Her eyes widened.

Yes. You got it straight. "So, angel? Do you know?"

Jane shook her head. Guy's hands went down to her waist, so slim he could cup her with one hand. He grabbed the ends of the belt and undid her robe.

"No?"

Bringing his hands to her shoulders, he pulled down her robe. It fell to the ground with a rustle.

Jane didn't object, but she closed her eyes, burning with embarrassment. She was still wearing her nightgown, but maybe she felt as if she were naked.

And yet, little one, he thought with gentle sarcasm, *I have already seen your bare skin, remember? More than this... and your heart-shaped ass, and your sweet, pink pussy—I could draw them in every detail.*

"When I want to buy a mare, or... or a puppy," he said, thoughtfully, "I go to the fairs or markets. Every Friday a cattle market is held in Smithfield, have you ever been there?"

He took a step away. Jane's nightgown was white, it resembled a Greek tunic. It was modest, full-length, and had no lace or ribbons. It had long sleeves and a tight collar, and this was nothing unexpected. Her breasts pushed against the fabric, closed by buttons on the front, because Jane was used to dressing and undressing alone.

"You have to answer me when I'm talking to you," he reminded her sharply.

Jane shook her head. She was stiff and tense, as if about to break.

"No?" He put his hand on her left wrist and undid the little buttons closing her sleeve. He did this with some trouble. His fingers were not very firm, because of the excitement that was taking over him.

He undid the buttons on her right wrist as well. Jane's nightgown was that kind of underwear he had always imagined on her. It had the clean scent of lavender soap and was immaculate white, with no frills and lace. He loved her simplicity, but it didn't matter. He would impose on her fluffy, colorful underwear. He would require her to embellish herself for him, to *change* for him.

"In a market, animals are exposed for everyone to look at," he said with forced calm. "You can scrutinize them, test their strengths and their weaknesses. And then, if you like what you see, you can buy them."

He undid the buttons at her chest, feeling her agitated breath brush over his fingers. Sliding her shirt down her shoulders, he slowly bared her skin.

"Tell me..." he murmured, kissing her neck, feeling her shudder against his lips. "Do you want me to buy you, Jane?"

Her coral lips trembled. She closed her eyes, nodding her head. How difficult was it for her? What was she thinking? He wondered if, despite everything, her chills were in part due to the caresses that were tickling her skin.

"Say it loud."

Jane swallowed against his tongue. She tasted like sugar, milk, and vanilla.

"Yes... yes," she whispered. "I do."

Guy smiled and his mouth returned to her cheek. He kissed it slowly.

"Good."

He placed his fingers under the neckline of her nightgown, and lowered it down her arms, letting it fall to the ground. He didn't look at her. With his cheek next to hers, his mouth on her skin wet with tears, he wanted to savor the moment he would see her naked, he wanted to postpone it and suffer in anticipation, relish it completely.

His hands went down to her waist. He reached her long knickers. He let his fingertips run over the cloth: her knickers were warm and practical, tied at the waist by simple ribbons.

That's not how you will be for me.

His hands were itching with impatience and excitement. He pulled the edges of the ribbons, and the force of gravity did the rest. With a rustle, Jane was naked, completely naked, against him, in the bright lamplight, with her clothes and her modesty at her feet. This realization made him ache with desire.

It took all his self-control not to look at her.

"Before I buy an animal," he whispered hoarsely in her ear, "I evaluate it carefully. I evaluate its structure... its temperament." He kissed her neck. He licked it slowly, preparing himself for what was about to happen. "That's what I want to do with you. And if you pass my exam, we will proceed with our deal."

Motionless, Jane was not even breathing. Guy had made her suck his cock a week ago, had made her climax on Christmas day... and it had been her first orgasm. But he had never seen her naked. He had only dreamed about her, he had dreamed about her breasts, he had dreamed about her pussy.

Now he could watch them. He could *enjoy* them.

He straightened his head and stepped back.

Jane raised her arms, over her breasts and mound, to hide from him. Perhaps unintentionally. Even so, her whiteness was blinding.

"Lower your hands."

She bent her head, eyes closed. Illuminated by the light coming from the lamp and from the fire burning with red flames in the hearth, she dropped her arms. At that very moment, an understanding struck Guy. Jane was... beautiful. He already knew it, of course, or at least he had thought he knew; but the perception of her beauty had been, so to say, from *outside:* he had read the admiration for her in other people's eyes—damned *men's* eyes— when she walked head down on the street, in the rapture of that young doctor at the hospital who even dared to *court* her; but for Guy she had always been *Jane,* just Jane. Jane with her blonde hair, Jane with her pink cheeks, Jane with her mouth with the upper lip fuller than the lower—with that mouth that always seemed to protrude in a sulky pout.

Beauty...

Now, she was naked and white, and her eyes were pleading, wonderful—and Guy really saw her, as if for the first time, and her grace, her candor enchanted him. He felt her scared breath like it was his own, he felt it inside his lungs, inside his gut and heart.

Her body was perfect. Both slender and feminine, with rounded hips and a slim waist. Her blonde sex was under a white belly. Her breasts... were breathtaking; Guy had imagined them a million times, but he couldn't even get closer to reality. As clear as milk, and her small areolas were pale pink...

Guy's eyes got lost; finally, they stopped on her navel, the most innocent part of her body, yet his salivation increased. A tiny, lovely button, it seemed like a cup... what did the Bible say?

A cup of delights.

In that luxurious room, with the crackling sounds of fire, mad desire grew in his lower abdomen. Burning, sexual excitement ached in his loins. Tossing her on the floor, taking her right now, right there. That was all he wanted.

I can't wait any longer.

You have to wait.

No, I have to FUCK her.

But he did have to wait. He closed his eyes; he filled his lungs with a deep breath of air. There were steps to take. Lessons to be taught.

He opened his eyes. Swallowing hard, he moved toward her, and when her nipples touched his robe, he stopped. He would enjoy them, tasting them with his tongue, making her mad with lust.

Not now.

The room was not cold, yet countless goosebumps dotted the silky skin of Jane's arms. Fear. Guy lifted his hand and touched the curve of her left breast. The response was immediate. Her nipple hardened with fear.

"Good girl." He used a softer tone. The sweetness of receiving a gentle word from her tormentor—oh, Jane didn't know this sweetness yet, but she would discover it quickly. And she would do anything to get it. The carrot-and-stick technique, what else? It worked for animals... it would work for her as well.

Guy's fingers went down again, to her sternum, then up to her neck. He cupped it. "Open your eyes."

She did. Her nose was reddened, but she was trying to control her tears. To send them back. Distraught with panic, she burned and trembled at the same time.

"Turn around, Jane. Let me take a good look at you."

The shame would kill her. She wasn't breathing, her skin was as hot as the fire in the hearth. *I can't do this,* her eyes said. *I can't, Guy.*

He just retreated two steps. To get a better view.

Jane closed her eyes. And turned. Her long hair was gathered into a single thick braid that swirled down her back between her shoulder blades, and her backbone continued this line to the wonderful curve of her ass. God, that ass. High, round. Two symmetrical buttocks as tempting as a cream cake.

Jane clutched her legs together. Under his dark-blue silk robe, Guy's cock peered out between the flaps, furious. *Let me get out of here, damn you!* Guy had put on the largest breeches he had, but they were torturing him, squeezing his dick in a fucking prison.

Hold on, buddy. You are going to have fun... a lot of fun.

"All right. Turn to one side."

He wet his lip with his tongue. Behind his breastbone, he felt pride, power... a kind of pulsating need that seemed like pain. And in his balls... in his balls it burned.

"Guy, please..."

"Don't, Jane. Don't you *dare* complain. Just obey me."

Did he hear a sob? He did not know. Jane turned to her left, showing her profile to him. Her breasts were round, the line of her butt was magnificent—her sacrum formed a sensual comma in her spine.

"The other side," he ordered, hoarsely. "Let me inspect your other side, too."

Jane sobbed distinctly and did as she had been told. At her feet were her nightshirt and robe.

Trampled. Useless.

Guy admired her for a long time. Her glowing skin. Her erotic and innocent figure. The fire was about to go out, and only the sound of their breathing remained in the room.

"Hmmm," he finally said. "I'm not sure I like you."

Mortified, Jane raised her hands to her breast and groin, covering herself. She bent her face and a tear, despite his prohibition, fell from her eyes.

She believed him, and Guy couldn't help but smile. *Good heavens, you are so naïve.* "Don't cry," he said softly. "You're not so bad. There are only... a few details I want to check better. Get on the bed," he ordered, indicating it with a nod. "We'll end your examination there."

Jane didn't drop her hands. Keeping herself covered, she lifted a shaking leg and moved, stepping over the nightgown and the robe at her feet. Dressed only in a pair of white slippers, she went to the bed, walking uncertainly. When she got there, ready to sit down, Guy added a few words.

"Get on the bed on all fours, Jane."

Shocked, she turned to him. Guy pointed at the bed as if it weren't possible to make her understand his command otherwise. Probably it was exactly so. "On all fours," he repeated with a cynical smile. "Just like a bitch for sale."

* * *

Jane closed her eyes. She had thought of dying when Guy had stripped her naked. When he had made her turn and had asked her to show every side of herself to him. She had thought nothing could be worse than to be treated like that.

Now...

No, she couldn't do it. Guy had humiliated her more in ten minutes than she'd thought possible in her entire life.

Besides, what was the point in obeying him? He would break their deal anyway. Her heart sank, she was oh so conscious of her own small value. She had submitted to him, she had done everything he had told her to... and he would send her away.

I'm not sure I like you.

Guy didn't find her attractive. Of course he didn't—and he would never. His mistresses were fascinating, sophisticated, and Jane... she was not. She could wear luxurious underwear—she had been certainly wrong not to do it—but she could not look like one of his women. Not even with a hundred lace nightshirts. Not even in a hundred years.

Why did you bring me here, then? Why, if I am not good enough for you?

With a stranglehold on her chest, tightened to the point she could barely breathe, she turned toward the bed. Placing her hands on it, she bent over, showing Guy the obscene part of herself. She moved slowly. Rigid. Embarrassed beyond measure, she bent her other knee, and was a virgin on a white bed.

On all fours.

"Face the headboard."

She turned, obeying. The white fabric that covered the head of the bed was vaporous, princely. She hated it. She hated *Guy*. Guy who, ten feet away, was studying the line of her back, her straight arms ending in clenched fists.

"Good."

Guy's voice was smug. He knew he had the power to humiliate her, and he was enjoying all of this in the cruelest way.

A blaze of shame ran through her body, burning her belly, breasts, face. She could feel his eyes on her. He was judging her. He was deciding whether or not to buy her. He was deciding if the line of her body was tolerable, if her breasts were to his liking. If her buttocks were...

She dropped her head forward, biting her lip to keep from crying.

You're evil, Guy. So evil.

He moved. She heard him coming and closed her eyes. Guy stopped by her side, standing. He was still wearing his elegant dressing robe. He seemed at ease. Putting a finger under her chin, he raised her face and turned it toward him.

Jane opened her eyelids. She knew what he wanted. To look into her eyes. His were as black as night, bright with brutal stars, while he smiled down at her.

"Do you want me to buy you, Jane?"

"Yes," she whispered, weakly.

"Fine. Let's proceed, then." He took her face with one hand, between his thumb and forefinger. "The first thing I do when I choose a puppy is to evaluate its temperament. Do you have—" he smiled cruelly "—a good temperament, Jane?"

"Y...yes."

"Prove it."

He put his hand in front of her face, and her heart jumped as she understood what he wanted her to do. She opened her mouth and stuck out her tongue completely, as he had taught her. And then, she began to lick his palm, moving her head up and down... up and down, in a grotesque imitation of... of what, exactly?

Guy looked down at her with a self-satisfied smirk. "Oh, that's perfect, little girl... you seem quite docile, after all."

I'm not an animal. I am not an animal, Guy!

He moved his hand away, and she swallowed her humiliation.

Taking her braid in his hands, Guy undid the ribbon that was tying the bottom end of it. Strands of hair slipped down the sides of her face. Soft and shiny, they touched the mattress.

Guy sank a hand in that gold. "When I buy a bitch," he said, stroking her gently, with a kind of shocking sweetness, "I check everything, Jane... also her hair."

Jane closed her eyes, trying to breathe rhythmically, not allowing her body to demand more oxygen.

"Yours seems passable."

Her arms were sore, she felt like they couldn't support her prostrate body anymore. She shivered despite the heat she felt.

"You're too thin." Guy placed his hand on her back and moved it back and forth, with an open palm. "If I keep you here, you will have to eat more than you did tonight."

How could she eat? She had eaten almost nothing since Christmas Eve. Her stomach was in knots, and it was for this reason that she had lost five pounds in a week.

"Is that clear, Jane?"

"Y...yes. Yes, Guy."

"Every night, you will welcome me with luxury underwear," he murmured as, his palm open, he moved up and down over her back in a gentle caress, "or naked, if you prefer."

The light coming from the fireplace was dampened, but the room was hotter than before. Or was she, her degradation, to warm the room up?

"All... all r-right."

"You won't be allowed to leave this house unless I tell you. You'll be free to read, write, go into the garden, when I'm not around."

The orphanage, Guy... please don't take it away from me! She didn't say that aloud. She could not talk about her children in such a moment.

"When I get back home," continued Guy, and she noticed how frighteningly huge and hard his erection was under his robe, "I'll call you if I want to see you. And you will do *whatever* I tell you to do."

"Yes, G—"

She stopped, because he had put his left hand under her body and, cupping her left breast, was touching it slowly. He took her hard nipple between his thumb and forefinger and rolled it, causing a jolt that ran to her groin and turned her legs to jelly.

The air came into her mouth with a hiss, and Jane dropped her face forward, letting him touch her, handle her, caress her... as he pleased.

God, forgive me.

"Your breasts..." Guy murmured. "Your breasts are good enough, I think."

The hand on her rear moved farther back, over her buttocks.

Jane clenched her fists, hurting herself with her short nails. Guy cupped her left buttock, then let his fingers slide down her tense thigh.

A wave of mortification burned her. She wanted to cry, cry for hours. It was not fair. What he was doing to her was not fair. *I am not an animal, Guy. We grew up together, and I cared for you.*

I cared for you so much.

He moved his fingers up, stopping them behind her thigh. Going farther up, he touched her vulva which, even though Jane kept herself closed, her position inevitably exposed.

"Hmmm," he murmured doubtfully.

Leaving her breast, he moved toward her bare feet, where he could get a better view of her private parts.

Distressed, Jane turned her head to him.

"Look ahead," Guy said abruptly, "or I'll put blinkers on you."

She turned to the headboard again, shocked by shame and frightened by the mistake she had just made. She clenched the white blanket in her fists.

"Spread your legs."

Jane closed her eyelids, everything went black, and she moved her right leg about five inches to the side.

"All right. Stay like that."

Guy's hands rested on her buttocks, and she involuntarily flinched. He was... God. She remained still as Guy spread her buttocks and ran his thumbs between the crack, touching the shameful little hole in his movement.

"Do you like being caressed here?"

Yes, she was supposed to answer *yes,* but how could she do that? Guy was shaming her.

"Tell me you like it, Jane."

"Please... please, Guy!"

A heavy slap on her ass made her jump. "Say it."

"I like it," she murmured in shock.

He resumed his light caress, and... God, she thought. Not again, God, *please* don't let him...

Guy parted her buttocks with both hands. And, astounding her, he spat in the crack.

"God, no..."

The heat of his saliva trickled down between her buttocks, on her anus, and a finger, no, not there, please!

"Your ass, angel..." said Guy, his voice both mocking and hoarse, "your ass meets... uh, fully... the requirements I need."

His finger was an arrogant intruder, perhaps only the tip, perhaps only half of it, moving up and down her anus, both uncomfortable and relaxing, not painful, no, violating her in such a despicable place. In her belly, she felt wicked spasms, and below her navel, and in her legs. Obscene, sinful sensations, that she couldn't accept...

Please God, make him stop...

He did not stop. He continued with insolence, moving his finger inside her, back and forth, and slid the other hand underneath her, down her belly, to brush her hair sex. Jane flinched at his light touch. With weak legs, taking in terrorized breaths, she stayed immobile and submissive to him.

"Oh, but look at that..." Guy murmured, pushing a finger between the lips of her vulva. "You're getting wet, little Jane..." She heard him laugh softly, laughing at her mortification. He moved his finger up and down, touching her in a way that made her shiver. "You like this game, don't you..."

He stroked her arrogantly, near the small knob hidden between the lips of her slit. Jane felt her vagina grow moist, and she knew, she had learned, what that tension in her limbs was. She breathed with her mouth open. It was humiliating and cruelly tempting—there was nothing else but him and his hands and his presence.

And his power...

Guy moved both hands over her, taking possession of her body, and stole away from her any chance to breathe normally. To think normally.

"Put your elbows on the mattress..." he commanded without interrupting his caresses, "let me take a better look at you..."

Jane blinked. Her elbows? Did he want her to put her elbows on the mattress? But that way...

Heavens, no.

Guy slapped her hard on her buttocks, and she groaned with pain.

"Jane, what are you supposed to do when your master gives you an order?"

God. God. She took a breath. "I... I obey..."

Guy slapped her buttocks again.

"I obey!" she sobbed. And she did. She buried her face in the pillow, resting her elbows on the bed. She felt the air hit her wet, fully exposed pussy.

"Good girl... and now you'll let me look well at you, won't you, Jane?"

"Y-yes..."

He chuckled. "This is the way I like you, angel... docile... and obedient..."

His fingertip reached the button at the beginning of her vulva. It was little, yet very sensitive, and an enemy to her. It craved his caresses, it craved to be touched; Guy provoked it, depraved and slow, moving his finger around it in small, languid circles. And the noises his hand was making against her lubricated flesh... they were sloppy, shameful sounds.

"Your cunt, Jane..." muttered Guy as the forefinger of his left hand got drenched with her juices, and the other finger, on her anus, penetrated her rectum, "your cunt satisfies me. Very much..."

His hands were rubbing her mercilessly, and her bottom moved up and down each time his forefinger penetrated it, each time he came closer to the small knob that protruded... that begged to be fondled by him.

"It's a wet cunt..." murmured that damned, damned demon behind her, and he moved his finger farther down, to her vaginal entrance, pushing the tip inside her.

"And it's hot, and... and horny... isn't it?"

Damned... oh, so damned... "Y...yes..." she gasped. His finger invaded her vagina just an inch or so, and Jane found herself lifting her hips, inviting him deeper, more inside her. Indecent instinct that drove her to soften her body, to welcome him, indecent because it wanted more, and it knew there would be more... soon, Guy would give her so much more...

"Oh, this little virgin wants to be filled..." Guy laughed softly and moved his finger forward, brushing the small, sensitive portion hidden in her intimate lips, and sliding between her sexual fluids. "But you have to wait, Jane... you have to beg me for that..."

Into her anus, between her nether lips, these two fingers were abusing and melting her, taking her to heaven and condemning her to hell.

"You can't wait to be fucked, my little girl..." he murmured as she could no longer hold back the moans and breathed noisily, moving involuntarily against his hand. "You want my cock inside you, don't you..."

"Yes..." she said, beside herself. "Yes, Guy..."

Forgetting her scandalous position, forgetting the cattle sale, only that craving inside her remained. That liquefied, hot chocolate that spread in her belly, in her thighs, in her pussy lips. It was a warm, wonderful torture, a delightful pain because it preceded ecstasy, and she was close... so close...

"And you'll do everything... everything I tell you..." He touched the little button between her wet intimate curls, ending the slow torment of his finger moving around it. "Everything, Jane..."

She arched with pleasure, bringing her head backward. "Yes! Oh yes!" It was a broken cry, in the arousal that was taking her near to orgasm. "Yes, Guy, I'll... I'll do everything... oh, please..."

Guy's hands stopped. Abruptly. Before she could reach the climax. With her elbows on the mattress and her hands gripping the pillow, with her ass and pussy between her master's hands, Jane groaned in frustration. Lowering her face, pressing her forehead into the pillow, she managed to swallow the *no!* she wanted to shout so badly.

"Your examination is going well," murmured Guy, withdrawing his hands from her hips and groin, leaving her exposed to the cold. "Straighten your arms now."

The effort to obey his command was enormous. Finally, Jane got back on all fours. Guy stroked her back with his damp hand, and slowly moved to the left, leaving the places he had so obscenely fondled. "You soaked my hand," he said huskily, putting it in front of her face. "Clean it, Jane."

Melted and weak, Jane began to lick his hand. There was her taste, her... *juice* on it. The thought made her burn with shame and lust. She licked his palm. Then his fingers. Guy put the index and middle fingers in her mouth. He slid them in and out.

"Jane, you're doing... well, very well indeed..." He pulled his fingers out of her mouth, and a drop of saliva ran down her chin. "Now turn toward me, like a good girl."

With her hands, she shifted on the bed, ending up with her face in front of Guy's crotch. He put a hand on her nape and, pulling her hair, lifted her face up. Then he undid his dressing robe. He was stripped to the waist. His chest was muscular and wide, covered with dark hair. Just a thin line of hair was on his hard stomach, running from his navel into his breeches. Jane's eyes could not linger on his mighty pecs or his abdominal muscles, because his underpants, long to the knee, were strained by the enormous bulge of his erection.

Guy reached for the buttons that closed them. He undid them with deliberate slowness.

"Don't close your eyes."

He dropped his underpants to the floor, and his arrogant penis sprang free before her face. Dark with blood and excitement, hard and with bulging veins... majestic as she remembered. Guy pulled her face near it. There was no need for words. Jane stuck out her tongue and began to lick it. She felt dizzy as she savored its base—oh God, it was so hot, so throbbing, so silky. Its taste was the same as a week ago: warm bread, clean

113

sweat.

It was Guy's taste.

"Oh, you... you're *really* an angel, aren't you..."

An angel on all fours. She should hate what she was doing, but between her legs she was wet, she felt the air slam against the secretions of her vagina. Guy's eyes were on her, he was *watching* her, and she could feel immoral excitement in her legs, in her breasts... between her thighs. She followed the big lower vein of his cock with her tongue, for the pleasure of his eyes, for the pleasure of this man. She licked it gently, carefully... *thoroughly*. From base to tip, soaking it with generous saliva, as he had taught her on Christmas Eve. She tasted the slit at the head of his rod, its slightly salty flavor, running her tongue over it several times, recalling the warm streams that had filled her mouth.

"Roll your tongue, Jane..." he panted. "Roll your tongue around the tip..."

You will do everything I tell you.

And Jane, shamefully aware of her submission, rolled her tongue around the large tip of his cock. Guy stroked her head with both hands, moving his fingers behind her ears and making her shiver, and she hated him. She hated him. Oh God, how she hated him, but it was no use repeating this to herself, because his taste didn't seem obscene to her, and all she could think about was to lick him. Give him pleasure.

"Lift your eyes, Jane... look at me, my angel..."

His voice was muffled; even he was losing his impassivity in having her here, with his penis in her mouth, feeling her tongue, her lips, her saliva on him.

Aroused and lost, Jane looked up. That devil—that beautiful, cruel devil—had his mouth half-open, his eyes fixed on her, on the tongue she was moving with a sloppy sound, and this took away her breath, yes, this made her feel ashamed of herself, but her belly didn't cool down, her belly contracted with cramps in time with each lick she gave him, each caress he gave her on her neck, on her lobes, dissolving her with need. Making her forget morality. Honor.

Herself.

* * *

Guy mustered every ounce of will, every drop of strength in his body. This was the best sex game, and the most difficult to sustain, he had ever played.

"Jane, you... you are *so* good, oh, *Jesus*... so good..."

He closed his eyes. He was too aroused, and he didn't have to come in her mouth. It was hard, it was fucking hard to keep control of himself. He had caressed her before making her suck his cock, he had left her unsatisfied, and the effects were, God... *magnificent*. Simply magnificent.

Jane's cheeks were red, and she, panting, was licking him, moving her head up and down, closing her mouth sideways over his rod, sensual, passionate. Guy pushed her head down lower, to the base of his penis. "Lick my balls, angel, show me... show me heaven..."

Bastard, yes, he was. He was taking full advantage of her and was madly enjoying this moment, her total surrender. Jane was defeated... completely defeated. With the utmost care, her tongue was tracing wonderful lines over his balls... such sweet lines; and she was beautiful to watch. She kept her arms straight, and her back made a sensual arch before her buttocks. With her face buried against his balls, her tongue was licking him all over. Oh, this was heaven.

In front of him on all fours. Yes, that was her place—and it felt so right. So perfect.

"I like the way you make me feel your tongue, you're... you're lovely..."

It could not last much longer, this game, if he wanted to finish it inside her. With an incredible effort of will, he guided her mouth up to his cock again. With her hair down her back, Jane was obedient, burning... passionate. She was moaning lightly as she licked him. He'd taken her close to orgasm, and she was still hot, *so* hot. Guy could not help but compare her Christmas Eve blowjob with this one. Now she was excited beyond reason, while she had been just prostrate back then. The line between cruelty and sex games was blurred and irrational. Unfair, too. Later Jane would hate herself for the abandon she was showing him, but now she wasn't just licking him, she was... *savoring* him.

Guy smiled, and his pleasure joined with a satisfaction he'd never felt before. Holding her head with both hands, he pushed the tip of his cock between her lips. With a mouthful of him, Jane let him guide her back and forth. She moved not only her head, but also her body, and her gorgeous ass went back and forth, back and forth for her master.

"Look at me, Jane..." He stopped her head, enjoying the sight of her with a mouthful of his cock. "Oh, you *love* to be my slave... you are enjoying all of this, aren't you..."

She had to answer; she nodded, and his penis, between her lips, moved up and down. Guy felt a spasm in his crotch. Jesus Christ, he was about to come. He pulled his cock out of her mouth and closed his eyes, breathing hard to regain control.

He had to be the strongest here, but God... *God!*

"Yes, I think... I think you're good enough," he murmured after a while. He looked back at her. She still kept her mouth ajar, waiting, as tame as a puppy. Guy stroked her face with his dick, wet from her saliva. First on one cheek, then the other.

"We can take the next step now," he murmured huskily. "Because you passed the test, angel. I'm buying you."

15.

"Lie down."

Jane left the on-all-fours position Guy had imposed on her during their foreplay. Resting her bottom on her heels, she looked at the pillow in which she had sunk her face as she raised her buttocks. Rolling on her back, she put her nape on it. She covered her breasts with her left arm and lay down, stretching her legs. Her right hand ran to her groin to cover the soft blond hair between her legs.

Soft... and wet. Guy smiled as he admired her from above, standing beside the bed. *I know that, little one. You are a bit late for modesty, don't you think?*

"Take your hands away," he said softly. "I want to look at you."

Jane swallowed. She brought her arms to the sides of her body, and Guy's eyes lingered on every inch of her. She was so white, lying on the fluffy bed, with her legs crossed. How many times had he dreamed of her like this? Thousands, millions?

Did one of these fantasies come close to reality?

Just one miserable fantasy?

The lamplight was bright and prevented her from hiding. Standing beside the bed, Guy filled his eyes with her. A virgin on a bed. Her blood would stain the blanket soon. Red spots on pure white. The thought gave him a sort of dizziness.

"Spread your legs."

Jane's beautiful breasts lifted in a panicked breath. She obeyed. She parted her legs a few inches. Passion glazed her eyes, but there was something else, too. Fear. She was a virgin, after all, although definitely flushed by the preparation of a few moments ago. And Guy would hurt her. He would hurt her no matter how attentive he would be. He had never been with a virgin, but God—he looked down at his hard-on—he was big even for the experienced women he fucked in brothels or in their husbands' houses.

He touched Jane's belly with his hand. His fingertips reached her mound in a promise of pleasure. Jane's breathing tensed. Her lips slightly parted.

116

Her intimate hair was golden. Wet for him. Guy pushed his finger between her nether lips, brushing the little prominence among the soft curls. Sweet juice wet his skin. He slowly brought up his hand to her breasts, feeling the shivers on her silky skin, shivers of cold, fear, and desire. He stopped on her turgid nipple; it was of a pale pink that his mouth would make more intense.

He had all the power, here. All the power of a man over a woman.

There was only a damn rule: he had to take it slow, because excitement threatened to make him mess it up. To make him hurry. He should not hurry. With his fingers, he played around her nipple.

"Are you ready for me, Jane?"

"Y...yes."

No, you're not. Dropping the robe that still covered his shoulders, he stood naked next to her. *But you will be. Soon.*

Jane's eyes widened. Guy knew he had a beautiful body. Women kept repeating it to him. He didn't care. When you're an earl, your noble title is all you need to get laid. He used his muscles for something else—for the Nights of Knives, for beating some son of a bitch when he wanted to let off steam, and for never succumbing to anyone. Now that he was reading involuntary admiration in Jane's eyes, he appreciated all the secondary benefits of having such a body.

Look at me all you want, little angel.

Jane met his eyes, saw his gratification, and flushed. She closed her eyes, and her chest rose and fell quickly.

Guy smiled. He lay down beside her, close enough to feel her presence, but not enough to touch her. For now, he had to be content with this. Heat rose from her body, along with an intoxicating scent of hawthorn and sugar. He felt his head spin, and the palms of his hands became sweaty. Bringing his arm behind her head, he kissed her cheek, then moved down to her neck, savoring her vanilla-and-flowers aroma. He let his other hand go down to her left breast. He cupped it gently.

Wait, Guy.

Wait.

God, he could not. Moving closer to her, he touched her belly with his exaggerated erection.

Wait, Guy.

She isn't ready yet.

Jane was breathing rapidly with her mouth slightly open, a mouth reddened for being used so thoroughly before. And so pleasantly...

Raising his head, Guy put a finger on her lips, to stop their trembling. They were soft and sweet.

He exhaled slowly. He was not a kisser. The women he slept with knew that the Earl of Ashbourne rarely kissed on the mouth, and only if strictly necessary to get a fuck. That was the rule.

Jane didn't want to be kissed, anyway. Not by him.

Jane opened her eyes, looking at him in a way that made his heart beat faster. Not only faster; in a different way.

It was beating in his gut, now.

Guy swallowed. He was the strongest one here. He should not forget this. He should do no wrong. Jane was like clay in his hands, and he would take her where he wanted. Period. Without hurry. He kissed her cheeks gently, to not scare her.

"Relax, little girl," he whispered hoarsely, "close your eyes and leave everything to me."

Jane didn't do as she was told. She stared at him, uncertain, her pupils wide with terror. "I..." she whispered, and bit her lip, as if not wanting to get out the words, but not being able to hold them in. "I'm scared, Guy!"

He smiled, and a memory of Jane as a child overlapped with the present. He remembered the braids on the side of her head, her nightgown with pink ribbons, and her cheeks wet with tears—the tears of a little girl who used to believe in him blindly.

I'm scared, Guy! There's a monster under my bed!

That little girl was gone, she had stopped believing in him for years, and Guy stroked Jane's cheeks, still as round and soft, still smelling of milk as then.

"I know, angel."

With his finger, he stroked her mouth. Jane's eyes were confused, and the gold irises hypnotized him. Pure gold. He rolled his thumb over her lips. Jane closed her eyelids tightly. She would not want, she would *hate* his kiss...

But a virgin has the right to one little kiss her first time, doesn't she?

He brought his lips close to hers.

Yes. A virgin must be kissed her first time.

* * *

Jane closed her eyes. Guy had taken all dignity away from her. He had humiliated her, made her moan with desire, degraded her into a circus animal. Now he was about to take away the last thing she had left.

Her virginity.

With his thumb he was caressing her lips, opening them with his gentle pressure. Did he think back to when he made her suck his penis? Did he think of her on all fours?

Her breathing became more agitated. She didn't open her eyes. Her heart slammed in her chest with dull thuds. His hard, big manhood was pushing against her right side. And his finger over her mouth was touching, caressing, playing. Jane swallowed. Now he would put it into her mouth. He would push it between her lips, and then he would tell her...

Jane opened her eyes. Amazement overcame her fear. Guy's mouth had come down on hers. Light and gentle, he was sucking her lips but didn't force them open. He touched them with his tongue, without parting them.

He was *kissing* her, and she recognized his taste; she had already savored it, once, many years ago. Her stomach did a somersault. Without thinking, she lifted her hands to his shoulders—to defend herself, maybe, but then she gripped them, to seek support from his muscles of steel, from his heat. Behind his left shoulder, to the touch, there was a portion of uneven skin, raised and indented under her fingertips; a scar, a burn?

She closed her eyes, enjoying this moment of total sweetness. Feeling at home as she had not felt for years—for nearly eight years, wasn't it?...

"Is my kiss so terrible to you, Jane?"

Terrible?

Guy leaned over her, his chest covering hers. He had a mild scent, of Marseille soap; he washed himself with laundry soap even as a child, and that memory warmed her. Guy's tongue slipped into her mouth, and she let him in. It was her duty, yet she was absurdly grateful to him for giving her this tender kiss. She had thought he would never want to kiss her on the mouth.

Didn't she disgust him? For what she had done with his penis a few minutes ago?

Guy met her tongue. Jane held it still, she didn't play with him. She felt him smile against her lips.

"You taste delicious, my little angel... delicious..."

And she felt like crying. Did he know what she was thinking? Did he say these words for this reason?

But Guy really seemed to love her mouth. He sucked it greedily, savoring every corner. Sliding his hand behind her back, he held her close and, lifting her leg, he wedged his knee between hers. He didn't weight her down, he warmed her, yes, warmed her, supporting himself on his right elbow to not crush her with his pounds of muscle and strength. His manhood, only it, pressed arrogantly against her, and Jane tensed.

Inside? Inside her?

Guy left her lips, panting. "You're so sweet, Jane..." He accompanied these words with small, warm kisses on her cheek. She blinked her eyes, in which a shiny veil of tears had appeared.

Tears of... happiness.

You are so sweet.

A gentle word on his part, and she felt like she had never been happier before. Guy kissed her neck in that disconcerting way Jane had come to know—he not only kissed her, but he licked, and bit her. His warm breath brushed the saliva on her skin, making her shiver with embarrassment and pleasure.

119

He went down, down—and his mouth was between her breasts.

"So soft and... and fragrant..."

Jane moaned as his mouth rested where she was white. Where she was pink. Where she was turgid, rotating his tongue.

"Oh, down here... down here you're soft, Jane..."

Guy's dark head was on her breasts, and Jane didn't want to look at him, didn't want to, but she *had to* look. It was outrageous... it was beautiful. Her belly twitched painfully, and she couldn't look away as he twirled his tongue over her nipple.

His tongue was warm. It was masterful. Dishonestly masterful, and Jane hated it and wanted it over herself. He was so gentle, like a devil, *her* devil, while he licked her, and bit her slightly. When he cupped both her breasts, touching them together, Jane arched, allowing him to touch her better, to humiliate her better, but she didn't think of this, she didn't want to think of this...

Guy put his hand down to her groin, starting his rhythmic caresses again, with his curious, shameless fingers. He found her wet. Her dense juice welcomed his fingertips, in thick hot drops. "Now you... you are ready..." he muttered hoarsely, "aren't you, little one..."

"Yes..." she said panting, and with an act of courage she would never do in full possession of her mental faculties, she placed her hands on his head, grasping his dark hair in her fists. Between her legs, his finger had found its way, a moist way, sweet and eager, so ingloriously eager, for his caresses. "Yes, Guy..." she gasped with no pride, raising her hips against his palm. "Oh yes... yes..."

* * *

Guy was sucking Jane's nipples as his hard-on, further down, begged him to hurry. He had just to slide one finger inside her. Then two. Preparing her. He had never been with a virgin, but technically he wasn't without knowledge. He pushed his fingertip into the entrance of her hot pussy. Then he stopped, resting his forehead on her shoulder.

Only a small piece of skin. He would tear it.

Why do you want to ruin her life, Ashbourne?

He wanted only to free himself from a bloody obsession. A hunger that had grown over the years and from which he could move on only this way.

He pushed his finger a little further, and stopped again. Was it possible to deflower her with just his fingers? Guy had asked himself that question earlier and, restraining himself, he had pushed only half a finger inside her.

Half a fucking finger, for chrissakes.

He continued to fondle the outside of her sex, his palm on her wet hair, his finger at her entrance.

Why didn't he push his damn finger all the way in?

He wasn't a weak man, he knew what he wanted and what he had the power to get. His cock was pushing against her. It wanted to sink into her.

Did you make her cry her first time, Ashbourne? Did you feel good, when you took everything from her?

But no, Jane wasn't crying, Jane wanted him so badly. She writhed beneath him, her breathing was labored, her movements were excited and involuntary. She was clutching his shoulders and responding to his kisses... He had manipulated her to this point, he had taken advantage of her inexperience, so what?

"Jane," he murmured, returning to her sweet mouth, which responded with an inexperienced and tender passion to his kiss. "Jane, angel." He continued to caress her, her breasts, her pussy... without penetrating her.

Stretch her pussy with two fingers.

Stretch her pussy with two fingers.

Push just the head of your penis inside her, Guy. You won't hurt her.

She wants you, for fuck's sake. You have waited so long for this moment.

Take her.

FUCK her.

He went down to kiss her breasts.

His fingers left her entrance. With a groan of frustration, Guy put his hand to her vulva.

Jane arched beneath him, clutching his hair, as he licked her nipples, and sucked them, and rotated them between his fingers.

Why? Why?

* * *

Guy was on her breasts, his hand was touching her rhythmically between her thighs. His head was dark on her white chest. He licked her and Jane panted, grasping his hair, writhing beneath him. It was so beautiful... so beautiful. Her devil, her master... her Guy.

Don't make him stop; I pray you, God, send me to hell... but don't make him stop.

His mouth slipped lower, on her contracted belly. He stopped his hand on her sex, and Jane bit her lip to keep from begging him to touch her again, to free her from the tension building in her loins.

Please, Guy... please...

But he put his hand lower, under her leg, and lifted it up.

"Guy... Guy..."

Licking below her belly button, he lifted her other knee. He spread her legs, keeping his hands under her thighs.

"My little virgin," he murmured against her skin. "My little angel."

Her vagina was ready, waiting for him. Her instinct knew how a man makes love to a woman.

Guy moved further down. Did he want to look closely at her shameful parts? Did he want to look at her like...

"Guy!" she screamed.

He wasn't just looking at her pussy. He was...

"Guy... no, that's... that's... oh, God... my God..."

Where before there was his finger, now there was his tongue. "Everything's all right..." he murmured, scandalous, on that part of her body so forbidden, so obscene; "I just want to find out... how angels' flavor tastes..."

He licked her, moving his tongue between her sex lips, rotating it among the curls, giving gentle strokes to her most sensitive skin. Jane felt his warmth, his saliva. Good heavens, it was what *she* had done to *him* earlier, and had Guy felt that pleasure too? That wonderful pleasure, a pleasure that couldn't be wrong? The sight of his dark head between her legs, on her blonde pubic hair, and his sucking, moving, moistening, was too much. Jane put her hands on the pillow, clawed it, arched.

"Oh, Guy!..."

An overwhelming wave of joy flooded her aroused belly; she closed her eyes and wept for absurd emotion, as her master held his tongue still against her little button. Something inside her twitched and soaked her and him with her orgasm—and his mouth drank her juices.

Against her hypersensitive skin, Guy made a sound of animal satisfaction, and a dense hot stream wet her legs. His semen. He had come as well, jerking off, without asking anything else of her.

Jane's heart was beating fast. Lost in a blissful moment. Slowly, Guy moved his head to her belly. He gave her a light kiss on her navel. Jane, dreamy, brought a hand to his hair, without opening her eyes.

He kissed her body, moving up slowly. To her breasts. Her neck. Placing his mouth to her ear, he brushed her skin with his lips wet with her juices.

"Welcome to Ashbourne House," he whispered.

16.

Had someone told Jane Hartwell that she could sleep during her first night at Ashbourne House, she would have told them they were crazy.

Yet it was so; she was sleeping in her new, big bed, feeling warm and fuzzy inside. She was serene, oblivious to the wild emotions that had agitated her lately. She hadn't felt that way for years... for many years. She... she remembered a storm, yes... yes, she had felt this way during a storm, a storm that had happened long ago... and even back then it was nighttime, but Jane was at 7 Courtnell Street, it was summer, and there was an attic room she had to reach at any cost...

Courtnell Street, 12th August 1840.

Jane looked up, toward the stairs leading to the dark attic. There was a candelabrum halfway up, but its candle was extinguished. And behind the corner, right at the top of the staircase, ghosts were waiting for her.

She turned to her right. The first-floor hallway was lit by a candle for the night, and it was much less frightening than the stairway to the attic. The latter was sinister, narrow, immersed in total darkness.

Everyone was sleeping in the house; it was two in the morning. A summer storm had awoken Jane. The storm even now was blowing against the windows, whipping the walls with an oblique and strong downpour; and terror, pure terror, had prevented her from staying in her room. As the second, explosive clap of thunder had roared, she had run out of her bedroom... and then she had frozen in front of the narrow attic stairway, immersed in the dark.

Outside, a bolt of lightning flashed through the rough shadows of the night and flooded the house with light. Jane's paternal grandparents' portraits, hanging on the walls, suddenly seemed to have terrible grins on their faces.

Jane tensed and put a hand to her chest. Soon would come the thunder, the loud thunder. She knew after the lightning comes the thunder, she was nine years old, she was grown up now. She also knew that lightning was only clouds running into each other. So there was nothing to be scared of.

She was scared to death.

A few feet from her, there was Rona's bedroom and, connected to it, her father's. Jane could run to Rona in two seconds flat. Her stepmother would welcome her with sweet words, and even a sort of glad gratitude. Both of them would be happy, and so why not run, right now, to her?

Jane looked back up at the stairway immersed in the dark.

She clenched her teeth, took a breath, and placed her hand on the handrail. With a mad rush, she began to climb the steps separating her from the attic.

Her heart was thudding against her chest, her legs were as stiff as broomsticks.

The rain was slamming angrily against the house; the windows shook as the wind howled, trying to sneak into the interstices.

At the nineteenth step, it came. The thunder. The house shuddered, Jane felt the ground sway beneath her feet. She froze, between the stairs and the corner.

The wooden girders, up in the bare ceiling, could barely be seen in the dark, and the sound of the rain was like rocks hitting the windows.

Jane gripped the handrail.

Keep going.

Her legs didn't respond.

She could not. She melted with terror, she couldn't breathe. Clutching the handrail, she crouched on the top step. It was dark, there were awful noises, and there were monsters—monsters stretching out their hands to her.

Jane closed her eyes and sobbed, unable to move. She couldn't walk the fifteen feet that would save her. Claws would take her, right now; monsters' hands would come down from the beams, and then they...

"Jane?"

"Guy!"

She opened her eyes and leaned around the corner. And she saw him, standing in the middle of the doorway, holding a candle that illuminated the short corridor.

"Guy!" she repeated, sniffling with relief. She jumped up and ran to him, embracing his legs. Jane hardly reached his navel, because her stepbrother was a teenager, she just a little girl. "There was a monster," she sobbed while a lightning lit the attic walls around them. "There was a monster, and... and it wanted to take me!"

Guy did not return her embrace. "God, not again, Jane..."

"It wanted to take me, I'm telling you!"

"Then why did you climb up here, if you say there are monsters here? Why didn't you stay downstairs?"

124

"It was not..." she cried, "it was not here, the monster! It was in m...m...my room!"

"In your... oh for God's sake, it's just a storm! There is no monster."

"Yes there is! It's under my bed, and it has..."

But then came a thunderclap, and it took the words out of her mouth. Jane jumped and, resting her forehead on the bare belly of her stepbrother, she hugged him with all her strength. He was wearing only his breeches, as he was used to doing on summer nights, and Jane calmed down as she felt how solid his abdomen was.

"Please, let me stay the night with you."

"Are you out of your mind? If my mother finds out, I'm a dead man."

She hugged him more, like a little crab louse clinging to him with all the strength of her thin arms. "Guy, please don't throw me out... it's under my bed and... and it's got claws!"

With his arms resting at his sides, Guy sighed. "Oh, Jesus." He put a hand on her shoulder and pushed her inside his bedroom. "All right then," he gave in, puffing, "but tomorrow you've got to go as soon as light breaks. If my mother catches you here, she'll cut my throat. Is that clear, goddammit?"

Jane brightened up. She stopped crying immediately, though she was still sobbing out of reflex. She ran a hand along her cheek and nodded with conviction. He closed the door and turned to face the room. There was only a table used as a desk, a chair, and some books in the bookcase on the left wall. And in the middle of the room, with a white nightshirt full of pink ribbons, there was the most unbearable thorn in the side in the whole story of stepsisterness.

Oh very well. So, once again, he was risking being sent back to his boarding school, just as it had happened a year ago, and all just because of this stupid little girl. She was afraid of monsters. At nine years old, she was afraid of monsters.

"Why the heck didn't you go to my mother, if you were scared?" he asked grimly. His eyes were swollen and his hair was messy from sleep. "Or to your father?"

Jane sniffled. *Lightning is only two clouds running into each other, there is nothing to be afraid of. And the thunder is not a monster's sound coming from under my bed.* Guy said that there was no monster at all under her bed, and she believed it, especially now that she was with him and with his muscles and his courage.

"Why have you come up here, Jane?"

"Because you are the strongest of all!"

Guy rolled his eyes, but he couldn't help but surrender to her logic. As a matter of fact, he would never deny the words she had just said, not even under torture.

"Get into bed," he grunted, yawning. "Do it quickly, Jane, or I'll take you back to the hallway and I'll leave you there in the dark."

Jane took a step to do as she was told, then stopped. She looked up at one of the wooden beams in the ceiling, the one over Guy's desk.

"Can you show me how you pull yourself up with one arm?" she asked hopefully.

"Are you kidding? It's the middle of the night."

Outside lightning flashed again, illuminating the attic room. Jane bit her lower lip, giving him a doubtful look. "Are you no longer good at it?"

Guy straightened his shoulders. "I'm *definitely* good at it."

She smiled and her irises shone with a thousand golden flakes. "It doesn't matter if you are not," she consoled him with kindness. "I'll protect you."

The thunder came, inexorably, and Jane jumped, embracing herself tightly.

Guy shook his head in resignation. "Just once," he muttered. "But first, get into bed."

"Yes, Guy." This time, Jane hurried to do as she was told, running to his bed and jumping on the unmade sheets. Guy put the candle down on the floor and climbed up on the desk.

He couldn't reach the beam, his fingertips were over ten inches away from it. He jumped, and because of the faint candlelight—and because he was sleepy-eyed, damn Jane—he almost missed the catch. He managed to cling to the beam by one hand, then clenched both his hands firmly onto it.

Jane clapped her hands happily.

"Keep quiet, you ninny."

The beam was cubical, a pain in his palms, but it was thin enough to allow him a good grip. Guy breathed slowly and removed his left hand from the beam.

His distrustful, annoying stepsister thought he was no longer good at it, did she? He'd show her how wrong she was. Dangling by his right hand alone, he pulled himself up. His arm muscles tensed, and he felt like flying as his torso got over the wooden bar. From up there, he looked at Jane, then stretched his arm and went down lower. Again. Up, down. One, two. Three times.

Jane was staring at him from the bed, enraptured, like a chubby blonde angel with immense golden eyes.

Guy put his left hand up on the beam to do the exercise with that arm. He let his right hand down, and then he repeated the exercise one, two. Three times.

"I knew you were the strongest!"

Guy made an annoyed grimace, under which he hid a silly smile.

He brought both hands up to the beam, and giving himself a push, he jumped down to the floor. Landing on his bare feet, he made a dull sound that mixed with the storm's.

"Now it's time to sleep." He took the candle and, moving to the bed, placed it on the nightstand. Then he turned to Jane and pointed his finger toward her. "Tomorrow, disappear before dawn, is that clear?"

She nodded quickly.

"Good," Guy muttered. "Now get up from the sheet." He said so, but then he didn't give her time to move. Grasping a corner of the sheet stuck under her, he tumbled her down to the floor.

"Ouch!"

Jane made a thud as she fell off the bed, and *obviously,* she began to whine.

Guy ignored her and slipped under the sheets on the left side of the bed, turning his back on her. "I'm blowing out the candle in three seconds. One, two..."

"No, wait!"

Jane stopped whimpering and took a corner of the sheet, slipping under it.

Guy blew out the candle. In the darkness, the sound of the rain seemed stronger, as well as the wind flapping against the windows. Jane turned on her left side, toward her stepbrother's back. She went closer to him. She didn't touch him, she knew how much he hated it when someone touched him. Yet she was close enough to feel the warmth of his body.

Guy was strong, the strongest in the world.

Then came the lightning. Jane froze. *I'll be brave, I'll be brave, I won't be afraid of some stupid thunder.* As the thunder came, she squeaked like a mouse. She clutched herself to her stepbrother, holding him with her right arm from behind and her left hand on his shoulder. Clinging to Guy like that, Jane squeezed him, ready to fight to stay in this safe position. She didn't want him to turn her away from that warm, solid shelter, but she knew he would.

The storm kept on beating against the windows, marking time.

Guy tensed and remained motionless. He did nothing to welcome Jane. Not even to send her away, and after a while she relaxed, resting her forehead against his back. Guy's muscles were hard and invincible, and his smell was good, like Marseille soap and biscuits. Outside, the wind was slapping against the windows with violence, and the lighting and thunder continued to rumble their concert.

"Guy?"

"Hmm?"

"Will you marry me when you grow up?"

"Sleep," he snapped. "Just shut up and sleep."

Jane mumbled something, squeezing him more. She wanted to argue, she felt offended, but her hand was resting on Guy's stomach, rising and falling to the rhythm of his breathing, and his skin was warm against hers. It rained outside, and the noise didn't stop; Jane closed her eyes without realizing it, and after a few minutes she was asleep, oblivious to the storm and the thunder.

She awoke only in the morning, as the dawn painted the world in pink shades, and the sky was clear of black storm clouds. She smiled joyously, snuggling better in Guy's arms. He was still sleeping, but at some point in the night, he had turned and had hugged her in her sleep, as if to protect her from all the monsters.

17.

Jane opened her eyes to the timid winter-morning light. For a moment, her mind was empty. Confused. Then she remembered some words.

Welcome to Ashbourne House.

She didn't move.

Next to her, Guy was sleeping on his stomach, with his face turned toward her. He was sleeping without the pillow. He had thrown it to the floor, and his black head stood out against the white sheet. His breathing was regular, deep. A little noisy; he was snoring lightly.

Jane covered her breasts with her forearm. The dull morning glow came through the window. Surely it was past seven; her father must have been awake for a while.

The man lying next to her was sound asleep. He had a relaxed expression, his forehead was smooth, not furrowed, for once. His lips were slightly parted, his nose outlined its cracked profile against the whiteness of the sheets. Sticking out from the heavy blanket, his muscular shoulders were caramel colored. There was a scar on his left shoulder, and Jane realized that it was the one she had felt under her fingers the night just passed. It was cross-shaped, formed by two jagged white lines joining in the middle, four inches long.

How had he got that scar?

She knew nothing about him, even though he had grown up with her as a brother.

She blushed.

As a brother...

She looked at Guy's arrogant profile, his closed eyes, his straight eyebrows. No, she hadn't considered him a brother for many years now. Since Christmas 1847, maybe, when he, drunken, had assaulted her. Or maybe since April 1844, when things between them had changed forever.

Maybe even before that.

Certainly, she would never see him like a brother again.

My little angel, Guy had called her before kissing her on her lady parts... before making her climax in his mouth.

My little virgin.

She was still a virgin, she realized with a start. Why?

Hadn't he liked her enough to take her?

The minutes were passing. The memories of their night came back to her more clearly. She remembered what he had done to her... and what she had done to him.

Guy's touch had made her melt in his hands. And... and his caresses, he had dared to...

She swallowed.

And his words. Hot, whispered words. Even tender, at the end.

Would he be tender, now?

Guy's breathing was relaxed. The light coming from the window was bright—worryingly, increasingly bright. Some noises came from outside her suite, in the corridor. The servants had started working; God, it was late. What about... waking Guy up?

Oh no. Waking him up was out of the question. If he got angry...

She bit her lip. But everyone was awake already! The servants. Her father. Sitting up with the blanket tight over her chest, she stretched a trembling hand to his left shoulder where it protruded from the blankets.

"Guy," she murmured. *Please God, don't let him be cruel to me.*

Don't let him send me away.

Guy muttered something and pulled the blanket over his head.

Jane swallowed hard, her heart beating wildly. "Guy," she repeated hesitantly. She held the blanket over her chest. She'd give anything to get dressed, but she had the impression—actually, she was certain—that Guy would not like such initiative on her part. And she didn't want to upset him again. Never again.

"Guy?"

His eyelids moved quickly. He squeezed them together. He opened them slightly.

His eyes widened.

They stared at each other in amazement, as if they didn't expect to be together there.

The room was cold, and Jane shuddered—but an unbearable heat suddenly flooded her face and belly. How was that even possible?

Guy blinked. And then he gave a slow smile. "Angel." With a sound that resembled a grunt, he turned on his back, then looked at the window. "What time..." He turned to her in disbelief. "What the hell time is it, Jane?"

She drew back in apprehension. "It's... about seven, I think. Past seven."

"Seven? Oh, Jesus." He covered his eyes with his forearm. "Jane, I don't live in a world where there are such things as 'seven in the morning'. Wake me up in a couple of hours."

He turned his back to her.

"Guy!"

He didn't answer, pulling the blanket over half his head.

"Guy."

She touched his shoulder, with cramps of fear in her stomach. Touching him, after what had happened between them, was difficult beyond imagination. Panicked concern was pushing against her bladder. God, she needed the chamber pot. "Guy, open your eyes, please. My father knows I get up early. Please... he's probably waiting for me already."

"Oh, for pity's sake." He turned on his back again, with a grimace on his face. "Come here," he said sleepily, getting his arm out of the blankets and reaching out for her. "Try to keep me awake, angel."

* * *

"Guy..." Jane murmured, clutching the blanket between her fingers. She drew back. "It's late, really late."

He snorted. He had opened his eyes, and it had taken a huge effort on his part. And what did that girl do? Well, she slipped away from him, and moreover, she covered herself! And only the sight of her breasts, objectively, could wake him at this time of the morning.

Oh, little one, how many things I have to teach you.

He reached out, grabbing her wrist. Leaning forward, he imprisoned her head with the crook of his other arm. He pulled her toward his mouth. Jane winced but let him catch her; Guy, sleepy and a bit clumsy, kissed her, tasting her flavor in the morning.

She was sweet even in the morning.

He loosened his grip, turning it into a caress. With her hair down, she was sweetly soft, and her tongue was tender and hesitant. Guy closed his eyes. The moment was so comfortable, it was rocking him in such a beautiful...

"Guy?"

Jane shook him gently on his bare shoulder.

He groaned and opened his eyes again. "Are you really asking me," he yawned, "to get up at this time, from now on?"

He held her tight. Between their bodies was the blanket, and Jane grabbed its edge, making sure it didn't slip away. She seemed calmer after this maneuver, and she softened against him, laying her face in the crook of his neck. Guy closed his eyes, stroking her head.

Was he being too gentle to her? Oh well, he would make her pay for everything later. Yes, yes, of course, there was still the matter of his carrot-and-stick strategy, but really, carrot, stick, he was too sleepy for this crap now.

"Guy?"

"Hmmm."

"Don't go back to sleep."

Oh damn. Did Jane wake up at seven in the morning?

Every morning?

That was a problem. In the morning, he had the reflexes of a stone and the aggressiveness of a pillow. He cupped her nape in his hand and, gently pulling her hair, he made her lift her head. He was sleepy, it was seven in the morning, and nonetheless, he realized he had never woken up in a better mood.

Jane was warm with sleep, and soft. She was looking at him imploringly, her eyelids still swollen after sleeping. Poor little girl, who knew how much courage she had needed to wake him up.

"So you don't want me to get back to sleep." He touched her lips with his index finger. "Well then, you must do better than this, angel."

He drew her to him for another kiss. It was slow, but her taste made his hydraulic system move. Or the circulatory system. Whatever; in short, his cock hardened. He touched her shoulder through the blanket. Jane resisted with her arm.

"Guy..." she murmured tensely. "It's late."

He raised his face. "It's seven in the morning. *Seven.*" The more he repeated it, the more it seemed inconceivable. He took her hand and pulled it under the covers, to his chest.

She closed her fist. "So, aren't... aren't you going to send me back to Courtnell Street?"

Guy blinked. Send her back *where?* "Not if you will be obedient," he said against her ear.

He moved the damn blanket away and, finally, Jane's warm breasts were against his chest. He put his hand on her back, and closed his eyes, remembering the night just passed... how white she was. And the way he had touched her on the bed... oh God, yes, definitely that was a game they would play again. Perhaps Jane would even like that kind of pet-play, with time.

Now, however, she was completely restless.

"But..."

"But what?" muttered Guy, rubbing his palm on her left buttock. He guided her hand over his chest, and her reluctant, embarrassed caress made him smile. "What about stopping to talk and, uh... touching me a bit, angel? For a pleasant, you know... awakening..."

He dragged her hand to his belly, but Jane closed it into a fist.

"Guy... Guy, it's late..."

"Late, late. Late for what, for God's sake?"

"My father and I have breakfast together usually. And..." she swallowed, "and in the morning, I teach the children of the orphanage on Moorhouse Road, so I have... I have to be there by nine." She said it quickly, almost like she was trying to hide her slight insubordination by speaking that way.

The orphanage, of course, the St. Mary Orphan Refuge.

Lifting her head by her hair again, Guy looked at her and his eyelids narrowed. "Oh, really," he said flatly. "So, you're telling me you have to be there by nine." He scratched his face, thoughtfully. "But tell me, when did I give you permission to go there, exactly? I can't remember. Maybe because it's early morning."

Jane bit her lip. "Guy, please, I would... I would like to keep taking care of those children. Please..." she blushed, "please let me go there. It's just a few hours in the morning."

She seemed to exhale the air all at once. She had made her request—a simple request, and she was a simple girl, after all—and it must have been difficult for her. She had even managed to look at him.

Ah, little Jane. Guy knew that the St Mary Orphan Refuge was important to her, and now he realized something else. He could use it as a blackmail weapon even better than her annoying father.

"A few hours in the morning," he repeated slowly.

"And... a few afternoons."

"Ah. A few afternoons."

"Those would be... just for the hospital. I'm used to giving my help as a nurse, and... and it would surprise my father if I suddenly stopped," she added quickly, her voice trembling with anxiety.

Her father. Jane was a clever angel, wasn't she? *But forget the hospital, Jane. There are a lot of diseases there, not to mention the young bastard doctor who dares to woo you—these are things I'll keep away from you, especially that mentioned bastard. And as for the orphanage...*

"I don't know," he said blandly, his hand caressing her back. "I don't think you've done anything to earn it."

"Guy..."

"Shhh. Now I'll explain a little rule to you, all right? I'll teach you what to do when you want something from me."

He propped himself up on his right arm, which swelled with muscles and veins. Sitting up, he dragged her up with him, resting his back against the headboard.

Jane covered her breasts with her arm. He took her wrist and pulled it away. "For starters, I'll look at you as I please," he said, watching her breasts—her beautiful breasts, ready to be kissed, which responded to his every caress with turgid and erect nipples. "And you," he put her hand on his shoulder, "you will touch me."

Jane breathed in quick inhalations, red with embarrassment. "H...how?"

"You could start, uh... moving your hand on my shoulder... yes, like that... and on my chest, too."

Jane touched him timidly; with wide eyes, she followed his bulging biceps, the big veins in his hard arms. In her eyes, mixed with embarrassment, was also an involuntary admiration for his sculpted body. What had Mrs. Delisle told him, while he was banging her on her husband's desk, ten days ago?

Earl, you... you have the body of a god...

And now, Guy could fully appreciate the compliment. Pushing Jane's head down on his chest, he murmured, "Kiss me, Jane... let me feel your delicious mouth..."

Jane swallowed hard, taking a breath. Then she did as she was told, with delightful submissiveness; she kissed his neck, his chest, his nipples. Now, that was a nice way to start the day. If he couldn't fuck her, he sure wouldn't get bored.

"You can also lick me, angel."

She *had to* do it. And she did. Guy liked her gentle, caressing tongue on his skin, through his dark chest hair. He held her still on his nipples and led her hand down his abdomen, then down lower, to his cock, already arrogant and eager, guiding her in a slow stroke.

As he pushed her head down, on his navel, then further down, Jane's breathing became difficult, but she did not resist. She kissed the head of his cock and then, after a moment's hesitation, she began to lick it.

"Oh yes... good girl..."

He threw the blanket aside, and watched her crouch between his legs, red with embarrassment but meekly obedient. She licked his penis all over, balls included.

"Take my dick in your sweet little mouth..."

She opened her mouth wide and started sucking his cock, with her hair falling over her face and her lips reddened.

"Oh, yes, yes... like this... you're a naughty little thing, aren't you..."

Many women had played with his dick, but he had never experienced such a feeling of power, such a feeling of invincibility.

"Open your eyes, Jane... look at me while... while you suck my cock..."

She obeyed immediately, willing to please him. Her sweet lips welcomed him, rubbing his glans; her saliva and warmth were lovely. Jane maintained eye contact with difficulty, her eyes were full of shame as she moved her head up and down with the utmost diligence; and spasms in Guy's crotch warned him that it was time to take his prize. He didn't want to slow down—it was late, and maybe he couldn't even delay his orgasm, he was too excited.

"Good girl... oh yes, like that..."

He moved in her warmth, enjoying her blowjob to the fullest, without remorse, without altruism. She had to learn, hadn't she, the better way to ask... to ask him something...

"That feels so good..." He grabbed her head with both hands. "Here it comes, little Jane... I'm coming, I'm... oh God, God, yes..." He held her still as his cock erupted. Hot streams of semen filled her mouth. "Swallow it down, angel, I know... I know how much you love it..."

Jane obeyed with a slight shudder, closing her eyes tightly. She didn't miss a drop of his hot semen, obeying his command to the letter. Satisfied, Guy pulled her head away from his cock, lifting her face toward him. Jane was flushed, her lips swollen. "A great way," he whispered hoarsely, "to start the day..."

Holding her hair, he dragged her upward. He encircled her waist with an arm, snuggling her against his chest. Her breasts, soft against him, were his morning cushions. For a few minutes, he couldn't speak, relaxed and weakened by his wonderful orgasm. The light outside was getting stronger, even though he had been way too quick to come.

Ah, what a blissful moment...

He took a breath and lifted her head. Jane's eyes were closed, her face red. Poor girl. She wasn't used to sucking his cock yet, and that was hardly the breakfast of her dreams.

"Open your eyes."

He was tired of this attitude of hers—looking at him for not more than three seconds. Jane opened her eyes, blushing. Shame clouded the gold of her irises, but there were no tears. Good. Guy relaxed, leaning back against the headboard. It was a good sign.

He stroked her swollen mouth. "Tell me how I taste in the morning," he murmured with a smug smile. "I'm curious to know."

Jane knew at once what he meant. She widened her eyes in a silent plea.

"Tell me, Jane."

She closed her eyes. "A little..." she whispered, resting her head on his shoulder. "A little... bitter."

Guy chuckled. He lifted her face and brushed her mouth with his. God, he loved to kiss her. Jane would have to resign herself to that. "Really?" he asked, bending his head down to lick her neck. "I will eat more fruit, then. A whore once told me that fruit makes ball juice sweeter."

Jane stiffened against him. *What's wrong, little girl? Don't you like to be compared to a whore?* But she was a whore too, after all. His *virgin* whore.

"Do you know how *you* taste?" he asked in a whisper.

Jane held her breath and shook her head.

"Deliciously sweet," he murmured on her skin. "Like apples and sugar, little one."

She hid her face in the crook of his shoulder. "So, are you satisfied with me?" she asked, caressing his skin with her gentle breath.

Guy laughed softly. "Oh, Jane, Jane..." He lazily stroked her hair, holding her to his chest.

"Is that a yes? You... you didn't..."

"I didn't what?"

"T... take me." She raised her head shyly. "I'm still a virgin, aren't I?"

Guy's smile remained on his lips, but the look in his eyes changed, softening in a strange way, almost melancholy. "Yes. Yes, you are."

"But... why? Do you prefer keeping me..." she swallowed, tense, "...on probation, for a while?"

He blinked, and then his smile widened, reaching his eyes and removing that sort of bittersweet regret from them. "On probation..." he repeated, amused. "Yes. Yes, consider it this way, angel. And if you are obedient... and docile... I won't break our deal."

Jane bowed her head. "Oh," she murmured, wounded.

Poor child, she believed him. She would deny him nothing during the next six months... she would satisfy him in any way he desired. She was completely in his power, and this thrilled Guy strangely, almost painfully. "Ask me again for permission to go to your orphanage," he whispered, stroking her cheek.

"Guy, may I go..."

"No," he interrupted her, letting his hands wander over her body. "Beg me, angel. Implore me."

Jane blushed with shame and a hint of anger she couldn't hide. "Please, Guy," she said after a moment, in a humiliating whisper. "Please, let..." she closed her eyes, because he had brought his hand to her pussy and was moving it slowly, "...please let me go to the orphanage."

Her pussy was wet. Perhaps the blowjob had aroused her, Guy thought, and that was another good sign. A very good sign. He slid a finger between her legs, without wasting time. It was late, wasn't it?

Circling his finger around her clit, he placed his other hand on the tight hole of her bottom and slipped his fingertip in it, making her moan. That little ass... Guy would fuck it, and soon. Now he pushed his fingers back and forth in her anus and between her viscous sex lips. She was already swollen, soaked with excitement.

"I love apple pie, Jane..." he whispered. "You taste like my favorite dessert, angel, so... so I'll need to eat you often... you want to be eaten often, don't you..."

She gasped, and her moans, and her sopping cunt, very clearly appreciated the prospect. God, Guy loved to see her like this... he adored making her lose control. Jane spread her legs, leaving him the space he needed. Putting his hands under her armpits, Guy lifted her to her knees, to have her breasts in front of his mouth. He sucked her nipples as he started to touch her again. Jane squirmed, sighing with a pleasure impossible to hide. Guy licked her breasts, her neck, to take her to the limit. He probed her asshole with his middle finger, caressing her pussy as well. Just a few more minutes and he would bring her to orgasm. Jane was sensual and passionate, and it was breathtaking to see her lost in these sensations, to have this power over her: a power that didn't depend on his blackmail, but only on her desire. He liked pushing her to enjoy his touch, his tongue, his caresses, forcing her pride and her ego, because she did love, oh yes, indeed she did, she loved to be touched, and caressed, and kissed by him.

With an effort of will, Guy pulled his mouth from her breast, looking up to her face. Jane was breathing heavily, her cheeks were red, her eyes closed. Throwing her head back, she did not try to hide her delight. Her delicate pubic hair dripped as Guy's fingers slid between her pussy lips, wet with sweet juices. Jane was about to climax, and Guy would have liked to admire her coming... hear her moaning, see her convulsing surrender in front of him.

Not this morning, damn it... not this morning.

He stopped his hands.

Jane opened her eyes, lost and pleading, looking at him.

I'm sorry, little one. He raised his moistened hand to stroke her face. "It's late, isn't it?" he murmured. "Your father must wonder where you are."

She blinked, breathing heavily. Guy looked away, otherwise, he would fail in his purpose: he wanted to leave her unsatisfied this morning. With one motion, he moved her aside and, turning his back to her, sat up on the bed, stretching out an arm to pick up his breeches from the floor. He got up, putting them on without looking at her.

"All right, you may go to your orphanage," he said casually.

He picked up his robe and put it on. His slippers were at the foot of the bed, neglected; he put those on as well and felt strong enough to turn around. Jane had covered herself up to the neck with the sheet. Her cheeks were flushed and her mouth was open, stunned... and twisted in a wounded grimace.

You don't want me to go away now, do you, Jane? Your body is begging for me... but I won't allow your orgasm to come. Not now.

Guy smiled. Alternating satisfaction and dissatisfaction, that was the rule. "I want you to come into my study this afternoon," he said, enjoying her frustrated expression. "At three o'clock, angel, don't forget it." And she would not forget, Guy could bet on it.

18.

It wasn't the first time Guy had entered his stepfather's factory. He had done it before, and he had tried to forget it as soon as possible. Now, the sharp smell of flowers and grease, oils and solvents, assaulted his nostrils, bringing to mind the afternoons of years ago, when Charles Hartwell, who had never really resigned himself to his stepson's coldness, used to drag him there "as a father with his son." On those occasions, Guy sat in a corner with a bored expression on his face, or to put it better, this happened on his *good* days. On his bad days—which, of course, happened a lot more often— he began to break alembics, jars, and working tools to force his stepfather to bring him home.

He'd have liked to do it now.

"Is this really necessary, Mr. Hartwell?" he shouted over the noise of the press near them, which was mixing semi-processed products.

"Of course it is," Charles replied, giving him the "my stepson is an idiot" look. "You must know the people you will work with."

Guy, work here? No way. He had no intention of spending his mornings in this hell of smells and noises. Someone would do it for him, of course. A supervisor, someone able to manage the situation.

It was a terrible situation, judging from what Guy was seeing.

They were in a large room of about two thousand square feet. Shelves full of finished products covered the walls. These products were ready to be delivered to the stores placing orders with Hartwell's Perfumery. Soaps, creams, bath oils. Not perfumes, though. Perfumes were sold only in the retail shop owned by Charles Hartwell, named "Hartwell's Flower"—and this was hardly a manly name for a shop, Guy thought.

Around them, a dozen people—all the factory staff—were working chaotically. Too chaotically; the division of labor between artisans and simple workers was not clear. Some were packaging the scented creams, wrapping the jars with lilac paper, and for no reason whatsoever, they suddenly went to the press to get some hair oil. Everyone seemed to do everything, bumping into each other in the middle of the room, wasting time at the worktables.

It wouldn't take much to make this factory productive. Probably would be enough to divvy up the workload in a more rational way, and, of course, there was an urgent need to modernize the existing production tool. For God's sake, Charles Hartwell managed it just as he used to do sixteen years ago. It had not changed a bit since Charles used to take Guy there as a child.

Guy shrugged. It was not his job. They needed a capable manager... and to find a manager, Guy needed Stephen, who gave his best in boring stuff like that. But there was a slight problem. Stephen hadn't shown up today. And he should have done. Stephen was Guy's accountant, it was his job to provide legal advice and secretarial services to Guy. It wasn't a pastime. But surely, Stephen was still upset about what he had found out yesterday. He was a prude to the bone. He couldn't accept Guy's blackmail of Jane, nor the way Guy had enslaved her to his will. But it was a revenge Guy had every right to take, and Stephen could go fuck himself. Guy would not go to his house, no, this time he wouldn't look after him. God, he was so disgustingly tired of rescuing his friend from his opium addiction. This time, Stephen could save himself on his own.

Guy put a hand over his eyes, rubbing them nervously. Anyway, Stephen wouldn't do drugs because of the blackmail of Jane, would he?

"These are essential oils, see?" shouted Charles.

Guy raised his head, and his stepfather showed him a barrel. "We make them according to the season and flowering time, when..."

"Mr. Hartwell, let's move from here! I don't understand a thing of what you are saying."

"And there is nothing new in that, big boy." Charles smiled and Guy felt like slamming him under the press. "All right, all right," said his stepfather, amused, understanding his stepson's intentions. "If you're afraid of a little noise, move over there. I'll have a few words with George—" he pointed to a man with white hair pouring oil into an ampoule "—but I'll join you in a minute."

Guy sighed. There was no way to escape this conversation. And Charles would make it as tedious and long as possible. Guy left him near the press and headed toward the farthest wall, covered with shelves full of colorful soaps. The sawdust scattered on the floor muffled his steps. On the way, he avoided by an inch a plump young woman who was hurrying around the room, as if the soap in her hands were vital. Charles had introduced her to him a few minutes ago, along with the rest of the staff, but Guy couldn't remember her name. He motioned to her to stop her apology, and went on to the back of the room. He could feel the eyes of the workers upon him. He scared them, whether for his elegance or for his noble title, he could not say. Certainly, he was the proverbial bull in a china shop, Guy thought, passing near a table covered with alembics and jars.

He reached the shelves. The noise over here was almost as loud as near the press, and the scents were strong as well, but at least Charles wasn't with him. Guy sighed and looked at the soap bars that filled the shelves. The soaps were packaged individually, one on top of another, grouped by the color of the paper wrapping them. Each color represented a product line, whose name was written on the label pinned down on the edges of the shelves. Red Sky, Green Water, Yellow Fairy... a dozen names not too imaginative, under the yellow, lilac, blue rows, like an extra-large candy store.

Guy's eyes wandered on the shelves. He didn't know he was looking for something until he saw it: a bar soap wrapped in pink paper, in the left bottom corner, about fifteen feet away from him. There were only four pieces left. They didn't have a label below them, as if they were leftovers forgotten there. Guy moved in that direction and dropped to one knee to take a bar. He brought it closer to his nose, inhaling deeply.

"We reserve the pink soap for Miss Hartwell," a shrill female voice over his head informed him. "It's made only for her."

Guy looked up toward the voice but remained kneeling, half-closing his eyes in his most charming look—or rather, what he considered to be his most charming look. It always worked with women, and with the young woman standing at his side it would work as well. She was the plump woman he'd bumped into a few moments ago. She was a few feet from him, placing a light blue soap on a shelf, and was giving him many admiring glances. Bumping into her once could be an accident, twice, definitely not.

"Made only for Miss Hartwell, you say?" he asked, standing up without haste. He had recognized Jane's soap, of course. It was the same one her father used to bring her from the factory when she was a child. It was a special soap, and Charles brought it only to her. Rona preferred another type, covered with lilac paper; and when Guy was at Courtnell Street (and not imprisoned at his boarding school), he used to buy himself white laundry soap in a small store at the corner of Artesian Road; he never wanted to use the soap made by his stepfather.

He smiled at the memory of his teenage rebellion, and once again, he brought the soap to his nose. Even wrapped in that way, and in the chaos of the factory's odors, he smelled the scent he knew so well. It was Jane's scent, and it went down into his lungs like a strange balm, both soothing and burning. Violets and hawthorn, Guy thought; but the soap was missing something, and it was Jane's natural fragrance, which was delicate and sweet like nothing else.

"Yes," replied the woman at his side, taking one step in his direction. "And if you ask me, my Lord, it's a real shame."

The girl wasn't even five feet three inches tall, but she was good-looking and, judging from how she was studying him with false shyness, definitely available. She had rouge on her cheeks, and her mouth was red-hot, although thin. With a few coins, he could get her into his bed, Guy reasoned as usual. But, though this young woman seemed clean, and despite her full, firm breasts (a thing that never hurt), the thought of slipping between her legs left Guy indifferent, almost annoyed. The night just passed had been the best overall sexual experience he had ever had; and there had been this morning, too... Jane's sweet mouth had sucked him, she had pleased him with all of herself. She had been warm and submissive, and he couldn't help but think back to when he had left the room: she was bursting with need, her beautiful face was flushed with dissatisfaction, and she was aching for his caresses—and for *him*.

Oh, Jane, my little angel. You'll make me a boring, monogamous man.

Guy took a breath to dispel the arousal that these thoughts had triggered, and he didn't allow himself to pull out his pocket watch to check the time. It was still morning, damn the world. Eleven in the morning, to be optimistic, and brooding about it made little sense. No matter how much he cursed the hands of the clock, it was still a long time until three in the afternoon.

"That's a pity indeed," he told the young woman, who was looking at him like a dog looks at a bone. "It smells good, it's..." He cleared his throat, thinking of Jane again. "Delicate and fresh. How come Mr. Hartwell won't sell this product line?"

The young woman giggled in a way that had nothing to do with their present conversation. "I just started working here," she said looking at him from below her eyelashes. "But someone told me—" the young woman came closer to him, brushing his coat with her breasts in a touch that was hardly by chance "—someone told me that there was a product line of this fragrance, years ago. Mr. Hartwell withdrew it from the market when his wife died... his first wife, I mean. He had created this fragrance for her, and..."

"Rose, you can get back to work now," Hartwell muttered behind them. He had arrived but Guy hadn't heard his walking stick. What on earth could one hear in this cacophonous hell?

The girl jolted comically. "Yes, Mr. Hartwell," she said deferentially, squaring her shoulders and abandoning the kitten tone of voice she had reserved for Guy. "My lord," she greeted him, taking a bow that revealed a generous portion of her breasts. The girl had unbuttoned the top button of her dress, Guy realized with amusement. Probably she had done it before approaching the shelf under the pretext of the soap bars. And in her eyes he could read a not-so-veiled promise. *Come and find me whenever you want, 'my lord', and I'll let you play an enjoyable game in my décolletage.*

Guy smiled with a nod, as if to say that he had understood and that he would certainly do it. It wasn't like him to hurt a girl's feelings, after all. He was a gentleman, wasn't he? *But I'm sorry, little kitten. I will be too busy for the next six months.*

Rose brightened up under his seductive look. She winked and straightened herself slowly, then walked away swaying her large buttocks.

Charles watched her with an expression between puzzled and amused. "Well, this is insane," he murmured. "I always considered her a god-fearing girl."

You understand nothing about women, do you, Charles? "These are the downsides of being an earl, I guess," Guy said, shrugging. He handed the pink soap bar to his stepfather. "It's an excellent fragrance, I've always thought so." He changed the topic abruptly. "If you market it, sir, it could help you get back on your feet. Stop being so damn sentimental, and start thinking of dirty money."

His stepfather took the bar of soap and rolled it through his fingers with a pensive expression. "My company started with this essence," he said in a low voice. "Personally, I think it's the only good one I ever created. I named it 'Mary Jane's Beauty.' " He looked down and curved his lips in a distant smile. "When my first wife wore this perfume, she used to smile and tell me that even she had one beauty at last." He shrugged weakly. "So you see, I will never market it again," he concluded simply.

"Your incomparable romanticism leaves me speechless, sir," Guy said. "And here I thought pragmatism was an essential characteristic of businessmen. How foolish of me."

Mary Jane's Beauty, indeed. Oh, that was so damn typical of Charles Hartwell. Snorting in exasperation, Guy let his eyes wander at the other product lines on the shelves. Among the names written on the labels, no one proclaimed "Rona's Beauty."

"You never created a perfume for my mother."

Charles raised his eyebrows. "Are you asking me if I loved her, big boy?"

Guy hastened to raise his hands in denial. Damn it. Why hadn't he ever learned to count to ten before speaking? "No, please, I wasn't soliciting you for confidential information. You were a good husband to my mother, and that's all that matters to me. The best husband she could have." He squared his shoulders, because it wasn't like him to be ashamed of himself. "After the dreadful experience with my father."

"You don't want me to tell you anything confidential, that's a big surprise." His stepfather smiled slightly. "Nonetheless, I'd like to explain to you why there is no perfume with your mother's name on it."

"Mr. Hartwell, really, it isn't..."

"I have created other perfumes over the years, although I haven't for some time now," Charles interrupted, rubbing his forehead with the back of his hand. "I could have told Rona one of these essences was for her, but the thing is... see, Guy, your mother and I... how can I put this? Our marriage started as a business contract. Maybe you suspected it. Rona had a good income, I ran my small company, and we both needed help. I was always traveling, and Jane needed a mother; and you—" he smiled, leaning heavily on his cane "—you needed a father figure. Or so I thought at the time." He shrugged, watching the soap between his fingers. "Then time passed, and things between me and your mother... changed. I stopped traveling so much, and, well... maybe late, all right... but I learned to love her. And she learned to love me as well. All in all, it was a good marriage, in the last few years especially." He lifted his head. "But I couldn't create a perfume named after her. Weird, isn't it? Maybe some perfumes happen just once in a lifetime."

Ladies and gentlemen, here is Love with a capital *L*. According to Charles Hartwell, of course. Guy rolled his eyes. Damn the world, he knew it would come to this. When one doesn't get laid, one gets sentimental. That was Hartwell's problem. His stepfather most likely hadn't gotten laid for ages. His first wife had died giving birth to Jane, and given the reputation of the 3rd Earl of Ashbourne, Guy's mother probably had felt revulsion toward sexual intimacy. Maybe Rona and Charles hadn't even consummated the marriage; their childless union was a clue among others.

"Yeah, maybe," answered Guy, suppressing a sigh. "But, changing the subject... have you ever thought of using a brothel's services, Mr. Hartwell?"

Guy's non sequitur unbalanced Charles, who widened his eyes in a rather funny way. He seemed unable to find a suitable reply and remained silent for long, blissful seconds. "Now, that's what I call leaving someone speechless, son," he murmured finally, "and I must admit, if your goal was to make me stop talking, you succeeded. Although, let me tell you, talking about sex with your stepfather is not quite respectful."

Guy bowed his head in sarcastic contrition. "I'm sorry, sir, but please, don't send me back to boarding school."

Charles was four inches shorter than Guy, but their height difference seemed bigger because Charles was bent over his cane. Now he straightened up, with the authoritative look that, sometimes, he had given him as a child. "No, wait a minute. Your mother may have been wrong sometimes, and I was away for most of the time, so I sure couldn't intervene with full knowledge of the facts. But about this specific subject, I clearly remember you swore that you didn't care, that you *loved* boarding school. And now, you're claiming you didn't like it?"

Guy clenched his jaws. *Have you ever known the pride of saying "no" before someone else says it for you, Hartwell?* "Of course I liked it," he said dryly. "I was just kidding. Now," he said, abruptly changing the topic once more, "shall we start our conversation about your business? Besides, come on... what the hell would be difficult to understand, here?"

In the corner where they were talking, the noise was a bit less deafening, but Guy's ears were ringing and he could not wait to get out of there. The artisans were around their worktables and, some feet away from him, Rose was returning to the shelves, bringing another soap bar, yellow this time.

"First, you will stay away from the women working here," said Charles, looking at Rose with a sigh.

"You're breaking my heart."

"Don't make fun of this, it's essential for the proper functioning of the company. Romantic involvements are never good in the workplace."

"All right, I won't hit on that big-breasted Rose." Guy sighed emphatically, raising his hands in surrender. "Are we done?"

"We're just getting started, big boy." His stepfather nodded toward a side door. "Let's go to my office. The girl over there won't rest until you stay here." Puffing, he leaned forward to put the soap back down, but Guy stopped him placing a hand on his shoulder.

"I'll do it for you, Mr. Hartwell."

He took the soap from Charles and dropped to one knee, putting the soap bar on top of the other ones. He managed not to bring it to his nose again, with an effort of will. God, Jane was already too much in his thoughts. Her soap was just what he needed today.

"Are you ready?" Charles asked.

Guy took a breath and stood up. Charles's lecture... his damn lecture on the factory! Charles needed a mistress, and soon, otherwise, he would be on Guy's heels during the next six months—his six months in paradise.

As his stepfather guided him toward the office, talking about customers and orders, Guy began to think about two or three women of his acquaintance who could be just right for Charles. Stephen would not help him with this plan, it was obvious. What a moralistic asshole his friend was, damn it.

Guy had to do it alone.

19.

Knock. Knock.

Sitting at the desk in his study on the first floor, Guy checked his pocket watch and smiled. Two minutes to three. What a good, good girl. He put the watch in his pocket and took the newspaper from the desk. He unfolded it, leaning back in his chair and having a look at the latest news: a robbery in a respectable Londoner's house, a new pony—oh, my goodness—for the little princess, Napoleon III, that restless Frenchman... and then, the headline on which his eyes rested: "New horrible murder by the Gang of Knives."

From the door came another timid knock.

Guy didn't put the newspaper down. "Come in."

Jane opened the door. She was wearing a white flowered dress. It was elegant, with some lace and ribbons, nothing excessive. Not a turtleneck dress, of course, though it had a modest neckline. All right, Guy decided, he didn't mind being the only one to see her treasures hidden under the cloth.

He folded up the newspaper and put it back on his desk, as if she had interrupted him. "Good afternoon, angel."

Jane blushed violently. "You wanted to see me, Guy?"

"Oh, yes," he smiled, "I wanted to... *see* you."

20.

It was the second of January 1852—this blissful, beautiful new year, Guy thought. Almost stunning, because Jane was in front of him... in his house, at his mercy. In his office, now, for her first... *training lesson.*

Their first afternoon was about to start. Jane had arrived on time, three o'clock sharp. She had knocked at the door timidly, and now she was near the sill, over twenty feet away from him. Guy was sitting at his desk. He was very much enjoying the sight before his eyes. Jane was frightened, and embarrassment and panic flushed her face. She knew she was his sex slave and was prepared to fulfill his every desire. But she would be much more than this.

She would be his beautiful revenge.

"You wanted to see me, Guy?"

Oh, how shaky her voice was...

"Oh, yes," he smiled. "I wanted to... *see* you."

He stood up, and Jane gulped. She was more than uncomfortable, poor little girl. What had happened between them in the last few hours had left her shocked, and, more important, had taught her to be submissive and obedient... at his disposal. This thought gave Guy a shudder of excitement.

"Today I'll explain a few things to you," he began in a gentle voice. "That way it'll be faster next time."

Walking around the desk, he sat on its edge, bringing his arms behind himself and placing his palms on the mahogany wood, which always kept some comfortable warmth.

But Jane's warmth definitely attracted him more.

Almost the total length of the room was between them. Standing by the door, Jane seemed ready to run away.

But you can't, little one, can you? "There's one thing you must do when you get in here," Guy explained quietly. "That is, close the door behind you, you ninny."

With her unsteady hand, Jane closed the door with a weak thud.

"And you have to *lock* it," Guy added.

Jane fumbled at the lock with her trembling fingers, until she got the difficult click.

"Good. I see that you learn fast." Guy narrowed his eyes, studying her delicate figure, silhouetted against the dark wood door. "The second thing you have to do," he continued with a smile, "is to remain near the door. You aren't allowed to come closer to me, not even to talk to me, unless I give you permission. It's possible that, now and then, I won't have the desire to... *deal* with you, but I want you here just in case. Understand?"

Jane nodded. Then, perhaps remembering that a gesture wasn't enough, she blushed more and added in a whisper: "Yes, Guy."

"Good girl. Of course," he added blandly, "you must be ready for my use, if I happen to want you. So, the third thing you must do—" he smiled, anticipating what would come "—is to undress yourself."

Jane looked like she couldn't breathe. She swallowed several times and didn't move, as if she couldn't grasp the implications of his words. Submitting to him would become a habit for her, but logically, it would take a while.

"Jane? Did you hear what I just said?"

She blinked. "Y...yes. Yes, Guy."

"Then do it, angel. Take off your clothes."

Jane breathed heavily, lifting her chest in a quick rhythm. After a moment, she brought her hands to her neckline and began to undo the buttons that closed the front of her dress. The first one exposed some lace under the fabric. The second one, a bit more.

"No, you're doing it wrong."

Jane stopped her hands with a mortified expression. "Why?" she asked in a small voice.

"You're too slow and reluctant. You must be more willing to meet my requests. More... enthusiastic."

Straightening up, Guy moved behind the desk. He opened the top drawer, kept locked by a small key he always carried in his inner pocket. There were various documents inside and, rolled up in the right corner, there was a long black strip of leather. A sort of belt Guy had bought just for Jane.

Guy took the golden buckle in his fist. The belt was a little rigid because of its never-used leather. He began to wrap it around his hand, and, after a few loops, he dropped his hand to his side. The tip of the strap brushed the floor.

"Let me give you an incentive, little one," Guy said nonchalantly, moving before the desk again. "Either you are naked within five minutes—" he swayed the belt slightly "—or I'll punish you for every second of delay."

He pulled out his pocket watch and opened its cover with a flick of his thumb. It was six past three or, to be more precise, six and twenty-two seconds past three. Guy put the watch back in his pocket.

Jane's eyes filled with terror. And with a kind of pained, wounded shock. After a moment, her hands hastened to her neck; she undid the buttons with trembling fingers.

Sitting casually on the edge of the desk, Guy enjoyed the spectacle of her clumsy panic. He enjoyed seeing her open the buttons on her back and spreading her dress over her shoulders. Jane had to do everything alone. She should offer herself to him.

Sniffling, she dropped the dress, pulling the sleeves off her arms. She fought against the ribbons tightening her waist until the sound of a rip revealed that she had finally got rid of them. Her dress and her puffy petticoat fell at her feet, leaving her covered in white stockings, a long chemise of the same color, and a bodice. The light fabric of the chemise hugged her sensuous hips.

The room was not cold, yet goosebumps dotted Jane's arms. It was the sign of her fear. She was moving awkwardly, with her head down.

"Keep at it, angel," Guy urged her, his voice tinged with derision, as she was even lacking the innate grace that distinguished her because of her frantic movements. "Maybe you'll make it."

He was pushing her to become clumsy for him, ridiculous for him. It gave him a painful pleasure, in his belly and in his heart. He felt a strange emotion in seeing her prostration. He could ask her so much... he could ask her *everything*. His fist tightened on the golden buckle. Guy felt the cold metal and the immense power coming from it while Jane was taking off her light leather shoes, pulling her garters and stockings down. She took them off with increasing anxiety; the seconds were passing quickly.

She put her hands to her bodice. It was beige, with elegant ribbons closing it. Jane unfastened them, and the flaps opened over the white chemise below. Her high, firm breasts pressed against the fabric. Jane put her hands on her shoulders, and then stopped. She turned a pleading look on him.

Guy took out his pocket watch and checked the time. "There's a minute and a half left, angel," he informed her with studied indifference. "Maybe you shouldn't waste time."

Jane swallowed convulsively. Bowing her head, she dropped the bodice to the ground and pulled her chemise down. It ended up on the floor like an old rag. Beautiful and white, her breasts were naked in the full afternoon light. They were so damn perfect.

Only her long, fluffy knickers remained. The ivory silk was shining just for Guy. Jane looked up, and her eyes flushed with unshed tears as she met his gaze. He was calm, unflappable—except for the massive erection bulging beneath his trousers, of course; about this, he really couldn't help himself. "Lower them," he said softly. "Take off your clothes... take everything off for me."

Take off your decency too. And Jane did it. She pulled the edge of the ribbon closing her knickers and they fell to the ground with a rustle. She lifted her graceful little feet and stepped over them, leaving the pile of clothes at her side.

Idly opening his pocket watch, Guy checked the time. It was eleven minutes, eighteen seconds past three. He smiled and put the watch back in his pocket. He had taught that little girl a lesson.

"Great," he murmured with a mocking smile. "You *are* willing to please me, then."

Jane had her arms stretched alongside her body. Keeping her face down, she didn't try to cover herself. In her hurry, a lock of hair had escaped from her bun.

"Look at me, Jane."

She lifted her face. Guy wanted her to feel his abuse to the fullest. He wanted her to sense his eyes on her breasts, on her sex.

He loved to watch her. He would never tire of that. She was delicious, slim and white. Guy wondered if his opinion about her body was impartial, or if it was the hunger he had for her that made her look so perfect to him, so pure and divine.

"Well, angel," he said mellifluously, "let's see if you were paying attention. How many things have you learned so far?"

"T...three," she said, her voice heavy with humiliation. Even the skin of her neck flushed with impotent anger.

"Good girl. And what are they?"

She clenched her fists.

Yes, little one, I'm having a ton of fun, Guy's eyes replied to the silent question in hers.

"I... have to lock the door. I have to stop here without speaking. And I have... to get undressed for you."

"Oh, you're diligent, aren't you? Only one thing remains, but it's simple, so don't look at me with such frightened eyes. Actually, I would say..." Guy looked her up and down, with cruel anticipation, "...that it will come naturally to you. Once you have stripped naked—" he smiled as his heartbeat increased "—you'll get down on all fours, angel. And you'll wait there, near the door, until I tell you what I want from you."

Jane's eyes widened. Motionless and naked, she closed her fists in a reborn, though useless, pride.

Oh, but you can't refuse me anything, my little slave. You can't. Because I'm the one in charge now.

He wouldn't repeat himself; Jane had to understand she belonged to him. She had to learn to obey him without objection. With a slow out-breath, Guy took a step forward, swinging the belt in an open threat. Jane realized how important this moment was; her eyes widened in fear. She remained still, perhaps trying to work up the courage to defy him; yet, before he got to the center of the room, Jane bent her knees.

With a smug smile, Guy stopped. He was taking away any dignity from her, and the power he had over her felt so wonderful. Why was that? Why did it feel so right, so necessary?

Forcing herself, Jane touched the ground with her knees and put her hands on the cold, light marble floor. She bent her face down, showing the top of her head. From above, Guy admired her sharp shoulder blades, her straight backbone, the soft curve of her buttocks. White goose pimples dotted her arms. It wasn't because of the cold; the fire was strong and lively in the hearth behind the grate and the room was exaggeratedly hot. Guy had wanted it that way just for her.

Just for this moment.

He took a breath, filling his lungs with savage satisfaction. He walked toward her. When he stopped, his trousers touched her hair.

"Every afternoon," he said hoarsely. "You'll do these four things for me every afternoon. Got it?"

Her head moved, nodding. From above, Guy looked at her on all fours, naked, submissive... and unable to lift her eyes.

That's your place. "I didn't hear you."

"Y...yes. Yes, Guy."

"Fine. And what did I tell you about these annoying tears of yours?"

From her head, completely bent down, came a humiliated sob.

"You're wetting my boots," he scolded her. "The salt will ruin them."

"S... sorry, I'll... I'll stop it right now..."

"Your apology isn't enough. Clean them."

Jane reached for his left boot, moving her hand to remove the tears from the shiny black leather.

"No, that way you'll ruin it more, Jane. Try it with your tongue."

Her hand froze on the leather of his boot. "No, Guy..."

He raised his right foot and put it heavily on her nape, pressing her head down.

"Obey. Clean it with your tongue."

Jane sobbed and rested her elbows on the floor, bending under his foot and finding herself with her mouth in front of his left boot. She sniffled, trying to hold back the tears.

"Lick my boot. *Now.*"

He couldn't wait to see her do it. Impatience gave him almost physical pain; it swelled in his lower abdomen and against his breastbone. And when Jane stuck out her tongue and placed it on the tip of his boot, Guy had to remove the foot that was pressing her head down and set it on the ground, or he'd have fallen because of the brutal feeling of victory that exploded in his chest. Seeing her in that position, and hearing the sound of her gentle tongue crawling on the leather of his boot, was magnificent, was heavenly. Almost scary.

"With your whole tongue," he murmured, taking a breath and planting his feet firmly on the ground. "Stick it out for me and... and move your head while you do it."

Jane obeyed, and her bun moved up and down along with her generous licks. Yes, God, *yes*. There was justice in this world, at last. Guy tilted his head to look down at her tongue on his boot, the glittering saliva traces it left behind, and Jane's eyes, that she, to not memorize the moment, kept closed.

But you'll remember the taste. You'll remember it forever, my angel.

"Well, now... the other boot," he ordered in a husky voice, and Jane shifted her face to his right foot.

Her head moved in the servile gesture par excellence, and it was brilliant gold against the shiny black leather.

"Your *whole* tongue, Jane. Stick it out completely, be a good girl."

Their roles were clear once and for all. After submitting to *this,* for her, any further attempt of rebellion would be impossible. Like keeping a shred of pride. Annihilated, she licked his boot as Guy wanted her to. In that position, with her elbows on the floor and her face close to his feet, her back was white and beautiful, and her bare ass was high and inviting as it moved along with her head and her velvet tongue.

"Yes," muttered Guy, breathing through his teeth, looking down at her with a sardonic smile; "they are *very* clean now."

He pushed the tip of his boot under her chin, lifting her face. It was red and her expression was shaken, her golden eyes veiled with tears of agonizing mortification, her shoulders trembling with suppressed sobs. She closed her mouth, pressing her lips in a pained line.

"Do you like to lick my shoes, Jane?"

She swallowed and her face, wet with tears, clenched achingly. "N...no."

"Oh, angel. Wrong answer."

Guy raised his boot and placed the tip to her lips. He made slight pressure. Jane's eyes widened, but, opening her mouth, she let it in. Tears streamed down her cheeks as she, submissive and shocked, took the tip of his boot in her mouth.

"There, see, you like it," he panted, pushing it a little back and forth.

Jane opened her lips to his thrusts; she was beautiful, she was *his,* and God, was it actually happening? Shaken by the triumphant emotion in his gut, too unstable for this game, Guy knew he had to interrupt it. He pulled his boot from her mouth and placed it on the floor. Its tip shone with her saliva.

"Let's try again, little one..." he said, his voice choked with satisfaction.

"Do you like licking my shoes?"

She nodded, shocked. "Yes," she sobbed, "yes, Guy..."

"I like it when you do it, too. I *love* it."

He took a deep breath. There was a kind of aching excitement inside him, pressing against every part of his body.

"Sit up on your heels," he ordered, his breathing rapid.

Jane did as she was told, sitting up and putting her hands on her knees. She was trembling, and small sobs escaped from her contracted lips. She didn't even try to conceal her nakedness.

"Spread your knees," Guy commanded urgently; his desire was becoming uncontrollable. He wanted to touch her, kiss her tears, taste them. "More than this, angel... here, yes... yes, like that," he approved as Jane opened her legs about a foot apart. "Bring your hands between your thighs and touch the floor with your knuckles. Keep your back straight... straight, Jane, let your arms squeeze your beautiful tits together... yes, that way... as if offering me your nipples to suck."

Jane's breasts, pressed between her arms, swelled even more because of her erratic breathing.

Guy leaned over her and stroked her cheek. "That's a good girl..." he murmured, rubbing his thumb on her lower lip. At his feet, bent to his will—for so long he had dreamed of it. For so long. "Open your lips," he ordered in a whisper, "and stick out your tongue."

It was kind of hard to speak with a steady voice. Guy was excited and... invincible, yes, he felt that way; immortal. And Jane's sweet tongue, after an instant, showed its tip between her soft, pulpy lips.

"Jane, little one..." he muttered roughly, while his thumb played with her mouth, "you are far beyond my expectations." With an effort, he dropped his hand. "This is a posture I'll tell you to assume from time to time," he said; his testicles were quivering with wild desire, and speaking was problematic. "When I tell you 'sit like a good puppy,' you must sit on the floor like this. Understand?"

She nodded, unable to speak, unable to *think*, overwhelmed by what she was submitting to. God, what power... what magnificent power it was, having her at his feet like this: stripped of clothes and pride, sitting on the floor with her tongue stuck out and her breasts pushed together, while her golden pussy almost brushed the polished marble...

She was finally debased, yes—debased from her pedestal of self-righteousness and innocence.

There was no innocence left for her.

No dignity.

"Well," he said softly. "Now you know everything you need to please me. We can begin to... *play*, angel."

At last.

21.

Jane was shocked.

Sitting naked on the floor was only a small part of how miserable she felt. She couldn't breathe normally. Her inhalations were shallow; they didn't get to her belly, they swelled her turgid breasts between her arms, increasing her devastating embarrassment.

God, when would this first, terrifying afternoon be over?

Guy was standing. With his black trousers, no jacket, and a dark waistcoat on his white shirt. The boots at his feet were wet with her saliva and tears. Jane had licked them, oh God—she had licked their dust, she could still taste it in her mouth. Her humiliation had been complete, but even more terrible was, now, this waiting without words, with him watching her from above. He held a belt in his right hand, a long leather strap that, lying along his side, brushed the floor, swinging slightly.

The floor was hard; there were no carpets near the study door. Sitting with her heels under her buttocks, Jane felt a slight pain where her knees touched the ground; her ankles pressed against the cold marble. Guy's study was large. Almost severe on its left side, where a massive, dark, gothic desk delimited the working area of the room. It was less formal on its right side, where the huge fireplace was elegant and noiseless, and a brown leather sofa, with an armchair of the same color at its side, invited one to sit by the fire.

Now we can begin to play.

Jane was terrified. More than her nudity, more than her posture, it was what she had just done, the way she had pressed her tongue against Guy's leather shoes while he looked at her from above, to make her feel like nothing—like a slave.

His slave.

He was standing in front of her.

Her master.

Jane had never felt him more powerful. Or crueler. He stretched the hand holding the belt toward her cheek and lightly stroked her skin with his knuckles. Then he dropped to one knee. His warm breath touched her ear as he brought his face close to hers, in a caress that gave her a thrill. And made her feel fear—exploding fear at her heart.

She didn't want to stay there anymore, no, no...

"Are you scared, my little angel?" Guy asked her softly, and Jane tilted her head toward him, involuntarily, for the gentle tickle of his words on her skin.

"Y...yes," she murmured with her eyes closed.

"Don't be." Guy moved his hand to her hair and began to remove the pins from her bun. "Do what I tell you to do, and everything will be fine."

Her hair fell to the sides of her face. Jane wore a simple hairstyle, and Guy threw the hairpins on the floor. He was gentle; he tickled her slightly with his fingertips. When he finished, he brought the belt under her hair, behind her neck. Jane didn't understand right away what he was doing—then she opened her eyes wide.

"No..."

Guy smiled. Encircling her neck with the belt, he inserted its end in the golden buckle.

"Now, now, what did we just say about the obedience you owe me?"

He pulled the belt tighter around her neck. There were no holes near the end of the belt, the ones that should have been used to fasten it to one's waist; there was just one hole, far too close to the belt buckle.

That belt wasn't a belt at all.

It was a *leash*. With a collar of the right circumference for her neck.

Jane closed her eyes, stunned with mortification. Guy secured the prong and straightened, holding the end of the belt—no, of the *leash*—in his hand. The collar was custom-made for her: loose enough for a finger to slip between the leather and her neck, tight enough for her to feel it against her skin in a humiliating reminder of how low she had sunk.

"Come with me, Jane," he said gently. "Follow me... on all fours."

Guy stood up, pulling the leash towards himself. The fly of his trousers was stretched tight over his bulging erection. He towered over her, and Jane hated him, oh, how she hated him! Her breathing rose with tears held. Swallowing hard, she leaned forward, putting herself on all fours again.

When Guy moved, Jane crawled behind him without protest. She was well aware of the scene they were enacting. Her palms were sweaty with shame, and she left wet handprints on the polished floor.

Before her, Guy's boots clattered on the floor. He pulled her leash without brutality, careful not to go too fast. Glancing over his shoulder at her from time to time, with a hint of a self-satisfied smile on his face. Jane tried to focus only on putting one hand in front of the other. One knee in front of the other.

She was not just his slave, she was also his...

No, *no!*

The hard floor was gone, replaced by a soft red carpet. Before her eyes, there were arabesques on a dark background with thin gold trimming; stylized flowers in complex motifs on the expensive Persian carpet.

Guy stopped in front of the right wall, not far from the fireplace, where a large tapestry, in tones of green and ochre, was hung. Jane hadn't noticed it before; she had watched only Guy. Guy reading a newspaper with indolence, sitting behind his inlaid desk; the polished shelf of the desk, and its legs carved into four tigers... or were they dragons...?

"Jane."

She swallowed and tried to be strong. When she looked up at him, Guy's dark eyes locked with hers, shining with pride and desire. He looked at her in a caring, almost sympathetic, way.

"Now," he murmured softly, "sit like a good puppy."

The light from the two large windows of the study was bright. The fireplace warmed the ample masculine room. The green and ochre tapestry showed an autumn scene; trees full of yellow leaves, and red, orange, dark green ones, against a pale blue sky.

Jane had licked his boots, she had let him lead her on a leash. Guy was breaking down the boundaries of her self-respect one by one. Why was it still difficult, in the name of God, still so difficult?

She tucked her heels under her buttocks, sitting up. Her collar tightened, and Guy raised his hand to ease her movements. Jane spread her knees and placed her fists between them, squeezing her breasts with her arms and touching the soft, warm carpet with her knuckles.

"Good girl." Guy moved to the tapestry and reached out to its lower left corner. He lifted it aside, and when Jane saw what was hidden under the tapestry, she retreated, covering herself with her hands. The collar tugged against her neck, and Guy pulled her forward.

No, no...

"Put your hands down, Jane."

No, no!

Guy came closer and gripped the leash in the middle of its length. Without warning, he bent over and whipped her right buttock in a painful snap.

"Take your hands *off.*"

Jane bowed her head. Her stricken buttock burned, her deplorable posture made her want to disappear. With a sob, she brought her hands between her knees once more, touching the carpet.

I don't want to, I don't want to, I don't want to...

Guy stepped back, sliding his hand up the leash again. He lifted the tapestry and hooked its lower left corner to a nail in the wall.

"Tell me what you see."

A master with his... bitch. This was what she was seeing. Hidden behind the tapestry, incongruous and unexpected in such a place, there was a mirror, six feet high, four feet wide.

"I see... us," she sobbed. The carpet's pile touched her vulva and she felt like dying.

"Why are you crying? Don't you like to watch yourself?"

Jane shook her head. She didn't even try to speak.

"Why not?"

"Because..." she swallowed and felt the salty taste of tears on her lips. "Because it's degrading, and..." *And shameful. And demeaning, and I hate you, Guy... how I hate you.* She couldn't continue; tears welled in her throat, and she wasn't allowed to cry, but God, she wanted to cry... she wanted to cry forever.

"Degrading?" Guy came closer to her, and his trousers touched her head.

"Yes," she said, her voice broken as tears fell. Tears of anger, pain... humiliation.

In his hand, the tip of the leash stuck out about four inches. Guy brought it close to her left cheek. "Is this degrading?" he asked, gently caressing her skin with it.

"Yes..." *Yes, you devil... yes!*

"And this, little one?" He bent over, touching her left breast with the tip of the leash, titillating kindly her hardened nipple. Jane nodded with a sharp snap of her head.

A tear slid onto her breast. Guy smeared it with the belt, all around the whiteness of her skin. It was a gentle, sinful touch; had Guy hurt her, it would have been easier; but this way, as he was treating her like an animal and teasing her with his perfidious caresses, Jane thought she could die of shame. Why couldn't she order her own body to reject the physical sensations—the pleasant, carnal ones—Guy caused her?

Guy cocked his head, as if considering her answer, and then straightened.

"I see." He moved behind her; in the mirror, his black trousers stood out against Jane at his feet. She was glowing with whiteness and gold against his blackness.

He bent down on one knee, putting himself at her level. He had a massive physique. His shoulders and arms, covered by the white shirt, invaded the wide mirror. Jane didn't want to look at their image in the mirror, yet her eyes sought him, inevitably, as the eagle seeks the sun.

Guy buried his head in the crook of her neck, and his lips touched her shoulder. With his tongue, he traced a hot, wet path on her skin. Bringing the leash in front of her body, he moved it over her breasts, between them. It was a soft touch on her most sensitive skin, which involuntarily

156

responded to these disturbing caresses.

"It's degrading, you say?"

Yes, it was; the flat, black belt, tied to Jane's neck and held in his hand, was stroking her, *fondling* her...

"Don't cry, my angel, don't cry..." Guy whispered, his words like kisses on her damp skin. "Look how beautiful you are... how can you call it *degradation?*"

The things in the room were in the mirror. The bookcase on the opposite wall, the desk, the sofa. The large oil painting of a nighttime lake, with its fog and moon reflected on calm water. And then, there were the two of them; Guy with his mouth on her skin, with his black hair against her blondness, licking her neck, warming her, giving her chills throughout her body, trembling shivers in her belly; and Jane with her bosom pushed forward, touched by the leash from the nipples to the areolas, to the white, full curves.

"It's not degrading, Jane... it's... it's beautiful..."

His voice was warm in her ear. He placed a gentle hand on her hip, and the other hand, holding the leash, dropped between her legs. With the tip of the leash, Guy began to rub her sex lips, parting them, masturbating her with the black, polished leather strip.

"No..." she whispered. God, it was too shameful. The black belt went up and down between her intimate folds in a rhythmic, diabolical way. It slipped through her nether lips and touched the sensitive little button at the beginning of her womanhood, insistently... tenderly. It began to move more easily; sweet juices were helping its motion; shy juices, at first, then more blatant; cruel, viscous juices, they slid absurdly from inside her belly to the curls of her pussy, lubricating her, as if it was *good* what Guy was doing to her, as if it was *right*...

Guy smiled against the crook of her shoulder. "If it's degradation, my little angel..." he murmured, raising his face and licking behind her earlobe, "then degrade yourself... degrade yourself for *me.*" Keeping one hand on her left buttock, he pushed her upwards. "Lift yourself a little, angel... here, just like that..." He put the leash under her buttocks. The black strap from her neck came down between her open legs and beneath her ass. Behind her, Guy's hand grabbed the tip of it and began to move it back and forth.

"N...no..."

But he had no pity. In the room, the noise of the fire mingled with her sighs of surrender, as Guy kept on masturbating her with the symbol of her slavery, and licked her neck, and wet her with his saliva.

"See, Jane... you enjoy... staying here..."

He was hot behind her, he was strong. His fingers knew her body better than she did; and from between her legs came the sound of soppy arousal, and she couldn't help it, oh God—she just couldn't help it and was burning with this wicked excitement.

Guy bit her earlobe. "You got your leash wet, naughty girl," he gasped against her, "you wet it all over..." He lifted the leather strip in front of her face, showing her the mess on it; his free hand ran between her thighs, where thick juices soaked her. "Now," he murmured, "you have to clean it up..."

"No, Guy..."

"Shhh..." He bit her ear gently. "It's an order... lick it, my little one... lick it..."

Her face looked flushed and confused in the mirror. Lost and subjugated, she stuck out her tongue. While Guy stroked her pussy, Jane licked the leash. She wiped her own juice with her tongue, slave of a devil, and of a pleasure she didn't want and she couldn't even understand.

"Is it degrading, my angel?"

"Yes... oh, yes..." she sobbed. If she was an angel, she was falling down: Guy's hand, his body against hers, her own taste on the black leather... the fever she felt in her belly along with the shame. She was crying for it, but she was also *enjoying* it, God, how was it possible?

Guy put his hand to her mouth, replacing the leash, and Jane licked his palm, his fingers, without waiting for his order. Guy was masturbating her without giving her a breather, without allowing her to think clearly.

Her master... her demonic master...

With his hand, damp with her saliva, Guy cupped her breast, rolling her nipple between his thumb and forefinger. Jane shivered against him, and Guy's hands started to run over her body, her bosom, between her swollen pussy lips. Finally behind her, over her anus. Carefully, he slid the tip of his index finger into it, still soaked with her vaginal fluids.

"Oh, yes, you're degrading yourself..." he murmured, "but I am the *only* one who can see you like this, my angel... and I am the only one who can tell you to do it."

She turned her head toward him; Guy caught her lips with his own, and this broke down any further resistance on her part. He was dominating her, with his touch, with his gentle hands, even with his fingers, two fingers now, that were pushing between the crack of her buttocks, widening her tight butthole.

"Yes, submit to me, angel... seeing you like this is... is wonderful..."

Hearing these words, feeling his hands, even wearing a collar for him, gave her a strange emotion, which could only have one name, a terrible name, *joy*. How was it even possible, as mixed as it was with devastating shame? But Jane couldn't think right here, right now; she was all body, belly, squashy melting. And wet, shamelessly wet; her sexual fluids dripped between her legs and moistened the carpet. She was hopelessly surrendering to his will, to his touch; and Guy's hand rubbed her vulva without giving her a pause, his fingers in her anus widened it insolently. Wonderful, Guy had said; and then, Jane moved her groin back and forth, panting, seeking the fingers that were masturbating her, that were *enslaving* her—with her head turned to Guy, she kissed his face, she licked it like an affectionate puppy.

"Oh, Jane... you're such a sweet... sweet little girl..."

It was unconditional capitulation, without honor. This man, he treated her like... like what? But it had been earlier; now he was touching her, he was kissing her, he was gasping close to her, as if she were important to him, as if she had power over him. He had told her she was beautiful, hadn't he, he had said...

There wasn't the dust on his shoes anymore, there wasn't Smithfield Market here... and her belly melted and shivered. Her collar didn't tighten, the warm colors of the tapestry in the mirror were sky and amber, and *yes,* she thought, *you're my master Guy, you really are...*

But cruelly, her master slowed the pace of his caresses. He smiled as he felt the sudden tension of her body. "No, don't worry," he murmured, "I won't leave you unsatisfied, my little Jane..."

He undid the two rows of buttons closing his trousers, then he lowered his breeches. The hot tip of his penis touched the cleft between her buttocks.

"I want to teach you a new game," Guy said in a choked voice. He put his hand on the back of her head and pressed it forward. "Rest your elbows on the carpet and lift your little bum up, my angel..."

Jane's heart began to beat terribly. But she was there to obey him: scared, swelling with desire, she leaned forward. Her face, flushed in the mirror's reflection, reminded her how much she should have been ashamed of herself. Yet, as Guy put his hands between her thighs and spread them wider, she humored him with lewd speediness. She put herself in a fully open position, well aware of his eyes which, behind her, weren't missing anything.

"God, what a sight, Jane..."

With his waistcoat and shirt still on, kneeling behind her, Guy stared at her buttocks. In his hand, he held something... a small round jar, which he had taken from his pocket.

"I have to prepare you a little," he explained in an unsteady voice, "but don't be afraid, angel, I'll be... gentle." He took some jelly from the jar with two fingers and placed it on her anus. The jelly was cold and pleasant; Guy smeared it, then inserted his fingers into her tight asshole, lubricating it.

"Guy, what..."

"Shhh... everything's all right..." He cupped her buttocks in his palms, rubbing and separating them. "Wonderfully right..."

A terrible doubt rose in Jane's mind. She kept her eyes up to look in the mirror, and when she felt, and saw, the head of Guy's manhood pressing against her anus, she gave a little cry of shock. *There?* Did he want to get in *there?* But it was against nature and... and he was big, so big!

"No... no, Guy, I don't like this!"

"Just relax, angel... let me... let me play with you..."

He pressed his large glans into her little hole, inserting his thick velvet knob. The length of his penis was still out, visible in the mirror. Jane tensed, waiting for his thrust, but he moved forward just a little, stroking her buttocks tenderly.

"Relax," Guy repeated, and he moved his hand to the front of her body, between her thighs, titillating her soft wet curls. "Now we'll make this beautiful, my angel..."

He touched her between her legs in a fast rhythm and, from behind, he pressed more against her. Half an inch at a time, until half of his cock was inside her. It was so wide; she was tight and Guy filled her to overflowing, she felt so full... full of him. It was... not painful, no; uncomfortable, yes. Guy began to move, he...

He was inside her.

His penis went back and forth in her tiny, lubricated hole. Guy held her left hip in one hand as he watched, mesmerized, her violated buttocks, pushing deeper. His face shone with manly pleasure. It was the pleasure of *sodomizing* her; and there was more, in the impudence of that scene, and in her own physical sensations, which took Jane off guard. The discomfort became a bulky massage, and when Guy reached for her hair and gripped it in his fist as if it were reins, the slight pulling on her skin absurdly excited her. Swollen with need, her sex dribbled under his fingers. Jane arched, gasping. His presence inside her was her ignominy, for heaven's sake, her unnatural ignominy, but it was *him,* inside her, it was *Guy*...

"What a divine ass, Jane... my God, you're beautiful..."

He rode her in a brazen way as she, with her buttocks in mid-air and her elbows on the floor, spread her legs wide open to make him sink more deeply inside her. He didn't push himself all the way in: he already filled her completely with half his penis. The sense of fullness made her close her eyes; it was Guy, he was inside her, and this thought gave her an inexplicable happiness. His manhood was moving in a sensual, possessive rhythm, rubbing between her tight and slippery flesh. His fingers were on her pussy, touching her, soaked with the liquid silk pouring from her. Wet sounds echoed in the room as the sensitive pearl between her nether lips swelled. Jane's belly tensed. She was about to climax, she knew it, and foretasted it with joy, and cursed it. No, she mustn't enjoy this, but the shocking pleasure came, and throbbed inside her, and lapped through her body, defeating any dignity she had left with hot, long waves of delight.

"Oh, Guy..." she gasped, "Guy!"

She came copiously, with choked cries, lowering her face to the floor and convulsing in a violent orgasm. How degrading *that* was, she didn't ask herself; Guy's heat exploded within her and she welcomed his hot shots of cum with wild emotion; his thick semen filled her, he buried himself inside her to the hilt, for the first time, slapping his balls against her ass and plunging into it with no mercy, with all his desire, his size, and his power.

"Oh my God, Jane..." he gasped, gripping her hips, "God, yes... *yes...* "

Jane, relaxed and loose, didn't open her eyes. She was content, while the last remaining contractions shook her body. If she opened her eyes, she would see her own face flushed with pleasure; the face of a slave, of... of a bitch, right?... who had come between the hands of her master.

The fire crackled in the chimney place. How much time had passed? Jane was coming to her senses. She didn't want to come to her senses.

What had just happened...

Guy slowly came out of her. "No," he said as she began to move. "Stay still."

Breathing softly, strengthless and wobbly, Jane rested her forehead on the carpet. A hot liquid dripped down between her buttocks, wetting her thighs. It was his seed, mixed with the juices of her own, scandalous orgasm.

Guy sat on the carpet behind her. Jane had still the collar around her neck; she didn't move. She remained with her legs wide open, and let him watch her violated ass, and the sperm which, slowly trickling down her skin, marked her indelibly.

161

22.

Jane tossed and turned beneath her blankets, and her silk nightgown rustled. She looked toward the window. Was the world still out there? She had kept the curtains opened, as she always did, because she loved waking up with the sun. But now, the night was dark, surrounded by obscurity, and she could see nothing. Between her buttocks, she was feeling a slight pain, from the anal sex of the afternoon: Guy had behaved like he enjoyed, uh... her *presence,* but now...

She wrapped the blanket more tightly around herself, biting her bottom lip.

But now she was alone. Guy hadn't joined her in her bedroom, and a jumble of thoughts was running through her head, preventing her from sleeping and making her twisting and turning in the bed. She couldn't help but think back to all that had happened between last night and this afternoon; the way she had changed for Guy in a single day; and the doubt that, maybe, he had already tired of her...

He had whispered to her some cryptic words in the afternoon, and his voice had sounded urgent, almost overwhelmed by a pressing emotion... but what emotion was that? And what did his words mean? They had seemed so important to him...

You're degrading yourself, my angel, but I am the only one who can see you like this...

These words haunted her in the warmth of her empty bed; and the short sleeveless nightgown, which she had worn just for him, made her feel like a high-class prostitute. Guy had told her she was beautiful, and she... she had thought he enjoyed being with her...

She swallowed hard and put her hand under her nose, sniffling out the incomprehensible bitterness she was feeling. Jane didn't know whether or not Guy was at home. It had to be two, maybe three in the morning.

She heard a noise of creaking wood, and her heart began to beat wildly. After a while, she began to breathe normally, with an illogical regret in her chest. It had been just one of an old house's typical noises. No, Guy wouldn't join her; he was tired of her for today. Or maybe, he was tired of her, period. She would find out soon, tomorrow morning perhaps. It was only a few hours till dawn, but this night seemed endless to her.

* * *

As Guy walked into the narrow corridor of the crumbling basement, a rat ran right in front of him.

Oh, perfect.

He pushed open the door at the end of the corridor and entered a large room. It was damp, windowless, and there was a musty cave smell. Mouse feces and cobwebs decorated the place; four bright torches illuminated the basement. Everything was abandoned to dust and cockroaches. In the middle of the room, on the dirt floor, was a square red box, about one foot on each side. The noise coming from the road was loud; two brothels and a gambling house were located on Dorset Street.

This was the kind of place one chooses when they have to meet someone without attracting attention.

Three men were already in the room. They were wearing long dark cloaks. One of these men, with hair so blond it was almost white, was leaning against the left wall. He was flipping a sharp knife into the air, catching it each time between his palms by the blade. He didn't look to Guy.

Across the room, there were two men sitting at a small table. One of them, about thirty years old, raised his head from the papers he was reading and smiled, nodding politely to Guy. Now that was what Guy called aristocratic etiquette. After all, the man's name was Stuart Cavendish, he was the 6th Duke of St. Court, and, incidentally, he was one of the richest men in England. Guy returned the nod, and Stuart lowered his head again. The Duke was studying his papers with the same attentive expression as the one a conscientious student would wear. As a matter of fact, he had the haircut of a student as well: his light-brown hair was perfectly in place, just curled at the ends. He looked like he was about to go to the theater.

In front of the Duke was a young man, who was the Duke's opposite, like in a distorting mirror. First, he was a toddler, well, sort of: not twenty years old yet. In addition, his brown hair was tousled messily. And his posture had 'lower-class' written all over it. He was rocking on the back legs of his chair in a precarious balance, and his restless swinging was not at all reasonable. For God's sake, the chair's wood would probably break under him in a minute. Even if the boy's body was slim, still adolescent, the chair was worm-eaten.

The young man threw a sullen look at Guy. "Hey, the Third Knife is here, let's ring the bells," he said with scornful sarcasm. "Let's welcome him like the diva he is. Fuck happened to you, Number Three, was your ass on fire, or don't you even remember how to read a clock?" His strong cockney accent rang raspily in Guy's ears. *For shit's sake,* he thought, Paul Bailey was a low point for the Gang of Knives. He had no self-control, he was disrespectful, and he was always in the mood to pick a fight. Guy had opposed his admission six months ago, but the other members of the Brotherhood had outvoted him. That was something Guy hadn't got over yet, so he approached Paul and kicked one of his chair legs without warning.

Paul felt down with a heavy thud.

"You son of a bitch!" the boy yelled.

Guy threw up his hands to parry the knife that Paul, getting up, had pulled from his cloak with amazing speed.

"Oh, I'm so sorry, Fifth Knife," Guy said, grabbing Paul's slender wrist and twisting it up behind his back. "You're so small I didn't see you."

"Let go of me, you bastard!" Paul grunted. His knife fell to the ground with a metallic clang; Guy grinned and slammed the boy's face on the table, rubbing his cheek up and down on the wooden surface.

"You forgot to say *please,*" Guy said above his head. "Learn a little respect, kid."

Ignoring Paul's awkward squirming, Guy turned to the Duke who, on his part, just lifted the papers from the table, so they wouldn't drop to the floor.

"Sorry I'm late, First Knife," Guy said politely, immobilizing Paul's legs with his own. "I had a little discussion with a drunken man. About the whore he was raping, actually."

The Duke didn't seem impressed. "Did anyone notice you, Third?" he asked in his calm, drawling voice.

Third, Fifth, First... they called each other that way, even when they were alone. Their names were numbers. They indicated the order of their admission into the Gang of Knives. So far, there were five Knives, until they accepted further members. The K-Gang was growing slowly: it had been founded by only two Knives five years ago. They had admitted Guy a little over three years ago.

"Maybe that drunkard's nose will remember my fist," he replied thoughtfully. "But he will remember nothing else—not even his own name."

Stuart smiled. His languid velvety-brown eyes had a look of amused surprise. "You seem in a good mood tonight."

In a good mood, my ass. He was in a *terrible* mood, because he had had to leave Jane alone tonight. It was an unbearable thought. Dear God, what a waste of delights. Yet, much to his surprise, Guy realized that yes, he was strangely serene. The hours spent with Jane had left him with a feeling of burning contentment, and not even the prospect of the incoming K-mission could erase it. He could still feel Jane's warmth on himself, and her scent, and her hair and her eyes... and for God's sake, what a glorious moment had been, when he had fucked her virgin ass...

He took a breath, trying not to think about it. What would happen was Jane's antithesis. Guy was used to facing the Nights of Knives in the same way as one would face a bad smell: nobody likes the stench, right? Nobody wants to smell it, they don't want to let that fetid air into their lungs; but they need to *breathe,* and then come on, inhale, exhale, let the stench fill their soul. And after three years, he had grown used to the K-Gang's meetings in the most crumbling houses, when the details of their missions hadn't been settled yet. He had grown used to their missions, always planned with the precision of a mechanical device—the places, the people involved, the words to say to the intended victims. He had grown used to the other members of the brotherhood, even to the boy who, crushed against the table, was squirming and trying to kick him away.

He had grown used to the blood, too. Plenty of blood. It would soak his clothes at the end of this very night. Afterward, he would throw these clothes away to leave no evidence. It wasn't pleasant, but it didn't matter. Because a K-night was just a job to do. To do it right. Even if it wasn't pleasant, it was necessary.

Like breathing.

"Shit, let me go, you assface!" Paul snapped.

In response, Guy pressed the boy's head against the table and raised his own knee between the boy's legs. Guy's knee remained still under Paul's balls in an explicit threat. "I haven't heard the magic word yet. Say *please.* "

"Go fuck yourself!"

Smiling, Guy lifted his leg and kneed Paul in the balls, not too hard, but enough to make him blow the air out through his teeth, along with a couple of profanities. Guy was satisfied with this and he let him go, stepping back.

Paul straightened up. The handle of a knife appeared from under his sleeve, touching his palm.

"Are you going to stab me, Number Five?"

Paul's face flushed. He felt humiliated by his own physical weakness. Unfortunately for him, he wasn't any good at close combat. He was even worse than the Fourth Knife. With the blade, though, he was the best of them. He was the fastest, the most lethal. He had many daggers hidden under his sleeve: he could have thrown at Guy one of them at any moment, had he really wanted to.

"I just want to reshape your ugly face with this blade, Third. Just one caress on your cheek."

"Oh, come on, don't be like that." Guy leaned toward the boy and gave him a pat on his face. "If you behave, I won't tell Number Four how I made you cry."

Paul shifted abruptly, and Guy laughed. Snubbing his ridiculous threat, he looked around. "Speaking of Number Four," he said in surprise, "where is she? Hasn't she arrived yet?"

"I told you we should never have accepted a whore in the Gang." The voice of James Sutherland, the man standing to Guy's left, sounded cold, almost metallic. "What did you expect from a slut like her?" Leaning against the wall, Sutherland kept throwing and catching his 11.5-inch knife. His gray eyes followed the knife's trajectory with hypnotic attention, the blade coming down fast between his palms without cutting them. His right hand missed two fingers: his ring and little fingers. That didn't prevent him from being fatal when he threw daggers and knives.

"We took a vote, Second," the Duke of St. Court reminded him patiently, without looking up from his paper sheets. "And you lost. Four is one of us, and you have to show her respect."

"Respect," Sutherland replied with an icy smile. "The same respect I show my dog."

"I told you we should never have admitted a shithead in the K-Gang," said a feminine, sensual voice from the doorway. Isabelle Smith stepped forward and stood before the red box, with her hands behind her back. "What else did you expect from a piece of crap like him?"

Guy smiled. Isabelle was used to people's contempt; perhaps she was even comfortable with it. She kept her chin lifted up. Her face was pink with rouge, her lips were as red as ruby wine. Like the other Knives, she was wearing a long dark cloak, but everyone would notice her on the street. Below the hood, a blonde wig with cheap curls framed her heart-shaped face, and her slim, light-footed body didn't go unnoticed.

Stuart stood up, stretching his long legs. "It seems everybody's here. Shall we begin?"

The Knives nodded. Everybody reached Isabelle in the middle of the room, arranging themselves in a circle around the box. Their positions weren't random, they followed the order of their numbers. From One to Five. Guy was the Number Three: to his left was Isabelle Smith, to his right James Sutherland. A few feet away, Paul Bailey no longer had an insolent look on his face; he had a tense, almost solemn expression.

Next to Paul, closing and starting the circle, was Stuart Cavendish, the 6th Duke of St Court. He was the First Knife.

Everyone turned toward him.

"Lord Unwin is waiting for us in a carriage down the road," Stuart told them in an apologetic tone. "He's tied, gagged, and willing to cooperate. I had a small stroke of luck this afternoon. I won't bore you with the details, let's just say it's no longer necessary to set up a complex plan for catching him. So..." he took a step forward, reaching out to the box on the ground, "let's draw lots, shall we?"

Stu and his rhetorical questions. But the news pleased Guy. They had already caught their victim, good. Tonight would be a cakewalk.

Stuart put his hand in the box. It contained five folded pieces of paper. The Duke drew out one of them and, opening it, read the number written on it.

"Tonight," he announced quietly, "it is up to the Number Three to throw the last knife."

Guy took a breath and nodded. No, it wouldn't be a cakewalk, after all.

* * *

At some point during the night, among doubts, fears, and pathetic tears, Jane had fallen asleep. A troubled, restless sleep. She was dreaming, and in her dream, Guy was keeping his left side toward her, standing in front of the study's window. He was dressed as he had been in the afternoon, with his dark waistcoat. His trousers were tucked into his black boots. Jane was on all fours, naked; but she didn't feel shame, she felt lonely, because Guy wasn't paying any attention to her. Tall, strong and distant, he was watching the garden outside the window. The afternoon light shadowed his long eyelashes, his black eyes, his nose a little crooked in the middle.

Guy, what did I do wrong?

She wanted to ask him, but she couldn't command her lips to move in her sleep, so she babbled meaningless whimpers.

What didn't I do right?

"Shhh..."

No, tell me what I did wrong, tell me...

Guy turned to her, finally. He bent over her, stroking her back with his hand. "Everything's fine, my angel..."

For a moment Jane felt happy, completely happy. He had touched her, she was still his angel. Then she opened her eyes and found herself in the bed, under the blankets.

The hand on her back was real. And a moment later, a bare arm wrapped around her waist. Her heart began to slam hard, and this pulled her out of her sleep completely. She blinked, holding back the burst of emotion burning inside her.

"Guy?"

"Get back to sleep, my angel..."

Sleep? What time was it? Outside it was dark, utterly dark. Guy was in her bed, lying behind her. He had come to her, at last. And now he was hugging her under the covers. He was shivering while pressing his strong, muscular chest against her back. His fresh, clean soap scent filled Jane's nostrils. Soap... had he taken a bath in the middle of the night? In the kitchen, the fire was out at this hour; and judging by his unusually cold skin and chills, he had washed with cold water. Probably he hadn't had the patience to heat the water. He hadn't even woken his valet to have him do this task, but then again... why had he felt the pressing need to bathe? Why hadn't he simply waited until morning?

A painful thought gripped her heart, a sharp emotion she didn't want to name. An emotion that years ago she had sworn she did never feel again. Not again, please, not again. She couldn't, she...

"Guy..."

He kissed her neck, pressing his body against her back.

"Guy, why are you trembling?"

"It's nothing... nothing, little one..."

Jane swallowed. Guy was stiff and tense; his voice was a whisper. Why had he gone out that night? Where had he gone? There could be plenty of reasons... couldn't there? Perhaps he had joined a boxing match, perhaps he had gone in some gambling house; perhaps he had *not* made love with another woman. Taking courage, Jane turned toward him.

"Guy, where... where have you been?"

He didn't answer, he just held her, putting his mouth on hers. Even his lips were cold. Jane placed her hand on his stubbled cheek and instinctively, in the room's darkness, she returned his kiss.

This was the same man who, the next morning, would make her kneel in front of him, smiling at her mortification; he was the man who, ignoring her tears, would forbid her to work as a nurse, not allowing her to go to the hospital anymore, not even once, not even to say goodbye to the doctors and to the nurses and to the sick; and in the following days, alternating pleasure with humiliation, he would give a new and shocking meaning to the term *submission*. Yet, this night he had joined her just to hold her, without asking for sex or obedience, and he was shaking with cold as he had years ago when, as a child, he had been pulled out from the Mole; Jane hugged and kissed him with passion, with no logic, warming his mouth with her own, and feeling him relax, finally, between her arms.

23.

Guy stepped into the opium den in St. Giles and tried to make his way through the crowd of stoned addicts. Goddammit, of all the stupid people in the world, the very stupidest was Stephen Weymouth. Guy was in the den's common room. Around him, the smokers breathed opium from their pipes. Lying on dirty mattresses, they stared ahead and saw nothing.

W., you idiotic ass.

Guy had never got high on opium. Even before the Gang of Knives, he had used violence to vent his anger. That was why boxing was so important to him. He loved fighting until he felt pain all over his body. Releasing his anger that way wasn't just therapeutic, it was intoxicating.

Like the smoke in this den.

There he is.

Guy saw his friend from a distance. Stephen was lying on a mattress, with his arm bent under his head and his forehead on the crook of his elbow.

Oh God, what a pathetic loser.

Guy moved forward, pushing away a couple of people. He ignored the skinny oriental prostitute who had approached him with the classic question: what did he wish, pipe, opium, or sex? *None of that.* Guy stared at Stephen, abandoned on the bed like a corpse waiting for vultures. *I just want to make this jerk spit his teeth out.*

Stephen hadn't gone to the den's back room. Of course he hadn't: he couldn't afford it. He was just lying there, making a pitiful display of himself. Once again, Guy thanked God for his friend's financial problems. Certainly Stephen hadn't got as high as he would have wanted to. Little money equals little opium, this is how the world works, and this was just fine with Guy. He had never been one to waste words. He didn't give Stephen huge lectures about his addiction, he prevented Stephen from achieving economic independence. He paid Stephen's bills. Stephen worked for him as his secretary, or accountant, or, more often, as his punching bag. Guy also paid the rent on his friend's small house in Bolton Street, and the wage of Stephen's tall and pale butler. Stephen couldn't complain, for his pantry was always well stocked at Guy's expense. And, every now and then, Guy gave him a few quid for everyday expenses. That was all. No cash for the loser.

Despite this, Stephen had managed to buy some opium. Perhaps he had put aside the lousy pounds Guy gave him occasionally like a miserable beggar.

For fuck's sake, W., have you got no shame?

No one had dared to lend him money, that was for sure. Everyone knew that the 4th Earl of Ashbourne was sworn enemy of whoever gave credit to the younger son of Baron Weymouth.

And no one wanted the 4th Earl of Ashbourne as an enemy.

Opium addicts always find a way to satisfy their vice, though, and Stephen was the proof. His hair was greasy and dirty, pulled back in a ponytail not redone in days. Surely he hadn't combed or washed it since the first of January, the last time Guy had seen him.

Stopping in front of the soiled mattress, Guy leaned over and, closing his fist on his friend's messy hair, raised Stephen's head.

Stephen didn't react, letting Guy handle him like a dead body. After a few moments, he opened his eyes, and his pupils dilated as he saw Guy. Good. He wasn't that high if he had the good sense to shit himself with fear.

"Get up, dickhead." Guy accompanied these words with a sharp tug at Stephen's hair.

Stephen placed his hands on the mattress. He had lost weight in the last six days, was it possible? And he smelled musty. Jesus Christ. As soon as they got to Bolton Street, Guy would throw his idiotic friend into a vat of cold water, no, *icy* water.

Stephen blinked. "Did the Earl leave His house today?" he asked sarcastically. "Why aren't you at home fucking your sister?"

"Keep your voice down, you asshole." He pulled Stephen toward him, lifting him bodily and kicking him in the testicles with his knee.

Stephen groaned, and this sound filled Guy with satisfaction.

"Let's get the fuck out of here," he ordered. "If you say another word, I'll rip your balls off."

He picked up Stephen's cloak, lying on the mattress in the same way as its miserable owner had been, and dragged his friend to the door. Stephen doubled over and let Guy move him like a bent puppet. The Asian whore, the same one Guy had seen before, approached them. She looked terrified, but she had no alternative but to hold her hand out in a silent request. Oh, it was like that, then. Stephen the Asshole had smoked on credit.

"Send the bill to Ashbourne House," Guy said abruptly. "And next time you give him credit, not only won't you get paid, but I'll also burn this place down. Is that clear? Tell your boss."

She nodded quickly, stepping back. Guy took five pounds from his pocket and handed them to her. "Let me know if you see him going around this place again," he said. "And you'll get more."

He pushed away a haggard man who was leaning on the wall and walked to the door, keeping his hand tightly gripped on Stephen's hair. Stephen let Guy drag him without a fight.

Outside, there was a carriage waiting for them. It was not the big one with the Spencer family's insignia; it was an anonymous, small carriage. Guy used it to reach the most degraded areas in the city.

Soho fully fell into this category.

Guy pulled Stephen toward the carriage, but his friend resisted. Maybe the chill night air had woken him up.

"Get in the carriage, you asshole."

"No."

No? "Do you want me to rearrange your face before we go?"

Stephen put his hand on Guy's wrist. His eyes were bleary, but perhaps not only because of opium.

"Get your hands off me, Guy."

The few times Stephen had called him 'Guy' had been dramatic ones. Oh, damn. Guy got off him, letting his own hand fall.

"Come on, get in the carriage," he said quietly, hoping to avoid a discussion in one of the most dangerous areas of London. He threw the cloak to Stephen; it fell into his arms as if by chance.

Guy couldn't see much in the lamplight. Among the cracked houses, there was laundry hanging from the strings stretched between the walls. The dirt street was covered with slush and ice, horse dung, and human feces too. The inhabitants of the street were used to emptying their chamber pots out of their windows. Under the dome of the dark sky, the smell was a mixture of shit, alcohol, and wet ice.

"Thank you for paying my share of opium, Ashbourne." Stephen spoke with a thick voice, but he didn't stutter. "Anyway, this is the last money I'll take from you. Now, go the fuck away and leave me alone."

He was pale and emaciated, and he moved languidly because of the opium. He casually draped the cloak over his shoulders and tried to tie the laces around his neck. His hands were shaking, and the result was a pathetic knot, as pathetic as him. Good heavens, he would have really deserved to rot inside that stinky den. But he would have done drugs all night, spewing his soul out of his ass.

Guy had had to prevent this. He had always prevented Stephen from throwing away his life, since Eton. Why does a friendship start, why does a friendship become stronger among narrow alleys stinking of piss and vomit? Guy didn't know, he didn't even care. He just accepted it.

He bolted toward Stephen, grabbed him by the lapel and dragged him to a side alley, away from prying eyes. He released him with a shove. Unbalanced, Stephen fell to the ground, on the days-old snowdrifts. A cat, frightened by the noise, jumped a few feet from them, emerging from the shadows of a corner; it was skin and bone, with gray, damaged fur that was ripped out in patches. Maybe it wouldn't survive the cold night, yet it hissed at them arrogantly and, without begging for food or heat, fled, leaving its refuge.

Stephen didn't scream when he fell. Maybe he was hurt. Maybe he was cold. Maybe he had too much opium in his body to feel anything. "Have you tired of her already, Ashbourne?" he asked bitterly. "In what, one week?"

Towering over him, Guy clenched his fists. "You're judging me, that's rich. Look at you, W." He spat to his side, on a heap of snow darkened by dirt. "You make me vomit."

"Oh, really? Why, because I have enough remorse to be disgusted with myself? Because I want to forget I'm the one who helped you to ruin an innocent girl?"

"Because you're a spineless shit, that's why. You're just looking for any excuse to get high, you pitiful sack of dirt."

"Well." Stephen pointed to the alley. "Go away, then. Leave me alone and just go the fuck away."

Yes, Guy should do it. Besides, now or later, what would change? He knew he and Stephen wouldn't stay friends forever. Guy didn't believe in forever.

"Come on, Steve. Let's talk about this at home."

He didn't reach out to him, even if he was dying to do it. His hands itched with the need to pull Stephen up by the hair and give him a strong shake.

"I'm not going anywhere with you, Guy. I don't know you... I don't know who you are anymore." Stephen shook his head. "I remember a boy who used to beat the bullies at Eton... are you still that boy? No, you... God! You're raping an innocent girl!"

"Stephen..."

"Who are you? Who the fuck are you, Guy Spencer, 4th Earl of Ashbourne? Don't touch me!" He moved away from him abruptly, without standing up, crawling on his ass over the snow. He showed no dignity, yet, to Guy, he seemed dignified anyway. "As far as I know, you are abusing who knows how many women. Every month, you withdraw a mountain of money from your bank account... I'm your accountant, aren't I? Yet you won't tell me what you do with this money. Why do you need it? Do you use it to buy virgins to rape?" He leaned his back against the wall, lifting one knee and resting his forearm over it. He buried his face in the crook of his elbow. "You're really your father's son, Ashbourne, for Christ's sake...

you really are."

These whispered words hit Guy one after another, like stones to his chest. "You really think so?"

Stephen looked up, studying him sideways, as if seeing him for the first time. "I don't know what to think."

Guy took a breath. He had to leave. He had to wash his hands of Stephen. What was the point in standing by him?

Fuck you, Steve.

"If I really were that revolting, I wouldn't need to inflate my bad reputation with false news, would I, W.?" he asked flatly. His objection was reasonable, and Stephen knew it. Stephen was the only one to know it, as a matter of fact. It was Stephen himself to leak fake stories to the newspapers. It was Stephen the one who paid women to tell lies about Guy. That was why such pieces of gossip went around, rumors about seduction and abandonment, about rapes and brutality in the dungeons of Ashbourne House.

They were all lies.

"This is another thing I don't understand. Why have you continued your 'wicked-earl charade' after your mother's death, Ash? Why do you still need a sadistic reputation?"

Indeed, why did he still need it? Guy took a deep breath. "I can't tell you why."

"No, of course you can't. How very convenient."

No, it wasn't convenient *at all*, and a blaze of anger ran through Guy's body, corroding him like acid. "Do you want to know why I can't tell you, you useless piece of crap on two legs?" He turned toward the corner where the opium den was and pointed it. "Because of *that*. Because I can't tell important stuff to a drug addict. Because some secrets can save lives, Stephen 'I-Am-a-Saint' Weymouth, and I can't blurt them out to a pile of shit like you. When you smoke your opium, you no longer can distinguish your mouth from your ass. Good God, you'd betray me for a puff from your rotten pipe."

Stephen raised his eyebrows. "Wow, what a speech," he said in a disgusted voice. "I'm weak and you're strong, right? You know secrets that... what the fuck did you just say?... ah, yes: that 'save lives' " He made a bitter laugh. "Then go. Go save lives. Go save *Jane Hartwell*. She will thank you, I guess."

"Steve, bloody hell. I do nothing wrong with the money I withdraw from the bank."

"Nothing wrong... yeah, I bet on it."

"Stop this fucking sarcasm! You know who I am, even if you say you don't." *You know me, Steve. You do.* "And as for Jane," he went on tensely, "she owes me. She's just paying a debt. No, I'm not talking about money," he added, raising his hand before Stephen could object, "I'm not talking of fucking money."

Stephen looked down, staring at his own hand, still resting on his knee. "So tell me," he said after a moment, with a strange, almost sweet sadness. "Am I supposed to accept your blackmail to her, without even knowing why you hate her?" The cold made his lips blue, but Stephen didn't seem to notice it. "Am I supposed to deal with you fucking her against her will?"

On the sidewalk, rivulets of water were mingled with ice, crunches of snow sounded along with the screams coming from the main street.

"No, I..." Guy took a breath, and the air filled his lungs with sharp crystals. "I didn't fuck her, W."

His friend raised his head sharply. "What did you just say?"

"I didn't fuck her." Guy's tone was more than annoyed. It was frustrated. "Jane," he clarified in a low voice. "She's still a virgin."

"Are you kidding me? Are you telling me you have been in abstinence this week? As chaste as a fucking eunuch?"

Guy hesitated. "I didn't fuck her," he repeated only. He wouldn't talk about his and Jane's sex games. He would mention to nobody the cuddles and the caresses he gave her, and the way he alternated gentle words with cruel, demeaning demands. His carrot-and-stick strategy was working as expected: Jane already looked at him as a puppy looks at its owner, with the same timorous adoration. But this was between Jane and him. It didn't concern Stephen. Guy wouldn't speak of Jane to him, nor to anyone else.

Stephen put his hand on the wall and got up with difficulty. Guy didn't offer him his help. With relief mixed with exasperation, he looked at his friend's clumsy attempts to get back on his feet.

"Did you fuck any of your whores in the last few days?" Stephen held himself up with an unsteady hand placed on the wall. His lips were trembling from the cold, and the mist coming from his mouth was not so different from the smoke into the den. Stephen didn't look dazed anymore, and that meant trouble. Soon, his need for drugs would come back, and stronger.

God, what a mess.

"No, you didn't, did you?" asked Stephen as Guy didn't answer. He moved his left hand over his butt and shook the snow from his soaked trousers. "Do you honestly expect me to believe in your sexual-abstinence bullshit?"

Guy remained silent once again. What the hell could he reply?

"No, I'm sure you're having sex with your stepsister," Stephen reasoned loudly. "But perhaps... perhaps you're not fucking her pussy. Am I right? That's what you mean, don't you? What do you do with her, are you fucking her in the ass?"

Guy raised his index finger toward him. "I won't talk about this. Is that clear?"

"No? You're forgetting a little detail, you piece of shit. It's my fault if you can use her as you please."

"Do you really believe so? Then you're a deluded moron. I have a score to settle with that girl, and I'd have managed to have her anyway, with or without your help."

"And you aren't fucking her. You want me to believe this." Stephen raised his eyebrows. "Mr. Horny Cock has his sister in his bed, and he isn't fucking her."

Guy felt his hands itch. No, he wasn't fucking her. Well, not in her pussy anyway, and it wasn't easy, not damn easy at all. He wouldn't talk about that with Stephen. It was something between Jane and him, just between them. Bloody hell, sometimes his desire to deflower her was so strong, it made him grunt with frustration. He was leaving her a virgin for another, still unknown, man. He hated this man already, he couldn't even think about that. Damn the world, and damn, *damn* his own scruples. Had Stephen known how this thought was eating Guy alive, he would have respected him, he surely wouldn't have that disgusted look on his face. And had he known the need Guy had for her, had he known how the prospect of leaving her alone tonight made Guy's gut burn with regret and longing...

Oh shit.

Guy looked at Stephen. Tonight, he wondered? *One* night? That hope was as optimistic as it was unrealistic. Guy wouldn't come home for a week, at least week. That was the time he needed to bring Stephen back into the realm of the living, beating all the opium out of him.

"I'm not a saint, W.," he snapped. His voice was a frustrated growl. "But I'm not the asshole you think I am. I haven't ruined her, she..." Guy swallowed. *She will be free to marry whoever she pleases in six months. If she wants, she will be free to marry even for love, and this husband will be some caring, boring shithead who will make her happy.* He couldn't say it aloud; perhaps because of the cold, perhaps because he felt so fucking tired. "I haven't ruined her," he repeated in a low voice.

Stephen straightened his shoulders, moving away from the wall. "You aren't fucking her," he murmured. Guy's depressed tone had sounded so sincere in cursing his situation, it had removed Stephen's last doubts. "You really aren't, are you? But why, Guy? Because I told you so?"

Guy hesitated. Was this the reason? Or were there other unspoken reasons, related to his own weakness—stupid, pathetic reasons that haunted him? "I don't know, all right?" he said, hardening his jaw. "I'm just not fucking her. Why the hell must there be a reason?"

Stephen looked at him in perplexity. "You aren't fucking her," he repeated softly. "But—" he frowned as if trying to solve a difficult puzzle "—but you don't know why you aren't. That's perfectly logical." He looked up and something passed between their eyes. Stephen's lips curved in an involuntary smile. "Perfectly logical," he repeated, and a hysterical giggle escaped from his mouth.

"Stop it, you idiot."

"And now *I* am the idiot..." Stephen's chuckle grew up, and he leaned his back against the wall to not fall again. "Holy Jesus Christ, Ash," he said, shaken by this absurd shot of laughter. "Who is the idiot...?"

"You, of course," snapped Guy, and his lips involuntarily curled up. He tried to restrain the impulse. It was so stupid, all of it, this scene, this stinking alley, their argument; and a moment later, there were *two* idiots laughing like fools—the younger son of a baron and an earl, doubling over with uncontrollable laughter like drunken commoners in a slum of London.

24.

Jane is just paying a debt.
No, I'm not talking about money... I'm not talking of fucking money.

7 Courtnell Street, 9th April 1844. Afternoon.

Guy was standing with his back to the door ajar and, as he heard the wooden floor creaking outside the small attic room, he allowed himself a smile.

What a nuisance, that little girl...

He continued packing his bag. Tomorrow, he would return to Eton college. Easter vacations had flown by quickly.

And as always, the mentioned nuisance had been around him all the time.

"Jane, stop spying on me from the door," he said a few minutes later, for she still hadn't mustered the courage to come in. "You're making my neck itch."

A snort came from behind the door. "I'm not spying on you. I'm just looking for something out here."

"Yeah, sure."

He put a white shirt in his bag. He appreciated something about 7 Courtnell Street: he was free to dress as he pleased here. At Eton, he had to wear his uniform: black jacket, stiff tie, and starched shirt—that *damned* starched shirt, as rigid as cardboard.

"Don't you believe me?" Jane pushed open the door and entered his bedroom with aggressive steps.

Guy turned to her and blinked. *Little girl*, he had thought of her just a moment ago... but Jane had grown during the last three months, when he was at his boarding school. For starters, she no longer had braids; her hair was loose on her shoulders, silky and fair, shining like a small sun. And she had gotten taller. There was something else about her... something that had nothing to do with her height or hair. Guy had noticed it a week ago, as soon as he stepped in 7 Courtnell Street, but this awareness kept on stunning him. The light coming through the window stroked her white, still-childish dress, emphasizing the small, but unmistakable, swelling of her breasts. That swelling wasn't there in January; and her hips... was it possible they had become a bit round? Her body no longer resembled a broomstick, did it?

Guy felt vaguely uneasy.

What the hell was he thinking? Jane wasn't even thirteen years old, and she was childish for her age. Compared to him, she was just a kid.

"Why are you here?" he asked abruptly.

"I told you. I lost something."

"Yesterday you came and said you lost your book. The day before, you were looking for your drawing folder..."

"It was really *you* who took my drawing folder!"

Guy couldn't help a smile. "Well, so next time you'll learn to not throw breadcrumbs at me when we have dinner."

As he said so, Jane's expression changed; the corners of her mouth curled downwards. "I didn't think Rona was looking at me at that moment. I'm sorry, Guy."

"Yeah, you've already said that." He shrugged. The day before yesterday, his mother had seen Jane throwing breadcrumbs at him and, of course, Rona had blamed *him* for that. She had turned to him with her usual oh-no-my-cruel-son-is-bothering-little-Jane look and, to avoid hearing her tedious complaints, Guy had got up from the table and gone up to his bedroom. Shortly after, Jane had knocked on his door with a slice of apple pie in her hands... her peace offering.

Guy turned around and picked up the book resting on his nightstand, tossing it into his bag. "I can't find my Eton lapel pin," he said, closing the bag and putting it on the floor. He turned to his stepsister, narrowing his eyes in an inquiring look. "Did you happen to steal it?"

Jane blushed furiously. "I don't steal!"

"Oh."

'Little Nuisance' Jane shifted from foot to foot. "I haven't stolen it, Guy," she repeated without looking into his eyes. "I've just... *borrowed* it. Until, you know... your summer vacation."

Guy sighed. He knew it, he could have bet on it. Jane's curious habits were comprehensible only to her: whenever Guy was about to leave, for example, she stole something from him. It was a different thing each time. Usually, Guy would notice something was missing from his portmanteau as soon as he arrived at Eton. Sometimes, these things were easily replaceable, such as a shirt, a tie or a pen. Other times, they were important, like his homework notebook or his uniform jacket. He couldn't grasp why Jane chose one thing rather than another. Even more, he couldn't grasp why she took these things from him: every time he came back to Courtnell Street, in fact, she returned the stolen stuff.

And she would steal something else.

And the cycle would begin again.

"What about taking something else instead?" he asked hesitantly. Jane's embarrassment moved him in a silly, almost annoying way. "You could take my tie... or one of my shirts, maybe?"

Jane lowered her face, shrugging. He saw her chin tremble with held-back tears. Oh, damn. "All right, keep that damn lapel pin," he said, sighing. "That's all right, I'll just get caned with ten strokes on my hand for having lost it. No big deal."

Jane lifted her face. "Will that hurt you?" she asked apprehensively. Her tears were already gone, and Guy rolled his eyes. What an idiot he was. He had given up at the first hint of tears in her eyes.

"I won't even feel it," he said, shrugging.

"Really?"

"Hey, you see these muscles?" he asked, feeling insulted. He made a fist and bent his right arm at the elbow to display his biceps under the shirt. "The caning never hurts me."

The caning hurt like hell, actually, but Guy never screamed or cried when a teacher caned him, so this wasn't a *total* lie.

Jane cocked her head to one side, widening her golden eyes. "Your muscles... are bigger than this winter," she murmured with naïve admiration. She looked into his eyes, and Guy's heart began to beat in a jerking way. A sort of premonition made him pull his shoulders back.

"May I touch them, Guy?"

No, no, no, no.

He didn't answer, he simply held his breath. With a sense of inevitability, he watched her as she came closer to him, like a fawn watches the tiger and knows its end is near. Jane was surrounded by the afternoon light, her dress was white, and her hair sparkled, long and loose over her shoulders.

Like when you put a foot wrong and fall down... fall down.

No, no, no, no.

When she was less than a step away, her scent hit him as if he had never smelled it before. He felt dizzy and wanted to turn around and leave, but he stood stiffly, his arm still bent while Jane reached out to his biceps. Her scent was the same as ever, a light soap's aroma of violets and hawthorn flowers... but there was a new nuance in it, what was it?

Jane's fingers rested with a slight warmth on the sleeve of his shirt. She gently squeezed his arm. "Come on, tighten it hard," she prompted. "Pull as hard as you can."

But he wasn't able to think. When had she become a woman? She was, perhaps, five feet one inch tall. Guy, seventeen and a half years old, was over five feet eleven inches tall, and time would add new inches to his stature. Standing with his arm bent without pulling, weak as he had never felt before, he looked at her from above. He had managed to avoid this moment for a week; now here it was.

"Guy?"

She was so close. Her just developed breasts touched him, and her eyes... he felt himself sinking into her eyes. Jane's face was raised to his, and she was staring at him with a certain look... *her* look, the way she had always looked at him, with loving, trusting, limpid eyes. What beautiful eyes she had. An eye color Guy had seen only on her. Her eyes were still too big for her face, because she was, God, just a child.

Just a child compared to him.

"Jane..." he murmured. He didn't understand anything; he didn't know what he was saying. "Will you miss me a bit when I am away, little one?"

Thereafter, he would often think back on this moment, on the madness that had caused him to consider right something that was wrong; and he wouldn't be able to understand why his brain had got confused, why his eyes had become glazed looking at Jane, why his lips had uttered words he should have held more than any other secret.

No, no, no, no.

Jane blinked. She opened her mouth slight but didn't answer. Her eyes were wide open. Was she afraid? But not of him; she couldn't possibly be afraid of him. Jane adored him, and when he was with her, even Guy didn't hate himself; he dreamed of being different from what he was. *It's the blood of the Spencers that runs through your veins,* his father, the 3rd Earl of Ashbourne, had once told him; *you can't change it.*

But he could, with Jane he *could* change it. He put his left hand to her round, pink cheek. Her cheek was still childlike, and Jane tensed at his new, unexpected touch. Why was he stroking her cheek still sweet with milk?

"Because I'll miss you, little one," he murmured, bringing his face near to hers. Her scent intoxicated him, and, like doves from a cage, absurd words escaped from his mouth. "I'll miss you like crazy."

His biggest secret. And he was betraying himself in this helpless way. He was revealing how much pain he felt every time he had to leave 7 Courtnell Street. It was like taking a knife and cutting off a piece of his own heart. And the time had already come: tomorrow, he would leave again. He wouldn't see Jane for many, too many months; and at Eton college, he would spend the days thinking about her, not even on purpose, but involuntarily, almost without realizing it; during the day, when someone would talk to him about his father, when he'd look at the blue sky, or during the math lesson, Jane's face would flash into his mind without invitation. That little girl who had always believed in him, Guy Spencer, the son of the devil, rejected even by his own mother.

Jane—she was his lifeline, his safety net... his angel.

She always had been.

No, no, no, no.

But she loved him, didn't she? She would love him forever. He had tested her affection time and again, he had rejected, bullied her, but Jane had gone back to him, every time. He could trust her. It was *time* to trust her.

Guy took a breath. He closed his eyes and, defenseless for the first time in his life, he put his lips on his angel's.

25.

What a damn hangover. Leaning against the carriage seat with his eyes closed, Stephen Weymouth was feeling every street's pothole right in his stomach. The Ashbourne Method to get him out of his opium-induced stupor was to make him drink like a fish. And it had worked, all right. But now, after having spent the last seventy-two hours swallowing a lot of whiskey and vomiting, Stephen was like a rag used to clean a latrine.

"We're almost there," his captor said, and Stephen opened his eyes. The light hit his irises, and his head ached with the sting of a thousand needles.

Guy looked at him without the slightest compassion. That asshole. He had drunk as much as Stephen, but this morning, when he had pulled him out of bed by the hair, he hadn't seemed to be affected by the same hangover that Stephen was. The damned Earl of Ashbourne appeared elegant, almost refreshed, in his black overcoat, with his walking stick and cylinder hat resting on the burgundy velvet seat beside him.

"How the hell do you do that?"

"How the hell I do what?"

"You look so disgustingly... rested."

Guy smiled, and a light flashed in his eyes. Stephen knew what his friend was thinking about—or rather, *whom* he was thinking about—before Guy answered.

"Jane wakes me up at seven in the morning," Guy muttered. "At seven *o'clock,*" he repeated outraged. "These three days in your home have made me feel alive again. It should be illegal to wake up before eleven. I will propose a law about that to the House of Lords."

Stephen tried to ignore the twinge that had pierced his gut when Guy had mentioned his stepsister's name. It was just the hangover, he decided. Just the hangover. "While I drank that damn whiskey, what were you doing, were you spitting it out all the time?"

Guy paid the whiskey in Weymouth's house, like everything else in his apartment at 31 Bolton Street.

"For one thing, the stuff we drank at your place is too disgusting to be called whiskey," Guy said. "And second, I threw it down more than you did."

Stephen grimaced and, remembering the amber liquid he had forced down the days before, he felt a retching in his throat. He fought it back with a shudder.

"You know what?" he murmured wrinkling his lips. "Maybe it's better you don't mention whiskey to me right now."

Guy grinned. But Stephen didn't misunderstand the expression on his friend's face. Guy wasn't in the carriage with him at that moment. Guy was already home. With Jane.

Another twinge, a mixture of anger, pain, and frustration, filled Stephen's chest.

This reaction was unfair, and he knew it. Guy was his friend. He had stayed with him for the past three days and nights. He had slapped his face, he had made him drink the whiskey. He had purged the opium from his blood. And now, he was bringing him to Ashbourne House, to keep an eye on him. That was definitely an act of deep friendship.

How could Stephen ask him for more? How could he ask Guy to give up on Jane Hartwell, to give up his mysterious reasons for revenge? Guy hadn't taken her virginity. He was leaving her intact, and this meant one secure thing. He would set her free in six months as he had sworn to. And he hadn't seen Jane for three days: to a man as obsessed as him, it had to have been an eternity. Now Stephen had recovered a presentable—well, barely respectable—appearance, so Guy was taking him to Ashbourne House. Having Stephen stay at Guy's place was the best solution for everyone. What else was Guy supposed to do? Was he supposed to stay with Stephen in his house on Bolton Street? Come on, Stephen's apartment was little and wretched. Stephen didn't want to move from there because he didn't want to be kept in a luxurious house like a whore, but the domestic staff at 31 Bolton Street had just one member, the butler. And yes, Stephen's whiskey was of poor quality because even Stephen had pride, and he couldn't accept expensive stuff from Guy.

So, he should thank Guy. He had to thank him right here, right now. But when the carriage stopped at Ashbourne House, he snorted and never said, "Thank you, Ash."

* * *

Jane tried to insert the needle into the silky, white fabric in her hand, but her fingers were shaking too much.

"Haven't you heard anything from the Earl yet, Miss Hartwell?" Lady Susan asked.

Jane gulped. After a breath, she raised her head to her companion. A *lady's* companion. Apparently, an earl's stepsister had to have a lady's companion. Guy had chosen Lady Susan Emerson for the task. She was the widow of a viscount and the sister of a penniless earl. Her husband's death had left her no legacy to support her needs. Guy hired Lady Susan the previous week, and Jane hadn't protested. How could she have protested? She was supposed to never object Guy's decisions. Yet, against all her most pessimistic expectations, Jane had realized she liked Lady Susan's company. She hadn't found her to be as shallow as Rona had always described the noblewomen. Perhaps it was because Susan was an impoverished lady. Jane didn't know why, but she felt almost at ease with her. It was a strange thing, considering that Susan was her opposite. She was self-confident, imperturbable, and she always knew what to do, both at home, with the servants, and even at St. Mary Orphan Refuge, where she could put the director back in her place with one word. She didn't seem to like the orphans very much though. She differed from Jane in this too: she always avoided any contact with the children.

And she was beautiful. So naturally elegant. She was maybe thirty-five years old, but her strawberry blonde hair showed no sign of gray, and her eyes were an odd blue, they seemed almost violet. Sometimes, they got veiled by something... bitterness, perhaps, or disenchantment. Jane couldn't understand what it was.

"No, not yet," she answered, while her heart squeezed in her chest. And why, in heaven's name? What did she care if Guy hadn't come home in three days?

"I can see you're worried about him."

Jane, *worrying* about him? Not at all! Guy was her master, her cruel master, and these days of freedom had been heavenly. Yes, exactly right, she wasn't missing him at all, she wasn't worried about him, she hated him; she hated him to death; she didn't want him to come back, she...

"Miss Hartwell?"

Jane blinked. "No, I'm not," she replied with an effort. "I'm just... a little surprised, that's all. It's the first time he's been away from home."

Lady Susan smiled. "You've been living here for what, ten days now? The first time in ten days is not indicative, is it? Don't worry, Miss Hartwell. Your stepbrother is used to staying away from home even for weeks, informing no one. Or at least," she added lightly, "Mrs. Robinson, the housekeeper, told me so."

"But..." Jane closed her mouth. *But he no longer lives alone. Now he should inform my father.*

Now he should inform me.

Oh, Guy, Guy. She clenched the embroidery between her hands. He was missing since Wednesday evening. Today was Sunday. Without a message, a hug, a... a request to her. Jane hated him, had she already mentioned that? The thought that he could be hurt somewhere didn't worry her. At all. It didn't torture her the idea that he could have been assailed, or wounded, or...

Oh, Guy, where are you? What happened to you?

Lady Emerson put her embroidery down and laid a hand over Jane's. "He's a grown man, Miss Hartwell," she murmured softly. Her voice was hoarse and low, as if she had just come out from a room full of smoke. "Really, stop torturing yourself this way. Maybe you're used to remembering him as a child, but he's no longer a child." She smiled. "By the way," she added with a vivacious voice, trying to change the subject, "I'd like to know how he was as a child. Did he look so menacing even then?"

Jane swallowed hard and tried to smile. *Menacing* and *Guy*, these were two words that had always gone together. Even in 1836, when her stepmother had introduced him to the Hartwells for the first time. It was the day of Rona and Charles's wedding. Jane wasn't even five, but the memory had remained indelibly in her mind. She could almost visualize Rona before her eyes, the way the morning light coming through the window of the east living room illuminated her. Rona hadn't the sweet smile Jane had come to know and love during the previous months, when Rona went to visit her at her uncle's house. Rona always smiled while teaching Jane the nursery rhymes that helped her get rid of her stuttering. But she wasn't smiling now. Guy had just arrived at 7 Courtnell Street, and something indecipherable shadowed her stepmother's face as she turned toward the door and called out: "Guy, come meet your new sister." Jane had looked at the threshold. Her shyness mixed with excitement at the prospect of having a big brother, a real, *whole new* big brother. A child showed up in the doorway, and he was startlingly different from his mother, with his dark complexion and dark eyes. He was a child who looked almost like a man, so tall and strong he was.

That child saw her and, without a word, he stuck his tongue out at her. Then he ran away.

"Miss Hartwell?"

Jane roused herself from these memories, under Susan's watchful eye. "I don't remember," she lied, blushing. "The fact is that he was older than me. Almost five years older, so we didn't speak much to each other." But Jane's childhood had revolved around Guy's arrivals and departures. As a child, she had always been waiting for him, she had always been following him around to get a word from him. Even when his words were rude.

Even if his words were rude, she was happy anyway.

"Yet the two of you were close, weren't you?" said Lady Susan, and Jane felt her face getting warmer. "Otherwise, you wouldn't be here now. And you wouldn't be so sad about his absence. Sometimes stepbrothers are better than real brothers, there's nothing to be ashamed of."

Under Susan's casual tone, Jane could detect a sort of unhappiness. Nobody could affirm that Susan's family was a supportive one. Guy had told Jane so—she closed her eyes, and heat rose up to her neck and went down to her groin at the same time—he had told her so while they were lying in bed, and Jane's heart constricted. She remembered that morning. It had been four days ago. He had returned at dawn, as it had happened before, and he had been... unusually sweet. In a wonderful way. He had embraced her tightly, he had caressed her with urgency; he hadn't fallen asleep and, kissing her with growing passion, had made her climax with his mouth, whispering that she was beautiful. He hadn't called her a slave. He hadn't told her she was just his plaything...

And that very night, he hadn't come home.

Was Lady Susan right? Was he out having fun?

And if so... *how* was he having fun?

Jane bowed her head over her embroidery, and her hand trembled. Maybe Guy had grown tired of her. Maybe he had satisfied his needs with another woman. Well, so much the better. Jane couldn't possibly miss the times when he took her against nature, or when he filled her mouth with his seed. He watched her swallow it all with a rapt expression on his face, and she hated him, didn't she?

She swallowed.

Yes, she hated him. And she hated when he touched her, and gave her a shocking pleasure, making her behave like a wanton creature, like a... a whore, and his voice in the morning, yes, she hated it as well, even if it was a sleepy voice, devoid of any cruelty. Because although Guy was gentle sometimes, he remained a devil, *always*. He made her crawl on all fours like a bitch, he used her as a footrest, he ordered her to lick his boots, for God's sake!

Jane sank her head between her shoulders, as if to hide.

He was mean, oh so mean. He smiled when he humiliated her, and then he whispered, *you like being my slave, Jane... you love it, don't you...*

"Really, you should stop worrying about him this way," repeated Lady Susan, startling her. "The Earl of Ashbourne is the last man something bad can happen to. I can't say the same, of course, for the people who dare to cross him." She smiled. "They can definitely happen to end up with their nose or ribs broken, and by the Earl's very hand. It also happened to my husband once."

Jane's eyes widened. She was interested in what Susan was saying, at last. "Did Guy hurt your husband?"

Susan bit her lip. Suddenly she seemed to realize she had said something improper, and her discomfort wasn't lost on Jane. In a situation like this, just three weeks ago, Jane would have apologized and changed the subject; she would have done everything not to upset a woman like Lady Susan Emerson.

But now she couldn't. She needed to know all about Guy, she wanted to know Guy, she wanted to understand him. If only it were possible.

She waited for Susan's response.

* * *

Well, that was a legitimate question, wasn't it? Susan sighed. She was disappointed with herself for having uttered those unwise words. Lowering her head, she silently cursed herself in English and French—and even with a few Russian words, her grandmother's native language. "Yes, he did," she finally answered.

This short answer couldn't satisfy the girl in front of her. No, of course it couldn't.

"But... how can you possibly be still his friend?" Jane asked. "If Guy hurt your husband..."

Susan could easily understand her astonishment.

Oh, I can, ingénue, she thought. *I can be his friend, all right.*

The Earl of Ashbourne had beaten Maxwell, 3rd Viscount of the House of the Emerson.

And yes, the Viscount's wife was still Ashbourne's friends.

Any guesses why, ingénue?

But how could Jane imagine why? She was like a blonde, naïve little butterfly. Only her curiosity about Ashbourne had made her say more than a few monosyllables.

I didn't remain his friend after he beat my husband, silly. I became his friend because of it. More than a friend. "Well, my husband and the Earl repaired their friendship, afterward," she lied. "And a woman in my position, you know, can't be rigid in denying her forgiveness."

Jane nodded with a sympathetic light in her eyes. Susan had known her only for a week, but she would bet that no, Jane Hartwell couldn't really understand her. Jane had a too-high sense of honor, she could never pretend benevolence. But Susan could. In the last year, the widow Viscountess had smiled at everyone. She had even smiled at the two people she hated most in the world, namely her brother-in-law's wife, the new Lady Emerson, and her brother-in-law, who had become the new Viscount Emerson after Maxwell's death. Her *magnanimous* brother-in-law. He had allowed Susan to stay in Maxwell's home... in exchange for occasional sex.

Susan shivered with disgust.

He couldn't even get it up. What a pathetic, impotent man. He was sixty years old, bald, and fat. There was always a rancid stink about him, and his breath smelled like chicken entrails.

No, Jane Hartwell. You don't know what one can do out of necessity.

Susan felt her chest tighten as if icy water flooded through her lungs. She was at Ashbourne House out of necessity, what else? She was here to escape from the new Viscount Emerson, as disgusting as the previous one.

Her heart constricted at the thought of what she was supposed to do here. It was a weird reaction, considering the situation she had been in before.

"I'm sorry I made you feel sad," Jane murmured.

Susan raised her head. *It's not you the one who makes me sad.* It was Susan's fault, just hers, because she was a silly fool. Guy Spencer, the Earl of Ashbourne, had hired her for a specific purpose, so what? What was the problem? She was a loose woman, everyone knew that. Why did it bother her that Ashbourne considered her a prostitute too?

He hadn't even hired Susan for himself. No, of course not. In exchange for a large sum of money, Ashbourne had asked Susan to seduce a man she had never met. The Earl had been sure she would accept the "job" he was offering her. And he had been right. She had accepted his offer. She was here at Ashbourne House. So, she was a prostitute. Officially.

"You didn't make me sad," she answered, rousing herself from these thoughts. Jane smiled, and Susan, observing her red-rimmed eyes, once again realized something. Not only had the sweet girl in front of her fallen in love with her stepbrother. No, she had *madly* fallen in love with him. Susan had noticed her love for him the first moment she had arrived here, when the Earl had introduced her to Jane. And every time he was present, Jane got completely confused. She turned pale, she blushed, she glanced sideways at him all the time, hanging on his every word.

Poor silly girl. Her heart would break when she finally understood that Ashbourne could never reciprocate her feelings. He wouldn't take advantage of her love to seduce her, at least. Many considered him a libertine with no honor, but he wasn't. Susan knew the reason why Guy Christian Spencer, the 4th Earl of Ashbourne, had broken Maxwell Emerson's nose, so she knew something for sure about him: Ashbourne could be a bastard in a thousand ways, and he was insensitive like a wall, yes, that was for sure too, but he would never, ever seduce an innocent girl.

"Miss Hartwell, don't be afraid for him," she said quietly. "The Earl is used to a certain kind of, uh... *fun.* It's not unusual that a man like him would stay out for days."

Jane turned pale.

I'm doing this for you, ingénue, Susan thought. *You need to stop loving him.* "Perhaps you'd prefer I don't raise this topic with you," she said, feigning embarrassment. She could guess the answer.

"No, I..." Jane blushed. "I hope you're right. Has he..." She closed her eyes, squinting her eyelids as if a sudden headache throbbed between her temples. "Does he have a mistress, to your knowledge?"

"More than one, I suppose," Susan said lightly. "Your stepbrother is... quite popular among the ladies. Surely you happened to read the gossip newspapers. They always write about his scandalous love life. They accuse him of having never courted a proper girl to marry. Not even one, can you imagine?" She shook her head emphatically. "For the most eligible bachelor of the *ton,* this is a serious allegation."

"Most eligible," Jane repeated in a whisper.

"Didn't you suspect? You should see the unmarried young ladies—and their mothers too!—when he happens to make his appearance in public. At the rare balls he attends, there are always four or five girls fainting with admiration."

Jane herself was likely to faint, and Susan decided it was time to comfort her, but without lying to her. Jane had to know the truth. Truth saves you from pain, even though knowing it is a form of pain too. "He cares about none of these ladies, anyway."

"Doesn't he? Why?"

Susan laid her embroidery on the couch and leaned forward conspiratorially. "Now I'll tell you a secret," she whispered, even though they were alone in the light-blue, ground-floor living room. "A secret that must remain between us. My husband was a friend of your stepbrother's, as I told you." That was a lie. But it was improbable that Maxwell Emerson, as dead as he was, would deny it. "Maybe you can't imagine this, but sometimes one drinks a little too much between friends. And drinking loosens the tongue, you know. On one of these occasions, Lord Ashbourne said he will never get married. Never ever."

"Never?" Jane asked, turning pale again. "Why?"

Certainly not because he doesn't like the ladies, ingénue. "He blurted something about the bad blood of the Spencers," Susan said in a detached voice. "As I told you, it was drunken talk."

"Bad blood, he said?"

"That's right. The Earl of Ashbourne said he'll never father children. The Spencers will end with him, he swore it."

He had really sworn it. He had said these exact words, about three and a half years ago, while he and Susan were lying on a large bed with deep-red silk sheets. *You could kill my husband and marry me,* Susan had replied with a sad smile. *I can't have kids.*

The Earl had smiled gently. They had just made love. Pulling an arm out from the sheets, he had taken her hand and had kissed it. *You shouldn't assume that's necessarily a bad thing,* he had murmured. *Some women do not love their children.* The bitterness beneath those words had been barely there, but perceptible nevertheless, and Susan had sensed an emotion in him, a certain... vulnerability. It had astonished her. The Earl of Ashbourne always kept a distance between himself and others. And between himself and Susan.

"Oh. Two ladies talking closely together."

Jane's and Susan's heads whirled toward the door. A young man with long light-brown hair was watching them from the doorway. He was smiling, as usual. The younger son of Baron Weymouth always smiled. He was an opium addict, that was the word on the street, and judging by the green face he had at this moment, he had just passed through a bad crisis. Was he there looking for Guy, Susan wondered? Everyone knew that Stephen Weymouth made no move without the Earl.

Weymouth turned to someone still hidden by the wall, and Susan knew she had been mistaken. Jane also seemed to come to the same conclusion. She blanched, becoming as still as a mouse before a cat.

"I wouldn't go in there if I were you," Weymouth said to the person around the corner, smiling with amusement. "Two women sharing secrets are the most dangerous thing in the world, Ash."

26.

"And tell us, where did you recover this stray cat?"

Stephen Weymouth smiled. "No, you don't really want to know, Mr. Hartwell. Trust me."

Rather yes, Charles wanted to know where Guy had been in the last three days. But they were at the table having lunch, and good manners required him to reply in one way only. "Yeah, I guess so," he muttered. He was not at all convinced. Because if Guy had gone to whores during the past three days, as expected of a libertine like him, it would be good that Jane knew it, and as soon as possible. Charles took a breath and glanced at his daughter sideways. She was sitting on his left, her head bowed over her plate. As usual, yet there was a big difference from the past three days. Her hand didn't just hold the spoon, but occasionally she brought it to her mouth. She was *actually* eating, something she hadn't done since the previous Thursday. And she was... full of life. Her eyes rose from her plate and ran to the head of the table where Guy was sitting. And her cheeks were colorful, her shoulders jerked, her hands trembled.

Just as she was as a child.

And that was a bloody, predictable problem, wasn't it?

"Why all this mystery?" Susan asked. His daughter's companion was dressed with simplicity, in a dark gray that showed the whiteness of her skin and emphasized her full cleavage. There was one thing that Charles had to admit about his stepson: he had good taste in women. Lady Susan Emerson didn't go unnoticed, that was for sure. Maybe she wasn't as beautiful as Rona, but she was younger, although closer to forty than thirty. She concealed her age well. She wore makeup in a clever way, leaving her curls loose on her face, and she always managed to avoid direct light. The latter habit reminded Charles of his first wife.

Ah, Guy, Guy... you're not exactly subtle in your maneuvers.

Only a girl as naïve as Jane could believe Susan was here to be her lady's companion. Charles looked at his stepson with a mixture of affection and exasperation. Guy's sideburns were of the proper length, his face was clean-shaven, his suit elegant. He was a veritable gallows-bird, as good as new for

191

Sunday lunch.

Charles sighed. No, Lord Ashbourne wasn't very subtle, and he was behaving obtusely. Guy didn't realize that Charles had only one face in mind, Rona's. Rona had died in Charles's arms eleven months ago. His stepson—Mr. Subtlety sitting over there, bless his heart—really believed that sex was the cure to all ills. As a matter of fact, Guy looked carefree indeed. He was eating slowly and with a distant smile, apparently oblivious to Jane's adoring gazes, Charles's quizzical ones, and Susan's charming ways.

As the staff entered to serve game and sauces, their conversation stopped. In the last days, only Charles and Susan had talked. Charles had talked with Susan to be polite, Susan had talked with Charles because there was a contract that forced her into it. Well, of course this was supposed to be a secret between Susan and Guy, but the reason why his stepson had hired Susan was crystal clear to Charles, even if he couldn't say it aloud.

Anyway, five people at the table made a great deal of difference.

Guy got up to carve the meat. At first, there had been squabbles between him and Charles about who should do the carving. "It's up to you, Mr. Hartwell," "No, it's up to you, Guy." In the end, his stepson had become convinced that it would be too much effort for Charles. Charles would have stood up, sat down, prepared the slices of meat for everyone.

Too difficult for a cripple like him.

And fall in love again, Guy? Don't you think it would be too much effort for me? I buried two wives, son. Two pieces of my heart. I'm all out of it, now.

"No, no mystery whatever, Lady Susan," said Weymouth as the servants came out. "It's just self-preservation." Shrugging, he reached toward the tray, serving himself a small piece of pheasant. His greenish face was probably related to his lack of appetite.

Susan giggled, and Charles decided to get to the bottom of that matter. Also, he wanted to find out the reason for Weymouth's green face.

"We haven't seen you the last few days, Mr. Weymouth," he began slowly. "Have you been out of town?"

The young man fiddled with the fork on his plate. "I've had... some health problems," he said with barely perceptible hesitation.

So, he had had health problems. He didn't look fine, that was certain. In ten days, he had lost weight, and dark circles underlined his brown eyes. His sideburns, long and unkempt, were too messy for someone like him. He seemed the type of person who cared a lot about his appearance. Yeah, health problems. It was the most logical explanation. Although, if one wanted to be picky, his red, half-closed eyes reminded more of a terrible hangover than fever or flu.

"Completely resolved, I hope."

"Oh, yes." Weymouth glanced at his friend sitting at the head of the table and grinned. "Completely."

"There's even worse news, Mr. Hartwell," said Guy with a smooth voice. "We won't get rid of him. Weymouth will give us the dubious pleasure of his company for the next few weeks."

"Are you going to stay here, Mr. Weymouth?" Susan shook her flowing strawberry blonde hair, provocatively pulled up in a bun in the middle of her head. This hairstyle left most of her curls loose over her shoulders. She gave a wide, white smile. A seductive one, Charles thought. Probably it came to her as naturally as breathing. "That's great news."

"Great news?" Weymouth grimaced. "I'm not sure, Lady Susan. Oh, that's not because of you and Miss Hartwell, I mean, you both are adorable. The fact is, Ashbourne has told me he wants me here to make me recover from my flu, but I rather think he's going to hand me some poison, passing it off as medicine."

"Oh, you don't mean it! The Earl has a heart of gold, doesn't he? Moreover, Miss Hartwell is an excellent nurse, so you'll be cared for properly."

"Really? Are you a nurse, Miss Hartwell?"

Jane gasped. "No," she responded quickly, saying her first words during the entire lunch. "Absolutely not." She looked frightened, and Charles frowned.

"Oh, come now, of course you are," Susan corrected her in a gentle rebuke. "Don't be this modest, Miss Hartwell. Yesterday, we went to the Christian hospital, Mr. Weymouth, and you wouldn't believe what a warm welcome they gave her!"

"No, I..." Jane spoke quickly, "...I went there just to inform Dr. Kenneth that... that I'd never go there again."

"Really, Jane."

Guy's voice was slow and quiet. Everyone turned to look at him. He was watching Jane, and Jane was watching him.

She was as pale as a ghost.

Charles pressed his lips together. He would say nothing, no, he would *not* intervene. Rona had always protected Jane, she had kept her stepdaughter in a bubble, and what was the result? Jane's timidity was beyond measure, and fear painted her face every time she went out by herself.

Charles wanted Jane to decide for herself, to fight by herself. She *could* do it. She had done it when she had mustered the courage to keep going to the St. Mary Orphan Refuge alone. After Rona's death, Jane hadn't stopped going to "her" children. Later, she had started going to the hospital as well, a little more distant from 7 Courtnell Street.

"I just told him that, seriously, Guy," Jane murmured, and Charles clenched his fists in hearing her subdued tone.

Don't apologize to him, my child. He's not the one who decides for you.

He watched his daughter's blonde hair, wisps escaping the bun and curling over her forehead.

You have your mother's blood. Don't forget it.

But what would the combative, formidable Mary Jane Gardiner have done to guide her daughter? What would she have told her? Jane had her mother's eyes, had her blood running through her veins, but she was falling in love with the wrong man...

"I don't think you have to justify yourself, Jane," Charles said, unable to withstand her tension any longer. His father's instinct had won this time again.

Guy's eyes narrowed. "On the contrary, sir. I think she should."

Susan giggled to lighten the mood. "Oh, my goodness, here they quarrel about Jane again. It's not easy for a woman to live with a father and a brother so possessive. You know what I think, Mr. Weymouth? Getting a husband will be a liberation for her."

Guy clenched his jaws at Susan's words. Ignoring her, he continued speaking to Charles. "Hospitals are places full of diseases and questionable people, Mr. Hartwell," he said harshly. "Jane could get sick there. She could meet someone dangerous."

"Are you telling me you care about safety issues? It seems a little strange coming from the man who learned to box as a child. I mean, you never miss an opportunity to pick a fight whenever and with whomever." *Almost to the point of self-destruction, right, Guy?*

His stepson waved his hand in front of himself, impatiently, in his peculiar way of saying "bullshit" without using the actual word. "I don't want her to go there again," he repeated. "I'll tell the coachman to not bring her to places like that."

"She can go there on foot."

"She won't."

And in his stentorian voice, and in Jane's silence, there was a certainty that sent a chill down Charles's spine.

* * *

"You didn't eat much for lunch."

Jane looked at Guy from her bottom position and clenched her teeth, fighting the swollen emotion obstructing her throat. A kind of stone, but not tears, no. Guy didn't deserve her tears. This man for three days had been with other women and now, as if nothing had happened, had summoned her in his study and made her undress.

Then, he had ordered her: "Sit like a good puppy, Jane."

She had obeyed without protest. That stone in her throat was pressing and pressing. It wanted to strangle her.

Yet, she wouldn't say anything. She wouldn't ask him where he'd been the past three days.

With whom he'd been.

I hate you, Guy.

With her feet under her buttocks and knees spread apart, she kept her closed fists between her thighs, resting on the big red carpet that covered the right side of the study.

"You didn't even eat the cake."

Answering was not easy. Guy was watching her breasts; they, pushed together between her tensed arms, obscenely offered themselves to him.

It was hard to tell if he was punishing her for the hospital or simply he wanted to humiliate her, as had already happened.

But something was different now. Maybe not in him. Maybe in her. There was slamming rage inside her. This rage wanted her to scream.

I hate you, Guy.

"I... couldn't," she said in a choked voice. "I was full."

The light in the study was strong. On the right side—their "recreation area"—the carpet kept her knees from getting hurt. The large leather sofa and the armchair on the side made the study like a living room.

"Full," repeated Guy. "But I told you I don't want you to lose any more weight, did I, Jane?" he said, as if reflecting aloud. "So, you'll eat it now."

He pointed to the low table in front of the sofa, a few feet from them. On it, there was a whole cream cake.

Please God, don't let him make me eat it all.

Certainly she would feel sick if she tried to. Fortunately Guy, approaching the table, took the knife and cut a slice. Very well—a large slice. But Jane drew a sigh of relief anyway.

With the aid of the knife, Guy put the slice on one of the two white plates on the table. Then he took it and, moving in front of her, placed it on the floor.

"Eat."

There was no spoon. She stretched out her hand to the plate.

"No. Without your hands."

Jane closed her eyes. *You didn't do this to her, did you?*
You didn't humiliate her.

She opened her eyes, and the slice of cake seemed immense to her. It was white and yellow, decorated with colored meringues and sugar flowers.

"Come on Jane, start eating, or I'll make you eat it all." He pointed to the cake on the low table. "Eat, and don't lift your head until you've finished."

With a sense of nausea, Jane placed her elbows on the ground, gathering her knees against her belly. She put her mouth close to the yellow cream of the cake. She opened her lips and closed them; a sweet and creamy taste filled her mouth. It was so big! Tears swelled her eyes. She blinked to hide them.

Guy placed his hand on her head. "Does it taste nice?"

I hate you. I hate you. "Yes."

"Fine."

He was smiling, she could hear it in his voice. He pulled the hairpins out of her hair, undoing her bun and making her hair fall into the plate—on the cake.

He stroked her back gently, then straightened and moved behind her.

"Keep eating, then," he said, "but... lift your ass into the air, angel."

Jane swallowed the bite with an effort. He wouldn't merely look at her, the devil. She untucked her legs and raised her buttocks, forming a perfect triangle on the carpet with her knees, mouth, and bottom.

"Very well, my angel. Now be good, spread your thighs wide for me."

She obeyed, and, from behind, Guy's fingers began to caress her buttocks.

That cursed. Cruel. Devil.

* * *

Jane's pussy called him. It was pink. Wet. Hot.

Take me, Guy. Fuck me.

Frustration made him groan. He spat on Jane's asshole and touched it with the head of his cock. He couldn't wait, couldn't wait a minute longer today, so he didn't do the necessary foreplay. He pushed himself into her urgently. Jane groaned, and Guy cursed himself. But either that or fuck her.

Poor, sweet little butthole; it was still a beginner, it needed to be fucked with more care.

"Eat your cake, Jane," he said, moving his penis slowly, to compensate the lack of attention of a few moments ago. "Eat, or... or I'll get angry..."

Cupping her buttocks in his hands, he pulled his cock in and out of her, inside her with half of it, stroking the glans when it went out. He wasn't touching her pussy, nor caressing her body. He didn't want Jane to climax.

To the hospital, my little one? Oh no. You shouldn't have.

Jane was holding her face up; her body moved back and forth in rhythm with his thrusts. She had stopped eating. Leaning over her from behind, Guy placed his hand on her nape.

"Eat," he repeated sharply. He pressed her face down, smashing it into the cake. He held it still, giving another couple of thrusts into her asshole, then pulled her head back by the hair, allowing her to breathe. "Lick the plate *clean.*"

He continued to push his cock through her little hole, gripping her hair tight in his hand, both to prevent her from slamming her face into the plate and getting hurt, and to ride her in the way he loved, with her soft hair caught between his fingers like reins.

Jane had lowered her face to the plate, her eyes on the cake, but Guy doubted she could swallow anything. He moved more quickly, taking his own pleasure.

This day was all his.

When his cock began to pulse, he came out of her and, taking a deep breath to prevent himself from coming, stood up with a hard effort. Moving in front of her, he reached down to her hair; he grasped it in his hand and pulled her face from the plate.

Jane was breathing with her mouth open.

"You haven't... haven't finished your cake..."

Cheeks, hair, forehead. She had cream all over herself.

"Don't you like it...?" he muttered, grabbing his cock with his hand and pumping it firmly. "Now you're going to like it, Jane..." he gasped, shaking with pleasure, "you're going to *love* it..."

He came on the plate: powerful, hot spurts of cum hit the cake. Stunned by orgasm, he put his hand on the back of the armchair for support. He closed his eyes, to enjoy these moments of total heaven. There was no noise in the room apart from the crackling fire, certainly not the sound of Jane's tongue licking the plate and eating her... *dessert*.

As he regained the use of his senses, he opened his eyes. Tears were rolling down Jane's cheeks, mixing with the white and yellow cream that covered her face. She was staring at the plate as if she couldn't understand what her master wanted from her.

Oh, but I bet you've understood, little one... you've understood just fine.

"Eat everything," he ordered huskily.

He raised his right foot. He was unsteady because of the pleasure he had just felt, but he was also determined to punish her. He pressed the sole of his shoe against her nape, pushing her head down to the plate. He waited until she closed her lips on the mess of cream and sperm, then removed his foot. planting it to the floor.

Slowly, he lifted his trousers up and went to the sofa, letting himself fall onto it without strength.

"When you've cleaned everything," he murmured, looking at her ass right in front of his eyes, "you can go, angel."

He took the newspaper from the little table and opened it with the sound of crumpled paper. It was all an act, he wasn't going to read any news. He wanted to enjoy the sight of her eating on all fours. Yet, a little discomfort stung his sternum as he watched Jane lick the plate clean. She was doing it dutifully, sobbing from time to time. Poor little girl, he thought with tender regret. He had denied her her orgasm. She would be sad for the remainder of the afternoon, until tonight, when he finally would cuddle her in bed. God, he loved to see her climax, as much as to climax himself. But she had done wrong, and she had deserved to be punished.

In the room the noises were muffled; the fire in the hearth, the stalactites of ice that broke free outside the window, the trampled snow in the garden.

Guy focused on the only sound he wanted to remember forever. Jane's tongue eating her... *snack*. It was wonderful to know that, on her plate, there was Guy too.

After a few minutes, Jane stopped licking. She had finished. Straightening her arms, she lifted her torso up, moving her mouth away from the plate. She remained on all fours. Guy expected her to crawl to the door, get dressed, and go out of the study. It was what he had told her to do; but she didn't move, and her beautiful, just-fucked ass looked more than ever like a heart, to the delight of Guy's eyes.

"You... don't treat her like this, do you?" Jane murmured in a suffocated voice.

"Her *who?*"

Jane lowered her face, her shoulder blades as sharp as vulnerable wings on her back. "Your mistress," she said feebly. "The woman with... with whom you've been. In the last three days."

Guy felt a protest rise on his lips. He was going to say, "I've been with that asshole Weymouth," but then he changed his mind. "If there's something you want to ask me, Jane," he replied, laying the newspaper beside him, "then turn around and look at me."

Jane took a breath that lifted her shoulders. She straightened her chest and turned around, sitting up on the floor with her feet under her buttocks. She put one hand over her breasts and the other over her pubic hair. What a silly girl. She still covered herself in front of him, despite the fact that he saw her more often naked than clothed. Her face was dirty with cake cream and framed by her blonde hair, which fell over her shoulders like a brilliant waterfall. Her mouth was slightly open, pink and soft, but a veil of tears and desolation clouded her eyes. "Have... have you been with another woman?" she asked weakly.

"Why are you asking?"

Jane bit her lower lip. "If... if you don't need me any longer..." she murmured, blinking to keep from crying, "then what happens to our deal?"

"Oh. That's why you want to know." Guy sat more comfortably on the couch, with his back against the cushions. "If I tire of you," he said nonchalantly, "our deal remains valid. I'll give you everything I promised you. Only if you don't obey me is our deal off."

"Are you tired of me?"

"Is that a hope or a fear?"

"I..." Jane's mouth bent downward; she looked inconsolable, even more than the first day of their deal. "I'd l-like to g...go, now," she stammered. "M...may I?..." She ran a hand over her face. She wanted to clean it, but she was trembling too much. She just got dirtier with cream and cake crumbs.

Guy took a deep breath. And then he capitulated. By God, he hadn't seen her for three days.

"No, you may not. Come here."

Jane didn't move, setting her jaws tight.

"Come here," he repeated. "You had better please me, Jane."

She swallowed. After a moment, she put herself on all fours, and, with her face down, crawled toward the sofa. Watching her come closer, Guy felt a kind of amazement. Good heavens, he had hated her for so many years. Maybe he had thought he would have been able to take his revenge by dirtying her. Dragging her down to his level. The fact was, she didn't seem dirty to him—damn it, she didn't seem dirty *at all*. Even if she was crawling toward him on all fours, even if she was covered with sperm and cream.

When she was in front of him, Guy took out his handkerchief and gently wiped it across her face. "You shouldn't have gone to the hospital," he said softly, "and you knew it perfectly well."

She pushed out her lower lip. "But you... you weren't *here,*" she protested, her voice trembling. "You weren't here, Guy! You sent me no message at all, you... you didn't tell me where you were!"

"I didn't tell you *what?*" He laughed, genuinely amused. "Jane, my little angel. I don't have to tell you anything. I can do what I please."

She drew back as if slapped. "I mean nothing to you, don't I? Nothing..." Slow tears came down her face sweet with sugar; her eyes were full of salty sorrow, and the law of gravity took care of the rest. "It means nothing what... what I do for you..."

Oh, hell. Placing his hands under her armpits, Guy lifted her to sit on his lap. He trailed his hand down to her right thigh. "You disobeyed me, Jane. And you did it on purpose, for you were mad at me." *Just like when you were a child.* He smiled unreasonably and, raising his hand, slapped her hard on her right buttock. She winced in pain, and one tear remained hanging from the edge of her left eyelid.

"This must never happen again, understand? Otherwise, I'll lock you in this house and throw away the key. Make me angry again, and you'd have to forget the St. Mary Orphanage, the money for getting its roof fixed, the presents for your precious orphans, and everything else I promised you." He gave her another slap on her bottom, and she squealed through her tears. "I should punish your rebellion for a long time," he murmured, placing his hand on her reddened buttock, "but today I'll be magnanimous." He smiled and began to stroke her gently between her buttocks. For a few days, he would stay away from that sweet little hole, but he would miss it. "So stop whining, you know I hate it." He kissed her cheek lightly. She was sugary and sticky—a tender, sweetly creamed Jane.

Still unhappy, she stiffened. "But w...where have you been, Guy?"

He grinned. "Did you miss me?"

"Have you been... with another woman?"

I wasn't with a woman, he thought, and opened his mouth again to say so. Then he shut up. He wouldn't tell her she was the only one he wanted to have in his bed. It would give her power, an immense power over him. He couldn't allow that. It didn't matter the way she was wrapping her arms around him as if she could not live without him. Her need for him was like a balm, yes, it eased his heart from the bitterness that had never left him over the years, but he wouldn't repeat his past errors. He knew Jane would draw back from him in horror as soon as he released her from this trap of sweetness and humiliation, pain and pleasure, which confused her and made her weak.

"I'm here now," he murmured, brushing her cheek with his thumb. He slid his hand down between her legs and began to touch her clitoris.

"Why... why didn't you stay... with her..."

"With *her?*" Guy chuckled and made her lie down on the couch, covering her with his body. He kept touching the folds of her sex. Jane was defenseless in his hands; she was so innocent, so sensual, and excitement took her by surprise every time.

Yet, she still spoke.

"Haven't you... haven't you been with another woman, then?"

Guy dropped down to suck her breast. "You know what I'm going to do, my angel?" he murmured. "I'll eat a little cake."

He reached out to his side, toward the low table, and dug his fingers into the soft, creamy cake, filling his palm with it. He put this hand between Jane's legs, smearing the cream all over her crotch. Then he lowered his head down farther and lifted her knees up with both hands, opening her fully to his tongue's exploration.

"I've never tasted a more delicious cake in my life," he murmured licking her pussy, relishing the sweet cream mixed with Jane's flavor, so much sweeter than anything else. She moaned, arching her hips toward his mouth, and after a few minutes, Guy gave her the orgasm he had vowed to deny her.

27.

A night with the Gang of Knives was always complicated; a *February* night with the Gang of Knives bordered on intolerable. Guy would like to curse, but he restrained himself. He was standing in the middle of a cellar. Next to him, on his right, was James Sutherland, a bit farther along was Paul Bailey. Stuart Cavendish, the 6th Duke of St. Court, was sitting at a table. He had a thoughtful expression on his face. With his elbow placed on the wooden surface and his chin resting on his closed hand, he was studying some papers where, presumably, he had rendered the graphical representation of the incoming K-mission. He had gathered the members of the Gang for a preliminary meeting, even though they had already agreed upon what to do. That usually meant a change of plan.

And it meant trouble too.

The grayness of the cellar differed from Jane's room, from her light, from Jane herself, as different as night from day. Guy stared at the floor of warped wooden boards. Jane had been living at Ashbourne House more than a month now and, damn it, he was not even a bit tired of her. In fact, with a kind of worry, he realized that each day was better than the last, despite the limitations he had imposed on himself. No, he had just *one* limitation during their sex games—her cursed, wonderful hymen he dreamed to tear but, damn it, he left intact. Nevertheless, their moments together made him feel... a giant. With her, he felt as if his body were filled from within with... with what?

Satisfaction, pride. And sometimes, he used another term: happiness. And that scared him to the bone. Jane's adoration for him was growing, as expected. She was more and more spontaneous in her kisses, craving both to give and receive them. She craved his touch, his cuddles. She no longer tried to hide the desire she had for him, and this was the evidence of his triumph. Still, she had not surrendered to him completely. Her eyes shone with tears of angry humiliation now and then. Like the day before, when he had made her run across the room on all fours... like a puppy, of course; he had been cruel, oh so cruel, and it had given him a strange emotion, a sort of a pain, seeing her debase herself that much. At the same time, he had felt

201

reckless exaltation for the power he had over her. And later he had comforted her, and Jane had abandoned herself in his arms, crying in mortification. *Why are you doing this to me, Guy?* she had sobbed into his chest. He had whispered tender words to her, without answering her question. He had caressed, kissed, licked her everywhere, making her climax two overwhelming times. *Shhh, Jane, shhh. Everything's all right, my angel.* It was a method as old as the world, nothing more than that. Stick and carrot again. He had often to remind himself it was just a strategy, when Jane was so sweet, so longing for him. It was worthless, it wouldn't last, it didn't even exist; he was just training her as a dog-trainer trains his best puppy; there was nothing else between them.

Nothing else, Guy; don't repeat your past errors.

Isabelle Smith, out of breath, walked into the cellar. She ran toward the Circle of Knives, stopping next to Guy with her hands behind her back. At the center of the circle, on the ground, there was the red box containing their names or, to be more precise, their numbers.

"Fourth Knife," Paul Bailey smiled. "Welcome."

"See, Five?" said Sutherland with a contemptuous smile. "I told you there was no need to worry about her. When she's late, it's because she never leaves a client before he blasts in her throat. She wants to slurp his jizz, you know."

Isabelle tilted her head to one side, batting her long eyelashes. "Oh, but I'm never late because of my clients, Second, honey. They come quickly with me, you should try."

She was aware of provoking Sutherland with her kittenish ways. It was a dangerous game. She disturbed Second's rigid sense of order. But Isabelle Smith resembled Guy in this: she never quit a game once it had started. "A man attacked me out here, and it was kind of unpleasant," she added thoughtfully. "By the way, now he's upstairs. Well, what's left of him," she corrected herself with a scowl. "And if it's not a problem, maybe one of you could help me clean the mess later."

Sutherland turned to St. Court. "She did it again, One. Jesus, even tonight she has drawn a lot of attention to herself. Let's throw her out of the K-Gang before she screws everything up."

Stuart raised his head from the papers with a patient expression on his face, but before he could answer, Isabelle intervened in a honeyed voice. "But if you throw me out, Second," she said frowning, "then you must kill me, mustn't you? I know too much about the Knives. You couldn't let me live." She lowered her hood, revealing a cheap, long copper-red wig, and pursed her lips in a childish way. At twenty-four years old, she was still really good at it. "Oh," she said, smiling sensually, "now I understand. You'd like to do it, wouldn't you? To sink your... *blade*... into me."

Sutherland's lips contracted in disgust. "You're just a whore," he said coldly, "and you should learn to keep your filthy mouth shut."

"You said something bad, honey. Maybe I should spank you a little."

She wasn't joking. Isabelle Smith wasn't just a prostitute, she was a dominatrix, the most requested of Regent's Park.

"Yeah, maybe it will do you good, Second," Guy said. Sutherland was his superior in the Gang's hierarchy, being Knife number *two*, but Guy couldn't fucking stand him. "And now I'll tell you a secret, Number Two, a secret that will be useful in your life and will take away that broom stuck up your ass. Sex is sex. And it's good. So, if you're scared to be chained to Four's table," Guy smiled wryly, "reassure yourself, it's not that terrible. It just takes some time to remove the wax from your balls afterward."

Isabelle smiled brightly. "Do you still remember, Third?"

"One of the best experiences of my life."

Guy smiled, winking at her. They had had sex just once, a year and a half ago, after one of the bloodiest nights in the K-Gang's history. To Guy, it had not been easy letting her immobilize him, but Isabelle needed it. Back then, she was just a novice, covered with blood and shocked; and she had felt the need to go back, to regain control over herself. So Guy had relinquished his own control to her—and it had been one of the most difficult choices in his life.

The Fifth Knife blinked, looking first at Guy, then at Isabelle. "You... you and Four..."

"Oh, don't stutter, you baby chicken," laughed Isabelle. "If you pay enough, you can have me anytime you want."

Guy cocked his head to one side, assessing Paul. "No, Four, he's too frail. That thing you did to me with the pliers..." He shook his head, with an emphatic shudder. "Wait a few years, it's better."

"Aren't you even ashamed to talk about it, Third?"

Sutherland's voice sounded slow and cold. Guy was not surprised to see contempt in his eyes.

"Ashamed?" he asked, just as coldly. "Ashamed of what, Second... of the pleasure I felt while fucking a beautiful woman?"

Isabelle's smile softened; Guy was always the gentleman, after all. "Thank you, Third."

"You're welcome, sugar. But don't do those bad things to me again, please."

She laughed, and a look of understanding passed between them. Guy didn't regret the help he had given her that night, but it wouldn't happen again. They were too similar to really want each other. They had become friends instead, and that was kind of nice anyway.

Isabelle nodded to Sutherland. "What's wrong with him?" she whispered to Guy with a smile. "He looks like he swallowed a lemon."

"Swallowed? Someone has stuck it up his ass, more likely."

Their whispers were loud enough to be heard all over the room.

"You know, Third, I think he's jealous," Isabelle murmured. "I'm sorry, Second, honey," she said with an adorable twist of her lips, "but you must pay double if you want me to bang you as well. My price goes up for the weepiest clients. I can't stand the ones who whine like a little mouse when I burn their balls."

Sutherland's eyes narrowed. "I want to give you a piece of advice, Isabelle Smith," he said, breaking the rule that prohibited them from calling each other by their real names. "Try to never be alone in a room with me, not even by chance."

There was nothing playful about the promise in his eyes, and Guy felt uncomfortable. He squared his shoulders and opened his mouth to give him a warning, a not at all friendly one, but the Duke of St. Court anticipated him.

"All right, we can get started."

All of them straightened their postures, as soldiers on parade in front of a general. The First Knife joined them, completing their peculiar circle.

"Sorry for the delay," he began with his drawling voice, "but I had to think about some details. First of all, I must inform you we will not hunt Mr. Seabright and Sir Blakemoor tonight, and we will not split into two teams."

"Why the fuck not?" Paul stepped forward. "What Luke and Josephine Goddard are, shit? For fuck's sake, they're just kids, and they suffered such..."

The First Knife raised his hand to stop him from speaking. "We will catch Seabright tomorrow night, Fifth Knife. He will pay dearly for what he had done to those kids."

"What if he buys other children in the meantime?"

"If there is any time left, we will take him tonight, but later. No," he halted Paul's protests with his raised hand, "there can be no objection. We have a priority. Mr. Trowbridge."

A small gasp of shock came from Isabelle's lips. Guy's heartbeat increased too. Nine people had organized the infamous St. Valentine's Massacre of Innocents three years ago. Nine souls as black as shit were guilty of having killed no less than 30 kids in only a night. The nine filthy men had become a target of the Gang of Knives since then. Finding them was not an easy task: after the Gang of Knives had killed three of them, the *Valentinos* had realized they were dead men walking and had gone into hiding. The K-Gang had found two of them anyway, one hiding in Constantinople, another one in Paris. It didn't matter how distant you were: when the Knives wanted you, they got you. The K-Gang had sent mercenaries to catch the two Valentinos. And then, the Knives had inflicted on them the punishment they deserved.

Four Valentinos were still alive.

Trowbridge was one of them.

"At last," Isabelle murmured. She straightened her posture, pulling the wig off her head and revealing her short, curly black hair. Any coquettish expression had disappeared from her face. Any light. Only granite-hard coldness remained in her eyes.

"Where is he, One?" Sutherland asked.

"He hides in a house in Philpot Lane."

"Has he come back to England?" Guy asked. "He's crazier than I thought."

"Tomorrow is 14th February," Stuart replied simply, and a sudden understanding struck Guy like a physical blow.

"Jesus Christ. He's going to repeat the massacre."

"I think so. That's why we have to catch him by tonight."

"And we must beat the names of this year's Valentinos out of him," Sutherland murmured. "Nine people, I would guess, like the last time."

"How are we going to catch him?" Guy asked.

"You and I will take care of it, Three. We're going to make a social call: Trowbridge won't refuse to meet us."

"We took Cringlewood this way just three months ago. If someone sees us with Trowbridge, we'll blow our cover."

"Nobody will tell anything about us. Dead men don't talk."

"Whoa, wait a moment. Do you want us to kill all the witnesses? How many servants are we talking about, Number One?"

"They're soldiers, not servants. Don't worry, Three, they know whom they're protecting."

They were pieces of shit then. Guy relaxed and didn't interrupt Stuart again. The Knives had happened to kill innocents people. Once, it happened to Guy too. It had been a mistake, but ghosts don't split hairs when they want to haunt your sleep with remorse.

The First Knife explained the plan he had delineated. He had received the news of Trowbridge's presence only an hour ago, but Stuart's analytical skills were amazing. He was the perfect field marshal. He gave the Knives any detail they needed for their mission: Five would guide the carriage, Four would play the madam of a brothel. Two would be "by chance" in that brothel.

"Is everything clear?" he asked.

The Knives nodded. Trowbridge had only a few hours left to live. This certainty was so beautiful. It expanded Guy's lungs, it made his head pulse—it made him thank God for having created him a murderer.

"Fine." Stuart took a step toward the box in the middle of the circle, reaching out to extract the number of one of them, the one who would throw the last knife. Before he could touch one of the five folded pieces of paper inside, a flying dagger got stuck in the box, piercing the red cardboard. Stuart looked up at the Knife who had thrown it.

It had been Isabelle.

"There will be no extraction, First Knife. Trowbridge is mine." Her cheap wig was on the floor, like a red stain on the dirty wooden boards. Suddenly, Isabelle seemed very young with her short hair. Any light had gone out from her green eyes.

"We are not here for personal vendettas, Four," the Duke said, straightening his back. "It's the first thing we told you when you joined the Gang of Knives."

"He's mine," Isabelle repeated. "You cannot take this away from me, Number One. You just *can't.*"

Three years ago, on Valentine's Day, Isabelle's daughter was four years old. She would be four years old forever.

Guy took a breath and put a hand to his forehead. "Let's leave Trowbridge to her, One," he said, knowing he was suggesting a rule violation. But if Isabelle hadn't the right to rip that filthy pig apart, who had this right then, in the whole crappy world?

"Exceptions lead to failure, Number Three," the First Knife replied calmly. "They undermine the organization, they make us weaker. This is why the procedure must remain the same. We need the extraction to be done."

"Trowbridge is the first Valentino we have found since I joined the Gang," Isabelle protested. Her face was pale under her makeup, in contrast to her red lips and black cloak. "Don't take this away from me, First Knife. Please. I need it. *Please.*" The dominatrix was imploring. The dominatrix was losing control.

Guy respected Stuart Cavendish. He understood him, he knew that everything the Gang of Knives was, it was because of him. The Duke was the founder and strategist of their brotherhood. His inflexible rules, his hierarchy, his exasperating rituals—all this stuff was necessary, for it helped the Knives understand each other with no words. But now Guy didn't know whether to laugh or scream in frustration. Holy shit, the procedure, really?

The organization?

"Why don't we take a vote on it?" he proposed with clenched teeth, keeping his voice in check as much as possible. A vein began to beat on the left side of his face. His jaw was tight, his fists closed hard.

Stuart drew his thumb and forefinger to the bridge of his nose and closed his eyes. "All right," he said after a few moments, opening his eyes. "All those who agree with the Third Knife, to change procedure for tonight only, allowing Four to throw the last knife without extraction," he looked at them one by one, "raise your hand. You, Four," he added apologetically, "can't vote."

It was obvious, for the vote concerned her. Isabelle could do one thing only. She could watch the other Knives as they decided if she had the right to murder the man who had raped, tortured, and killed her daughter.

Paul Bailey raised his hand, with a solemnity that made him look like an adult.

Isabelle met Guy's eyes, and he nodded. He understood how important revenge was in life. It was the meaning of life sometimes. He raised his hand.

First Knife's negative vote was predictable. Only the Second Knife remained; all eyes turned to him.

Sutherland shook his head, showing no emotion.

What a son of a bitch.

Isabelle lowered her head in bitter defeat. The vote had ended in a tie, but when this happened, the senior Knives' votes were decisive. In the Gang's hierarchy, First and Second were higher than Guy and Paul. They had won this vote.

"I'm sorry, Number Four," Stuart murmured, sympathetic but nevertheless inflexible. "If it makes you feel any better, and for what it's worth, just think of this: whatever the outcome of the draw is, you will see Trowbridge die. It's more than a lot of us can say."

He leaned over the box and removed the knife stuck sideways. A precise cut remained to disfigure the box; Stuart picked it up and shook it. He laid it on the ground and pulled a piece of paper from the inside. His hand trembled slightly as he unfolded it.

"Tonight's last knife," he said, "will be thrown by... Number Four."

* * *

The air outside the wooden shack was cold. A red glow illuminated the tip of Stuart's cigar; he was leaning against a tree near the entrance. Guy wrapped his cloak tighter around him. What a fucking cold night. It was still dark, but it was not long before dawn. Damn it. It had taken longer than expected to get the names from Trowbridge: all the Knives had questioned him, each Knife with his or her own methods. They weren't even sure Trowbridge had told them the truth. Anyway, his interrogation was over. Guy could smell the blood soaking his cloak and his gloves. He would take them off at the end of this long night. The Knives had still a task to do: they had to move Trowbridge's corpse to Albany Street, in front of the place where the St. Valentine's Massacre of Innocents occurred.

The problem was, Trowbridge wasn't a corpse yet, and it was getting fucking late.

All the executions took place in this shack. The vegetation hid it, and the surrounding area was marshy and unhealthy. The Knives could reach the shack with relative ease, through a secret passage that began from the Duke of St. Court's palace. The passage exit was just five hundred yards from here.

There was a faint light coming through the cracks of the boards nailed to the windows, but it didn't illuminate the trees and the weeds around. One could see just thin blades of light cutting the dense blackness of the February night. The three Knives outside didn't feel the need to light a torch. They remained in the dark, where not even the shy crescent moon, hidden behind the clouds, peeked through. Not even the stars. Only Stu's cigar was visible when he took a hit off it. It was the Duke's only vice, and he hardly allowed himself to smoke anyway. Drugs were forbidden in the K-Gang; tobacco was permitted. Stu's cigar had a strong but not unpleasant smell, like a fire made with green eucalyptus and mint branches.

Guy's breathing moistened his hood that, according to the rules, he was keeping lowered over his face. He felt warm droplets on his skin. The creaking of the vegetation was soft, muffled by a frosty mist. With his hands in his pockets, Guy could feel the slime of blood dripping from his gloves.

The shack's door opened, illuminating the outside. The Fifth Knife came out and closed the door behind him, making them plunge into the darkness again.

"Is it over?" Sutherland asked, leaning against the shack's wall. He was invisible in the darkness, and his voice seemed to come from nowhere.

"No," Paul Bailey said with a voice too deep for his still adolescent body. Harsh emotion stained his words. "She hasn't strangled him yet, she wants... to make him bleed to death."

"Well, she better get a fucking move on. If daybreak comes, we won't have the time to bring Trowbridge's body to Albany Street."

"For Christ's sake, Second," Paul snapped, "how can this be a job like any other to you? They killed her daughter. Can't you understand how she is feeling?"

"Understand her?" A slight laugh came from the darkness. "No, I *don't* understand her, Five, but I do understand something. Where do you think she was while the Valentinos kidnapped, raped, and murdered her daughter? She was screwing a client, that's where." The sound of a disgusted spit echoed in the night. "Do you know why she's in there? Do you know why she needs to see that scumbag die? Because her daughter's death was her fault, and hers only. Had she been a caring mother, it would never have happened. She's deluding herself. She thinks she can wash away her guilt, but you know what, you little shit? She can't."

Guy approached Sutherland. He slammed a fist against the shack, a few inches from where he had supposed Sutherland's face would be. He hit the wood, making a dent into the old rotten wall. Even if he had punched Sutherland's nose, he wouldn't have given a shit.

"Don't you ever dare repeat this bullshit to Four," Guy hissed close to Sutherland's face, "or I'll kill you, Second. You hear me?"

Sutherland didn't move or seem impressed by Guy's threat. He had probably heard Guy coming, and he would have been able to defend himself. He hadn't even tried. "What a fuss you're making, Third," he said mockingly. "Your emphasis is quite wasted upon a whore, don't you think?"

"A whore who happens to be *my friend,* you dickhead. To me, the shit coming from her ass is worth more than your life. If the First Knife didn't vouch for you, I'd say you're not better than the scumbag who's dying in there, and you know what, while we're on the subject? I wouldn't mind if you got the same treatment sooner or later. So—" he moved closer to him, touching Sutherland's hood with his own "—watch your mouth from now on."

"What a coincidence," said Sutherland in a tone both thoughtful and amused, "I think you're a dickhead too. As a matter of fact, I don't just think so. I know it."

Guy's palm grabbed Sutherland's throat, while his own neck began to prickle. "What the fuck do you mean?"

"I mean," Sutherland said, lowering his voice to a whisper only the two of them would hear, "that when a man blackmails his stepsister into sex with him, well, he falls fully within my definition of *dickhead.* So, Ashbourne," he grabbed his wrist, and Guy, stricken by his words, let Sutherland push his hand away, *"please,* don't tell *me* what is moral and what is not."

Guy felt the ground giving way under his feet. How had Sutherland found out about Jane? Oh, shit. Probably he'd done research on Guy, as he did on every Knife. He certainly did not lack money. And now he was hanging a Damocles' sword over Guy's head. If the Knives ever decided to rescue Jane from him...

Guy's heart rebelled at the idea. No, hell *no.* On July 1st, he would give her up, but now... now it would be easier to cut off his own arm. How could he explain to Second what Jane meant to him, why his blackmail was so right, so necessary?

"It's not what it looks like," he murmured.

Second laughed derisively. "Yeah, it never is, is it?"

The shack's door swung open, and Isabelle stared at them blankly. She had no wig; blood stained her face.

"He's dead," she said without emotion. "Let's go to Albany Street."

* * *

Jane opened her eyes. Behind her, a gentle mouth was kissing her nape. She didn't move, holding her breath. She was lying in her bed, on the right side. It wasn't her usual side. Had Guy made her turn? Was he aware of having woken her?

Maybe. He continued to kiss her, going down her spine.

She hadn't heard him come home. It was early morning, the light peeked through the open curtains already. Her breathing became fast as he reached her mid-back, where her spine naturally arched. One of his hands moved to the front of her body and softly squeezed her breasts.

She could no longer hold back her moans, the sensual desire that, for the unfair world's logic, Guy always aroused in her. Had he woken up before her?

Had he just come home?

"Ooooh..." she gasped, as he licked her back, returning upward to her neck.

"Good morning, sleepyhead."

"You... you're already... oh, Guy..."

With his hand, he descended inside her thighs, teasing and making her want more.

"God, how much I want to make love to you, Jane," he murmured in an ardent, almost desperate tone.

"Why don't... why don't you just do it?"

Guy let out a frustrated groan against her shoulder. "Because I'm a damn good boy, that's why."

He, a good boy...?

She couldn't think about these words right now, even if they were pretty strange on her master's lips. Guy turned her towards him, kissing her hungrily. He lowered his mouth to her neck, to her breasts; but he was in a hurry, in an almost anguished frenzy, and ran down to her sex. His lips danced over it, and he began to lick her all over, both angrily and tenderly. When he was this passionate, when he treated her like this, without cruelty, and sweetly, oh so sweetly, Jane found herself defenseless. He melted her down completely, in a way she didn't want to analyze. Because if she allowed herself to think about it, she should admit something she didn't want to admit, she would whisper something she desperately needed not to whisper. Something she was *already* whispering, for she couldn't hold these words back any longer, she simply couldn't, not anymore, not now that she was coming in his mouth with no shame, while extraordinary waves of pleasure lapped through her body with dense, wet contractions.

"Oh Guy, I... I love you... I love you."

28.

"Why are you watching them from afar? Why don't you get closer?"

"Beg your pardon?"

Stephen pointed to the children, sitting around the table in the common room of St. Mary Orphan Refuge. "The kids over there. I can see you'd like to be sitting next to Miss Hartwell."

Lady Susan shrugged. "You're mistaken. I don't feel comfortable with children."

Stephen remained silent. Perhaps he had brought up an unpleasant topic. Lady Susan, widow Viscountess Emerson, had no children; maybe thinking about that made her sad.

The room where they were had been repapered recently; Stephen could still smell the glue. The furniture was bright and new, shining with light colors. These were improvements made at Guy's expense. Well... at Jane's expense, actually. She was paying for each of these things. She was paying with her body, like a whore, and Stephen felt ashamed with guilt at the thought.

Two large sofas were placed at right angles to each other, against the walls at the back of the room. Three little children were sleeping on them. Actually, the three of them were sleeping on the same sofa; it was a curious habit, common to the younglings of the human race. A massive oval table stood at the center of the room; it could easily accommodate sixteen orphans. Nine orphans were already sitting there; five little boys and four little girls. Jane was sitting with them.

It was the second time Stephen, along with Susan, accompanied her to the orphanage. Today, just as it had happened two weeks ago, it surprised him to notice how this place transformed his best friend's victim. Jane didn't seem the same shy girl who never spoke at Ashbourne House. She was laughing cheerfully while teaching the older children to read and making the younger ones draw animals. Just a little earlier she had played with the kids, running after them around the room. Perhaps, in such moments, she could forget she was Guy's sex slave.

Stephen hoped so.

"Miss Hartwell is an absolute angel, don't you think so, Mr. Weymouth?"

"Yes, I do," he said. *Angel.* Guy called Jane like this from time to time, whether or not there were people around. "I can't say the same for the children around her."

Susan laughed. "You're referring to the kick Henry gave you a few moments ago, aren't you? But that's your fault, Mr. Weymouth. You shouldn't have been considerate to Jane. Helping her to take off her overcoat at the entrance was a big mistake. That kid is jealous of you."

"He's eight years old at most!"

"He's nine. Anyway, the deepest loves blossom at that age."

The deepest hates, too. How old was Guy, when he met Jane for the first time? Not even ten. Somewhat like that Henry kid, who looked sullen as he spelled out words with the other orphans. He had cobalt-blue eyes and fair hair, but a big purple burn on his left cheek sadly disfigured his otherwise beautiful face.

"The Earl of Ashbourne is going to secure a good marriage for his stepsister, isn't he?" Susan asked, drawing Stephen from his thoughts. And as usual, the habitual, painful twinge of guilt grabbed his stomach. Goddamn it. He should never have helped Guy in achieving his wicked plan. Never. He had been living at Ashbourne House for two months now, for Guy had decided Stephen was too spineless to live alone and had taken the house on Bolton Street away from him. During this time, Stephen had realized how much his friend dominated Jane Hartwell: totally. Frighteningly. Jane even seemed to *breathe* to the rhythm Guy wanted her to follow. It was enough that Guy cast a glance at her, and Jane blushed; another glance, and she ate what she had just refused from the waiter; another one, and a whispered *no* turned to a hasty *yes*. Poor sweet girl, she debased herself to please her pitiless master. Like the big bastard he was, Guy enjoyed her embarrassing submission with an arrogant, satisfied smile on his face.

"Yes, he is," Stephen replied with an effort. It was not a lie, not really, even though Guy would let Jane marry someone only after... well, *afterward.* Stephen blushed, but his shame was not enough to end his friendship with Guy. Stephen would stay loyal to his friend no matter what, and that sucked, and he knew it.

"Do you think there is a nobleman suitable for her? Someone who can truly appreciate her sweetness, I mean. It would be a shame if she became as cynical as we are."

Stephen looked at Susan sideways and chuckled. "As *we* are?" he repeated. "Come on, you're not cynical at all, Lady Susan. And neither am I, please believe me."

"Aren't we? I'm sorry to disagree... as for me, at least. I'm not talking about you. You're not disillusioned by what hides inside the high-ceiling buildings, I guess."

"High-ceiling buildings, that's nice. You know, I like this definition for the *ton.*"

"What did I just tell you? You're cynical, Mr. Weymouth."

Stephen raised his hands in surrender. "All right, I give up."

Was Lady Susan cynical, Stephen wondered? She had had an unhappy marriage. Perhaps she had been a romantic girl once, but years had brought her down to earth. The Peers of the Realm well knew her promiscuous behavior. Guy had fucked her too: Stephen had caught them in bed together at Ashbourne House once, but luckily Susan was sleeping, and she hadn't noticed him.

So you're telling me you're cynical, Lady Susan... I think you'd just like to be cynical.

Oh, that was so typical of Guy, Stephen thought in exasperation. Guy had brought home a woman who had been his mistress... and not for fucking her himself, of course not, he had asked her to seduce his *stepfather*. It was another of his friend's manipulative plots. Stephen wondered if Charles Hartwell had figured out his stepson's scheme. Stephen thought so, since Jane's father always managed to avoid Lady Susan.

"You know, Mr. Weymouth, judging from the way you're looking at Jane, I dare say you admire her a lot."

"Beg your pardon?"

"Oh, you know what I mean. Does the Earl think of you as a suitable husband for his stepsister?"

"Are you kidding? Ashbourne wants the best for her."

"Well, I think you're quite nice yourself. You are kind, young, good-looking. What more could one ask?"

"I'm also spineless," he added quietly. "You forgot to mention this, Lady Susan."

"Oh, but Mr. Weymouth..."

"No, please, there's no need to say something nice about me. I'm not fishing for compliments. It's just a fact."

Susan smiled. Shrugging, she gave up. "I won't try to contradict you if you don't want me to. But this makes it more difficult to understand. The Earl wishes her to marry well, yet the only man he placed near her is you."

This was a slippery slope. Stephen brought his hand to his forehead. "As far as I know," he replied cautiously, "it's Jane who is the one refusing to meet anyone. She never agrees to be introduced to the men who pay visits to Ashbourne House."

"That's true," Susan sighed. "And the Earl says nothing about that. Yet it would be important for Jane to change her attitude. Stephen Algernon Weymouth, may I speak bluntly?"

"You just said I'm a cynic. You're calling me by my terrible middle name. So yes, you may, of course."

Susan smiled. "Miss Hartwell is in love with the Earl of Ashbourne."

Stephen felt the ground shifting beneath his feet. "Where did you get that idea?"

"Haven't you noticed the way she looks at him?"

"With awe. How else? She's shy, and he's such a tyrant." *And he uses her body in every way, except one.* Susan didn't know this detail, and that was why she was so flagrantly mistaking the tension between Guy and Jane for love. But all Jane could feel for Guy was hatred, my goodness.

What else could it be?

"When the Earl disappeared for three days, in January," Susan said without emphasis, "Jane stopped eating at all. Probably she stopped sleeping as well."

Maybe she had hoped Guy was dead, Stephen supposed. "Well, he's her brother. She was just worried about him."

"He's just her *step*brother." Thoughtful, Susan looked at Jane who, at the table, was staining the nose of a child with some ink. "She needs to meet other men. *Decent* men," she added eloquently, "and I could use your help for this, Mr. Weymouth. I think you're a fine man."

"I don't believe it's a good idea to force her in meeting someone, if she is uncomfortable with that, Lady Susan."

"I don't want to force her. I just want her to take a look around. Her passion for the Earl is a predictable event, don't you think? It's predictable and *sad,* for he will never marry her. You and I know that for sure, don't we? Mr. Weymouth, Jane deserves to meet other men. Other types of love. She needs to be introduced to suitable, nice men. Am I supposed to take this task upon myself alone?"

Stephen sighed. Other types of love, had Susan said so? But it wasn't love, what Jane felt for Guy, Stephen was sure of that. Anyway, what could be the harm in introducing some admirers to her? As beautiful as she was, her success was guaranteed, and maybe she would regain a little confidence in herself.

"All right, I'll help you," he murmured. "Even if I'm not entirely sure it's a good idea." *In fact, it will be a remarkably bad idea, my dear Susan, if Guy happens to find it out.*

29.

Anyway, the deepest loves blossom at that age.

7 Courtnell Street, 9th April 1844. Afternoon.

Up in the attic of 7 Courtnell Street, a boy and a girl were sharing a kiss. It was the first kiss for both of them, but Guy wouldn't have admitted that even under torture. He hated being such a loser: not only had his classmates been kissing for years, but some of them had already had sex.

Guy hadn't, and it was his fault. He had never hit on girls, and the funny thing was, he could understand why only now. He had refused his classmates' sisters' advances. He had ignored the housemaids who smiled invitingly at him—and they were *everywhere,* for God's sake: both in his friends' mansions where he sometimes stayed as a guest, and even here, at Courtnell Street!

He had always avoided any romantic or sexual involvement. And the reason... the reason was clear, at last.

It was a beautiful reason.

He had waited for years just to seize the perfect moment, the perfect girl.

It lasted only an instant, and, in the following years, Guy would wonder why he remembered it as so dilated in his mind. The reality was that he put his lips to Jane's, and after a moment a shocked whisper coming from the doorway made him draw back. What his mind would reiterate like a mental torture, in the following years, was a sum of a thousand details: Jane and her lips slightly parted beneath his; her taste... of sugared almonds, and sweet tea with milk; her scent, her warmth; his own blood running madly through his veins, his belly contracted with emotion; and Jane's soft skin, and her round cheek cupped in his hand. And his heart, flapping everywhere, and her tongue, which he wanted to taste, and he knew how to do it, for some strange instinct, or perhaps because Jane tasted so good, God, so *good*...

"Oh, my God... no."

Guy jumped back. He immediately knew whose voice it was. The horrified whisper had come from the doorway, and he swallowed before turning to the door. Rona was standing there. She was motionless, with her tight bun and her black high-necked dress. She was staring at him and Jane, her eyes wide with panic. Her expression said that her worst fear had just become a reality.

And Guy hadn't heard her coming up the stairs. Completely in the rapture for Jane and the magic of this moment, confused by the fog in his mind and by the painful thought of his imminent departure from Courtnell Street, he hadn't heard the stairs creak, he hadn't heard his mother's footsteps, he hadn't noticed anything... anything but Jane.

"Mother," he murmured, raising his hands and stepping back, putting more space between himself and Jane. Then he didn't know what else to say. Mother, what? I'm not kissing her?

Jane hadn't turned toward the door. She was watching Guy with parted lips, her eyes wide open. She didn't seem aware of Rona's presence.

Lord, what a mess.

"Jane." Rona squared her shoulders, calling her stepdaughter softly. She didn't enter the room. "Jane?" she repeated since her stepdaughter seemed not to hear her.

Jane blinked, blushing suddenly. She turned to Rona. "We..." she muttered with a small flinch, as if only at that moment had she grasped the implications of her stepmother being there, in the middle of the doorway. "I just wanted... I mean, we..."

"She just wanted to wish me a nice trip," Guy said. His mother looked at him, and he felt uncomfortable. The look in Rona's eyes wasn't anger; it was shocked awareness for the oh-so-terrible thing that had just occurred.

Rona slowly looked away from him and turned to Jane. "Honey," she murmured, "could you go downstairs? Your father is looking for you."

"Rona, we just..."

"Go, Jane." Rona's tone was tired but very, very sweet. She moved to the side and motioned for her stepdaughter to come out. "I need to speak to your older brother alone."

Older brother. It was a simple definition—and such a cruel one.

"But we..."

"Go, Jane," Guy interrupted. It was useless to postpone the confrontation with his mother. It would happen sooner or later. "Go to your father."

Jane bit her lip. Trembling slightly, she reached the threshold. As she was next to Rona, she opened her mouth to speak again, but her stepmother shook her head and, placing her hands on Jane's shoulders, she led her into the corridor, escorting her downstairs, perhaps to ask Charles to watch her.

Guy hoped his mother would not come back. Maybe she'd decide to forget about this little incident, maybe she'd...

He heard her faltering steps on the stairs again, and sighed. After a moment, Rona appeared on the threshold and did something she had never done before. She moved one foot forward and entered the attic room, closing the door behind her.

Guy swallowed. His mother was facing him... alone? It was difficult for her to even *look* at him; if possible, over the years, the situation had worsened. The more he grew, the more his mother looked away from him. And now what? Would she cry? Would she threaten to kick him out? God, Guy hoped she would not make a scene for a simple kiss. To be fair, he had to admit that their kiss should have seemed... odd to Rona. Menacing, even. Guy was tall and had broad shoulders; his body was built of muscle on muscle, his strength and size grew day by day with tough boxing training— his special way of venting his energy and anger. As a matter of fact, he almost looked like a man; while Jane was thin and petite. She was just a little over five feet tall, and her face was still childish, the curves of her body nearly nonexistent. A tower leaning over a little flower, a giant eating a tiny girl—his mother must have seen something like that, and Guy could understand why her eyes were horrified.

What the hell had gotten into him, dammit?

Rona remained silent for a while, then her lower lip began to tremble. "Please," she whispered. "Please, don't hurt her. She's just a child."

"Mother, I really..."

"When your father raped me," Rona whispered, and her voice sounded desperate, "I wasn't even sixteen years old, Guy. The pain I felt... sometimes I still wake up screaming at night."

Guy's eyes widened at the mention of his father... and as he heard the awful truth behind his parents' marriage. He knew his mother had given birth to him at sixteen. Now he could understand why she had married so young, and why she had ended up with a husband with an evil reputation.

"Mother, I would never hurt Jane," he protested. He felt wounded. He took a step toward Rona with his hands raised and open. He needed her to know that she was wrong, that she had *always* been wrong, but the horror on her face grew, and Rona retreated to the door, as if she saw the terrible 3rd Earl of Ashbourne again.

Guy stopped. "Mother," he just called her.

"You... you have needs, Guy. Your father had them as well. Maybe you don't want to do any harm to Jane, not like he did to me, but..." she placed her hand over her eyes anxiously and said, "...but she's just a child, Guy, don't you understand that? Without even meaning to, you will take advantage of her. You were kissing her like a man kisses a woman... if the two of you had been alone, what would you have done to her?"

Nothing! I would have done nothing! He was about to shout these words, but then he remembered something. He remembered the weird emotion that, shortly before, had warmed his groin. He blanched and spun around, going to the window and turning his back on Rona.

God, he hadn't identified it when he was kissing Jane, but now he realized what that emotion was. If he lowered his eyes to his groin, he wouldn't see it anymore. But it had been there, hadn't it?

An erection had been there, dampened by his mother's entrance.

Oh God, no. He had never had sex, but he had masturbated in the last year. Because it was as his mother had just said, he needed it. Now, for the first time, he realized that Jane's face appeared in his thoughts sometimes, when he touched himself. Often. Always, God, always... and how could it be otherwise? He was always thinking of her. Only her face, nothing more than that, he wouldn't dare to imagine anything else, she was a little girl, a sweet, adorable little girl... But it was enough, because his penis swelled and then exploded, and white streams of sperm filled his handkerchief—and him with shame.

"Guy, you must stay away from her. Do you understand?"

Stay away from her? Guy had a dizzy spell and propped his hands against the window sill, touching the damp glass with his forehead. "Please, don't send me to Mr. Blackwood," he begged softly, swallowing his pride. Mr. Blackwood was Guy's legal guardian. He had been the best friend of his father; he had often accompanied the 3rd Earl of Ashbourne when hunting. Guy had been forced to go hunting with them too.

He shook his head to wipe these childhood memories away. He was no longer afraid of Gerard Blackwood, nor of anyone else in the world; but he didn't want to stay away from Jane, not until adulthood, in the name of God, he didn't want to. He *couldn't*.

"No, I... I'm not going to do it," his mother replied, her voice pained. "He... God, he's like your father. But..." A terrible hint of doubt stained Rona's words. "But Guy, Jane is in danger around you. You must satisfy your... your instincts... with some other woman. An *adult* woman. Jane knows nothing of life, you are almost a man, and this... this is not right."

I gave her just a kiss, a little kiss!

But that wasn't exactly true, though, was it? He was a liar, a lousy liar. He wanted her as a man wants a woman, and if they had been alone that afternoon, maybe he would have pushed her on his bed and... God, what would he have done to her?

Was he a monster like his father?

He bowed his head. He felt so defeated... so humiliated. He looked at his tight knuckles on the window. A few minutes ago, he had taken advantage of Jane, and it had been so easy. This frightened him the most: he hadn't realized how wrong his conduct had been; all had seemed so right to him. So natural.

The seduction of the devil.

"Guy, if you want money... you can ask me for all the money you want. If you need it to... to look for some... company. Female company. To... please, Guy. You must placate your needs elsewhere."

This was clear. Simple. He had been a stupid, stupid, *stupid* moron. What had he been thinking, by resisting his natural need to have sex? Why was he still a virgin? He had wanted to preserve himself for Jane—ha! Doing so, he had become a danger for her, and he hadn't even realized it. He had been like a bullet in a loaded gun.

He took a breath and straightened up, looking at the street outside. "Five pounds," he said.

"I'm sorry, what?"

"I need five pounds. I... I'm going to do what you just said, Mother. I'll no longer be a threat to the little one."

It was spring, but the road in front of him had no color. There was only pallid gray out there, and a persistent, annoying drizzle.

All right, then, he thought.

If this was the price to pay, Guy would pay it; and perhaps, he hoped while closing his eyes in panic, there would be no need to stay away from Jane. Good Lord, if he couldn't see her for years... that would drive him crazy.

A woman. He needed a woman. Meanwhile, he would wait for Jane to grow up, and then...

He squared his shoulders.

Then he'd marry her. Of course he'd marry her. For some reason, through some inexplicable bond, Jane had never abandoned him, despite his bad attitude, his sullen words, his sulky behavior. Not even his bad days had scared her, those terrible days when he remembered his father and a certain fawn in the woods—a beautiful, bleeding fawn in the woods.

Despite all the wrong that was in him, Jane... Jane loved him.

A veil of emotion clouded his eyes. Impatience and hope dampened his bitterness. Yes, hope—hope of a future with her. Only a few more years, he needed to wait for only a few years. On the 5th of November 1847, Guy would turn twenty-one. Jane would be sixteen, and Charles would let him marry her, even against Rona's wishes. Or Jane and Guy would elope, it didn't really matter. Only, it couldn't be right now. He had to wait. He *could* wait. And in the meantime, he would be content to just talk with her, to just look at her, without the risk of losing his head as had happened this afternoon.

He had to do one thing, just one thing, before seeing her again.

He threw his head back, closing his eyes as his stomach clenched.

Right now. He had to do it right now. He could no longer put it off.

His throat hurt, and it was absurd. Why on earth did he feel like crying? He was about to lose his virginity, and that was a good thing. And later... later he would be able to go to Jane and reassure her, with no danger of behaving like mad again; he would explain to her that it had been a mistake, their kiss, but she should not be afraid of him, because he would never hurt her.

Never.

30.

Her hands and knees on the floor. Her dignity—it no longer existed. As well as her clothes, which she had taken off quickly a few minutes ago, letting them drop on the floor. With impotent rage, Jane stared toward the desk. Guy was sitting there; he had turned his chair sideways, toward the window; with his legs stretched out in front of him, he was reading the newspaper.

He didn't even look at her.

She hated him. When she was herself, she hated him. As she did in moments like this. It was the greatest humiliation, staying on all fours waiting for a gesture from him.

She lowered her head and swallowed. She could not understand herself. She could not understand why licking his boots was still better than this indifference.

She could not understand why an awful *I love you* occasionally slid from her lips, treacherously, just when she was not in control of herself. She didn't love him, she hated him!

Do you understand me, Guy? I hate you!

He rustled the newspaper by turning the pages. While doing this, he gave her a brief look, and a smile came to his lips. "You're funny, you know that? You look like a puppy waiting for caresses."

Hit by this statement, Jane set her jaw. "I don't want your caresses," she replied harshly. Around her, the light coming through the large windows was bright, hugging everything in the study. This March day was clear, and the sky was free of clouds, although its blue color was still tinged with the pallor of winter. The cold, outside, was wintry as well; Guy's study, however, was warm. Even too much so for a dressed person; Guy always kept the fire lively to prevent Jane catching cold.

He was such a considerate master, wasn't he?

Jane clenched her fists on the floor.

Or simply, he preserved her health so he could use her without breaks.

"Don't lie to me, Jane," he said, amused. "Your adoration is something I find gratifying. After all—" he lifted the left corner of his mouth in a smile that often appeared in Jane's mind, at any time of the day "—every master dreams of possessing a devoted slave."

His words mortified her and, at the same time, his eyes watching her made her belly flutter. She hated him even more for that. No, no. He always humiliated her, he wanted her to kneel before him, he... he even ordered her to eat on the floor, good heavens!

"I don't adore you," she hissed angrily, "I hate you!"

Guy chuckled, returning his gaze to the newspaper. "You want to make me angry, don't you? Well, it's not working. I know why you say it—you'd rather be punished than ignored. All right, then. Come here." He said these words, full of emphatic condescension, still keeping his eyes on the newspaper. "Let's see if I can do something to send your pout away."

Jane swallowed. With anticipation in her whole body, she crawled toward him. The air of the room caressed her naked body, and between her legs, treacherously, her pussy began to moisten. Moving around the desk, Jane stopped in front of Guy's shiny black boots.

Holding the newspaper to the side with one hand, he leaned his torso forward towards her. He was wearing a white shirt and a dark gray waistcoat, with a fresh scent of Marseille soap mingling with starch. His elegant dark trousers fit perfectly his muscular legs.

He lifted his hand to Jane's head, stroking her hair in long, top to bottom.

"Here's your caress," he mocked her with a slight smile, "now you can stop looking at me in that imploring way."

He was so close, his lips just a few inches from her face. Jane couldn't help but stare at him, lost in his eyes. He had just compared her to a puppy, but she couldn't think clearly when his eyes met hers like this. Guy's hand moved slowly through her hair, and he was beautiful when he smiled, he really was. His eyes sparkled under his long dark lashes. That morning he had been so sweet to her when he had woken up, why couldn't he be like that even now? He had kissed her and had held her tight in his arms, had told her she was beautiful...

Guy withdrew his hand and opened the newspaper again. "You can go back to the door."

What?

Jane flushed with indignation. "I'm not imploring you," she snapped. "I'm here just because you forced me, otherwise..." She bit her lip, stopping herself just in time.

Guy lowered the newspaper, raising an eyebrow. "Otherwise, what?"

Jane lifted her chin. She was playing with fire, she knew it, but dear Lord, when he behaved like this, she lost control of herself. Simply.

"I can't tell you," she replied through gritted teeth, cursing the blackmail which prevented her from standing up and slapping him. "You'd get angry."

He smiled kind of tenderly, and remained silent for a few seconds, as if the sight before his eyes were very, very nice indeed.

"Today you can," he murmured softly. "I give you permission. Finish what you were saying, I won't punish you."

Jane swallowed and, looking up at him from beneath, she said in one breath: "I'd spit in your face, Guy Spencer, Earl of Ashbourne!"

Guy blinked. Then he laughed. Heartily, throwing back his head and with a full, hoarse sound. It wasn't the reaction Jane had expected from him and, definitely, it wasn't what she had hoped for. She wanted to make him mad! She wanted to hurt him, she...

"Oh, really," he said, still chuckling. "So you're telling me that, at this very moment, you'd rather not be here. And if I told you to suck my cock, you'd be disgusted, because you don't like the idea at all. Is that right?"

Ouch, ouch. Perhaps she'd better have kept her mouth shut and gone directly back to the door. There was a dangerous light in Guy's irises, but she didn't want to take back what she had just said. Risking a lot, she nodded. Her lungs burst and pushed against her ribs, fear mixing with the excitement for the challenge she was throwing to him.

Guy took the newspaper with his right hand, leaving it dangling on the side of the chair, and leaned toward her.

"I said you could speak, little Jane, but I didn't say you could lie to me."

"I'm not lying."

A piece of wood fell in the hearth, clanging against the fireplace's iron grate with a slight thud.

"Aren't you? Well, I can check it right now. Turn around, angel, let me see your beautiful ass."

Jane's breathing became more difficult. "It's not right! I had your permission to..."

"Now."

She startled. Guy still had the power to frighten her, even if he had never physically hurt her... not for real, at least. She moved on her hands and knees, turning around.

"Put your elbows on the floor. And spread your legs."

Oh God...

Anxious, not knowing what was on her master's mind, Jane rested her forehead on the carpet. Guy was behind her, looking at her... and he knew that sight very well, the damned devil, didn't he?

As his fingers touched the entrance of her vagina, Jane couldn't help but let out a sigh.

"You're wet."

Jane blushed. But his touch, and his words, excited her more, and the moisture between her legs thickened, revealing her pathetic bluff. She wanted him, yes. It was an absurd, sinful desire, but Lord forgive her, she craved his touch. She wanted him to caress her; she ached with the need to hold him tight... she looked at him as a shipwreck survivor looks at a passing vessel: when you are overboard, it doesn't really matter if the vessel is sailing under an enemy's flag, does it?

Guy's finger touched the sensitive bit of flesh between her sex lips, very lightly, so she couldn't accuse *that* of turning her on.

"More than wet... sodden, I would say," he murmured, amused. He stretched out his hand to her head and pulled her backward, catching her off guard.

Jane groaned and, seconding his moves, she sat on the ground.

Guy made her turn toward him, with her hair tight in his fist. "You're a liar, Jane Hartwell. You can't wait to give me a blowjob."

"I... I..."

"Admit it. And I'm warning you—don't lie again."

Intimidated, she swallowed. "Yes, it's..." *false, false!* "...true." No, they were just the words he wanted to hear, just that, just...

"Then beg me, you velvet tongue. Beg me to let you suck my cock."

"Guy, I..."

"Beg me, you liar. Get on your knees and tell me you want my cock in your mouth."

It's not true! It isn't!

He opened his legs to give her space; she, blushing with mortification, kneeled between his legs.

"Please..." she whispered. "Please, let me suck it, Guy."

He smiled and let her hair go. His hands went to the buttons of his trousers, unfastening them. After a moment his erection was free and majestic, waiting for a warm welcome. He took her hair in his hands and pulled her mouth down on his cock.

"If you insist, uh... angel..."

He had had a moment of difficulty in managing his voice as she had closed her lips sideways over his rod. The first contact always shook him.

Jane began to wet him with her saliva, then licked his glans, her tongue wrapping around it. Guy kept his left hand on her head. With the other, he lifted the newspaper and...

And he opened it again, with unbelievable gall!

Jane hardly kept herself from biting him. She tasted him, on the contrary, maybe because she wasn't allowed to do anything else, maybe because she just loved the hot aroma of his skin, the slightly salty flavor on the head of his penis, the slit from which, soon, his sperm would shoot out and fill her mouth.

She licked there with particular passion.

Guy didn't look at her. Not even once, the goddamn man, while she used her lips, tongue, hands on him, sucking him with the dedication of a slave. Jane knew he was enjoying *every* moment of it, because his penis couldn't pretend indifference. Still, she felt used, kneeling like that between his thighs, while he was reading the latest news and moved his hand to turn the page or absently give her a pat on her head.

Look at me, Guy... I'm here... here for you.

Only at the first spasms of orgasm did he finally put down the newspaper and grab her head with both hands.

"Here, Jane..." he murmured in a choked voice. "That's what you wanted so badly..."

He arched to push himself better in her mouth and filled it with his cum, watching her swallow every spurt through half-closed, satisfied eyes.

When she moved her mouth away, with a little sucking sound, he closed his eyes, with his head back, sprawled on the chair. Fully delighted.

Frustrated, Jane swallowed again, his taste in her mouth.

After a few minutes, Guy's hand stroked her head again. With languid movements, he sat more properly in his chair. He had a beatific smile on his face.

"Turn around," he ordered huskily. "And spread your legs wide open, little velvet tongue."

Her heart jumped into her throat. Blushing furiously, she obeyed. On all fours, she turned until her buttocks were right before Guy's eyes. Face down, she rested her elbows on the floor, touching the carpet with her forehead. She spread her legs, and when Guy's fingers brushed against the entrance of her sex, her humiliation was complete.

"Look at me, Jane."

She turned to him again. Her body was flushed with agonizing embarrassment, her shame was unbearable. She knew her pussy was wet, completely wet and hot with unstoppable arousal. And Guy knew that too; he had touched her damp flesh between her legs, and she could no longer deny it.

Guy smiled, his eyes shining with arrogant satisfaction. "Say 'thank you.' "

She lowered her eyes. "Thank you," she whispered.

"Good." He closed the fly of his trousers with expert gestures. "Now you can go. I'll see you tonight at dinner."

He smiled and took the newspaper, unfolding it in front of him. He went back to reading, without looking at her anymore, leaving her aroused and terribly, painfully dissatisfied.

31.

Jane walked toward the living room. As she reached the threshold, her eyes widened. She stepped back to the corridor. She couldn't back away farther—behind her was Lady Susan.

"You're not going to cut and run, are you, Miss Hartwell?"

Cut and run? Who, she? Jane turned to Susan, swallowing. "I'm... I'm not feeling well."

"Of course you're feeling well. Come on, come with me into the living room."

"Please, let me go back to my room."

"I'm afraid you can't," said Mr. Stephen Weymouth, appearing behind Susan. It was a full-blown conspiracy! "These young men are here for you, Miss Hartwell. And they don't bite—at least, last time I checked they don't. Besides, your stepbrother wishes you to meet some new people."

"Guy? Was it Guy who invited... does he want me to *meet* these men?"

Stephen gave her a kind look. "Of course," he replied in an as-matter-of-fact tone. "Ashbourne would appreciate if you talked with them. You won't disappoint him, will you?"

Jane, disappoint Guy? She always did everything he wanted! But... meet other men, was it really possible?

Jane's heart stopped in her chest. As cruel as a whip, some words he had said to her suddenly echoed in her mind.

I'm a damn good boy.

His meaning became as clear as daylight.

For another man... he was leaving her a virgin so she could marry another man. Jane turned to the room. Another man who maybe was in there. God, she thought; probably... probably yes—that was it.

Feeling dizzy, she put one hand on the wall to support herself.

"Miss Hartwell, they won't eat you," Susan said gently. "Meet them. Just for five minutes," she added softly. "And you won't even have to talk to them. I'll do the talking for you."

At a glance, Jane thought she saw three or four men in the light-blue living room. She felt like crying. Like dying. How could she say no? If Guy

226

had said so...

With her breath caught in her throat, she looked at Lady Susan and Mr. Weymouth.

Had Guy grown tired of her? But this morning he had been sweet with her, and Jane had done everything he had told her, everything... wasn't it enough?

The blood drained from her face; her hands became wet with cold sweat. No, *of course* it wasn't enough; he wanted to set her free. He was looking for a husband for her, just as he had promised at the beginning of their deal.

Good heavens, was that news... *good* news?

Good news, she repeated to herself. Good news.

With her jaw tightly clenched, barely breathing, she raised her chin and entered the room.

Good news. Good news...

* * *

As soon as he arrived at Ashbourne House, Guy felt his hands itching. He would have liked to say it was some kind of premonition, except it wasn't. The carriages parked in the stable yard, with their noble insignia and glossy finishes, were a more-than-obvious clue. One carriage was Linville's. Another one was Barrow's. The blue one with the dragon... whose was it? Carruthers's, perhaps. Shit. Today was a damned Tuesday. Did courtship calls take place on Tuesday?

He entered the house and headed for the smallest living room, the gold and light-blue one, which was Jane's favorite room. They could *not* call upon a young woman who hadn't been officially introduced to them, holy crap, even Guy knew that—and *he* surely had courted no bloody marriageable girls.

Who had allowed these scoundrels to get into his house?

He dismissed the valet approaching him and, without putting away either his walking stick or his overcoat, he reached the living room. Damned Hartwell's Perfumery and damned, stupid time it made him waste.

He went to the door and looked into the room. It was full of flowers.

And of men.

The seats on the couch by the fireplace were occupied; Jane was on the left side, with Linville alongside her and Smithers a bit farther. Barrow was in the armchair at the side, Carruthers had retrieved a chair and parked his useless ass on it and, opposite him, Susan was sitting in the twin armchair. Plus, of course, there was Stephen Weymouth, the most annoying and self-righteous man in the world. He was also about to be toothless, given that later Guy would punch him until he spat out all his teeth. The chair his friend was sitting on was too soft to break his head, but Guy would smash it against him just in case.

Sitting with her sewing work between her fingers, Jane was keeping her face down, occasionally glancing at David Linville. Guy immediately nicknamed him David Big-Asshole Linville. As a matter of fact, Linville was worse than an asshole; he was an actual *decent* fellow. He was the penniless younger son of Marquis John "Gamble" Linville. Penniless, yeah, but good-looking and charming. There was a mile-long line of heiresses willing to marry him—no, not just to *marry* him, these ladies would jump into the fire for him and his ridiculous blond hair. So, if he had come on a visit to Ashbourne House, it wasn't out of despair. The young man was curious about the 4th Earl of Ashbourne's mysterious stepsister. He could find a woman with a large dowry anywhere, but Jane Hartwell was only here. Fucking hell, surely he was already in love with her. Who wouldn't be?

"Ashbourne," said Linville, seeing him before anyone else. It wouldn't have been otherwise. Guy was looking at him in a murderous way, thinking about how sharp a blade had to be to cut through his neck like butter. "Where have you been hiding your lovely sister?"

Sister? *Sister?* Oh God, Linville wouldn't come out of here alive.

Jane raised her face and set her jaw in an expression Guy well knew. It was a mixture of hate, pain, mortification: she happened to have this kind of look now and then, for example, when she wanted to know if he saw any women other than her. When he was late at night, usually because of the Gang of Knives, she got jealous. Guy had never given her any explanation for being late, so her look had been sort of justified on those occasions. In fact, he had found it gratifying. He was quite pleased to see her that possessive.

But now...

Why the hell wasn't she happy to see him *now?*

A thought burned his gut and ran up along his body like bile. She was among flowers, among men—adoring, young, even *decent* men. There was no congenital assholery in them. Barrow, Smithers, Carruthers. Linville, oh yes, let's not forget the cherub with blond curled hair. He was the only nobleman Guy would pay a pound for, if that pound could save his life.

"Ashbourne?"

He took a breath. "Who..." *the fuck* "...allowed you to enter my house, Linville?"

Marquis Linville's son smiled. "Your attitude is as adorable as ever, I'm pleased to see."

"Oh, don't mind him," Stephen said.

Guy nailed his friend with his stormy eyes. *You are the one behind this display of beaus, aren't you?*

Stephen ignored him. "He's friendlier than usual," he told Linville. "He normally welcomes me by knocking my teeth out. So, what were you just telling Miss Hartwell?"

Linville shrugged and turned to Jane.

Had they just cut him off in his own home?

"Well," the damn cherub said, and it was immediately clear whom he was talking about, "he knocked them out, Miss Hartwell. Both of them. Oh, you should have seen him, fighting alone against these two sailors with arms like trunks." He put his hands in front of himself to better show how big the sailors' arms were. He kept his palms opposite each other, something like eight inches apart. Yet Jane's eyes didn't widen to hear Guy's exploits. She was pale. Her shoulders were stiff, like the pose of one who had eaten a broom for breakfast.

Why?

Didn't she want him to stay here?

Guy clenched his teeth. Maybe she dreamed of getting married quickly. Maybe she hoped to get rid of him. He thought back to the words she had said to him that very morning, when she was more vulnerable. She was climaxing, and she had said...

I love you, Guy.

He wasn't stupid. He knew that the words said during an orgasm have nothing to do with reality. Yet... yet Jane brightened every time he said a gentle word to her. When he cuddled her. Jesus, sometimes he even thought...

Do you want to get away, angel?

Do you want to get away from me?

"Why don't you tell her about when I knocked *you* out, Linville?" he said abruptly. He took off his hat and gave it to the servant who had followed him. He did the same with his overcoat.

The Blond Cherub put his hand to the back of his head and laughed. "That's a low blow, Ashbourne."

Guy tightened his fists. A man shouldn't be as good-looking as David Linville, come on, that was ridiculous. Linville's face looked like it was straight out of a picture by some effeminate Renaissance painter. He was simply... simply... oh, fuck. He was simply too much. Like the red and yellow flowers he had brought Jane. In the name of God, they hit like fists in the sobriety of the little living room. Unlike most of the rooms of Ashbourne House, this one had a somewhat bourgeois furnishing, with its cherrywood decor and light-blue velvet on the walls.

Jane had not turned to Guy. She was resolutely ignoring him. Raising her head and blushing as she acted with more audacity than usual, she stared at David the Asshole Cherub Linville.

"Now, all of you," muttered Barrow, whose bald head shone like a cannonball in the living room. "I already told you. These aren't things to be spoken of in front of the ladies."

And here's a reprimand with no hint of irony. Ah, Barrow. Guy supposed that he must have been complaining all the time, while the rest of the group ignored him. Barrow was polite, morally impeccable, undoubtedly boring. No one would notice him even in an empty room. And speaking of personality, there wasn't that much of it in the room. Apart from Guy and Stephen, only Linville could be considered an interesting fellow—well, if you liked gentle, nice fellows, of course. Smithers never spoke because his ears had the deplorable habit of burning red with shyness whenever a lady was near him. Carruthers, on the other hand, was chewing a biscuit. He was a good guy, and very overweight too. He wasn't shallow, no; he could express his opinions with great sensitivity. Even too much of it, Guy thought, but he could guess Jane wouldn't mind such an attitude. His problem was that a plate of food shut him up. He was eating almost without realizing it, with a distracted expression on his face. He didn't even seem to savor what he was putting in his mouth. It had to be an idea of Stephen's: he surely had made Carruthers sit by the buffet on purpose. Guy had to give his friend that: he was diabolically cunning. *You have put the diamond among ordinary pieces of glass, haven't you?*

Among these men, Linville had a troubling chance to impress Jane.

"Well said, Barrow," Stephen approved. He had every intention of crucifying Guy, it was clear. "Ashbourne," he said, narrowing his eyes eloquently, "we managed to keep Mr. Hartwell away from home, and only one thing is worse than having the lady's father around when you're calling on her. Having her brother."

Brother. How funny. Stephen wanted to piss him off, as if Guy weren't already dangerously close to losing his temper. "Are you kicking me out of my house?" he asked with forced calm as he approached the group.

"You aren't going to join us, my lord, are you?" Susan interjected with a chuckle. "It would be a shame, for we were finding out a lot about you. If you stay here, you'll intimidate these men. Nobody will reveal any more of your secrets."

"Hey, wait a minute," Linville protested, raising his hand. "A few moments ago, Ashbourne said he knocked me out. Now, you're saying he intimidates me. I don't think I'll impress Miss Hartwell that much, if this keeps up."

He looked at Jane and smiled. To Guy's total bewilderment, Jane smiled in response. "You're mistaken, my lord," she said in an almost audible voice. "You already did."

This seemed to impress Susan and Stephen no less than it had Guy; they all widened their eyes. That girl over there, the one who was the source of Guy's orgasms for two months now, had her jaw set tight, and Guy remembered when she had taken his notebooks and thrown them into the fire as a child.

She had the same expression now that she had worn back then.

"Well, Jane," he said coldly, stopping next to her. "I'm sorry to hear that, because the men calling on you will have to follow some rules from now on."

Carruthers choked on the cookie he was eating. Stephen patted him on the back, and Carruthers, alas, survived. He began to breathe normally again.

There was no room for Guy on the sofa. Since he couldn't sit next to his angel—his angel who, very soon, would pay dearly for how she was defying him—he took a chair and sit in it with a sigh.

"We weren't expecting you, Ash," Stephen insisted as if Guy could possibly fail to grasp the concept. His friend was on his right side and, as it happens, the right jab was one of Guy's best punches. What a nice coincidence. Guy wondered if it would be worth using it. Swinging his fist out at his friend's cheekbone, well, *that* would be pleasant.

"Yeah, I'm sure *you* weren't." *You sent me across town to keep me away from here, you fucking traitor.* But Stephen's plan hadn't worked. Guy had missed the appointment he had with some boring lavender merchants. He had sent Charles instead. It had been Charles's fault: his stepfather had started his usual, annoying "Let's Discuss Your Unhappy Childhood" talk, and Guy had done the only possible thing. He had come home to take his pleasure with Jane.

Good plan.

Except for Linville.

"Rules to follow, you said, Ashbourne?" Linville asked, pensively. "Ouch. I feel like I'm inside one of those Oriental tales... you know, the ones where the suitors must pass deadly tests before wooing the princess."

"Miss Hartwell is a princess indeed," Barrow said. "The most beautiful I've ever seen."

Guy rolled his eyes. How many laughable poems would Barrow write to Jane in the coming weeks?

Note to self: shoot Barrow.

He looked around the room. Smithers and Carruthers wouldn't speak, thank goodness. The other two men's vocal cords, unfortunately, would produce some tiresome sounds as the air vibrated them. Linville's words would be the most annoying.

Guy leaned back in his chair with a relaxed movement. "Deadly tests?" he asked casually. "Not at all, Linville. In fact, there is only one rule if you wish to call upon my stepsister. That is, you have to beat me in a boxing match. Simple as that. You can try it immediately if you like." He looked at all the men with narrowed eyes. "I have a very well-equipped gym in the west wing of the palace."

Three and a half months. Jane would belong to him for the next three and a half months yet. She had to remember she was his property. She had to remember *why* she was in his house. He had been too kind to her lately, and that was what happened when you didn't follow the plan.

Stick, carrot, and you won't think about anyone but me, Jane.

For three and a half months yet.

And after...

Guy shook off the thought. After, he would tire of her.

That was all.

Linville grinned. "And you just said those tests weren't deadly! Tell me, may we challenge you all together, or are we supposed to do it one at a time?"

"All together, if you like. And you can tie one of my arms behind my back."

"Yes, we already know you are a rock, Ash," said Stephen, his voice exasperated. "You needn't keep saying it. Anyway, you seem not to have considered that, if the rules are indeed these, the only one who can call on Miss Hartwell will be, well—myself."

Linville looked at him in amazement. "Did you best Ashbourne?"

"Sure I did. More than once."

Guy snorted, annoyed. "A *couple* of times. Out of hundreds, mind you. And just because he jumps like a ballerina." He looked at Linville shaking his head. "I mean, he makes me dizzy. That's fully comparable to a low blow."

"The best boxers move quickly," Stephen said. "You are big, strong—and slow."

"I'm not at all..."

"Could you teach me your technique, Weymouth?" Linville interrupted, with a smile which was asking for Guy's punch, oh, how much it was asking for it, right against those white teeth of his. "I would like to win a match against him. I'd really love to—" he looked at Jane gently "—return to Ashbourne House."

"I was told there was a party in here," interrupted a slow, drawling voice from the doorway.

Everyone turned toward the door.

Guy first.

Oh, *shit.*

Weymouth jumped up from his chair. "St. Court," he said with a troubled expression. "What are you doing here?"

His grace walked into the room. "I came to visit the Earl of Ashbourne. Aren't I allowed to see a friend, Mr. Weymouth?"

"I suppose you are," said Stephen, tensely, "but it just so happens I have invited *my* friends this afternoon, and you are not one of them." He turned to Guy with an explanatory light in his eyes. *Get him out of here or I'll rip your guts out.* "Ashbourne, you granted me the exclusive use of this room," he improvised. "If you are a man of your word, I find myself in the invidious position of asking you to lead your... *friend*... somewhere else."

Guy got up slowly. He and Stuart shared a grim reputation. The *ton* considered them both sadists, and this meant many believed there was some kind of link between them, even if Guy and the Duke rarely talked to each other in public.

"That's true, I'm a guest in this room," Guy said to the Duke. He tried to hide his tension, which had come about for a very different reason than Stephen's had. "A very unwelcome one, by the by. That's a bit humiliating for the master of the house, I dare say—but whatever, my word is my bond. And to be honest, I think the topics you would like to talk to me about aren't appropriate for the sensitivity of the ladies. In fact," he said, looking at the men present in the room with condescension, "they aren't appropriate for the sensitivity of these gentlemen, neither."

St. Court laughed languidly. "You will allow me to pay my respects to Lady Susan, won't you? I am a gentleman, after all." He got close to her and bent to kiss her hand. "Lady Susan, you are as comely as ever." He turned to Jane with an insistent look. "I've heard a lot about your beautiful stepsister," he murmured without taking his eyes off her, "but the reality exceeds any description. Would you do me the honor of introducing her?"

Was the Duke enjoying playing this cat-and-mouse game with Guy? Or was he doing all of this just to fool the people who were watching them?

"No, St. Court," Guy said between his teeth. "You know, I don't exactly like the idea of you as my stepsister's acquaintance. I'm sure you don't mind me saying that. As a matter of fact, I dare say it will fill you with pride."

St. Court gave a distant smile. "Oh, I don't know. Now that I saw this beautiful creature, I might even decide to settle down. No, please." He lifted his hands and took a step back. "There's no need for you to leave the room because of me. I'll talk to you another time. Stay with Mr. Weymouth and his... *friends*." Smiling, he bowed to Jane and Susan. "I'll get out of your hair now. It's been a pleasure, ladies. Gentlemen."

He went to the door. The visit had been brief. It was just a warning the Gang of Knives was giving Guy, before they discussed his case in an official K-Trial.

By the doorway, his grace turned to Guy one last time. *Yes, the Gang of Knives knows your secret, Number Three,* the Duke's eyes told him. *And if you hurt Jane Hartwell, we will sharpen our knives, with your name on them.*

32.

Entering Guy's empty study, Stephen Weymouth didn't look at the desk or the leather sofa. He headed directly for the hidden door on the left side of the room. The wood paneling camouflaged the small low door; he opened it, and a musty smell assaulted his nose. There were shelves of old books on the walls. There were no chairs, just two stools crammed with other books and yellowed papers. There were no windows, either.

Leaving the door ajar to let in some light—and some air, bloody hell, you couldn't breathe in here—Stephen made his way to the shelves on the right wall. He reached out to the dusty registers of 1835 and put them down on a stool. Guy was methodical: he loved the whiskey, and of all whiskey, he loved Macaulay's the most. Macaulay was a Scottish business associate of his, a very ordinary fellow apart from producing the best whiskey ever; and hidden behind the 1835 registers, there was a bottle of whiskey Macaulay distilled in 1835. Maybe Guy had chosen this hiding place because he thought it was a brilliant one. Yes, he probably did. Anyway, here was the bottle with the yellow-and-red label, aged sixteen years, with its gently peaty nectar.

Brilliant, are you, my friend?

Stephen grabbed the bottle. The liquor glowed behind the clear glass. Question: where can you find so special a blend apart from Ashbourne House? That's right, Mr. Weymouth—nowhere else. And even better, this was the last bottle Guy had left.

Anyway, keeping it in a place like this was kind of a sacrilege, between the smells of stale paper, ink, and dust. But Stephen didn't give a shit. He was used to drinking everything, he didn't even like whiskey. Macaulay's bottle was in his hands, that was true, but that was just because he wanted to piss Guy off. Guy had annoyed him beyond measure this afternoon. And here was another question: what was the deal between Charles Hartwell and Stephen Weymouth? Oh, yes... Jane's father should have kept Guy *away* from Ashbourne House! That had *so* not happened.

So, swallowing Guy's last bottle—well, half a bottle, Stephen estimated by swaying the whiskey before his eyes—swallowing this half-bottle would make him feel better. Guy didn't mind the servants drinking his liquor; in fact, he would mind if they *didn't*. "Alcohol is for men, lemonade is for ladies, and water is for pansy-asses," he was used to saying like the big beast he was. But this whiskey here, well, this was a different matter entirely. This was a limited selection: Macaulay sent to Guy just one bottle every three months, and Guy usually kept it for himself. He had offered it to Stephen a few days ago, though. And he hadn't hidden his... "storage system."

Big mistake, old bean. Stephen took off the cork and swigged out of the bottle. *You know what? I think you're going to running out of your favorite whiskey, at least until your next trip to Scotland.*

He lowered the bottle, his throat softly burning from the liquor. He reached toward the stool and threw down the papers covering it, then sat down on it heavily. He leaned against the shelves and raised the bottle, gulping down a long swig of liquid fire.

Three and a half months. There were three and a half months yet before Jane Hartwell was free. Stephen took a breath and shivered. The alcohol was warming his bones.

Oh God, poor sweet girl.

She had such beautiful golden eyes, such beautiful shining hair. As he thought about her, rage ran like acid inside him. Susan claimed that Jane was in love with Guy. Susan was wrong, of course. She was wrong, wasn't she?

Stephen swallowed.

Because if that wasn't the case, what a strange and painful kind of love it was. Jane wasn't happy; she looked constantly scared, constantly insecure. She always watched Guy with eyes as helpless as a kitten's in a downpour.

Love, was it?

God, Stephen hoped not, but this thought had settled in his hard head and was gnawing inside him like a parasite. He raised the bottle and took another sip; he had already consumed over a quarter of its contents. If only Jane found Guy revolting, oh, everything would be so much easier.

Guy... revolting?

Ha!

Stephen swayed the bottle in his hands. If only there were a way to have her disgusted with him. But there was none, holy shit...

A usual pain gripped his stomach. He rested the back of his head against a shelf and closed his eyes. The alcohol was flowing through his veins, taking away his restless desire for opium. And his thoughts too. He felt lulled into a suspended sensation. Sleep, yes. That would be a blessing. He didn't fight the sweet mood that the single malt had generated. If Guy found him there, well, so much the better... Stephen certainly wouldn't deny him a fistfight...

When he woke up a half-hour later, with the bottle still in his hands and his legs sprawled, he realized that his nap in the archive hadn't been a *blessing* at all. Because from the study, on the other side of the door, came low voices and sighs.

Stephen felt his hair stand up on the back of his neck.

Holy Jesus Christ, *no.*

That couldn't be.

That couldn't be happening.

33.

Except it was happening.

"Oh, that's... that's so good, little one..."

Guy's voice sounded low, hoarse, and dangerously close. He and Jane had to be on the sofa.

Oh, fuck.

Inside the archive, Stephen soundlessly placed the bottle on the floor and turned to the door. From the inch of space between the doorjamb and the door came some light, agitated breaths, along with sobs, perhaps.

Please, God, don't let Guy be too harsh on her today.

How long had Guy and Jane been there? And... how long would it take before Guy realized the archive door was *not* closed?

Fuck... fuck fuck fuck!

Stephen stood up slowly. The stool creaked.

Stay still, you idiot. If they haven't noticed the door ajar until now, they won't notice it at all.

But Stephen didn't know how long they had been in there. And if he could do something, anything, to not be seen, he had to try to. If Jane knew of his presence... God, she would die of shame.

He took a step toward the door, sweat beading on his forehead. Not only were his shoes as narrow as mousetraps, but they also made a rattling noise when he bent his toes.

Calm down.

He had to calm down.

"Let me feel your tongue, naughty girl..."

And Stephen's calm got fucked up. Tensely, he took another step forward and reached out for the door handle. Then he stopped, dumbstruck. He couldn't believe what he was seeing through the crack of the door. That bastard... that bastard had asked her to...

"There, see... you *love* it..." Guy's voice was charged with amused cynicism. "You shouldn't have complained so much..."

Stephen clenched his fists. For a moment, he thought of coming out from the archive and pummeling his best friend.

237

But what would that solve? It would only mortify Jane Hartwell, and terribly.

He swallowed, shocked.

They both had their backs to him. Guy was standing, wearing his shirt. His trousers were down to his ankles. Jane was on her knees, behind him.

Her hands were on his buttocks, her face buried between them. She was of a heavenly whiteness. Naked and soft. The line of her back perfect, her nape left exposed by her upswept hairstyle, and her ass was lovely, round, and high.

"Soak me with your saliva, yes, oh, yes... you're *so* good at it, Jane..."

Judging by her muffled sobs, she was soaking him not only with saliva.

With shame, anger, and embarrassment, Stephen tried to ignore the irrepressible erection which grew inside his trousers.

"Stick your tongue all... all the way up inside me... yes, just like that..."

How dare he order her such a thing? Even a prostitute would refuse. Stephen had shared women with Guy, he had seen him having sex on several occasions. His friend had never asked for something so... so... oh fuck, what the hell could Stephen call that request?

Outrageous, wicked?

But words weren't enough.

Stephen couldn't see his friend's expression—certainly not an ashamed one, the damn son of a bitch—but the rhythmic movement his friend was making with his arm was unmistakable: he was masturbating with the utmost impudence. Jane was cupping his buttocks in her palms; his ass was firm and muscular, and Guy's olive skin was in striking contrast to her white hands.

"That's so good, angel... oh, *yes,* I'm coming... I'm coming, *God..."*

Guy climaxed, throwing his head back. Stephen saw the white streams of his sperm hit the floor beyond the edge of the carpet.

Jane kept her face between his buttocks. The soft rustle of her tongue continued, diligently, and it took a few seconds before her master told her to stop.

"All right, angel. That's enough."

She pulled herself back, resting on her knees, sitting on her heels.

There was no noise in the room; in Stephen's ears, only the rumble of his own heart.

After a few moments, Guy turned to her. Stephen drew his face back. His blood ran wildly, ran where it should *not.* Overwhelmed with guilt, Stephen repressed the urge to touch himself.

"Don't cry, angel," said Guy. He sounded amused, how could he be so mean? "Now I'll let you sweeten your mouth. Lick the cum on the floor, Jane... clean it with your tongue."

His slave... she was his slave for real.

Of all the horrible thoughts Stephen had had since he had found out about Guy's blackmail—and he had had many horrible thoughts about it—he'd never thought that badly of his friend.

That. Lousy. Bastard.

Stephen heard a slight, damp sound. Before he realized it, he moved his head closer to the door again. Guy had pulled up his trousers and tucked his shirt into them; relaxed and satisfied, he had settled on the sofa with his body facing Jane's buttocks. She was on all fours, with her elbows on the ground. She sobbed softly. She kept her ass protruded in the air and her thighs tight together; her feet, resting on the carpet, had a small, graceful shape. Guy was sitting with his body turned three quarters, showing Stephen his profile.

Fucking dangerous.

Depraved.

Yet Stephen didn't have the strength to stop looking.

"Spread your legs."

"Please..." Jane sobbed. From behind, her round buttocks, prominently exposed upwards, concealed from Stephen's view her head bowed over the floor. And her tongue, which was licking Guy's sperm from it. "Please, enough..."

Guy slapped her right buttock, making a sharp noise. "Spread your legs," he repeated.

Sobbing, she obeyed, spreading her pink pussy and her naked buttocks wide open. That was indecent... shocking. Stephen took a deep breath. He was hypnotized, angry, he didn't know, only his cock had no doubt, and it stood erect with the same, scandalous desire Stephen blamed his friend for.

Don't watch; don't watch, don't watch don't...

"Now, that's a good girl."

Guy leaned his torso over her. He touched her buttocks, running his fingertips between them, up and down. He pushed his hand farther down, to her pussy, moving his fingers with a wicked and experienced pace. He was a master for *real*, diabolically perfect. Not only had he all the power over her, but he also used it to the fullest, with no scruples whatsoever. After a few minutes, the sound of his touch grew thick and wet, and Jane's breathing became heavier.

"Oh, Guy..." she gasped, defenseless under his hands, "Guy, please..."

"You're almost there, aren't you?" Guy withdrew his hand, and she groaned in frustration.

"What do you want, my angel?" He brought his hand between her legs again. "Do you want me to touch you?"

She pushed her pelvis against his hand. "Y-yes..."

"What a naughty, naughty girl..." Again, cruelly, he withdrew his hand.

The son of a bitch. Stephen understood Jane's agonizing situation;

excitement and shame; he could understand her very well, for he, too, was terribly excited, and he, too, was ashamed of himself.

"Are you licking the floor clean?"

"Yes..."

"Good." Guy pulled back his shoulders, relaxing into the back of the sofa. "Don't stop, then." He lifted his right foot and brought it between his victim's wide open legs.

"No, Guy..."

"Shhh..."

Guy was wearing an elegant, polished boot; he began moving it back and forth, pushing its tip between Jane's wet thighs. She sobbed, but she was too aroused to regain control of herself, and Guy had no mercy for her. He kept rubbing her pussy with the tip of his boot and with his ankle.

"You like it, don't you, Jane... you like it so much..." There was mockery in his tone, maddening, infuriating mockery. "But keep cleaning the floor... use your whole tongue to lap up and down. Duty comes first, doesn't it, little girl?"

The noise of his boot sliding over her most sensitive part came along with the sound of her agitated breathing, and with her tongue licking the floor clean. Being touched in such a demeaning way was making her feel pleasure, and that was more than cruel, that was... immoral.

But morality had nothing to do with Guy.

"Are you licking every drop, Jane?" he asked, increasing the rhythm of the movements of his foot back and forth, harder, faster.

"Y-yes... yes, G... Guy... Guy... oooh..." Jane arched, quivering. "Guy!" she cried out, shaken by a violent, humiliating orgasm.

Guy stopped his foot and placed it back to the carpet. Jane let her buttocks rest on her heels, exhausted, touching the floor with her forehead.

Wide-eyed, and almost without realizing it, Stephen had put his hand to the swollen fly of his trousers, brushing himself over the fabric.

Guy had made her come... he had *actually* made her come. What kind of absurd relationship did those two have?

"Good girl," Guy said softly, "you've cleaned everything."

The fire crackled in the hearth. Stephen tried not to breathe.

Was it true humiliation? Was it just a sex game between them?

What *the fuck* was that?

Guy waited a few minutes before speaking again, giving her time to recover from her climax. Then, he said something so ignoble Stephen almost let out a loud curse.

"Now you've soiled my boot."

I can't believe this. God, he can't ask her to...

"Turn around, little one."

Jane obeyed, looking up at Guy with eyes red from crying and fogged with pleasure. Guy stroked her cheek. "Clean your mess up," he murmured, pointing to his right boot.

"Guy, please... let me go now..."

"Just a little." With his hand, he pushed her head down. "Just to let you know who's the one in charge."

His voice was gentle, somewhat sorry. Jane bent her head and, with her eyes closed, began to lick the boot, wet with her own juices.

Guy caressed her head. "How obedient you are," he murmured. "I like you just this submissive, Jane." He buried his hand in her hair and lifted her face. "This little mouth of yours hangs out in very strange places, doesn't it?" he murmured, brushing her lips with his thumb. Jane tried to draw back, but Guy clenched his fist in a handful of her hair. "Don't lower your face. Don't close your eyes. Answer me."

Stephen was expecting the usual "yes" from her, but Jane clenched her teeth. "I'm not worth anything to you, am I?" she said, her voice swollen with heartache. And then she couldn't take it anymore; she bursts into tears. "I'm just a t-toy to... p... p... play with and then... then pass on to others..."

Guy raised his eyebrows. "Others? Not for the next few months, certainly. You are mine, and mine only."

"Then why," she said between sobs, "why did you invite those horrible men today?"

"I did *what?*"

"You... invited those men?" she repeated, but a flash of doubt shone in her eyes, and her sentence came out with a timid question mark at the end.

"Of course I didn't," Guy replied, amazed. "Next time I see them, I'll let the dogs loose."

Jane's eyes widened. And, much to Stephen's dismay, she seemed to light up. She put a hand under her nose, still sobbing, and looked at Guy with a dazed expression. "So you are mad at me... because I *met* them?"

"Well, I don't see why that's surprising. You're for my use only, and it's obvious that..."

"You did *not* want me to meet them, Guy?" she cut him off, her voice shaking. "You did *not* tell Mr. Weymouth I had to meet them?"

"Mr.... *who?* God, what a son of a..." Guy paused, his eyes lighting with fury. After a few seconds, his expression relaxed, just like that; it was so unexpected, so weird, Stephen couldn't understand what was happening. Why didn't he look angry anymore? "What a son of a bitch," Guy concluded slowly. "Angel, when I want you to do something, I give you the order myself," he said with sudden sweetness. "Really, just the fact you thought I let an idiot like Weymouth talk for *me*, well..." Guy smiled. "That deserves a serious spanking. Come and put yourself over my knee."

She got up shyly. On her face was an absurd expression of relief, despite the physical threat Guy had just uttered. Threat that Guy didn't put into action; he just grabbed Jane's hips, putting her on his lap.

"Is this why you punished me, then?" Jane asked snuggling against him, as if his chest were a cozy nest, as if he weren't the man who'd made her lick his ass a few minutes ago.

Punished. The word struck Stephen. Guy had humiliated her so badly... because of Linville and the other men Stephen had invited this afternoon? Oh, holy shit. It was a curse, a fucking curse: whatever Stephen Weymouth did, it ended up hurting Jane Hartwell.

"I didn't punish you. I just wanted to play a new game with you."

She bowed her head with a sob, hiding it against his neck. "I... I felt so bad, Guy!"

"Come on, don't overreact," he muttered, wrapping his arm around her and rocking her gently. "That can't have been so terrible, can it? I remember a couple of things you did to me..."

"No, I wasn't talking about... about what you told me to do *now,*" Jane interrupted him, shaking her head against the crook of his neck. "I was talking about what happened in the living room... I was with those men and... and Guy, I thought that *you—*" her voice cracked "—that you were choosing a husband for me."

"Don't you want me to choose a husband for you?"

Jane drew back. "Are you tired of having me here?"

Guy's lips curled. "Don't get your hopes up about that." He lifted his hand and followed the contour of her face with his index finger. "You're mine for the next months, and flirting with that brat Linville won't do you any good."

"I wasn't flirting with him, I was just..." she turned her head toward Guy's hand, kissing it gently and, much to Stephen's bewilderment, spontaneously, for God's sake, she was doing it *spontaneously;* "I was just mad at you."

"Mad at me? Jane, my little one, you *really* want that spanking, don't you?"

Incredibly, she giggled. The sound of her laughter was a bit hysterical, chipped with the thorns still gripping her throat. "So, don't you want me to go out with Lord Linville tomorrow? I've promised him I'll go for a ride in his carriage."

"Do you want to go?"

"No. Absolutely not." She clung to Guy, putting her hands on his shoulders. "I just want to be with you."

"Are you flirting again?"

"No, I... God, Guy, how can you not understand?" Her words blew sweet and barely perceptible against his neck. "I love you."

Stephen forgot to breathe.

Look what a mess you've made, Guy, you prick.

But when Guy spoke, his voice wasn't tense. Or worried. Or excited. It was amused.

"Five minutes ago you said you hated me."

"I..."

"Shhh, angel." He put his thumb to her lips, stopping her from speaking, and lowered his voice, making it soft and reassuring. "You feel like loving me now, and it's normal," he explained with a strange emotion in his voice. "It always happens after an orgasm."

Jane fell silent for a bit, then, biting her lower lip, she asked: "You too?"

"What?"

"Do you happen to love me too after an orgasm?"

Guy smiled. "You're trying to distract me, angel, but it won't work. I said I'd spank you, and I will. Lie over my lap and let me redden your beautiful little ass, you insolent girl."

Jane grimaced. Her face was still wet with tears, yet as she blinked, her golden eyes shone, and she seemed not a victim, but a siren, unaware of her sensuality and therefore more dangerous. Without getting up, she moved on Guy's legs, putting herself in a prone position, lying across his lap with her face toward the desk. Her butt was round and white, a delightful sight against the black cloth of Guy's trousers. She stretched her legs on the sofa and placed her hands on its armrest, turning her head toward Guy in fearful waiting.

He placed his right hand on her buttocks. "Now you have to be brave," he warned her in a low voice. He raised his palm and brought it down sharply on her pale skin.

The noise was stinging, and she groaned with pain.

Stephen closed his eyes and turned his back to the study, leaning his shoulders against the wall. He was shocked, yes, but also terribly excited. May the Lord have mercy on his soul...

"Who's the one person you must obey?"

Holy Jesus Christ. This was the longest afternoon of Stephen Weymouth's life.

"You... you are..."

Another slap, another prickling noise, stronger than the first. Jane gasped in pain. Why didn't she fight back, dammit? Why did she look happy to be treated like this?

Stephen swallowed hard. That was a strange question coming from the man with an aching erection pulsing between his legs, aroused by the shameful scene he had been spying upon...

"Will you remember that from now on?"

"Yes, Guy, I... I will..."

There was another slap, but the noise sounded softer. There was nothing of punishment anymore, it had become a role-playing game between them.

"Will you meet other men again?"

"No... never again..."

The slaps stopped, replaced by the sound of caresses, increasingly humid caresses—and Jane's sighs of pleasure. Guy was masturbating her again.

Stephen stared at the wall of the archive, full of shelves up to the ceiling. He put his hand on his erection, embarrassed and angry, pinching himself to calm down. From the adjacent room came a strangled, quivering cry; it was Jane's second orgasm, this time by her master's *hand*.

In the archive, the air was thick with dust. Stephen's sweat was wetting his clothes. God, he was ashamed of himself for witnessing how Jane had been punished. It took his breath away... or was it arousal, maybe?

Oh, shit.

He raised his head to the ceiling and closed his eyes. He hated himself for having spied on them, but he hadn't been able to...

How much longer would it take? What the hell were they still doing in there?

Don't watch don't watch don't watch don't...

But he did, inevitably, like the weak man he was. He moved his eye closer to the crack of the door. Jane had turned supine and Guy was lying over her. They had covered themselves with a blue blanket and, among the many things that had shocked Stephen Weymouth today, he saw the most shocking of all.

Guy was cupping Jane's face in his palms. And he was kissing her mouth gently... lovingly.

God, what a son of a bitch.

34.

Susan was walking along Piccadilly. It was almost dark, but it didn't matter, for she would be in a carriage for the ride home. The middle of March's wind was still wet with sleet and was whipping her face. She wrapped her overcoat tighter around her waist, moving aside to make way for a woman coming from the opposite direction. The woman was pushing a baby stroller; Susan didn't turn her gaze to the baby, not even when she heard the infant gurgling from the blankets.

A moment, and it was gone.

Susan hurried and turned down Bond Street, ignoring the people walking in the luxury street. This afternoon had been a palpable success, she thought. More than Susan had expected. The young men Stephen had informally invited at Ashbourne House were nice fellows indeed. Well, apart from that devilish Stuart Cavendish, the 6th Duke of St. Court. He had kind of worried Susan when he had looked at Jane. How strange: he was handsome, his face had something gentle, even boyish in it, yet his appearance was just a deception by nature. According to the rumors, his soul was utterly despicable. Ashbourne had asked St. Court to leave immediately, anyway. Whatever business the Earl shared with the sinister Duke, he certainly would not allow him to approach his stepsister.

St. Court hadn't been the only one admiring Jane. Lord Linville had looked enchanted by her. And Jane... why, she had even *encouraged* him. What had she told him? "You already impressed me" or something like that; luckily, when Jane had said so, Susan had already drunk her tea, or she would have choked on it. David Linville, as gorgeous as an angel and as seductive as a devil, had a good chance to charm her. Twenty-three years old, a sunny smile and a disarming lack of artifice, he hadn't been able to conceal his pleasure as he heard Jane's words—and concealing one's own feelings is something a young aristocrat should learn as a child.

A little pain gripped Susan's heart. Inside her, satisfaction mingled with frustration. She stepped aside to avoid a puddle and almost collided with an old woman walking in the opposite direction. Smiling in apology, she pulled the scarf tighter and continued along the bustling cobblestone street. Now she was alone, so no one would read into her. She could finally admit something to herself. Seeing those young men calling upon Miss Hartwell had satisfied her, but had also made her a little sad. The fact was... well, attractive suitors and colorful flowers—and even a poem, bless Barrow's heart!—were intended for girls like Jane. Not for Susan Emerson, not anymore. And even in her youth, she hadn't enjoyed that sort of stuff very much. Her family had had her betrothed to a man thirty years older than her. Lady Susan Bridgewood's fate differed from the one waiting for Miss Jane Hartwell. The Earl's stepsister, without a drop of blue blood in her veins, would soon become a diamond of the first water among the ton.

"Good evening," said a man coming from across the street. His accent was vulgar; and even talking to her like that was rude. The man did not seem to realize how improper it was. With two fingers, he touched his top hat, gazing at her with admiration.

Susan did not reply and kept walking. She wondered if the man had changed direction to follow her but, turning with feigned indifference towards the center of the road, she noticed he hadn't. Stupidly, she felt hurt.

God, how she hated to feel envy.

I'm sorry, Jane Hartwell.

That was why she felt like this, wasn't it? Because yesterday she had turned thirty-eight, and although she had told no one, she knew that no man would look at her the way David Linville had looked at Jane Hartwell two hours ago. Not anymore, anyway.

She shook her head and turned into Regent Street. She was happy for Jane, she really was. She wished Jane would get married soon. Susan's need to save her was silly, perhaps, but she couldn't bear to see that girl live under Ashbourne's oppressive shadow. It was too sad to accept.

Girl, you're only young once.

There was only one thing left to do: wait for Linville to call on Jane again. And possibly with the Earl out of the way. Things had changed a little after Ashbourne's arrival, but Jane had ignored him, and Susan could not deny it had been a welcome change in her attitude.

She avoided another puddle and clutched her overcoat more tightly around her. She had decided to walk to make her cheeks get some color. Or to delay the inevitable, maybe.

A sweet scent in the air, coming from a shop along the street, informed her she had reached her destination. She looked up at the shop's new sign; it used to be smaller a couple of months ago. And it had been more delicate too. Now it surely attracted customers' attention. It was red and violet, painted with white flowers and blue roses. Among these blazing decorations, the shop's name was still the same.

Hartwell's Flower.

Come on, Susan.

She sighed. What had Guy Spencer said while hiring her for this... *job?* "You're so charming, Lady Susan, he won't be able to resist you."

But your "charm" hasn't worked a bit so far, my dear, her mother's voice echoed in her mind. Lady Colette Bridgewood had been dead for seven years, but she still didn't leave her daughter alone. She dispensed her advice, and above all, she stabbed her daughter's self-esteem. *You better seduce Charles Hartwell quickly, unless you want to be replaced with a younger, more attractive woman.*

But maybe you can't wait to come back to Lord Emerson, can you?

A shiver ran through Susan's body as she thought of her filthy brother-in-law. After him, Charles Hartwell was a big step forward. Hartwell was a good-looking man, and middle age suited him. It gave depth to his bright, dark-green eyes, like a sort of pensive expression that intensified his gaze. It was true that, because of the injury to his leg, his posture was not straight; moreover, he was too thin; yet, in a difficult-to-explain manner, his calm presence filled the space. He seldom joined her and Jane in the light-blue living room for tea; on these rare occasions, he had always managed to say something interesting. His peculiar way of speaking was slow, pensive, and never hasty.

And Susan would have appreciated these qualities of his... if he weren't the damned hypocrite that, alas, he was!

Susan, stop it at once. Open your legs wide, and...

Oh, shut up, Mama. Susan had met all sorts of awful men, bad, selfish, even vicious men. But at least, they never pretended to be nice guys. Not like Charles Hartwell. How condescending he was with everyone, even with the Earl of Ashbourne. And his voice... it was low, warm.

Oh, Susan hated his voice.

You're so charming, Lady Susan, he won't be able to...

She took a deep breath. She hadn't even *tried* to seduce Charles Hartwell so far, but she couldn't afford to lose her job at Ashbourne House. It would be a disaster. Now it was time to put a stop to her aversion to Charles Hartwell.

Guy Spencer wanted her to seduce his stepfather, very well, she would. Everyone knew Lady Susan was wanton. She had had many lovers, both as a married woman and as a widow. So, what was she waiting for?

She lifted her chin and pushed open the door of the shop. The bell fixed to the frame rang gently.

* * *

Sitting at his office desk on Regent Street, Charles Hartwell thought that Guy "Rabid Dog" Spencer had done a great job with the perfume shop. Charles had gone back to work two days ago and had realized his debts were reduced by a third already. With the account book in front of him, he had a look at Stephen Weymouth's neat calligraphy. Well, Stephen had been the one keeping the shop's accounts. Guy wouldn't dirty his hands to the point of doing it himself, would he?

Charles leaned back against the chair. The new chairs were damn comfortable. Especially his: it was a red-leather padded chair as big as a throne; in front of his desk, there were two other chairs, but they were blue and *smaller*.

"Yours has to be larger and more comfortable, Mr. Hartwell," Guy had said when he had shown the new furniture to him. "You must make it clear who's the boss here."

'Who's the boss.' *And changing the furniture of my office without asking for my permission, what else does it make clear, Guy, my son?*

His stepson had refurbished the whole room. Even the wallpaper. Now it was a pale gray; two months ago, it had been light green. The inlaid desk chosen by Guy—or by someone on his behalf—was big and dark, and its legs seemed bed columns rather than office furniture. Two twin bookcases, on whose shelves were the account registers, were against the right wall. Guy had bought even a safe: in the back of the room, four feet high and almost as wide, with a door similar to a ship's. It was impenetrable, or it looked so. It contained a little cash and the formulas of some Hartwell's perfumes.

As if someone could ever steal them.

From the window of the first floor, where the office of his central shop was, the onset of the dark prevented him from seeing the buildings across the street. It was only five in the afternoon, but it was a cold, sharp March. Into his office, a cheerful fire was blazing. Downstairs, in the perfume shop, a salesman was selling perfumes from a catalog that had not been renewed for four years. And four years had passed since Charles had created his last perfume. He hadn't named it *Rona's Perfume*.

And that hurt. This regret hurt.

The years he had spent with Rona had passed between talk about business, theater, poetry, cooking; about Guy and the little affection his mother showed him, about Rona's excessive apprehension over Jane. Rona had always been a beautiful woman, but she had strongly tried to look ugly when Charles was around, in order to keep him at arm's length. She used to pluck her eyebrows almost to the point of eliminating them, she used to leave the little hair on her upper lip; but her tight bun, the imperfections on her face, could never hide her beauty. And every time, Charles couldn't help but compare Rona with his first wife. The blonde and generous Mary Jane used to spread her arms and legs to him with the utmost love; the cheerful and *ugly* Mary Jane would have liked so much to be beautiful for him... and she had been.

She had been beautiful in Charles's eyes.

This was a comparison Rona had never won, not even after one night eight years ago, when she had called him in terror because she had had a nightmare, and the lamp, which she always kept burning, had gone out; and Charles had run to her and hugged her tight; they hadn't made love, but they had slept in the same bed... and not long after that, Rona's hand had touched him, and they had had other nights, perhaps not as overwhelming, not as passionate as the ones he had spent with Mary Jane—but they had been tender anyway, so why hadn't it been enough for him?

This hurt. It hurt that Rona, bleeding in the overturned carriage, before dying had whispered an unexpected "I love you" to him, and he hadn't had the time to reply, to tell her the lie that would have made her happy. And she was dead now, and it was late, too late for everything.

What was left to him was an office furnished by his stepson, with tons of guilt instead of knick-knacks.

From the door came a mild knock. Charles turned to it in surprise. Come on, who needed him in here?

"Come in."

Unpredictably, from behind the door appeared the curvy figure of Lady Susan Emerson. Charles wouldn't have expected such a move on her part. The revulsion that woman felt for him had seemed much stronger than her zeal toward her... well, uh—her *mission*.

Charles stood up, leaning on his cane. It didn't ask him much effort. The daily exercise the doctors hired by Guy forced him into had given good results.

"Lady Susan," he said, moving towards her. "What an unexpected pleasure. Please, come in and have a seat."

Susan smiled. "It seems like paradise in here, compared to the cold outside."

The woman was wearing a heavy black overcoat, tight at her waist. It surely emphasized her generous curves. Her hat was dark, as befitted a widow. Its decorations of lilac flowers and fruits, however, were certainly a bit improper.

Are you dressed like this for me, Lady Susan? What an honor. "Please sit down," he said, pointing at one chair in front of his desk.

"Oh thanks. No," she said, stepping back as he tried to help her take off her coat. "I'll do it myself."

Her reluctance to be touched was annoying. *Come on, I won't eat you up, you little virgin.* He shrugged and went back to his chair behind the desk. He couldn't grasp what Susan's game was. She was supposed to seduce him, wasn't she? It had been clear during the first days of her arrival at Ashbourne House. Afterward, her behavior towards him had changed. Charles didn't give a damn about it, but he couldn't help but wonder what he had done to arouse her aversion; and he wondered if the desk between them would be enough to restrain such an aversion.

He sat down, while Susan placed her elegant overcoat on the chair to the left and sat down on the one to the right. The padded chair made a light *whissssbh,* and Susan frowned, looking at it for a moment.

Charles couldn't help a smile. "Guy chose them."

"Beg your pardon?"

"The chairs. Guy chose them. I find them slightly embarrassing for my guests, but then," he shrugged, "it wasn't up to me to decide. The money is his."

Susan gave a smile that didn't touch her eyes. "I'm sure he enjoys helping his stepfather."

"Oh, I'm sure of that too. He never minds when his ego can grow." He reached under the desk and rang the bell for a servant. "Would you like to have some tea with me, Lady Susan?"

"That would be lovely." She gave him a seductive smile. That was a good move: she had a beautiful mouth. Full smooth lips, lightly painted in pink. And white perfect teeth, as bright as pearls.

Charles didn't want to watch her mouth. "Is there a particular reason you came to visit me, Lady Susan?" he asked a little too abruptly.

"I just wanted to take a walk. Do you mind?"

Charles tried to smile. "Not at all."

A knock at the door interrupted them. "Come in."

Jasmine, the shop servant girl, appeared in the doorway. "Did you ring, Mr. Hartwell?"

"Yes. Would you prepare some tea for me and this lady?"

"Yes, sir." She bowed slightly and left the room.

Charles looked at Susan. "And then," he said with a hint of irony, "how is your mission progressing?"

Susan blushed under the rouge of her cheeks. "I'm sorry, what mission?"

Making her uncomfortable was fun, Charles decided. "The one you and Mr. Weymouth had hatched to have Jane meet young bachelors," he explained quietly. "What else?"

"Oh." Susan didn't relax as he had expected. "There was no mission," she said with excessive cheerfulness. "It was just..."

"A mission," Charles interrupted her, finding it amusing to be rude. He used to do it with Mary Jane too. And God, how angry she got those times. "Weymouth informed me. In fact, he asked me to keep my stepson away from Ashbourne House."

"Except you didn't."

Charles leaned his back against the chair. "I didn't even try."

"That surprises me enormously."

He smiled. *Come on, Susan. You shouldn't be this sarcastic to a man you're supposed to seduce.* "My aim was to find out if Guy really wants Jane to marry someone," he explained calmly. "You were present. What's your opinion about it?"

"I couldn't tell," she replied evasively. "He wasn't particularly friendly with the gentlemen calling on her, but then, the Earl is never particularly friendly."

"Did he kick them out?"

"He just threatened to crush their bones."

Charles smiled. "And Jane, how did she act? I guess she said nothing the entire time."

"You're wrong." Susan lifted her chin, and her eyes twinkled with a peevish challenge. "I'll tell you, she was quite animated."

"Seriously? Did she talk to any of the men?"

"She did, yes. So you see, Jane has every intention of getting married soon."

"Glad to hear that. But, if I may ask... when did she start talking? Before or after Guy entered the room?"

"What does it matter? He arrived almost..."

"Before or after?" he cut her off for the second time, with a total disregard for courtesy.

Susan pursed her lips into a thin line. Her expression was telling him she was feeling the urge to knee him where the sun never shines. "After," she admitted through gritted teeth.

"I'd have bet on it."

"What do you mean? I assure you, there was one young man, and Jane didn't dislike him at all."

"Indeed."

Susan could no longer conceal her irritation. "If you were there, you'd have noticed it yourself."

"Except you didn't want me to be there. Neither did you want Weymouth to tell me about it. Am I right?"

Susan smiled detachedly. "I think fathers and brothers should stay away from their daughters' and sisters' suitors. Men are possessive about female relatives."

A knock on the door prevented Charles from replying. "Come in," he said, and Jasmine entered with the tea-things. The tray was almost bigger than her, and she wasn't precisely small. It was trembling dangerously in her plump hands. Charles breathed a sigh of relief when she laid it on the desk. The tray was loaded with a fine assortment of pastries and bread and butter. The porcelain cups were shining new, with delicate blue doves painted on a white background.

Jasmine bowed slightly and, after glancing curiously at Susan, got out the room. Charles watched the confectionery in the tray. He recognized some sweets with a pang. Small, delicate flowers of puff pastry... they had been

Rona's favorite ones. Their flower shape was unmistakable. The French pastry shop on the corner with Conduit Street made that kind of *petit fours*. Did Guy know that? Had he told the servants to buy from that bakery? Or was it just a coincidence?

The interruption had given Susan the time to put a brand-new smile on her face. "As I was saying, Mr. Hartwell, Jane showed interest in a young man. The younger son of the Marquis Linville. He's a handsome gentleman, and he and Jane had a nice long chat. This means..."

"This means she was unhappy." Charles put one sugar in his tea and turned the teaspoon slowly in his teacup. "Unhappy enough to talk to this gentleman. She used to react like that even as a child when Guy ignored her. She tried to draw his attention in every way, sometimes with an audacity no one would expect from her."

"You can believe that if you want," Susan said with ill-concealed impatience. "But trust me, she never looked at the Earl of Ashbourne. She only had eyes for the young Lord Linville."

Charles reached for a *petit four* and took a bite. It was Rona's, indeed it was; a deep melancholy filled his chest. He put it down on his saucer.

"Let me tell you something, Lady Susan," he said wearily. "Once Jane threw a spoonful of mashed potatoes in Guy's face. She was ten years old. We were having lunch, but it was not a simple family lunch, it was a lunch with thirty guests. The largest one we ever gave at Courtnell Street. Guy's mother... maybe you knew her?"

"Only by sight. She was a beautiful woman."

Charles fell silent for a moment. "Beautiful, yes—she was, indeed," he murmured, and paused to recover control of his voice. "And unfair, sometimes," he continued softly. "As in that case. She blamed Guy for the mashed-potatoes affair. She said he had provoked Jane, she didn't know how, but she was *sure* he did; and then she consoled my daughter because obviously Jane must have been wronged badly to overreact that way. Guy didn't try to defend himself. He got up from the table and went to his room. Forfeiting the dessert, by the by, and believe me, it was a not-at-all small sacrifice for him. But you know what, Lady Susan? Guy hadn't provoked Jane. During that lunch, he had been gloomy and withdrawn— nothing unusual for my stepson. He was sitting at the table without saying a word, ignoring everyone. Jane included. But my daughter couldn't accept that. She could stoically endure if he teased her, if, say, Guy pinched her, that was all right, she never complained about any of this. But if he ignored her..." He shook his head with an affectionate smile. "In Jane's defense, I must say she admitted she was the only one to blame."

"And didn't Lady Ashbourne... oh, I'm sorry. Didn't Mrs. Hartwell believe her?"

"No." Charles smiled wistfully. "Jane was kind of a little devil to Guy."

"He calls her 'angel.'"

"What he says seldom clarifies what he really thinks."

"Do you think he might marry her?"

Charles looked up from the tea that was cooling down in his cup. He wasn't expecting such a direct question. "That's a possibility."

"He says he won't get married."

"He might change his mind."

"But he couldn't make Jane happy." Susan leaned towards Charles, forgetting all the precautions she usually adopted to seem younger. She stopped hiding her face behind her strawberry blonde curls and shortened the distance between herself and Charles, without thinking whether or not her wrinkles looked more evident. "The Earl is not a bad man, but he's... reserved. He pushes everyone away, he doesn't trust anyone. Communication, to him, means to give orders. You should know it, since he grew up in your home. He would completely dominate Jane. He already does. She looks at him in a way... come on, it's obvious. Your daughter needs a different man, Mr. Hartwell, a man who can give her more confidence in herself. Someone who can make her bloom."

"Yet, she seems to want nobody but him."

"Of course, because *you* let this happen. If you knew about your daughter's feelings towards her stepbrother... why did you move to Ashbourne House? Just for this?" She waved towards the redecorated office with her delicate hand. "Is the Earl's money worth Jane's happiness to you?"

A flash of understanding crossed Charles's mind. "That's why you dislike me, then," he exclaimed. "You think I'm selling my daughter for my own gain." He felt relieved. It was a sort of harsh, bitter relief. Once, as a child, he had found a metal box buried in a field, and he had tried to open it for three days. He had hammered, burned, pierced the damned box until he had succeeded. Alas, the box's contents were disgusting. Whatever it had been, it was so rotten and stinky, he couldn't even identify it. Maybe dead worms, maybe decomposed fishes. Their nauseating smell had made him sick; but having the box closed on his nightstand, without knowing what it was, had been worse. The relief he felt now was the same as it had been back then, when he had opened the box and had been released from his strange obsession.

Susan blinked, returning to herself. "Of course I like you," she replied quickly. "I mean, sorry... I took an improper liberty."

Charles wouldn't allow her to put on a mask of politeness again. "Is that what happened to you, Susan?" he asked quietly, calling her without her title. "Did your father push you into an unhappy marriage?"

Susan stood up at once. "Now I must go." She grabbed her overcoat and, laying it over her arm, headed for the door. "I'm sorry to have bothered you."

"Lady Susan."

She kept on walking.

"Susan."

The woman stopped and straightened her shoulders. A second later, she turned around to face him.

"It's already dark outside," Charles said. "You can't go on foot. I'll call the coachman, and he'll take you back home."

35.

That evening, dinner took place in silence. Four persons sat around the table, and each was silent for their own reasons, still immersed in this afternoon's events.

Susan thought how stupid she had behaved in Hartwell's office. Why had she thrown away all her chances to seduce him? At this point, she could only hope Charles wouldn't tell his stepson. Susan couldn't afford to lose this job. Ashbourne paid her a generous salary, but it wasn't enough to live off the interest. She had a hundred pounds left in her savings account, and this money would fly away in a moment. Afterward, one thing only could she do—return to Lord Emerson. Or find a protector, as an alternative. *No way!* screamed her mother's voice. *You would be labeled as a fallen woman, and my daughter can't be called a whore, this just can't happen. You want to sell yourself, you can do it, my darling... if you do it secretly. It's fine as long as nobody knows. Didn't you learn anything from me?*

Charles Hartwell's thoughts were different. Every so often, he glanced at Jane: his daughter was quiet, but there was a relaxed light on her face that made her look like a porcelain doll. God, she was beautiful. She even seemed happy, sneaking a peek at Guy now and then.

Was Charles selling her? Susan's words roared in his head. What an unbearable woman! But was she possibly right? This doubt made Charles curse her. Without Guy's help, Hartwell's Perfumery would fail. Charles could not let this happen, but because of *Jane,* not for his own gain. This sounded even to him like a thin justification, since if he were a good businessman, his company wouldn't have fallen to ruin. His physical and mental weakness after Rona's death had slowed him down—oh, it had slowed him down way too much.

But he wasn't asking for Rona's advice. He had respected his irrational, fragile, and sometimes cruel second wife, but now he was calling his strong *first* wife, his beloved Mary Jane, for help.

Mary Jane, you've always known what to do. Please, tell me what to do now.

"So, Weymouth isn't feeling well," said Guy, breaking the silence.

It was Susan the one who answered. "Yes, unfortunately. His valet said so."

Guy felt a surge of irritation. *Not feeling well* for Stephen Weymouth was a sign of trouble to come. "I see." He took a sip of wine. The dinner was almost over, and the problem was, he couldn't dare to stare at Jane. She was literally shining tonight. If her skin had that color after some sexual play, he wondered what color it would have if a man filled her *completely*.

Better not to think about that.

I love you, Guy.

He had led her step by step to this point. She ate out of his palm, and his blackmail had little to do with what Jane was willing to do for him. And yet, this afternoon Guy had doubted her devotion to him. He took another sip of Château Margaux and didn't even taste it. Why was he so stupid? The anxiety he had felt a few hours ago still bothered him. Come on, had he believed Jane was interested in Marquis Linville's son, seriously?

Guy had got his revenge. Period. Three and a half months in advance of what he had expected, but why had he been so mad at her this afternoon?

He put his napkin down on the table. "I'll go and see what's keeping Weymouth in bed," he said, standing up. "Maybe I can manage to make him feel worse."

He glanced at Jane before turning his back to the table. He wanted her more than ever. And the situation, he feared, would not improve. Unless he decided to fuck her *fully*, of course.

He took a breath as he climbed the stairs to Stephen's room. Because of his friend's interference, he had punished Jane heavily. His angel hadn't deserved it. But to be honest, Guy didn't feel much regret. All right, all right, he was a bastard, but God, how he had loved the way she had licked his ass... it had been an act of total submission on her part.

Jane hadn't seemed too upset by this, anyway, no matter how demeaning it had been. Her sadness was due to different reasons altogether.

Nevertheless, it was time to yell at his friend.

And hit him hard in the stomach.

* * *

With his arm dangling out of the bed, Stephen Weymouth let the empty bottle fall from his hand. He heard it roll away.

The hell with it.

Jesus, everything was spinning around him. High-quality whiskey or not, it always made him nauseous. When he had sneaked away from the study of the bastard who, incidentally, was also his best friend, he was feeling like shit. Not even a "therapeutic" hangover had ever affected him like this. And he had thought: since things are this bad, why not make them worse?

Guy and Jane had left the office before Stephen, separately. Luckily, they had been late for dinner, and in their hurry they hadn't noticed the archive door ajar.

Luckily—ha!

How damned *lucky* he had been, hadn't he? Holy Jesus Christ, what an infernal mess. Stephen could still see Guy and Jane's sex games in his mind. And, more than Jane's extreme humiliation, it was the memory of Guy kissing and cuddling her that had shocked Stephen the most. They had been kissing and giggling under the blanket like teenagers.

Ash had never behaved like this before. He and Stephen had shared women more than once, because, come on, threesomes are always fun, aren't they? But, even on those occasions, Guy had remained distant, uninvolved, even too... *linear*. He was a pussy-lover, so he usually fucked the woman in her main hole, he took his pleasure, and gave her pleasure in return. That was all. He had never humiliated the women they had been with. And of course, he had never hugged or kissed them after their sexual intercourse. Stephen hadn't supposed that Guy could kiss the way he had kissed Jane, with such tender care; in fact, he had never seen *anyone* kiss so sweetly...

This was a disaster. Susan had said Jane was in love with Guy, but it was worse than that. That girl was nullifying herself for Guy.

The door opened without warning. Lying on his stomach, Stephen made no move nor opened his eyes. He knew who it was.

"Get up, you asshole."

He half-opened his eyes. "Go fuck yourself."

Guy noticed the bottle on the floor. He bent down and picked it up. "Macaulay's whiskey," he said, frowning. "You *really* are an asshole." He approached the bed and put the empty bottle on the nightstand. "You don't even like it, for God's sake. Since when can you tell the difference between good and bad whiskey?"

Stephen felt increasing nausea. He didn't know if it was because of his friend or the liquor. "Since never," he admitted in a thick voice. "But it made a difference to *you.*"

"Oh, I see—you're pissed at me." Guy picked up a seat by the small table on the left corner of the room, carried it to the side of bed, and sat down. "That's not exactly news. Instead of wasting this nectar from heaven, why didn't you come looking for me? You could kick my butt instead. Hell," he said, watching the empty bottle with regret, "had it been a bottle full of pee, you wouldn't even have noticed."

I should have come looking for you, you just said, my dear friend? While you were getting licked where the sun doesn't shine?

God, Stephen wanted never again to think about that. Acrid sweat covered his skin. He turned supine and breathed with his mouth open. Guy was used to seeing him weak, and it bothered Stephen an awful lot. He had emptied the bottle an hour and a half ago, and he had also vomited in the garden, but he couldn't hold his alcohol. So, if his mind reasoned quite

257

clearly, his body was like crap.

"May I ask you why?" Guy inquired with overplayed indifference. "Why you are pissed off and why you murdered this lovely whiskey, I mean. Is it because of the new moon?"

Oh, wasn't that a good question. *You know what, old bean? While you were "punishing" Jane, I was in the archive room spying on you.* He blushed with shame as he remembered his own massive erection. That was why he had drunk all the whiskey afterward. He couldn't allow himself to jerk off while thinking back to Jane's punishment.

"You came back home this afternoon," he said in a faint voice. He was afraid that if he spoke louder than this, he would vomit again.

"Yes, sometimes I do. You know, this happens to be my home."

"You got in Jane's beaus' way."

Guy raised his eyebrows. "Oh, is that a surprise to you? By the by, don't try it again, W. Until July, Jane is mine, and mine only."

"And then what, Ash? Will you throw her away like an old rag?"

"Please, not again!"

"Do you know what Linville and the others saw when you entered the living room? An asshole acting like a bully in his own house. Do you know what *I* saw? A small vein."

"A small *what?*"

"A small vein. It throbbed in your temple. Right here." He tapped on his own temple with his index finger.

"What the fuck does that..."

Stephen sat up suddenly, putting a hand over his own mouth. "Hand me the chamber pot."

"Do you want to empty it over my head?"

Stephen's face contorted with nausea. "Hurry up."

Guy followed his advice, and rightly so, because Stephen, leaning over the side of the bed, threw up the last drops of whiskey left inside his stomach.

"I hate my body," he muttered, wiping his mouth with the back of his hand.

Guy picked up the chamber pot and went to the door. Nobody would believe he was the Earl of Ashbourne if they could see him now. He opened the door, turning his head away from the stinking fluid, and put the chamber pot down on the corridor floor. He was an asshole but not a sissy. He closed the door with no retching whatsoever.

Stephen sat up, his legs hanging over the side of the bed. On the nightstand was a pitcher of water—never was water so welcome—and Stephen poured himself a glass.

"If you could hold your alcohol, you would also be an alcoholic, just the way you are a drug addict and an asshole," Guy said, going back to his chair and sitting down. "All in all, it's better this way."

Stephen put the glass on the nightstand. He had spilled a lot of water when filling the glass with it, and now a small pond was on the nightstand's wooden surface. "Let her go, Ash."

"Oh Jesus Christ, don't..."

"For fuck's sake, open your eyes! That girl is like a puppet in your hands!"

Guy moved nervously in his chair. When he spoke, his voice showed no sign of discomfort, anyway. "That was my purpose from the beginning."

Stephen thought back to this afternoon. Jane's sweetness, and her need for sweetness, were heartbreaking. "Then you have fully achieved it," he said, too bitter even to be angry. "You may let her go. Holy shit, don't you see? She won't be able to be herself again if you keep her with you any longer. After just two months, she is your shadow. Perhaps it's already too late."

"You're wrong." Guy jumped up and went to the window, turning his back on him. "She'll forget me in a minute. As she has always done." With one hand, he pulled the ocher velvet curtain to the side and looked out in the garden. "I'll let her go on July 1st, not before. I'm not a eunuch like you, by God." He let the curtain fall back into place and turned around with a belligerent expression. Yelling at Stephen was always his last resort. "You haven't got laid in how long... three, four months? Hell, sometimes I wonder if your cock still works."

Stephen ignored the offense to his masculinity. "Well, yours works, doesn't it, and that's the important thing," he said wearily. "And strictly speaking, you aren't having pussy either, or so you have sworn to me. Don't you miss it? You can have all the pussy you want. Here's what we'll do. Let's go to Betsy tonight. You'll fuck her from the front, I'll fuck her in the ass, or in her mouth, maybe. Would you like to?"

Betsy was the whore they used to share from time to time. Usually it was Stephen suggesting the threesome; but, even though Guy preferred to manage the, uh... *situation* alone, he seldom said no. That was typical of him: he considered Stephen too shy to fuck enough—enough for Stephen's health, obviously: that was the way Guy's mind worked—so he was always happy to cooperate. And after all, to Guy... well, a fuck was a fuck. Nice stuff, no matter how you looked at it.

Or what position you took.

But this time he shook his head. "Not tonight, W."

It was the answer Stephen had expected. He thought back to the times the two of them had shared Betsy, then thought of Jane, of her innocent eyes, of her adoration—not hate, for God's sake; not rebellion—for his friend. What a difference.

A dangerous difference.

"Not tonight? Then when, tomorrow? The day after tomorrow? In the name of God, Ashbourne, find a pussy to fuck and leave Jane alone. Don't you realize you've gone too far with her?"

A thought flashed in Guy's eyes. "Are you in love with her?"

"And if I say yes, what will you do, will you kill me? Holy shit, look at you. You're jealous of a scrap of a man like me."

"Jealous, am I? Christ, you're the best at bullshit."

"Aren't you jealous? Is that what you want me to believe?"

"I just want *revenge* on her. I don't want her to shine like a diamond among the *ton*. I don't want her to have beaus. And as for me not fucking other women, I have physical limitations as everyone else, how does that surprise you? I can't throw my load around. Jane is here to repay me. To... for Christ's sake, never mind, all right? Call me a bastard, a pig, whatever. But jealous... come on, this is ridiculous, even for you."

Stephen put his hand to his forehead. A throb of pain tightened around his temples. It was just revenge sex to Guy, that was all. It could not be otherwise; and to Jane... Stephen didn't know, maybe it was arousal, lust, momentary loss of her mental faculties, but it couldn't be love, for no woman could love a man who humiliated her so cruelly. Just sex, he repeated to himself. And setting Jane Hartwell free was more necessary than ever.

"If only I knew what that girl did to you," he whispered. "I would feel less shit about this, Ash."

Guy shrugged and turned away, heading for the door. "I'll tell you this, W. Next time you throw up a very rare whiskey," he reached the door and went out, "I'll pour it back down your throat."

36.

If only I knew what that girl did to you.

Courtnell Street, 9th April 1844. Afternoon.

Jane lifted her hand to her mouth and touched her lips.

Guy had kissed her.

"Jane."

She blinked. In front of her, Rona was pale and upset. Jane felt completely light-headed. She tried to look normal, she knew that her face had a dazed expression, but... Guy had kissed her!

And... on the lips!

He, who had never given her even a little kiss on her cheek, had put his lips to hers and...

She blushed violently.

He had also touched her tongue with his.

Her belly twitched with slight, unexpected pain, which seemed like fear. But no, it wasn't fear.

Maybe a little.

She wanted to run to Guy and... and at the same time she didn't know what to tell him! Perhaps she wouldn't be able to look at him. Everything had changed between them, hadn't it?

"Jane, what Guy did is wrong."

She looked up at Rona. A thin strand of dark-brown hair had escaped from her stepmother's tight bun and stood out against the pallor of her skin. Oh dear, she was distraught. Jane had to reassure her. Who knew how vehemently she had scolded Guy! Jane would have wanted to eavesdrop at the attic door, but Rona had brought her downstairs and *locked* her inside her room. Unbelievable! Anyway, whatever Rona had said to Guy, Jane wasn't worried. Rona had a strange relationship with her son, pretty much like the relationship between stinging nettle and human skin, but Guy didn't care. He was afraid of nothing, nothing discouraged him, he was the

261

strongest in the world, and... he had kissed her!

He *really* had kissed her!

Jane couldn't grasp the enormity of it. She felt stunned, and didn't understand what Rona, who had got into Jane's room half an hour after the misdeed, was saying.

Misdeed?

Guy had said he would miss her!

He had *kissed* her!

This was the best day of Jane Hartwell's life.

"You're just a child, darling, you understand? Guy is a lot older than you."

Jane frowned. "Only four and a half years... Papa is seven years older than you," she objected reasonably.

"You don't understand, Jane, you are still young for... for certain things."

Certain things? "It was just a little kiss," she murmured, "surely it's not a bad thing..."

Her cheeks were hot. What a pity Rona had walked in on them while they were sharing their first kiss! Had it been their second kiss, or their third... but their very *first* kiss, the one Jane would never forget! And instead of being with Guy right now, she was getting a lecture from her stepmother.

Guy, she thought. And she smiled, tilting her head to the side. *Guy, Guy, Guy...*

"It's not about the kiss, Jane, you don't understand. He... could hurt you."

"Hurt me with a kiss?"

Oh, it was really too much. Guy was wonderful, and he tasted so good—chocolate and biscuits and...

"I was the one who went to him," Jane managed to say, blinking out of her daydream. "Guy just said goodbye to me, he..." Surprisingly, she felt her throat swell, and she burst into tears. A strong emotion had caught her offguard. "He said he will miss me, and... and he had never said it before!" She sobbed foolishly, but she was happy... oh, so happy! She couldn't hold it in, her heart would burst with joy. The memory of Guy's flavor, his hand on her cheek; his sweet words and the heat in his voice. He had trembled against her body, as if he had lost, for once in his life, his imperturbability, the coolness that distinguished him from all others in the world. And his scent was so appealing, and his warmth, and the light illuminating the attic room, and his Eton lapel pin, which Jane had already locked in her treasure box, along with some of Guy's buttons, a lock of his hair that she had cut a year ago while he was sleeping, a page of his notebook where Guy, at Christmas, had made a small drawing of her...

"Black... too black," Rona muttered, so softly that Jane barely understood. "It was bound to happen..."

What was her stepmother babbling about? She seemed a bit crazy. Had Jane not been so happy, and overwhelmed by her own feelings and tears, maybe she would have been afraid of her.

Rona looked at her. "Jane, Guy wouldn't have been content with just one kiss." Her face stiffened, trying to control her anguish, and she put her hands on her stepdaughter's shoulders. "Honey, you're still a child. I'd have liked to have this talk within a few years, but... but I need to talk about this now. See, Jane, men... they want something from women. They..." Rona took a breath and paused. She didn't seem able to continue.

Jane frowned. "What does Guy want from me?"

If he wanted to kiss her again, Jane wanted that too—and very much. She had the good sense to keep this to herself. Rona was agitated beyond belief. In fact, Jane had never seen her stepmother and her father kissing, or hugging, or whatever. Jane felt sorry for Rona, but really, she couldn't think of her stepmother right now. Not for selfish reasons, but because Guy occupied every corner of her mind. Like a river breaking its banks: it cares for nothing and no one, it takes everything away.

"Not only from you, my darling," Rona murmured. "He has some... needs. All men have them. He wants..." She shuddered, closing her eyes. "He wants to get inside you."

"He what?"

"Guy is... he's different from you. Physically. He has... a... between his legs he has this sort of..." She opened his eyes, distressed. "You've never seen it, have you? He never took off his pants in front of you."

Jane blushed to the roots of her hair. "No! Of course not!"

Rona breathed again. Her chest rose and dropped hard for a minute, then she gathered the courage to speak again. "Men have... I mean, between their legs, they have a... this kind of... snake, Jane. This... *snake*... it wants to go in there." She pointed to her stepdaughter's groin, and Jane's eyes widened. Without thinking, she ran her hands over her skirt, as if hiding her intimate parts.

"Women don't like it when the snake gets inside of them," her stepmother went on, "because it hurts, Jane. You understand me? They allow their husbands to do that, because it's their duty, but... little girls can't. They mustn't do it. It would be very painful, God..." Rona began to cry softly, "very painful, honey."

Jane crumpled her skirt between her fingers. What was this nonsense Rona was telling her? But of course, Rona was always telling lies about Guy. When Jane was a little child, she used to say there were ghosts up in the attic. And she still said Guy was an evil boy, but that wasn't true, it wasn't, it wasn't!

"He would never hurt me!" Jane exclaimed. "He has always protected me, and... and he also saved my life once, he... he loves me!" *And he will miss me, he told me, he actually told me!*

"Guy doesn't love you!" Rona exploded, making Jane jump. "Otherwise he'd have never tried to seduce you! He's... he's like his father, his eyes are scary, don't you see? Tomorrow he's going back to boarding school," she added trying to soften the tone of her voice, for Jane had moved away from her, "and you should stay away from him, from now on. I know you secretly write to him: I want you to stop."

Jane clenched her jaw. She would never stop writing him. She needed to write him: sometimes she missed him so much she couldn't breathe. It was the only way she had to keep in touch with him, and he read the letters Jane sent him. She knew he did. He even kept them; once she had found some in a wooden box under his bed. She had always written to him, and she would keep doing it. Perhaps Guy would even reply to her now!

"No, I won't! I love him, I..." Jane got up from the bed, angry. "I want to marry him!"

"This will never happen." Rona also stood up, going close to her, and Jane moved to the wall. "Guy is an Earl, and noblemen don't marry bourgeois girls!"

"You were the daughter of a baronet, and you *did* marry my father!"

"Jane! My God, darling..." Rona lifted a hand to her eyes. She had stopped crying, but, rigid and motionless, seemed to stand just by some miracle. "I didn't want to do this to you, I swear I didn't, but you... God, you don't understand... you don't believe me. So... come with me, Jane." She swallowed, trembling, and held out her hand; her face looked drawn, her jaw set tight. "Come with me. You're telling me Guy loves you." She gave a laugh that was a desperate sob. "You're telling me he'll marry you. Very well, come see what Guy wants from you... what Guy wants from every woman!"

"No!" Jane squeezed against the wall. "I'm not going anywhere with you! I'm sick of your lies!"

"Please, I promise you." Rona took a small step towards her. "I promise you I'll let you decide for yourself what to do with him. All right? I won't get in your way anymore. But first you have to see something."

Jane angrily ran her hand across her wet cheeks. Rona was pale and seemed on the verge of passing out, but Jane didn't feel sorry for her. How could she say something like that about her only son?

"Promise me you won't speak ill of Guy again!"

"I promise you—but first you have to come with me, all right? Right now. Hurry up, honey..."

Jane didn't take the hand her stepmother was offering her. "All right," she muttered, sniffling. "You go ahead, I'll come behind you."

Rona moved quickly, despite her tremor. In fact, she was almost running. It was weird, because her stepmother always moved hesitantly. She guided Jane along the hallway and then down the stairs, heading for the kitchen.

"Where are we going?" Jane asked, running to keep up with her.

"I have to show you something. Just don't speak, Jane," she said at the corner before the pantry room. "Whatever happens, you must remain silent."

Rona led her around the corner. Only her stepmother had the pantry-door key, because there wasn't a housekeeper at Courtnell Street, they had just two maids and a cook as domestic staff. And yet, the door was ajar, not closed; and, what was even stranger, from inside the little room came some indecipherable sighs—moaning sounds, like the ones cubs in a den would make.

Rona swallowed and stepped aside. She put a hand on Jane's shoulder. "Look... look in there, honey," she whispered, very low. "Say nothing, just look. I know this will hurt you, but... it is necessary, Jane, my child."

An odd terror stopped Jane from moving. Rona pushed her gently towards the door, and she, with stiff legs, found herself in front of the pantry room. She didn't understand; she wanted to run away; she didn't want to look through the crack of the door.

Those sighs were strange. And there were slight noises of rustling cloth, along with wet sounds—like a kid jumping into the puddles, but this sound was different, this one was scary, it was somewhat more... dangerous?

A woman's voice, which sounded like Rona's maid, Sophie White, said: "Give it to me... good... like that. It feels good, doesn't it..."

Jane's hair stood up at the nape of her neck. And something magnetic, like a cruel force she couldn't explain, urged her to approach the door and look inside.

She didn't understand right away.

Guy was standing with his back to her. His trousers were at his ankles, his shirt covering the top half of his naked buttocks. He was between Sophie White's legs; she was leaning her back against the wall, with her skirt tucked up at her waist.

With one arm, she was encircling Guy's shoulders.

Will you miss me a bit, little one?

Jane looked at them with empty eyes, prey to a shock that was slowing her reactions. She thought, foolishly: *Sophie is old, she is over twenty already...*

Guy moved his pelvis back and forth, between the maid's legs, *inside* her.

Because I'll miss you, little one. I'll miss you like crazy.

Sophie's eyes were closed.

The snake.

Rona wasn't lying to her. Guy didn't love her, he had never loved her.

Guy just wanted... he...

Jane took a step back.

Behind her, Rona tried to touch her shoulder, but Jane pulled away from her and spun around. She ran away.

This was the worst day of Jane Hartwell's life.

37.

"Emma Jones, aged six."

Flying in the air, a knife stuck into the wooden floor, a short distance away from the head of a man tied on the ground with his mouth gagged. One inch more to the left, and the knife would have cut off his ear.

Guy took Stuart's place. The Duke had thrown the first knife. Standing in front of the man lying on the floor, Guy took aim. The man was naked, immobilized on a brown carpet. Between his fat legs, the color of the carpet was darker: the man had pissed himself in terror. The members of the Gang of Knives had tied his ankles and wrists apart with four strong ropes. They had attached the ropes to four posts at each corner of the carpet, so the man's body formed a cross of flabby flesh. He was squirming, but he couldn't move an inch.

"Louis Robertson, aged nine."

Guy threw the second knife, which stuck as if the carpet were butter, a few inches from the man's right ear.

"Agnes and Rory White."

Isabelle took Guy's place in front of the prisoner. She threw another knife at the man, sticking it a few inches from his left hip. The man sobbed, writhing desperately. Snot was oozing from his nostrils. He could barely breathe with his nose filled with mucus and his mouth gagged. Between his legs, his penis was small and flaccid. It looked like a pathetic rotten mollusk. There was nothing manly about it, but then, probably there had never been.

"Matthew Johnson."

Paul took Isabelle's place and launched the fourth knife, which stuck into the carpet just a few lines away from the right side of the man's body. The knife hadn't gone so close by chance. The boy was a master with the blade; sometimes he brushed the victim's body without cutting it.

"But you didn't know their names, did you?"

James Sutherland took over from Paul. He tossed his knife into the air, catching it by the handle as it fell.

"You just bought these children like they were pieces of meat from a slaughterhouse. Emma Jones died of the internal wounds you caused her;

267

the other kids perhaps will feel better with time. But they'll never forget."

Sutherland threw the knife up again and then caught it with a firm hand. Two fingers were missing from his hand, his ring and little fingers. The man tied on the ground was looking at the blade, following its path in terror, up and down, with his eyes.

It was up to Sutherland to throw the last knife, hence the need for the carpet under the victim: it would be a bloodbath, like every time Sutherland was the appointed executor of the death sentence. The carpet would absorb part of the blood, and cleaning up the shack would be easier—well, at least Guy and the other Knives wished so.

"You didn't know their names, but perhaps you've heard of us," Sutherland went on. Under the thick hood pulled down over his face, only the Second Knife's gray eyes were visible. "We're the Gang of Knives, and the papers talk a lot about us. They say we kill *good* people. They say we are anarchists, like some sort of rebels, you know. Revolutionaries. But you and I know the truth, don't we, Millfort?"

He knelt between the man's spread legs.

"We know you are *not* a good person."

He touched the man's flabby belly with the tip of his knife. Through the cracks in the wooden walls came a cold wind from outside, even though it was the first day of spring.

"Do you remember how Ingham looked when we left his corpse in front of your house two weeks ago?" Sutherland threw the knife near the edge of Millfort's left hand. "His hands were missing." He pulled another knife from his sleeve and threw it near the man's right foot. "His *feet* were missing." He took another knife, throwing it a few inches from the man's head. Millfort sobbed with dread. "His *eyes* were missing."

Sutherland put his elbow on his knee, pensively.

"His dick *wasn't* missing. He still had it, hadn't he? We had stuck it down his throat."

A new knife appeared from under his sleeve. Sutherland threw it into the air and caught it back with his three-fingered hand.

"But you know what?" he asked discursively, as if talking about a horse race. "Dying was kind of easy for Ingham. Maybe you're wondering why. Well, I'll tell you. It's because my brothers—" he motioned to the Knives around them "—are benevolent. Yes, usually the other members of the Gang just cut off the victim's dick." He reached out with the knife to touch the mollusk between Millfort's legs. "And then used it to suffocate them. Sometimes they kill the prisoners even before they castrate them. Their hands, their eyes... they cut them off *after* their death. Just for show, you know. A sort of warning to swines like you."

The knife flew upward again; in the shack, the hoods down over the Knives' faces muffled the sound of their breathing. Everything was still except for the wind; banging against the windows, it made the torches' red flames sway.

"But you've been unlucky," he continued in a tone of regret. Millfort would find out how ironic Sutherland's tone was very soon. "Because tonight it's up to me to use the last knife—and with *me*, it's not only for 'show.'" He took some long silk strings from his pocket. "These?" he asked, lifting them. "I need them to not let you bleed to death. I'll tie them around your upper arms. Around your thighs. I have a beautiful ax, you'll see it soon. You'll *feel* it, for when I cut your hands and feet off, you'll be alive. When I spoon your eyes out. When I castrate you. Then I'll shove your cock and balls down your throat—and you will remember those children's names." He lowered his voice with a strange, heartfelt sweetness. "*This time*, you will remember their names."

He got up, and his tone became professional. "Edmund Herbert Millfort, you are here because the Gang of Knives has tried you. We have found you guilty of raping five children, killing one of them. The Knives have condemned you to a Level One penalty." He paused, perhaps to smile icily under his hood. "That is a sentence of death."

Guy exhaled. He had been holding his breath without realizing it. Behind him, the door of the shack opened. It was Stuart, going outside. The First Knife never witnessed the executions, unless it was his turn to execute the condemned man. Maybe this was why he had invented the Last Knife Rule: there was no collective murder; there was only one murderer for one victim. This way, the Knives didn't have to always kill. Plus, they didn't even know *if* and *when* they would kill, because the executioner's name was drawn by lot. That was why the last-knife red box existed. The Knives could live their days without thinking about killing. They could avoid seeing their victims die if they didn't want to.

Paul Bailey stepped back to the door and slowly left. What a change this was from the way he had behaved during his first two months as a member of the K-Gang. Initially, Paul had witnessed all the murders, in a childish way to show his courage. He even used to smile at Guy with condescending superiority, for Guy rarely attended the executions.

Two Knives would get soaked with blood soon. Sutherland, who had to throw the last knife, and Isabelle, who always appreciated seeing a scumbag die. And courage had nothing to do with her choice; it was only the desolate, helpless confirmation of her huge weakness. Everyone has their ghosts, and everyone exorcizes them as they can. Even Paul Bailey had finally realized it.

Guy moved to the exit and, stepping out, closed the door behind himself. He lifted the hood up to the bridge of his nose, leaving the upper part of his face covered. He breathed deeply. Outside, the air didn't taste of rust, sweat, urine, and blood. It was crisp and fragrant, and the night was still cold, yes, but clear. Out there, it was possible not to think that behind the shack's door a man was dying.

He approached Paul and Stuart. They were resting their backs against the wall of the shack. The weak light of a lamp, placed at Stuart's feet, illuminated the new-moon night.

The First Knife was lighting a cigar. The flame of the match shone clear and strong.

Guy took a breath. "Is there something you wish to say to me, First Knife?"

The tip of the cigar turned bright red. Stuart had lifted the hood up to his nose, leaving the upper part of his face covered, as Guy had done. He blew the match out with a single breath, then inhaled a mouthful of smoke. "And you? Is there something you wish to say to me, Third Knife?"

"Yes, actually there is. Don't come to my house ever again, you asshole."

Stuart chuckled. It had been five days since the afternoon—the first and the only one, no doubt about that—when Jane's beaus had set foot in Ashbourne House.

"You know, Third," Stuart said, "Second proposed a Level Four penalty for you."

In the Gang's language, a Level Four meant a broken leg and a scar on a cheek. The former to damage the body, the latter as a reminder to the soul: *don't you ever blackmail innocent girls into sex again, you dickhead.*

Guy rubbed his forehead with the back of his nail. So the Knives had discussed his case. His stomach froze, contracting as if filled with ice water. "Nice of him," he said, waiting to hear their verdict.

"Yeah," Stuart replied calmly; "but the Gang needs you with both your legs working, I daresay. So I voted against him."

And that was a good start.

"I voted against him too," said Paul, who was standing on his right side.

Guy closed his eyes and let out the air he had been holding in his lungs. Even if Isabelle had voted in favor of Sutherland's proposal—and Guy didn't believe she had—Stuart's vote was decisive in case of a tie. Mathematics is not an opinion. Sutherland's proposal had been rejected.

Oh, thank you God.

After Stuart's visit to Ashbourne House, Guy had thought obsessively about it; it was like a whole mountain of rock resting on his chest. Had the Knives decided to free Jane from him, Guy would have had no way of opposing it. He knew the K-Gang's methods and organization. They'd have found him anywhere, even if he had fled with her to the ends of the Earth. God himself couldn't do better than the Knives, when they wanted to right a wrong; and that was a good thing—except of course when you were the one in the wrong.

270

"That won't stop me from kicking your ass, if that's what you're hoping for," he replied to Paul, flaunting scornful nonchalance. But he was relieved. No... he was *incredibly* relieved. Oh God, he was happy... so happy. Jane would stay with him; until June 30, with him. The sweet air got down into his lungs, the creaking in the night and the wind in the trees was like music from a harp hidden in the dark. God, what a wonderful, magnificent first night of spring.

"I didn't do it for that," Paul said, his voice indignant. "I... I think you're... oh, screw all of this. You're a good Knife, that is. And... fuck yes, you're a great man. When you aren't being an asshole." Probably he blushed as he said so. The more kicks you give them, the more they respect you, this was man-cubs' strange logic. "If you're acting like this, with her," Paul added softly, "you must have your good fucking reasons."

"Do you have your good reasons, Number Three?" Stuart intervened.

"Am I still on trial?"

"No, you're not."

"Good. Then you'll understand if I tell you to go fuck yourself."

Stuart laughed quietly. "All right, Third Knife. Whatever. But I'd like to find out what that girl did to you." He took a pull on his cigar. "And why you are taking this revenge on her."

38.

"Angel, I know you hate it when I read the paper." Hot and rough, Guy's hands cupped Jane's naked hips. "So this time *you* will read it instead."

Read *what?* Standing in front of the desk, without a shred of clothes on her and with Guy behind her, Jane doubted she understood. She breathed with difficulty, tensing with anticipation. What was he up to? On the desk's wooden surface there was the newspaper; and Guy put his hand on the back of her neck, pushing her down and forward.

"Rest your elbows on the desk," he ordered hoarsely, "take the newspaper and... read it, angel."

Eager to please him, Jane bent over and held the paper in her shaking hands, unfolding its pages. Guy's palms moved over her breasts, and she sighed. She adored how he touched her in that way of his, both firm and sweet. His hands were large, dry, and—

"So, Jane?"

What? Oh yes... the newspaper. But seriously? Did he expect her to read, while he was sliding a hand between her legs?

He pinched her left nipple, and she jumped.

"Come on, start reading."

Yes—he *really* expected her to. As his middle finger moved slowly between her sex lips, Jane read the first headline.

"It's... it's s-still..." She gasped. Guy gently pinched her breast, and she felt his penis, inside his trousers, pushing against her. "S-still un... unknown the identity of the body f... f... found in Brushfield Street..."

Guy's hand twitched on her breast. "No, I've already read this one, angel. Switch to another page."

Turning the page? It was so *not* an easy task. Luckily, he withdrew his hand from her legs to lower his own trousers. Jane turned the page, and after a moment she felt his penis, hot and hard, against her buttocks. She felt stupidly happy, and if someone had asked her why, she would have died of shame. God, she loved to be the cause of his wild erection.

Guy brought his hand to her intimate lips and began to rub his penis between her thighs, masturbating her with that.

"The Parlia...ment..." she read, and started to move her groin against his palm, rubbing like a kitten. "A... aaaah... approves the La...aaah...law. On taxes!"

His glans touched the entrance of her vagina and Jane leaned on the desk, opening her legs wide. She pushed herself against his penis in a clear request.

"Jane, little one," muttered Guy, "it's hard enough resisting your sweet pussy. Don't tempt me like that."

He sighed, frustrated. He moved his hand from her breast to her buttocks, preparing her anus with his fingers. First one, then two, while with another finger he was massaging the eager little knob between her thighs, soaking it into her wet arousal. Oh God, it was so good, she...

Jane jumped as he slapped her bottom.

"You're not reading, Jane."

She hated him, she decided, arching over the newspaper and opening herself to his caresses. She hated his need to humiliate her, to test her obedience.

"The... the Peers have..."

And she loved him.

When he was sweet. When he chuckled against her shoulder. When he didn't want to wake up in the morning.

And right now. She loved him completely right now.

Guy pushed the head of his penis into her anus, and Jane concentrated on his heat, on the way he filled her totally.

"A... approved by the majority..."

Guy stroked her wet vulva as he moved back and forth into her butt, between her tight walls. "Very... very good, Jane... but don't stop, keep... keep reading..."

While he enjoyed her body brazenly, Jane gasped the words of the article as she was told. Her sweat dripped on the paper, as well as her saliva and her lubricating sexual juices. She moaned and threw open her legs, arching to her master. Sometimes she was able to look lucidly at herself. Sometimes she tried to see herself with an outside eye. But then came Guy—and everything else disappeared. There was only him. And his hands, both in front of her body now, torturing her with pleasure, and his penis thrusting in time with his caresses. The words went up and down on the paper, while he drove into her, abusing her, against nature, against morality, and it was so beautiful Jane screamed, reaching her ecstasy over the neglected article on domestic policy. Guy filled her with his hot, thick... splendid seed.

Jane rested her cheek on the newspaper. Guy eased from her body, and she remained with her legs spread apart as Guy had taught her. She heard him sit on one of the chairs behind her. And she let him look at her as he pleased. She was happy even because of this—of his eyes looking at her shame, of him watching with satisfaction as his cum slid down her violated ass. She was happy to please him. And unhappy, because...

Why, Guy? Why won't you make love to me?

After a few minutes, a slight noise informed her that her master had gotten up. A soft piece of cloth, in a moment, was between her buttocks. Guy wiped her skin with his silk handkerchief, mildly and gently.

Jane opened her eyes as the delicate caress ended.

"You can straighten up, little one."

She obeyed and turned, finding herself a few inches from his body; her breasts almost touched him.

"You can go," he said, pointing at the door; he had a slight smile on his face, his features relaxed and beautiful. "Enough for today."

Jane didn't move, and Guy gave her a quizzical look.

"Well, angel? Did you hear me?"

Hesitantly, she put her hands on her breasts. "I..." She pursed her lower lip, as she had when, as a child, she was sad and displeased.

"What's the matter, Jane, my little one? Is there something you want to ask me?"

"Would you... would you hold me, maybe?" she let the words out, flaring with embarrassment. "Just for five minutes?"

* * *

It was an easy word to say, "no." Two letters, one syllable. He'd held her tight this morning. Last night. And yesterday afternoon.

Every fucking day, holy shit.

Today his defenses had collapsed again. His need for cuddling her had got its way. Sitting on the sofa with Jane on his knees, Guy repeated to himself he should have said a damn "no."

"I don't know if you deserve it," he muttered, wrapping his left arm around her waist. Jane was still naked, but he had covered her with a blue blanket over her shoulders. With his right hand, he stroked her head where it rested on his chest. "You read the paper so badly, angel. I understood almost nothing about that law in Parliament."

She giggled. "Guy..." she murmured, lifting her face to his. "Would you give me a kiss?"

He gave her a one-sided smile. "Beg me to," he said, "and maybe I will."

Jane shook her head. "I won't beg you for a kiss, a kiss should be, you know—a... a gift."

Guy grinned. "You're just the same as when you were a little girl, Jane. Remember? You used to manipulate me in any way. And in the end, I always did what you desired me to do. But now," he said, becoming serious and lowering his voice, "now you have to beg me. It's time that you *learned* to do it properly."

"It wouldn't be a real kiss if I beg you for it."

"Just do it, then, we'll see if you're right about this."

Jane lowered her face. "Guy..." she whispered, putting her face in the crook of his neck. "Do you still hate me?"

Wait a minute, he thought between amusement and exasperation. Where was her shy request? Wasn't she supposed to beg him? Oh, Jane, Jane... With a sigh, Guy decided to let it go, and answered her question.

"A little, angel. Just a little."

"Is that the reason why you torture me like this?"

"Like this? What do you mean?" He lifted his hand to her breast. "I torture you when I touch you here?" He moved his hand down to her stomach, then farther down, brushing the soft tangle of hair between her thighs. "Or maybe... here?"

"No," she murmured with a sigh. "You torture me because you haven't made love to me yet."

Guy stiffened, stopping his hand. "What you give me," he said slowly, "is enough as payment for..." *For having thrown me away.* "For your father's debt."

"What if it weren't a payment? What if it were a gift?"

Guy lifted her from his knees and, putting her on the sofa, stood up at once. Turning away, he went to the window, placing his hands on the frame.

"You don't know what you're saying."

"Why don't you take my virginity, Guy? You did everything to me... why not this? I..." Jane paused, summoning up every drop of her courage. "I *want* you to make love to me."

"You did everything to me," had she really said that?

"I did *nothing* to you," Guy hissed, clenching his jaw. "Nothing, you understand? You won't have any regrets when this is over. But if I take your virginity... Jane, do you *really* not understand what you're asking me?"

"I understand that you're leaving me a virgin for another man. That is it, isn't it? But there will be no one else, ever!" Her voice became shaky, swollen with pain; behind him, Jane was weeping her slow, heavy tears. "How can you think I'd ever do *it* with someone who isn't you? I'd rather lick your shoes than be worshiped by anyone else... how do you not see that?"

Guy didn't allow himself to look at her. He didn't allow himself to run to her, to cuddle her. Outside, the fresh April greenness covered the plants in the garden; and the lawn, with its new grass and flowers, was colorful with yellow, pink, red petals.

"In a few months, you'll be a free woman," he said in a tone devoid of expression. "And you'll change your mind."

"That's not true, how can you believe that!" Jane was angry as well as weeping. Her voice was broken, hard to understand; but still, it was so passionate that for a moment Guy flattered himself that he could believe her. Just for a moment.

"I know you won't get married," she murmured more calmly, when he neither replied nor looked back at her. "I'm not asking you this, Guy. Just don't send me away in July." She raised her voice, desolate. "Please, I'll never ask you for anything more than what you're already giving me. Don't... don't you want to keep me here? With you?"

Guy couldn't take it any longer. He turned to her. She was beautiful, disheveled under the blue blanket, with her legs tucked to her chest. She was sad, she was... golden. Her hair, her eyes... her magic, everything about her wanted to make him forget who he was, once again, as it had happened years ago.

"I love you, Guy."

Believe it, believe it. But she didn't love him, it was just part of her training, and Guy knew it. He had blackmailed her, he had trained her, he had taught her to obey and enjoy her rewards.

So what? asked a little voice inside him. It was a sweet, seductive voice. *You have the power to do it forever, Guy; you have the power to manipulate her forever. Just do it. Keep her with you.*

His lungs became swollen, his heart began to slam into his throat. "Do you want to be my slave forever, is that what you're telling me?"

Jane nodded, hugging the blue blanket as if she wanted to hug him. She would be content with so little... she would be content to be treated in a servile, demeaning manner for the rest of her life.

And why not, after all?

Guy leaned against the wall, struck by this sudden, shocking thought.

It *could* be forever. Guy was no longer a child begging for affection, he was a man who could get everything he wanted. There was a strategy for everything... even for this stupid thing called love; and he would make Jane happy, he knew he would, she would be happy with him—well, for most of her days, anyway. And in bed, he would give her a pleasure that no other man could ever match.

It was a perfect picture.

He closed his eyes and lulled himself with this illusion. He didn't want reality to come crashing back on him, he didn't want to know how much he was deluding himself.

Please, just for a moment. Let me believe it just for a moment.

But it was already there, wasn't it? It was already there, close to his heart: a tiny, bastard worm, gnawing his soul with sharp teeth, a worm that was making the picture *so not* perfect...

Guy swallowed. The worm inside him was eating, eating his soul and his heart, and he opened his eyes.

"Don't you want children, Jane?" he finally let out, even if this question swelled his throat like a mouthful of choked food. "Because I won't have any. Ever. Do you understand what you'd have to give up?"

Jane wiped the back of her hand under her nose. Before speaking, she cleared her throat. "I... I have the kids at the orphanage, Guy. They love me, and... I won't have children, anyway. Not after you, not without you. Do you think I could... with another man? After *this?*"

"Jane, you..." He paused because he was a damned coward. *Jane, you mean it now*, these were the words on the tip of his tongue. *But you're wrong, angel; for I trained you like a circus animal, and once I set you free, you'll change your mind.*

These words didn't come out.

He could say other words: false words, cruel lies filled with contempt, words that would push Jane away from him. *You're just a whore to me*, he could say. *You're nothing but a slut quick to spread her legs. All over London, I have ten other sluts like you who enjoy my cock.*

Even these words didn't come out from his mouth.

Could he keep her with him a little longer?

A year, maybe? Two years?

God, he wanted her forever.

"Jane," he said going back to the sofa. He stopped in front of her as she looked at him with big eyes full of hope. "Jane, let's not talk about this now."

"But..."

"Hey. When I give you an order, I want you to obey it. You are my slave, aren't you? You said you like to be." He pushed her to the side, making her lie on the sofa. He lay over her, with his forearm under her head, supporting his body with his elbow to not crush her. "And now, I want you to stop talking about this."

Jane pursed her lips. She was sweet and unhappy, and he knew what he should do. He should stand up, tell her to pack up her things.

Leave me Jane, leave me right now, forget me for good.

He should tell her she was just a bitch to him; tell her he had tired of her. Let her go back to Courtnell Street, and, in a few days, make her meet a decent man, a man who would ease her pain and would make her forget these months at Ashbourne House.

This thought gripped his guts. As God was his witness, he would let her go on July 1st, but not now. He couldn't let her go now. Three months, he had three months with her... only three months.

I swear to you, God, I'll let her go, but not now, and you won't blame me for this— you can't blame me, for you're the one who made me like this. It's your fault if I am this killer, this monster.

This aberration.

Yes. God owed him at least that.

"Don't cry," he whispered. "Everything's all right, angel. I'm pleased with you. So much, my little one."

"Then... why don't you want me to stay here?"

"Shhh." He stroked her cheek. "Let's not talk about it now."

"Another time, then?"

"Another time, all right," he lied. He cupped her face with his hands and leaned gently to her lips. Once again, he was the one giving in, he thought as he kissed her. It was always like this with Jane; a witch, she was a witch, a siren to him. After a moment, her mouth hesitantly answered his kiss. She was still hiccupping with sobs, but she *did* answer his kiss. She raised her hands and slipped them into the neck of his shirt. She pushed it down his shoulders, revealing his muscles under the whiteness of the fabric. Maybe Guy should stop her initiatives—he was the master here, wasn't he?—but the truth was that he loved when Jane, taking courage, did something he hadn't asked for, just out of her desire to do it.

"Sweet greedy girl," he whispered, kissing her neck. "Are you trying to turn me on again?"

"No, it's that... I'm n-naked..."

"Seriously? I hadn't noticed."

Jane pumped a light fist on his shoulder. "Come on, you know what I..." she sniffled, tears still staining her delicate voice, "...what I mean. I'd just l-like to feel your skin. May I?"

"You can do to me whatever you want, angel."

She undid the buttons of his shirt and pushed it down, slipping off the sleeves and leaving the lower part tucked into his trousers. Then she began to kiss his chest. His shoulders. She did it with sweetness.

She was an imprudent girl.

"Are you sure you don't want to turn me on?" Guy asked huskily.

"I just want..." she stopped because of the kiss he gave her, deep and long, on her mouth, "...to hold you tight for a few minutes," she concluded when they parted.

Guy smiled and moved to her side, lying next to her and pulling the blanket over them. "Come here, then. Hold me all you want, angel."

39.

I love you, Guy.

Courtnell Street, 1844. Night between 9th and 10th April.

Motionless in Rona's bed, Jane tried to contain her sobs. She didn't want to wake her stepmother. It was the first time she had slept in Rona's bed, but it was also the only place where Guy wouldn't look for her, if he wanted to talk to her.

Jane didn't want to talk to him.

Her stepmother had tried to console her after... after what they had seen in the pantry room, but Jane had moved to a side of the bed, saying nothing.

Guy, clinging to the housemaid. With his trousers down, moaning strange sounds and sighs. Jane had turned and fled in shock. He had noticed nothing. He was too busy with Sophie the maid, wasn't he?

Jane brought her hand to her mouth, touching her lips with her fingers.

I'll miss you, little one.

Rona's breathing was regular. Jane thought of Guy sleeping in the attic room. It was his last night there. Tomorrow he would return to Eton.

And she hated him.

40.

"You know, Guy? The kids were delighted with the gifts you sent to the orphanage."

Without opening his eyes, he ran his fingertips through Jane's soft hair. "Hmmm." Lying on his back on the bed, with Jane's naked breasts against his chest, he was enjoying the moments following his orgasm. His angel had learned to wake him gently...

"They always ask about you."

He didn't even try to answer; he inhaled her scent instead. Jane's hair tickled his chin, and the sensation was lovely.

"Why don't you come there with me today?"

A man like him, with his bad reputation, among little orphans... God, it was... really, only Jane could believe something like this were possible.

"Guy."

"Yes... I'm not sleeping," he mumbled. "Just five more minutes and I'll leave. I promise you."

"Guy, I'm trying to *talk* to you. Could you at least answer me?"

She kept her head on his chest, moving her fingertips over his belly and down the line of hair leading to his groin. Her pout surprised him. She had climaxed just a few minutes ago... wasn't it all that mattered?

"Do you seriously want to talk to me at *seven* in the morning?" he asked in disbelief. *And maybe, do you even think I can follow what you're saying, with my head blurred and your naked body touching mine?*

"Anytime would be good for me," she grumbled. "This afternoon, maybe. What about it?"

She raised her head and looked into his eyes. He just thought, *How beautiful you are after an orgasm, with your hair disheveled and lips swollen and cheeks flushed with pleasure.*

"I mean, couldn't we, just for once, just... have some tea together? And... have a little chat, maybe?"

He cleared his throat before speaking. "Having tea together," he murmured, passing his thumb across her lips. "With our clothes on, maybe? Well, that's not really my idea of fun, to put it mildly."

"We never talk, Guy. We do only... these things together."

She blushed as she said it, and he smiled. God, he had been using her body for four months now, and, to him, she seemed still as naïve as the first day.

"*Only* these things?" he asked, pulling her closer to him. "Watch your mouth, Jane, don't say what we do is something of an 'only' to you, otherwise..." he yawned and wrapped an arm around her shoulders "...I'll have to spank your little ass red."

"No, I mean..." She buried her face on his chest. "I'm just saying I'd also like to *talk* to you, Guy. I'd like to spend some time together just *talking.*"

"You have plenty of opportunities to talk to me. At dinner, for example. You never say a damn word."

"But the others are with us!" Jane exclaimed, astonished by his dullness. "And I'd like to ask you so many things... *personal* things," she remarked with a lovely grimace. "I don't know that much about you, I don't even know—" she put her hand on his left shoulder, touching the scar marking it "—how you got this scar or... or where you go when you come back home at dawn." She looked up, staring at him with fearful suspicion. A fit of silly jealousy was shining in her golden irises. Oh, come on. How could she believe he had time to fuck other women? "I'd like to understand you a bit more, that's all."

He smiled. *No, you better never understand me.* "Jane, angel," he said, bringing a hand to her cheek and lifting her chin with his thumb. "This afternoon, I want you naked in my study, on all fours, near the door. And you'll be docile and obedient as I taught you. Is that clear?"

Jane stiffened in a mixture of embarrassment and disappointment. If the evoked scene also aroused involuntary desire in her, her expression didn't show it. "Yes, as you like," she whispered, and tried to move to her side of the bed.

Guy held her by one arm. "Hey."

Jane's shoulders rose imperceptibly in her way of saying: It doesn't matter, I don't care anyway. I don't really want to talk to you.

I don't care about your lapel pin, I don't care if there's a lightning storm outside, I don't care if you don't say goodbye to me before you leave for Eton.

Guy smiled. Jane hadn't changed that much by growing up. "Listen," he murmured, yawning. "I'll come with you to your damn orphanage, if you let me keep my eyes closed five more minutes."

The words had escaped from his mouth, as much to his surprise as hers. Facing an argument at that hour of the morning was clearly beyond him, but... seriously? To an orphanage? And then what, maybe would he play the part of the nobleman with a heart of gold? For God's sake, Guy couldn't be a do-gooder out in the open. It was important to maintain his sadistic reputation, he couldn't risk it just because Jane had a pout on her face.

He opened his mouth to rectify what he just said; but his angel had drawn her head back and was looking at him with eyes wide open, in amazement and delight. All his objections stopped in his throat.

"Oh, the kids will go mad with joy!" she exclaimed, clapping her hands and twitching over him in a delightful tickle. "They always ask about you, they... oh, thank you, I... I love you so much, Guy!"

She leaned toward him and kissed his mouth. Guy slipped his hand to the back of her neck, softly responding to her initiative. He liked it when she clutched him this way, as if she could not live without him. When she told him she loved him.

God, he liked all of it. Way too much.

* * *

"Hey, kids. I have a surprise for you."

Jane pushed open the door and entered the common room, where the children, sitting around the table, were waiting for their teacher.

And their teacher was *late* today... but with her cheeks red with happiness, for she couldn't wait to show her "surprise" to them.

The children, and Mrs. Barnaby, raised their heads in expectation. Guy was still out of the room behind the corner; Lady Susan had entered, stopping by the wall and trying to blend herself with it.

"Have you brought us a cake?"

"Jane knows it's not Sunday," said Mrs. Barnaby severely, "so no cake, right, Jane?"

Well, as a matter of fact...

Jane grimaced and searched for the words to explain why this was a special occasion. A voice behind her saved her the embarrassment, making her almost cry with joy.

"I hope you will make an exception today, Mrs. Barnaby," said Guy with his aristocratic, authoritative inflection, which always messed Jane's heartbeat up. "Jane said the kids would be thrilled with me, but I was not so sure. Then a cake looked like a good idea, for preventing them from biting me instead."

Jane turned to him. And it happened as usual: she stared at him as if he were an apparition. She couldn't get used to him. Day by day, his body, his face, his presence seemed more and more beautiful to her. His black hair, his V-shaped hairline. His dark eyes. His nose slightly crooked in the middle, his sculpted body...

Guy gave her a half-smile and doffed his top hat in an elegant bow, with the walking stick clutched in his hand. He was dressed in black. Jane had suggested that he could wear another color—"what about brown?"—but he had glanced at her with his "I'll Spank You for Your Impertinence" look and had dressed in his usual dark colors.

But the kids wouldn't be afraid of him, because he was... just perfect: a tall, strong figure standing in the doorway, with his broad shoulders and narrow hips. With secret pleasure, Jane realized that she was the only one in the room who knew that Guy had a scar in the shape of an X on his left shoulder; that on his right hip there was a strawberry birthmark, and Jane had licked that birthmark several times, with devotion, like every inch of his caramel skin...

She blushed.

Good God, why was he so gorgeous?

It was so unfair of him!

Mrs. Barnaby got up slowly. "Jane, you didn't say you would bring the Earl with you." The directress's tone wasn't exactly harsh. She was too attentive to the budget of the orphanage to be harsh with an *earl*. But obviously Guy's bad reputation frightened her, although she had never talked about it with Jane.

"I myself didn't know yet," Jane said. "But I was sure you'd be pleased. May I introduce him to you?"

"Yes, of course." The directress looked at him with inquisitive eyes. "Please come in, your lordship."

With all eyes fixed on him, Guy walked in slowly. Jane counted the children. There were fourteen of them, and sat motionless, as if in the presence of a scary monster.

Maybe they were afraid of him, after all.

Guy stopped beside Jane and the directress.

"Mrs. Barnaby," began Jane, "this is the 4th Earl of Ashbourne, Guy Spencer. And, Guy... this is Mrs. Barnaby, the priceless director of St. Mary Orphan Refuge."

"I'm pleased to meet you, Mrs. Barnaby. Jane told me a lot about you." Guy took the hand Mrs. Barnaby was holding out and bent to kiss it. Jane almost laughed as Mrs. Barnaby's eyes flash.

"She told me a lot about you too," Mrs. Barnaby said.

Straightening, Guy raised an eyebrow. "Really? I hope she didn't frighten you. I'm not *that* terrible."

"No. Your stepsister says the nicest things about you."

"Does she?" he murmured, then turned to the table where the children sat. "So, where are the brats I'm supposed to yell at?"

"Guy!" Jane scolded him.

He shrugged. "I never claimed to be the best person to deal with kids, did I?"

Jane rolled her eyes with an exasperated grin. "Children," she said approaching the table, "the Earl is just joking. And you—" she looked at Guy, her voice rebuking him "—come here and behave yourself."

Guy's eyes shone with amusement. It was the first time he had seen Jane here, in this place where she felt comfortable. She almost felt comfortable today too. *Almost.* She was in the security of St. Mary's walls, among her children who not only loved her, but also trusted her. Nobody looked at her with condescension here. Sooner or later grown-up people tended to behave in a patronizing way with her—like her father, Lady Susan, Mr. Weymouth. And Guy, of course... but he, definitely, was on a whole other level.

Or maybe having him here made her stronger. She was happy for her children; they had indeed asked about him. It might be in a confused manner, but they would understand the honor the Earl was doing them. But she was also happy for herself, because... because Guy was here for her.

Yes... for *her.*

Years ago, Guy had broken her heart. She was only a child back then, and he was a boy playing with her feelings. But they had grown up, and it was possible that now...

"Children," she said with a lively voice. "This very tall gentleman is Guy Spencer, the 4th Earl of Ashbourne, whom I told you so much about."

In front of the kids' fearful silence, Guy curled his lips in a small smile. "See, Mrs. Barnaby?" he whispered to the directress in a very audible tone. "Fortunately, I've brought the cake."

Jane glared at him. "They're just a bit scared of you. Children," she said, turning to them, "you need not be. I've known him since he was little, and you know what?" She leaned forward and cupped her hand to the side of her mouth, making her voice a whisper as if sharing a secret. "He wasn't any good at times tables."

Robert threw a surprised look at Guy, then leaned toward her, whispering. "Seriously?"

"Oh, yes," she lied boldly, feeling Guy's eyes on the nape of her neck. "In fact, he still isn't. That's why he'll stay with us today during our math lesson. And, kids... when I explain arithmetic, please be kind to him. If you can, pretend to make some mistakes in your multiplications. He'll feel smarter if you make some mistakes too."

The children giggled and relaxed in their chairs, looking at him with less awe. Jane felt a light tap on her left ankle. Guy had softly touched her with his walking stick. She was playing with fire, she knew it, and he would make her pay for this, but—and that was the important thing, the oh-so-important thing—*not* right now. He'd never humiliate her here, in front of her children, because... oh, it was so clear now... because he loved her!

She closed her eyes for a moment, overcome with joy.

Yes. She'd never allowed herself to believe it. Sometimes she had hoped for it, sometimes she had suspected it, but now he was behind her, poking her with his stick, and the reason *had* to be this. Perhaps he had wanted her in his home as revenge at first, but now he loved her. A bit, at least. Yes, he still felt the need to humiliate her, yes, sometimes he made her cry with mortification. Jane didn't understand why, but in the end it didn't matter, because she couldn't help but love him; and he...

Well, he was with her right here, wasn't he?

"So," Guy said, placing a hand on her arm. "May I sit at the table doing a little math?"

"May he, children? He's not good at it, but he's still an earl. He even knows the Queen."

"And I'm taller than Prince Albert," he added, in order to give strength to her point.

"But," said Joanna, a little girl who couldn't be easily fooled, "can we eat the cake, first?"

The cake, right. Jane looked at the directress. Mrs. Barnaby sighed.

"You're spoiling them, Jane."

"You're right," Guy intervened. "It takes firmness to handle these little rascals. Otherwise, look at the bad results you get." He pointed at Jane with a nod. "She was a *very* spoiled brat as a child."

The directress smiled. She actually smiled, at Guy Spencer, the infamous 4th Earl of Ashbourne! "Not so bad a result then," she contradicted him good-naturedly. "All right," she sighed, "but only for today. Henry and Edward aren't here yet," she added, counting the children at the table. "They went to the dormitory for their notebooks, and it's taking a little too long to come back. I'll go get them and then we'll start eating this blessed cake."

"No, I'll go get them, if you'll let me," Jane said. "Actually, I'd like Guy to come with me, to show him the orphanage." She pulled back her shoulders, giving him a cheeky look. "Maybe I'll convince him to donate some more money to our orphans."

Guy raised an eyebrow, with a clear promise in his dark eyes. She knew he would punish her, but who cared? Guy didn't really hate her. And he wouldn't let her go in July. He would keep her with him forever.

Simple.

Jane wanted to laugh. To sing. Since the beginning of the year—since the very first night with him—she had had moments of joy. Yet, these moments had always mixed with bitter ones, with annihilating ones. Now, she was completely happy. Maybe she had joy written all over her face, but Guy was the man she loved, the man Fate had chosen for her, and to whom Jane, alas, was happy to belong.

"What did I tell you, Mrs. Barnaby?" Guy said with a sly smile. "She is *so* very spoiled."

* * *

"Shall we go?"

Jane reached out to take Guy's hand. It was a gesture she wasn't supposed to do in public, but then again, Jane was hopelessly Jane. She was an artless girl, and she was as happy as Guy had ever seen her before.

Revenge. He was doing all of this out of revenge. To enslave her better, to make her more defenseless, to...

Oh, what did it matter? His palm pressed against hers, and he followed her out the door like an obedient child. God, everyone could figure out what was going on between them. Guy hoped the others would confuse his passion with brotherly affection.

He certainly didn't.

As he let her drag him down the hallway, a realization struck him. He had never seen her like this. She was confident. She looked like nothing could harm her. She was the kind of woman Guy thought she would become in a few years, after marrying, after having kids of her own. But she already was. He could see it; she wasn't just a shy girl, but a woman capable of handling a dozen children with firm sweetness. This thought gave him a strange pain. He already knew that Jane, after him, would recover quickly from what she called *love*. Now he was certain of that. She had a life beyond him; and what a wonderful mother she would be... how many wonderful children she would have.

Revenge, he had called it? Revenge against whom, he wondered. Himself, maybe.

Jane climbed a step, and then stopped, turning to him. Guy hadn't started to climb the stairs yet. Their eyes met almost at the same level.

"Thank you," she murmured.

They were alone. Guy smiled, raising his hand to her cheek. "Don't thank me," he said with an edge of melancholy. "You're going to pay for everything, little girl."

Jane couldn't misunderstand the threat and the desire in his eyes; she swallowed with concern mixed with expectation. "I know," she whispered. "I'll do everything you want me to."

"With total devotion, Jane?"

"Yes."

Guy's heart slammed into his chest with aching pleasure. "And you'll humiliate yourself for me, angel, won't you? You'll submit completely to me."

Jane blushed. Some things, among the ones he asked her, were still hard for her to bear, they still hurt her pride. These things told Guy he didn't have total possession of her yet.

But today you won't cry, you won't complain. Today you'll be happy to do everything I'll tell you.

Today you'll give me something to remember.

As if I owned you for real.

Without the courage to look into his eyes, Jane nodded. "Whatever you ask of me, I'll do," she said, rubbing her face against his hand, in want of a caress. She turned her head and kissed his palm in a show of sweet, spontaneous submission.

"I'm starting to think," Guy whispered huskily, "that I should do you more favors."

Jane opened her eyelids, maybe to reply, when a noise coming from upstairs made both of them raise their heads up. It was like something heavy had just dropped to the floor... or *someone* heavy.

"Good lord, what are they doing upstairs?" Jane exclaimed, and without further delay, she ran up the stairs. Guy took a breath, pushed away the emotions threatening to make him weak, and followed her.

* * *

The cause of the noise became clear as soon as they opened the door of the dormitory.

In the middle of the long room, between the beds lined up against the right wall and the basins for the kids' personal hygiene on the left, two children were fighting furiously. More precisely, one was beating the other. A blond kid with a severe chemical burn on his cheek, about nine years old, was sitting astride the stomach of the other child. He was slapping him with his open palm. His expression was contorted with rage, his raised upper lip showed his teeth in a feral way. There was something devilish about him, Guy thought, or maybe it was just his burned cheek that made him creepy.

"Henry! Eddie!"

Jane started to run toward them, but Guy stretched out his arm and stopped her.

"I'll handle it."

In two strides he reached the kids, bending down and grabbing the child with the burned cheek by the waist, picking him up.

"Your fight is over, champ," he said, holding him horizontally against his hip, like a battering-ram ready to break through a door. And judging from the way the kid was kicking him, and striking him with his fists, his very blond head had to be as hard as a battering-ram too. So, this bully couldn't even understand when he lost a battle, could he?

Jane ran to the child lying on the ground. "Edward!" she said with worry.

Meanwhile, the battering-ram kid kept on punching and kicking at Guy who, for his part, didn't even blink.

"Get off me!" the child yelled, struggling with anger.

"Now you and I will have a chat, champ," Guy said coldly. The child lying on the floor looked smaller and weaker than the one he was holding against his hip.

Jane was dabbing at the bruise of the injured kid with a handkerchief.

"What happened?" she asked, shaking her head in disbelief. "Fighting this way! Henry!" She turned to the child hanging at Guy's hip. "Why did you beat Eddie?"

The boy ignored her. "Let me go!" he shouted at Guy, punching him on his stomach.

Guy merely tightened his grip on him. "I'm the strongest now," he said, looking sideways at the kid. "It's not that funny anymore, is it?"

"Eddie." Jane looked at the child she was comforting. He was still in tears. "Can you tell me what happened?"

"I did nothing wrong," wailed the boy, sitting up. "I just walked in and... and Henry was there, with his cockroaches..."

"Shut up, you pig!" Henry struggled against Guy's side again, but he was a gnat compared to him. Guy approached the bedside table Edward had pointed at. He looked dispassionately at what was on it: three cockroaches, impaled on a pin, one on top of another. Guy wondered if Henry had watched them all die together, or one at a time.

"So much for your courage. You're brave, Henry, you really are. Jane," he turned to her, who was still kneeling on the ground to calm the bruised child. "Jane, please, lead, uh... Edward, right?... lead him downstairs, angel. And let the kids eat their cake, without me and Henry. I'm going to have a little chat with this..." he slightly shook the blond kid hanging at his side, "...champ."

Jane's eyes widened. "Guy, it's better if I talk to him. I don't know if you..."

"If I am the right person, you mean?" Guy smiled. "You asked me to come with you this morning and I did. Now I'm asking you..." *to trust me* "...to let me talk to him."

"But... he's just a kid, Guy."

"I know. Edward, go downstairs," he said to the child who had been beaten badly.

Edward was as skinny as a broomstick, and tears were still dropping from his eyes, but he probably was so afraid of this big scary man who was ordering him around that he got up at once. Without looking back, he ran from the room.

Being an earl with an authoritative frown was good for something. Not to mention that Guy was so massive he seemed to occupy the entire dormitory.

He walked over to Jane, keeping Henry at a distance from her. Jane said she loved him, but she still feared him, she feared his reactions. It was normal. Guy was the son of the devil, wasn't he?

"I assume that you've talked to him before," he said reasonably. "And it didn't work. So let me try to do it my way."

The kid at his side stopped struggling. Guy was expecting him to beg

Jane not to go; instead, Henry just watched her, waiting. For what? Her backstabbing? Looking at him from above, for a moment Guy felt like he was seeing a reflection of himself as a child.

"It's not an order, Jane," Guy added quietly. "I know you'd never obey me about this, but—just trust me, will you?" He stepped back. "But maybe you think I'm a horrible person, after all."

She shook her head. She glanced at Henry, but the child didn't move. He said nothing. It felt weird, seeing him so serious despite his awkward position, hanging horizontally like that.

"You just want to talk to him, don't you, Guy?" A thousand emotions crossed Jane's face. "For we..." she looked at the child, tensely, "...we do not use corporal punishments here."

These words hurt him. Good lord, she thought he would hit a kid?

"I'll just talk to him," he confirmed softly.

Trust, doubt, hope, fear... and then trust again. Jane bit her lower lip and swallowed. It was hard to believe in Guy Spencer, the son of the devil. But finally she turned around, going to the door. Entrusting one of her dearest children to him, she left the room.

41.

Guy and the blond child were in the middle of the long dormitory. Guy was still holding him against his hip, horizontally in mid-air like a spear.

Stepping out of the room, Jane had left the door ajar. He was sure she was behind it, eavesdropping, but Guy couldn't blame her. He himself didn't know what instinct had driven him to deal with this little bully. Maybe it was just because he was used to dealing with bullies; he had always done it, since his days at Eton College.

"So, champ."

Guy put Henry down, then stepped back. He expected to see the boy darting towards the door, about thirty feet away from them. It would be a good race.

Henry did not run away. He merely stared up at Guy with a defiant look. He had cobalt blue eyes, shining with anger and, of course, with fear, which the kid was trying to not show.

His fake bravado surprised Guy. It didn't fit with the first impression he had got of the child. Anyway, he didn't change his plan. He glanced around, looking for something that suited his purpose. He found it: in the back of the dormitory, between two narrow windows that badly illuminated the long room, there was a wooden notice-board covered with sheets of paper. At that distance, Guy could not read the words written on the notes, but they seemed to be some sort of lists. Rules, huh? They were never missing, no matter where you were.

"See that board over there, kiddo? Where papers are pinned up all over?"

Henry didn't answer.

"What's written on those papers? It must be something important, I guess. Something we can't rip off. Am I right?"

The kid still didn't answer. Wasn't he supposed to tremble or beg? He would begin now.

"But there is a small square of wood with no note covering it, can you see it, Henry? It's over there, at the bottom right corner." Guy looked at the notice-board, assessing its distance and position. "And you know what? It's

290

just what I need."

It was a square about two inches on a side. Guy bent down and pulled a knife out from his boot. It was a long, sharp knife. As expected, the boy took a step back, widening his eyes in fear.

"No, it's not for you," Guy stopped him with a wry smile. "And do you know why?" He straightened up and, raising the knife over his own head, threw it almost without aiming. The part of the board with no papers on it, as small as it was, was a target that looked impossible to hit. Yet the knife, flying quickly through the twenty or thirty feet of distance, stuck in the middle of it, sinking into the wood. Its 7-inch steel blade glinted in the sunlight coming from the window, swinging fast to side to side due to the force of the blow.

"That's why," Guy said to Henry, who was looking at the knife with wide eyes. "It's because I like *real* challenges. It's because I'm not a coward."

The boy blinked and turned to him. His eyes shone with admiration.

And that was something Guy had expected too.

"Neither am I a coward, sir," he said in a clear voice. His expression was so solemn, his ruined cheek didn't look so ugly anymore.

"Are you not? The kid you've beaten is smaller than you."

"Eddie—" Henry lifted his chin and his eyes gave out flashes of hatred "—Eddie deserved it. He's mean."

"Oh, I see." Guy pointed at the dead insects on the nightstand. "Am I to understand that they deserved it too?"

"The cockroaches? You're mad at me because of them?"

Guy sneered. "How could I possibly get angry because of some bugs? No, of course I'm not. They just make me realize that you're a coward, that's all."

"I told you I'm not!"

"Are you sure?" Guy smiled condescendingly. "Now forgive me, Henry, but I'm finding that hard to believe. Problem is, the cockroaches couldn't defend themselves. They were an easy target for you, weren't they? And cowards always look for easy targets."

He went to the back of the dormitory to take the knife stuck into the notice-board. It had been a calculated risk: and it had worked. He pulled out the knife by its handle, leaving a deep cut in the wood, and put it back in his boot. He felt the child's eyes on the nape of his neck. He straightened and, turning around, he looked back at Henry.

The child was beyond furious. He was hurt. "I. Am. Not. A. Coward!" he exclaimed with a kind of adult anger, which made him look older.

Guy walked to him. The boy pulled his shoulders back and, in fact, he showed uncommon courage in front of such a big man.

One, incidentally, with a throwing knife in his boot.

"No?" Guy stopped five feet away from him. "Why should I believe you?"

"Because..." The boy swallowed hard, and Guy saw a sudden pain in his eyes. "Because I wasn't the one who killed the cockroaches, sir."

Oh.

How was it that everything got complicated when the 4th Earl of Ashbourne was involved? Even when he had to do something simple like scolding a child, he managed to mess it up. Weren't children supposed to be easy to understand, for God's sake?

"You'd have done better to tell me that in the beginning," Guy muttered. But it wasn't Henry's fault. As Stuart always said, you must get all the facts before jumping to hasty conclusions. Yeah... but Guy would never learn that. He didn't have what it took to be a strategist. He was too impulsive, too aggressive; his fate was to be a common soldier, not a general, and that was it.

But fuck if it wasn't annoying.

Henry blushed at the undeserved reproach. "It's stupid to play with cockroaches," he said, embarrassed. "That's why I didn't tell you. I just catch them, I never kill them. Jane thinks I do, but I don't."

Guy sighed. Henry's hair was the color of wheat in summer, a little too long on his forehead, and his eyes were big and beautiful; but his left cheek... his cheek condemned him to walk with his head down, avoiding people. It condemned him to be alone... or with his cockroaches. Fear of rejection was such a shitty thing. Rejection—what an old, familiar story.

"Is that why you beat that child?" he asked, bending down on one knee and finally putting himself at Henry's level. "Did he kill your... friends?"

"They were *not* my friends." The boy looked down, but not fast enough to prevent Guy from noticing the angry shyness filling his eyes. "I just played with them."

"I see." To hell with the cockroaches. Guy rubbed his forehead. "I owe you an apology," he said, raising his head and staring at the child's amazing eyes. "You're *not* a coward, Henry. In fact, you were right to defend your..." He looked toward the nightstand and shrugged. "Well, whatever they were."

The child ran a hand under his nose. "I haven't been very good at it, have I?" he murmured as tears began to fall down his cheeks as by accident. "They're dead."

Guy got up and put a hand on the boy's shoulder. "But you tried to, and that's all you could do. That's all *we* can do." He looked at the nightstand, at the three disgusting, impaled insects. "Come on, let's bury them in the garden."

The child followed him, sniffling softly. "Sir?"

"Yes?"

"You won't tell anybody I cried, will you?"

42.

"Even Henry asked if Guy would come back, Papa!"

Jane's surprised voice rang out in the garden of Ashbourne House, where beautiful flowers bloomed in colorful pictures. Her father, sitting on a stone bench under the maple tree, smiled.

"Now, Guy being so sweet is weird. Maybe he emptied the sugar bowl into his tea at breakfast."

Susan held a puff of annoyance. Good heavens, Charles looked *so* pleased by his daughter's words. And so pleased with himself! Probably he would explode with satisfaction. As he threw a sideways look at Susan, as to let her know he was guessing every thought that was going through her head, she jumped up.

And she was supposed to seduce this damn hypocrite?

Never!

Luckily, the Earl hadn't mentioned her "mission" again, and Susan hoped he had given up his plan. To be more precise, the Earl had never said anything about *anything* to her. In fact, any time she had asked him for a private talk, he had replied he was too busy for that.

But it was damn time to talk to him in private. Jane's situation hadn't changed one bit. Weymouth hadn't invited unmarried men to Ashbourne House anymore, and wasn't it a pity after the successful afternoon of over a month ago? Jane had even refused to see Linville again, and that was incomprehensible; she had shown interest in him at first! In addition to all of this, Charles was exultant. He was deluding himself with the hope that he would become the Earl's father-in-law. And this morning, Ashbourne had gone to the orphanage with Jane; God, had the Earl no good sense at all? He had given her *tons* of false expectations.

"Excuse me," Susan said with a tight smile at Jane, carefully avoiding looking at Charles. "I have to come in for a moment, due to a little... *nécessité.*"

Charles nodded politely. "Come back soon, please, Lady Susan. We're going to miss you."

Since Susan had not said a damn word until now, his sarcasm was definitely not funny. She bit her tongue not to tell him to go to hell. After their catastrophic *tête-à-tête* in March, she had avoided being alone with him. With other people, she could manage the aversion she felt toward Charles Hartwell. And she felt *a great deal* of aversion toward him, especially now that he had got better and stronger, physically speaking. Damn it. He had become almost handsome, and that made her furious. It would even be enjoyable to bed him, and the fact that he was an insufferable hypocrite bothered her *badly*. Charles had got a healthy color because of the hours he spent in the garden. He had gained weight and energy. Now he could walk more easily: his damaged leg gave him less pain, and his handmade shoes made his handicap milder. He didn't even seem a cripple anymore.

Well, you know what? One day or another I'll trip you, Charles "King of Hypocrites" Hartwell, so you'll break your leg again.

Oh, come on, Susan. She forced herself to feel ashamed for her evil thoughts. She didn't like it when she was being mean. Exasperated with herself, she couldn't help but blame that obnoxious Charles Hartwell again.

Shaking her head, she came inside the palace. The entrance hall of Ashbourne House was intended to stun the visitors: it was immense and aggressive, and the prevailing colors were gold and red. When someone entered it, they unconsciously stopped, struck by the violent luxury welcoming them. Susan passed through the hall hastily. She wouldn't let the opulence intimidate her. She herself was the daughter of an earl, wasn't she? A *penniless* earl, all right, but whatever...

She walked through the corridor leading to the common rooms. She hoped to find Lord Ashbourne alone, in the armory or the paintings gallery. As she looked into these rooms, she sighed. He wasn't there. In Ashbourne House, even a man as big as Guy Spencer could hide. And if he was in his study, he wouldn't let her come in; if he was in his rooms, Susan couldn't knock at his door: it would be too improper.

With little hope, she reached the door of the large living room on the ground floor, the red living room, where the inhabitants of Ashbourne House spent their evenings reading and playing the piano, sometimes engaging in card or chess games. She looked inside and, with a little blow to her heart, she saw the Earl's tall, broad figure standing before the window, with his back turned to her. His body was powerful and strong, and Susan couldn't help but think back to how he looked when he was naked. An involuntary shiver gripped her belly at the memory. When naked, he looked like a Greek god: his physique was pure perfection. Not to mention the first time she had seen his *cock*... she'd almost been afraid of how big it was. Yes, Susan remembered it very well... as well as the pleasure his body had given her, and now she gave herself a moment to admire him against the afternoon light.

Come on, Susan. You'll enjoy this eye candy another time.

She sighed. Ashbourne was looking out the window, towards the garden, where Jane and Charles Hartwell were.

"Lord Ashbourne," she greeted him, entering the room.

He turned slowly. He didn't show a great deal of enthusiasm in seeing her.

"Lady Susan. What a pleasure."

Yeah, sure. "The pleasure's mine," she clucked, coming closer to him. "I've finally managed to catch you alone! Since I've been in your house, it has never happened, but perhaps you didn't notice. Your daily schedule seems incompatible with mine. I mean, in the morning I'm at the orphanage with your sister—" Susan didn't miss the quick frown on Ashbourne's forehead "—and in the afternoon, when you're in your study, there are strict orders to not disturb you, no matter what."

Ashbourne raised an eyebrow with aristocratic arrogance. "I'm a busy man."

"I hope you're not busy *now*. I'd like to have a couple of words with you. May I?"

"I hope it's not about that boring orphanage again. I have had enough of it for the rest of my life."

"No, it's not about it. Maybe you can guess what it is? I mean, I'm sure Mr. Weymouth told you about my doubts regarding... how can I put this?... regarding the, uh... the feelings..."

She paused. Facing the topic head-on by saying "Earl, have you happened to notice how madly in love with you Jane is?" would violate all the rules of social etiquette. But who knew when another occasion would arise; and after all, Susan and the Earl weren't exactly *strangers*. All right, they had had sex only three times, and their relationship had ended quickly—to be more precise, *Ashbourne* had put an end to it quickly, but still. It had to matter a little, didn't it?

Susan swallowed and decided to go on. "The tender feelings that Jane has... oh, good gracious, forgive me for speaking this bluntly. I'm talking about the feelings, Lord Ashbourne, Jane has for you."

Had she gone too far?

Judging by the Earl's expression, definitely yes: Ashbourne's face hardened into aristocratic disdain. The sunlight behind him made him look even taller, or maybe it was because he had straightened his posture in a silent, though very clear, menace.

"Yes, Weymouth told me about it," he replied, and an implicit warning sounded in his voice: *Stop this at once, Lady Susan.* "I gave him the same answer I'm giving you now: it's nonsense."

The large living room was in dark tones, and its classic, impressive furniture gave the room an out-of-time atmosphere. But the light coming from the large windows brightened the colors, despite the burgundy curtains; and the need for doing the right thing pushed Susan to muster enough courage to plead her cause again.

"I hate to insist," she murmured. Good heavens, they had slept together! Why was he looking at her in that intimidating way? "But you want me to chaperone your sister, and I'm spending a lot of time with her. I don't think I'm wrong, she..."

"All right, that's enough."

Ashbourne spoke with a stentorian voice. Susan had already heard that harsh tone of his. He had used this exact tone against her husband, the late Viscount Emerson. But he had never used it against her.

"This, Lady Susan," continued Lord Ashbourne, with a haughtiness he'd never showed to her before, "this is the last time I'll hear you mention this subject, to me or anyone else. I didn't bring you here as a 'chaperone,' even if you pretend otherwise. You seem to have many difficulties in completing the task I hired you for, but I strongly suggest that you focus on that, instead of minding my business."

Susan felt her cheeks warm up at this rebuke, more appropriate to a scullery maid than to her. She hoped that the rouge covering her cheeks would conceal the humiliation she was feeling. She was the widow of a viscount and the daughter of an Earl, not a lower-class servant!

To regain control, she pretended to be interested in the double bookcase across the room. It contained many novels, the favorite genre of the guests of Ashbourne House, who, very often in the evening, would read one or another book aloud by the fire. The actual library was in the opposite wing of the palace, with several volumes that would make a professor's head spin: books about art, technology, mathematics. Susan enumerated the various disciplines in her mind: that was stupid, but she needed it to calm down. When she thought she had succeeded, she finally spoke.

"Lord Ashbourne, once you told me you will never get married," she began hesitantly. "Have you changed your mind? Are you going to marry Jane? Of course, if that's the case, I'll stop worrying about her. But if not... I know that you'd never seduce her, don't get me wrong, but it's so obvious that she has... feelings... for you. Feelings that aren't just limited to sisterly affection. Today at the orphanage... how do you not see it? Earl, you..."

"Lady Susan," he cut her off, suddenly raising his hand. His gesture was so abrupt that he almost slapped her face, and Susan took a step back, feeling uncomfortable. "I feel obligated to remind you that you are just an employee in this house. *My* house. Start minding your own business, or I'll be forced to take some action."

What the heck was happening? Susan had expected an annoyed reaction from Ashbourne, and, in fairness, she knew she what she was talking about was none of her business; but what she was reading in the Earl's eyes was... fury. Was it possible?

"Would you sack me because I care about Jane?" she asked, puzzled. "Lord Ashbourne, you beat up my husband for abusing a maid, years ago. You're a good man, despite what people say about you. Why do you want me to believe you're not?"

She couldn't match the image of this man before her—this man frowning with fierceness, with his face hard and his posture stiff with anger—with the one of four years ago, when he had threatened to kill Susan's husband. Susan had witnessed the scene between Guy and her husband through the crack of the study door. They had been at Maxwell's house, and, with her nose between the door and the jamb, she had found out that her filthy husband, along with other noblemen, had raped a maid during a ball. Maybe the maid herself had told Ashbourne about the painful experience she had suffered, maybe Ashbourne had figured it out from the rumors whispered in some gentlemen's club. Either way, the Earl had gone to Maxwell's house and had threatened him explicitly. He had enough money and connections, he had told the Viscount, not only to ruin him, but also to buy him a new overcoat—a *wooden* overcoat. His threat had worked just fine. Susan's fearful husband had hastily signed a promissory note for two hundred pounds, payable to the maid, to get himself out of trouble. Guy had taken the note with a smile, and Susan would never forget that smile: because a moment later the Earl had closed his fist and hit the Viscount. His punch had been so powerful, Maxwell had flown to the ground. *Next time I'll make you swallow your balls,* Ashbourne had told him dryly, and then he had turned his back and walked out of the room. Barely breathing behind the door, Susan hadn't got away. She had waited for Ashbourne to thank him. Finally, someone had taught her husband a lesson, as he deserved!

One thing had led to another; and Susan and Guy had begun their brief affair.

How could the man before her be the same she had thanked years ago?

"You have a very romantic idea of me, Lady Susan."

A cynical smile surfaced on the 4th Earl of Ashbourne's lips. Susan considered him a very handsome man and, to be honest, she was a little infatuated with him; but now, all she could feel was fear. To calm down, she looked around the room; in the middle of it was the grand piano Susan had played just yesterday evening. Now it occurred to her that Jane had never dared to play it when the Earl was with them. Jane was very good at playing the piano, even better than Susan. Yet, she didn't play it when Ashbourne was there.

It was this realization that pushed her to speak again.

"No romantic idea whatsoever," she said, trying to believe what she was saying, trying to hang on to this certainty; "I *saw* you, remember? That morning, four years ago, with my husband. I saw what you did, and I admired you for that."

The Earl grinned. "Yes, I remember the incident you're talking about. I was very young, so I found it amusing to yell at your husband. But you know what? I kept the money he gave for the maid. Funny, isn't it? And I fucked that little slut myself a few days later. Maybe I fucked her the same night I fucked you too."

Susan felt dizzy. Ashbourne and she hadn't seen each other after their brief affair, but Susan had kept a wonderful memory of him. And over the last few months, he had behaved so kindly, so... splendidly, at Ashbourne House. To Charles Hartwell, to Stephen Weymouth, to Jane... to *her*.

In the name of God, who was the man in front of her?

"Don't be crude," she flatly rebuked him. When everything is falling down, you can always seek refuge in etiquette; this was one of the few good pieces of advice her mother had given her. "It's not like you."

"You don't know what's like me. Don't you ever read the newspapers? Don't you know what they write about me? I assure you, your late husband's scruples were stronger than mine. I see you're shaking your head... for God's sake, how old are you, forty?... and you are more naïve than a virgin."

Susan could barely breathe. "I believe none of these rumors about you."

"Don't you? Well, you're right. They are way too watered-down when compared to reality."

"You're lying to me."

Ashbourne raised his eyebrows. "Why on earth would I pretend to be worse than I am? Don't be silly, Lady Susan, if you can."

"But if so... why did you let me believe you were a better man?"

The fire in the chimney, fifteen or twenty feet away from them, wasn't too lively or noisy; it had been lit only to please the eye, because it was a warm, pleasant day at the end of April. Still, Susan had never felt so cold at Ashbourne House.

The Earl shrugged. "I always make sluts believe I'm a do-gooder," he replied with cynicism. "In my bed I want someone who really cares for me. Any guess why, Susan?" He glanced up and down her body, insolent. "The more the sluts like me, the more they'll be willing to *totally* please me."

Oh my God. Was that true?

Was it possible?

Had he only pretended to be a decent man, just because he wanted to fuck her better?

Four years ago, Guy Spencer wasn't even twenty-two. He was very young; still, Susan remembered he had always been unselfish during their sexual encounters, he had always been gentle afterward. But he used to be distant when they were together; and he used to barely talk to her. He kept it all inside. Susan was a married woman back then, and she was much older than him; theirs wasn't a serious relationship, and they, of course, couldn't go out in public together. That was what she had told herself to justify his coldness; but now a thousand details surfaced in her mind. She recalled his inaccessibility, the quick way he had tired of her. He had put an end to their relationship with a simple note, accompanying it with a rich necklace of pearls and matching earrings, as if he were getting rid of just any mistress. Susan also recalled, blushing with anger, how in bed she had indeed been... what did Ashbourne just say?... yes, she had been *willing* to please him. Very willing.

Guy Spencer, the 4th Earl of Ashbourne, was not only *not* better than the other men... he was the worst of all.

"I'm going to pretend this conversation never happened, Lady Susan," he continued with icy hauteur. "And here's some advice to you. I can speak plainly now, since I don't need your aged body in my bed anymore. I've hired you because I want you to fuck my stepfather. Just for that. No, don't jump at my words, don't look down. Listen to me because I won't repeat myself. Whether or not I want to seduce Jane Hartwell is none of your damn business. Another word on this subject and I'll send you back to your brother-in-law. Do you think I don't know what sort of... *benefit* you used to grant him? Of course I know. Everyone knows. At White's, he always speaks of his dearest sister-in-law. I even laughed with him over it a couple of times. You'll be pleased to know that he and I agreed about how good you are at blowjob."

Susan drew back in disgust. She had been looking surreptitiously at the Earl these past months. Oh, how charming he was! How many times she had wished she could have sex with him again! She had had these thoughts a lifetime ago; a minute ago. It had been just physical attraction for a masculine face and a sculpted body; now she was ashamed of herself for having desired him.

"I see my words offend you." The Earl smiled with brutal cruelty. "It's the first time you've seen me like this, I guess. And if you dare to breathe a word about this little chat of ours, you'll discover another side of me you don't know yet. I'm a vengeful bastard, Lady Susan. Keep this in mind."

Ashbourne's eyes burned with a genuine threat. Susan's bowels tightened with shocked fear.

"Hello there."

A cheerful voice coming from the door made Susan jump. With her stomach in turmoil, her eyes almost misted with shock, she hadn't noticed that Weymouth had just appeared at the threshold. Swallowing hard and blinking her tears back, she turned to him.

The young man had just come home. He was still wearing his hat and gloves, and he was holding a walking stick. He looked at Ashbourne and frowned. "Am I interrupting something?" he asked, his voice hesitant.

He was interrupting... what exactly was he interrupting?

What in the heck had just happened here? An earthquake, an explosion, what?

"You've been interrupting something since the day you were born," Ashbourne replied sharply. He turned to Susan with narrowed eyes in a last, silent threat, then he coldly bowed and strode towards the door. He left without further comment, bumping into his friend's shoulder as he stormed out.

Startled, Weymouth turned to Susan. "My heavens, you look very pale— and Ashbourne is as dark as a new-moon night. What happened, did the two of you have some sort of argument?"

She opened her mouth with no idea what she would say.

"It happened that your friend is a bastard dog, Mr. Weymouth!"

Oh, very well, just the words to tell the best friend of such an asshole. But Susan didn't know what she was saying... she couldn't even think, my goodness!

Weymouth blinked, then gave her an uncertain smile. "Then everything's normal," he said, trying to be witty. "For a moment you had me worried." He entered the room, walking over to her. "Susan, what did you say to provoke such a confrontation? I hope you didn't talk to him about Jane." Stephen took a deep breath. "God, I advised you not to, didn't I?"

"Of course you did, and you also promised me to separate the Earl from her. Your word is not worth much, I see, but then, you are *his* friend!"

"What did he say to upset you so?"

"He said he is a bastard, that's what he said! He boasted he's more than happy to be the bloody, filthy worm that he is. Is it true?"

"He..." Weymouth hesitated. Of course, he wouldn't answer honestly. Why on earth was Susan asking him? Stephen Weymouth would take Ashbourne's side. He always took his side. He was just the Earl's damned sycophant, he obeyed Guy Spencer like a servant; he sure knew what Ashbourne did, how disgusting he was; but then again, the Earl paid his salary, didn't he?

That was all that mattered, wasn't it, that was all that mattered!

No, not to me! Susan thought angrily. *Do you hear me, you filthy Earl of Ashbourne? Not. To. Me!*

"No, he isn't... no, Susan, no," Weymouth said in alarm. "Please, you're pale, you're worrying me. Sit down, please let me get you a glass of wine."

"I don't need any wine." *I just need to stick a fork in your master's eyes.*

"Lady Susan, please, listen to me. When Ashbourne gets angry, he says things he doesn't mean. He's not an evil man, I believe, no, I'm *sure* he isn't. But..." He rubbed his forehead with the fingertips of his right hand. "But to be honest, there are some things about him that escape me, and other ones that I can't tell you. I promise you something though. About Jane Hartwell, you've convinced me that we have an actual problem here. And I'm working on it. Seriously. Just trust me."

Trust him? He was a friend of... oh my goodness, what to call that vicious pervert? And she, Susan—how had she been so naïve to believe that there was a man, just *one* man, less disgusting than the others? With the Earl of Ashbourne, she had broken her number one rule: never, ever believe that a man is worth more than a worm.

"Susan..."

She had her eyes lowered, fixed on the light marble floor, her nails digging into her palms to control the impotent rage she felt. As Weymouth said her name so softly, she looked up at him again. He was just a young, weak-willed man. He himself had told her so weeks ago. Maybe he failed to see Ashbourne's faults; maybe he didn't want to see them. However, the concern on his face was real. His large brown eyes were kind and sympathetic.

Susan swallowed. She had worn a mask of indifference for so many years, and this skill *had to be* good for something. Since she had arrived at Ashbourne House, she no longer seemed good at pretending indifference. She wondered why. It must have been Jane Hartwell's fault. That girl knew nothing about the filth Ashbourne wallowed in. Nothing about Weymouth's weakness. And nothing, of course, about the moral compromises Charles Hartwell would make just to have an Earl as a son-in-law.

Above all, Jane knew nothing about the grime Susan had endured in her life; and she would never know. Susan hadn't been able to save herself, but as God was her witness, she would save Jane Hartwell.

At any cost.

"Of course I trust you, Mr. Weymouth," she replied more calmly, putting a tight smile on her face. *Pretend, pretend, and pretend. Don't confide in anyone ever again.*

Weymouth breathed a sigh of relief. "Good. I mean, it's not advisable to mess with Ashbourne. He's a nasty piece of work when he happens to be crossed. That is something—" he cleared his throat, embarrassed "—that I know beyond any doubt."

"And aren't you worried about yourself?"

Stephen gave a slight smile. "No, he won't lash out at me. So please, leave it to me. Give me a couple of weeks, all right? I'll solve everything."

A couple of weeks? No, Susan could not wait any longer. She had to open Jane Hartwell's eyes as soon as possible. That bastard Ashbourne was trying to appear as sweet as candy to seduce Jane, Susan was sure of it. The reason behind his visit to the orphanage was very clear now. His fake kindness this morning and the nastiness he had shown Susan a few minutes ago... God, if she needed some proof of the Earl's deception, she had it now. Alas, words wouldn't be enough for Jane Hartwell. If Susan spoke ill of her stepbrother, Jane would never believe her.

So, there was only a way to save the innocent girl from his stepbrother. Susan had to show her the monster he was. She had to move from words to deeds.

* * *

"How's the renovation work going at the orphanage, Jane?"

"Oh, very fine, Papa. The roof is rebuilt almost completely."

Under the maple, Jane was standing next to her father who, kneeling on the grass, was busy with a corner of calla lilies in bloom. The white flowers stood out against the green of the lawn, and Charles, with a little shovel in his hand, was planting the last flower into the damp soil. Both he and Jane had their backs to the house.

"Maybe Guy is trying to convince us he's a good fellow," said Charles, pounding the shovel on the moist ground.

Jane stared at the flowers. "I'm not sure, Papa. When Mrs. Barnaby took him aside to persuade him to donate to other charitable institutions other than St. Mary, he backed out."

"Really? What did he say?"

"He sounded cynical as usual. He said something like, 'Come on, Mrs. Barnaby'"—Jane changed her voice, making it deeper and aristocratic—"'you should know I'm not exactly famous for my heart of gold.'"

"So, these donations he's making to St. Mary aren't donations at all. Guy is helping the orphanage just because you work there."

Jane blushed. "I think so. I mean, you know what he's like."

Charles nodded. "He always tries to impress you."

No, he's just paying me, Papa. He pays me for... the things... I do for him. The donations to the St. Mary Orphan Refuge were her recompense for... well, for the way she let him use her like a sex-toy. Nothing else, and Jane well knew it. "But Guy is... impossible to understand," she reasoned aloud. She *had* to do it; she needed to speak about Guy, she needed to figure out who he really was. "If you'd seen him with Henry, Papa, he seemed almost... oh, I just don't know."

"Henry..." said her father. "He's the kid with the burned cheek, right? And if I'm not wrong..." He glanced at her teasingly. "He's your favorite pupil."

"I told you a thousand times. I have *no* favorite pupil. All the children are the same to me."

Her father looked at her from below, sideways, and she smiled reluctantly.

"Oh very well," she gave up. "Henry is my favorite. And this morning..." She became pensive, rubbing the tip of her cloth shoe into the green lawn. She was too lost in thought to realize that the grass stains would never be removed from her shoes. "You know, I didn't hear everything they said when they were alone in the dormitory. They were far from the door and were speaking too softly, and I think—" she snorted "—I think Guy knew I was eavesdropping, because he *never* speaks that softly. Anyway, what is certain is that Guy acted like a bully. As usual." She thought back to when she had seen him pull a knife out of his boot. She had taken a step forward, ready to intervene, but Guy had only wanted to draw Henry's attention. With her heart in her throat, Jane had resisted the urge to enter the room, leaving Guy to have his way. "And somehow it worked, Papa. Henry even paid attention to the math lesson. He spontaneously answered a couple of questions, and that's not like him. He usually keeps to himself and never joins in group activities."

Her father leveled the ground surface with the little shovel. "And now you're happy, but also a bit jealous of Guy's success. Am I right?"

Jane felt uncomfortable with her father's sharpness and shifted from foot to foot. Yes, he was right. Was it a bad thing, feeling that little bittersweet jealousy? "I just can't help but wonder," she murmured, "why Henry has trusted him... and hasn't trusted me instead."

Leaving the shovel on the grass, Charles grabbed his cane and started to pull himself up. Jane restrained the impulse to help him. The last thing he needed was to be treated like a cripple.

Charles stood up with relative ease. He had improved since he had moved at Ashbourne House. Guy forced him to do rehabilitation exercises every afternoon, and physical activity was working fine with his damaged leg. Of course Guy, like the diabolical master he was, wanted Charles to follow the therapy just to keep him away during the afternoon. It was a shocking thought: while her father was in the gym doing his workout with his therapists, in Guy's study Jane was on all fours, naked and obedient, ready to do anything her master told her to.

Charles sat down on the bench under the maple tree, in the pleasantly warm sun of the clear day. "Any thoughts on why he trusted him?"

Because Guy is magnificent, Papa. "I don't know, Papa," she replied without looking at him.

Magnificent, yes. The way Guy spoke, the way he moved... the way he did *everything*. He had run the perfume business for a few months, and more than half of her father's debt was repaid already. He took care of Mr. Weymouth who, as Lady Susan told her, was an opium addict with economic problems. And even for Charles, Guy had managed the impossible: he was deceiving him, obviously—if her father ever found out that Jane was Guy's sex slave, he would drop dead—but, though Guy's intentions had been mean at first, he had succeeded in giving Charles the will to live again. After Rona's death, he seemed to have lost it forever.

"Are you in love with him, my child?"

Pulled abruptly from her thoughts, Jane jumped. It was the first time her father had asked such a question of her directly. Perhaps, it was an inevitable step to overcome. Jane touched the white velvet of a calla flower, avoiding her father's eyes. "You love him too."

"You know what I mean."

Jane dropped her hand and stared at the flowers without seeing them.

What could she answer?

She had given up on Guy when she was thirteen, and in all these years, she had told herself she hated him. She had told herself she didn't want to see him again.

She had hated him, yes, she had hated him like no one else in the world; and since she *hated* him, she had never forgotten him. Since she *hated* him, she had never moved on. He had been a silent, cumbersome presence in her mind, in her heart. In her dreams... and nightmares. Even without realizing it, she had been always waiting for him, always waiting for the few days he would spend at Courtnell Street.

All of this, because she *hated* him.

Had it ever been hate, she wondered? Had it been hate *at all?*

And now she silently admitted something else, something that scared her to the bone. Eight years ago, when she had lost him the first time, it had been like dying inside. She had promised herself that never again would she trust him. Oh, the pain—the pain had been unbearable. The kids of the orphanage had saved her; they had helped her to bear the desolation Guy had left inside her.

She couldn't even think of losing him again.

But this wasn't going to happen. He loved her—he loved her, right?

Her father cleared his throat, and Jane swallowed. She lifted her head.

How could she tell her father all of this?

"See, Papa..."

Then she stopped speaking. Even assuming that Guy would keep her with him, he would never marry her; so, her father had to remain unaware of their relationship forever.

The problem was that she was no good at pretending.

"Do you mind if I leave you alone, Papa?" she said without looking at him. "Lady Susan wishes to show me a watercolor she did."

Charles sighed but, maybe noticing the emotions that were overwhelming his daughter, he didn't insist. "Sure, go ahead, honey. Best not keep your lady companion waiting. When she gets angry, she becomes unbearable. More unbearable than usual, I mean."

"Oh, come on. She's so sweet!"

"As sweet as gall," he murmured, closing his eyes and raising his face to the sun, whose heat was a blessing after the incessant rain that had fallen in the previous two weeks.

* * *

The heels of Guy's Hessian boots rang hollow on the marble of the long hallway.

Damn it.

He should never have hired Lady Susan Emerson. Years ago he wasn't a member of the Gang of Knives yet, so he didn't care to be cautious when he happened to act like an avenger. And of course Susan remembered what had happened between Guy and her disgusting husband.

That was a problem. It could blow his cover. At twenty-one, Guy had been a naïve young man with an unruly passion for justice. People don't easily forget things like that: every now and then, there was still someone who remembered about Guy's generous donations to the poor. Even worse, somebody still talked about the "lessons" the Earl of Ashbourne used to teach the bastards who took advantage of the weak. Just as it had happened with the late Viscount Emerson, Susan's husband. *If you do it again,* he had told him, before breaking his nose with a punch, *you'll end up in a drainage ditch, with your throat cut and rats eating your balls.*

And Lady Susan had heard these way-too-clear words.

God, he should never have hired her. How stupid he was sometimes.

Guy hoped he had convinced her that she had misunderstood him. He had told her that the incident with Emerson had been only a joke due to Guy's youth. In a way, he hoped that the woman, after their unpleasant conversation, resigned from her job; on the other hand, he would regret it very much. For two reasons: first, Jane liked Susan; second, Susan seemed to be the only other person to dislike Charles Hartwell apart from Guy. She so clearly couldn't stand Charles, and it was even better than having her seduce him. Guy enjoyed a great deal seeing his boring stepfather despised by the witty, beautiful lady. Someone could look at Hartwell and see no halo around his head, wasn't it nice for a change?

Guy had always had trouble dealing with halos.

He pushed the door open and stepped out, heading for the small part of the garden that Charles had begun to cultivate himself. The days were getting longer. May. It was almost May. Time was running out. Guy felt a pain in his chest, just like after a race. He looked at the flower garden. He didn't give a shit about the flowers; he just watched Jane and her father. Charles was sitting on a bench, while Jane was standing next to him, with her back turned to the house and to Guy.

She was a vision even from behind. Her large straw hat was frustrating: its brim was wide and fell over her neck, covering her nape and beautiful shiny hair. She wore a pink dress. Guy had often seen her wearing that dress: it was elegant, not too flashy. Of the thirty he had bought her, that foolish girl always wore the simplest ones.

305

He was still fifteen or twenty feet away from them when Jane turned around. She blushed and, before he reached them, she stepped away from her father to go inside. Just perfect. Guy had gone there for this: let her know to join him early this afternoon. He wanted her more than ever, and today Jane would do *everything* to please him. Like the big bastard he was, he was eager to make the most of it.

"Are you coming in, Jane?" he asked as she gave him an embarrassed smile. She looked tense; Charles must have questioned her. A sort of inquisition, most likely.

"Yes," she replied, glancing uncertainly at her father. "Are you staying here in the garden?"

Not for long, angel. I'll stay just enough time to keep up appearances with Charles "Halo" Hartwell. "Yes, I'd like to have a word with your father."

Jane opened her mouth as if to argue. Didn't she want him to talk to her father? An uncomfortable silence lasted for a while. Finally Jane, with no excuse to stay, headed inside. As she walked past him, Guy smelled her scent. And as always, he was surprised by how good it was.

With his eyes, he followed her while she walked to the palace. As Charles's voice called him back to reality, he realized that looking at her in such an eager manner had been a mistake.

A childish, definitely *stupid* mistake.

"Why don't you marry her and get it over with?" his stepfather snapped.

Precisely.

43.

"Why don't you marry her and get it over with?"

Precisely. What the hell was the matter with everyone today?

Guy let the air out between his teeth and turned to his stepfather. "Do you want a countess in your family, sir?"

Charles was sitting and Guy was standing, but he knew this would not intimidate Charles.

"Guy."

"You don't really believe I'll talk about it, do you?" Guy shook his head and turned to leave.

"We'll talk, big boy," Hartwell stopped him, and his voice was firm. "Or I'll take my daughter away from Ashbourne House this very day."

Oh for fuck's sake!

"We haven't taken up this matter in months, why now? It's because I went with her to that bloody orphanage, isn't it?"

"It's because today my daughter is as happy as a child left in a pastry shop, Guy. It's because she has started believing in a future with you."

Guy's heart began to beat irregularly. "Bullshit."

"No, it's not, and one of two things is happening: either you're leading her on, and then it's better that Jane and I leave before you do any more damage. Or you have serious intentions with her. You can't possibly have failed to notice the way she looks at you. It's the way you look at her, or maybe not, because in your case it's much more embarrassing."

Guy wouldn't allow Charles to take Jane away from him. He had another two months to be with her, two months of heaven before returning to his usual hell.

"If today I did something wrong," he said, his voice devoid of emotion, "I'll make it up, sir. I don't think Jane wants to marry me, but if it is true, and I stress *if,* it's not so big a problem. I mean, she'll just deal with the fact we can't get married. Maybe she will suffer for a couple of weeks—a couple of weeks *at most.* Maybe less, if the orphanage occupies her thoughts. She'll fall in love with someone else, and there will be no painful side effects."

"Someone else, is this your solution for a broken heart?" Charles raised an eyebrow. "That's really pragmatic, Guy, congratulations. Too bad that Jane had never fallen in love with anyone but you. And too bad that she had turned down no less than five marriage proposals in the past. Oh, but you already knew this, didn't you? And you knew they're good proposals too."

Yes, he knew, of course. And of course he would have prevented her marriage if she had accepted one of the bastards proposing her, for Guy had to get his revenge first. Luckily, she had refused any of those men before he had to intervene. But what was Charles implying?

Was he suggesting that Jane had refused these proposals because of *Guy?*

Oh, that was *such* colossal bullshit. Jane had forgotten him for years. He had returned to her life by using *blackmail,* for God's sake!

"Maybe none of them was the right man for her," Guy replied flatly.

"Oh, and who'll find the right man for her? You, maybe? Come on, you're not *that* stupid. You know you'll consider no man good enough for her."

Damn Hartwell and his more-than-reasonable objections. "You've thought of someone?"

"I've thought of you."

"In the name of God, Hartwell, stop it!" Guy snapped, cursing himself a moment later. *Calm, for fuck's sake, keep calm. It's just a test to overcome, some kind of training for when you have to give her up for real.* "She's your daughter," he went on, more controlled. "You can't possibly want something like that for her."

"Something like *what,* precisely? Something as terrible as you, you mean?" Charles laughed sadly, shaking his head. "Holy God, and here I thought I was the one with the lowest self-esteem at Ashbourne House. Guy, go on thinking of yourself as a piece of shit if you want, but please don't force me to repeat that I have a very good opinion of you. I myself would like to forget it."

Guy could not fake a smile, neither an amused nor a sarcastic one. "And regarding my father, do you happen to have a good opinion of him too?" Guy hated Charles Hartwell also for that: his stepfather could always pull out of him words he didn't want to say. Truths he didn't want to face. "My mother must have told you something. Just seeing her with me must have made it clear that my father wasn't exactly a happy memory for her."

"I know what sort of man he was, Guy."

"Some think he was insane."

"Well, I don't think so. He was just cruel."

"A perfect nobleman, then." Guy managed to put a difficult grin on his face. In fact, he didn't feel at all like laughing. "He raped my mother when she was sixteen, I guess you know that," he said in a detached tone. "He was forty. My maternal grandparents shouldn't have let him marry her, but my father could be quite persuasive when he wanted something." Guy was facing trouble in speaking, the words were shards that scratched his throat. "I think he kept doing horrible things to her. Maybe you know that for sure. I remember that my mother was always crying; certainly he was a less-than-exceptional husband. But you know what, Mr. Hartwell? He loved *me*. My father."

He lowered his eyes, looking at the calla lilies Charles had just planted. Guy had seen him do it from the window of the red living room, where he had stopped to watch Jane while she was outside; spying on her without her knowing, because... just because. Just to steal one more moment. Now he stared at one of the white flowers and, before realizing it, took its spathe between his thumb and forefinger and tore off a piece.

"He used to take me hunting with him and his friends," he said, and in his ears the sounds became muffled, as always happened when he thought of the early years of his life. "He pushed me to fight with children older than me. As I told you, sir," he said, looking at him with a hard smile, "he loved me. One day, he whipped a dog to death in front of me, because it had barked at me. It took him almost an hour to kill it." He allowed himself a moment to breathe deeply. "I didn't defend that dog, Mr. Hartwell."

"You would defend it now."

"It doesn't mean that everything's right with me."

I'm a killer, Jesus Christ, don't you suspect that?

Guy had channeled his nature into controlled forms, of course— acceptable, even *right* forms. He only killed filthy human beings, and he didn't even have fun as he did it. But then again, when God gives you a talent, it would be blasphemous to waste it, wouldn't it?

He tore another piece of the calla lily. It had been white and soft under his fingers; now the beauty of the flower was gone, just like that. It had taken Guy just an instant to destroy it.

"Would you hurt Jane?"

Guy looked up at Charles. Hurt Jane... physically? No, of course not. He never would. But he liked to see her submit to him. He liked her looking at him all the time. He liked to have power over her, he loved it when he made her lose control.

And what was that? Wasn't that "hurting her" as well?

"Let me tell you something about my father, Mr. Hartwell," he said flatly. "There are many rumors about the 3rd Earl of Ashbourne. Some said there are torture dungeons in his estate in Northamptonshire, even if I never found them when I went there. Some said many young women were forcibly brought to the palace and never came back. Once," he said, running his hand over his forehead, "a thief trespassed inside the estate. He died in a fall from a cliff while he was fleeing from the gamekeeper. That was what my father said to the constable. I myself had a talk with the constable a few years ago. He is a solid man, in his mid-forties, named Kennaway. He remembered the thief, a boy of perhaps fifteen or sixteen. The constable had found his body at the bottom of the cliff with his bones all broken. Because of the fall, of course. One of the thief's eyes was missing, perhaps it had popped out hitting a rock." Guy looked up at Charles. "But the thing Kennaway could not quite understand was how the thief had lost all his teeth. He had none in his mouth. Not even one. All of them were pulled out at the root."

He broke the stem of the white calla with a slight snap. Around them, spring was twittering, singing, rustling in the grass.

"When I moved here," Guy continued, "I found some of my father's old things. Memories, junk, trinkets he had kept for, I suppose, some sort of *sentimental* reasons. Including a box hidden behind a board wall. Inside it, there was stuff of little value: a medallion with a lock of red hair inside, a handkerchief with the initials BC—I never found out whose it was. Other little things: a couple of buttons, a shoelace. And a small black bag, about two inches on a side. Want to guess what was in that bag, Mr. Hartwell?" He raised his foot and crushed what was left of the calla. The flower in his hand was now only golden spadix, and Guy threw it into the bushes. He turned to his stepfather, his chest rising and falling with hard breaths. "There were twenty-eight teeth. They were white and strong; they certainly had belonged to a young person." He opened and closed his fists. "The thief I was talking about, you know? Well, I think my father pulled all his teeth out, one by one, torturing him in a thousand ways before killing him. Don't you?"

Charles did not answer immediately; he rubbed his forehead for a moment, lost in thought. "Is that why you won't get married, then?" he asked finally, with a heavy sadness in his voice. "Do you think evil is hereditary?"

"I won't father children," he replied only. "Never."

"Why do you think so badly of yourself, big boy?"

Guy did not answer. Ashbourne House was behind him, a gem in the middle of London. It was large, imposing, arrogant. What had happened within those walls when the 3rd Earl of Ashbourne was alive?

But it didn't matter, not really; because Guy himself was a killer. Guy himself had poison running through his veins, and he could not change it.

"You did nothing wrong, my muscular and dull boy," said Charles softly. "In all likelihood, you have fewer sins to confess than me, as far as... hey, don't go away, stop at once, Guy Spencer, damned Earl of Ashbourne!"

Already some feet away, Guy turned around without understanding why the hell he was still listening to his stepfather. "Sir, I should really..."

"Guy. Let's say, for the sake of argument, that your absurd belief about... hereditary evil, or whatever you call it, is true. Have you ever thought it might be enough, to Jane, to have you in her life—you and no one else?"

Guy remained silent, looking towards the trees of Green Park that soared into the blue sky not far from them. Yes, of course he had thought of it; moreover, he was sure to have the power to keep Jane tied to him forever. She called it love, he called it manipulation, but these were just words, after all. Without ever letting her know he had a double life, hiding any disturbing truths from her, he would make her happy, not every day maybe, but *many days*—countless moments of happiness.

"Jane... not a mother?" He smiled tiredly, looking at the green against the blue; the trees looked almost black against the afternoon light. "Having babies is what she was born for, Mr. Hartwell."

There. He had said it. And what he had allowed himself to dream of every now and then—in the morning, more often, when he opened his eyes and smiled at Jane at his side—didn't really matter.

"And so, what am I supposed to do, big boy? Just sit here and watch my daughter dying of love for you? Keep pretending nothing is going on here?"

"I told you, I will make everything right. I'll start looking for a new place for you and Jane to live. It will take two or three weeks at most." Two months. The two months which still belonged to him. "And Jane is not the little girl you believe her to be, sir. You happened to go to the orphanage with her, didn't you? So you already know that she's a woman with many interests. She has a life on her own. She'll be quick to forget me, she..." *She already did it once, long ago.* "She'll have a serene and happy life. Without me."

"She's *in love* with you. You know what that means, my stupid son? But of course," his stepfather looked at him with narrowed eyes, "of course you do."

"Are we done, Mr. Hartwell?"

"Mr. Hartwell," repeated his stepfather.

"Beg your pardon?"

"Mr. Hartwell. You still call me like that. You never called me 'Papa.' Not even 'Charles.'"

Guy shrugged. "I never was an easy child."

"As no child is. I was aware that your mother was unfair to you." He scratched his nose with the back of his nail. "But she had wronged you more than I imagined. She should never have let you spend time with your father."

"How could she oppose that, pray tell? She wasn't much more than a child herself."

"She was your *mother*. How was that your fault if you were a child born of violence? How was that your fault if you looked like your father?"

"Bullshit."

The man on the bench smiled. "Always the same, aren't you? Always thorny. You were like that as a kid too. Proud and angry. I shouldn't have given up on you."

"And you would have ended up with a bullet in your head. Once you came close to that, and frankly, I can't understand why you're so willing to take all the world's sins on your shoulders. Well, you know what, just go ahead and do it. If you want to believe I was a lovely child mistreated by a cruel mother, be my guest. That will never change the truth, Mr. Hartwell. My mother didn't mistreat me. She treated me just the way I deserved."

Hartwell started to reply, but Guy turned away, walking towards his palace. His stepfather called him again for the umpteenth time: no, enough. For today, enough. Guy ignored him and reached the entrance. He passed through the hall, finding himself in a long corridor dominated by dark colors, with neoclassical statues and paintings of family ancestors hanging on the walls. He hadn't made major changes to Ashbourne House; the presence of the 3rd Earl of Ashbourne, and those who had gone before him, was evident in many details. And in the portraits Guy hadn't removed. No one should suspect that his father's legacy was unwelcome to him; more important, he himself didn't want to forget his own origins.

But he usually avoided looking at them. In fact, he never looked at his father's large portrait. It was about halfway down the corridor, and every time Guy ignored its golden frame and ornaments. And of course, he ignored the *subject* of the portrait who, despite the brilliant frame, was an eye-catcher in a strange sort of way.

This time Guy stopped before it and stared at it. The man in the portrait looked like him: or rather, he had the aspect Guy would have at forty-seven, his father's age when the portrait was made, a year before he died from a fall off a horse.

In the big, bulky painting, the 3rd Earl of Ashbourne was dressed in a hunting outfit, with a brown jacket and a red scarf on his shoulder, probably added by the painter to brighten up the colors of the work. The Earl's dark hair and straight eyebrows were the same as his only son's; in his hands he held a rifle without smiling. Perhaps the painter had been afraid of the 3rd Earl of Ashbourne; perhaps that was why he had managed to catch the man's expression so perfectly. Without any explicit details of cruelty, the sparkle illuminating the very black irises of Guy Christian Spencer, the 3rd Earl of Ashbourne, made his gaze disturbing. He seemed to look back at his son as if he were alive. His eyes were like Guy's, in color and elongated shape, with the same long fine eyelashes; they were the very eyes Guy saw in his own mirror each morning.

Guy turned around and leaned against the wall next to the painting, putting a hand over his eyes. He felt sick... the same sickness his mother must have felt when watching him.

Either you kill or you are killed, my son.

He remembered this voice. He remembered the green woods and the sun's rays passing through the branches. Spring exploded around father and son on their first day of hunting together, and Guy was six years old: in his hand he held a knife almost bigger than he was. Bright and shiny, the knife had an odd shape: it was asymmetrical in order to cut better, as his father, the 3rd Earl of Ashbourne, had explained to him.

At Guy's feet lay a fawn. Its wail came up from the ground. The fawn was small, not bigger than a dog, with reddish spotted fur and eyes as velvety as chocolate. Its four legs were tied together, and its crying sounded like a child's.

Cut its belly open, Guy. Don't be a sissy.

At this point Guy's memories became confused. Surely he had stepped back, surely he had implored his father to let him go back home. His father had yelled at him and slapped him hard. Then his father had been the one who had done it, who had made a deep cut in the fawn's stomach, while holding Guy by his hair. The blood had splashed out, it had flooded father and son. And the smell, too, wet iron and feces, had covered them at once, like a red hot storm.

The smell came from the animal's belly, and Guy didn't want to see, and his eyes were closed, and he was weeping. The Earl had pulled him by his hair, pushing his face down onto the open wound.

Agonized, the fawn had made little gasps. Guy had tried to scream, but blood and guts were filling his mouth. He jerked, he kicked in the air, but his father had kept him pushed down, with his face pressed against the hot red river and the fawn's fur. The animal had stopped moving, Guy was breathing into its torn bowels. The blood went down his throat, and he coughed violently; he was suffocating, but his father had kept him there.

He had held him pressed there.

Either you kill or you are killed, my son.

These were the last words Guy had heard. He had passed out, he didn't know. He had woken up in his room, in his bed. His nightgown was white and clean, his hair was soft, there was no slimy liquid on it, so Guy had hoped he dreamed it all. But in his nose he could still smell the fawn's blood, in his throat there was an iron taste, and two weeks later he had raised a knife over a fox immobilized by a trap. He would never forget the eyes of the little beast as he had planted the knife into its belly. Nor would he forget the words his father had told him, patting him on his small shoulder.

Very good, my son. It's the blood of the Spencers that runs through your veins. You cannot change it.

Guy blinked. Around him, there no longer were the woods, there was just Ashbourne House. It was large, high-ceilinged, and full of light. The

313

golden cherubs on the ceiling had been shooting arrows and flirting immodestly for generations. Guy straightened, stepping away from the wall. The windows let in the sun, as bright as the knife's blade that killed a fawn long ago.

The blood running through your veins.

Guy thought about Jane. She had given him a kiss this morning.

She had given him a small, sweet kiss, and she had said she loved him.

Jane, my little angel. I cannot change it.

44.

As Jane saw Guy enter the light-blue living room, she immediately knew that something was wrong with him. He was stiff, his eyes flashed with dark light. Jane was alone, for Susan had not joined her; still, she was surprised when Guy, instead of telling her to follow him into his study, closed the door behind him, turning the key in the lock.

"Draw the curtains and come here on all fours, bitch."

Jane gave a start. She felt a pain in her chest—a silly pain. Certainly she couldn't expect him to be always as sweet as he had been just a few hours ago. She put her sewing work down on the sofa and got up. She reached the French window, drew the blue curtains closed, then turned to Guy.

Bitch.

She swallowed hard, and bent her knees without looking at him. He had never called her that. Although the "treatment" he reserved for her was more suited to a pet than a woman—she could not ignore it—it remained just a game if he called her "angel," didn't it? If she was his little one or his little girl...

But this term was so crude. So cold. It made the scene look... *real.*

It was just a word... so why was it hurting her so badly?

Her large, long skirt impaired her movements. It made her awkward, it made her ridiculous. With her palms on the floor, she went towards the tall figure by the door.

She looked up.

"There is a lot of mud out there," Guy said coldly. "I soiled my boots. Lick them clean."

Jane obeyed. With her eyes closed, she began licking his right boot, sticking out her whole tongue.

"Do it faster."

She quickened her moves, screwing her eyes shut as tight as she possibly could.

"If you don't watch what you're doing," said Guy, "you can't clean them

315

properly. Open your eyes."

Jane did.

"Good. Now shine them." He smiled cynically when she pleadingly looked up at him. "Don't look at me as if you don't know what I mean, Jane. Rub your pussy on my boots. Make them shine."

It was one of the things that embarrassed her more, moving and squirming over his shoes while he, smiling from above, enjoyed that indecent sight.

"Guy..."

She straightened her back, remaining on her knees. She took his hand and kissed it. Guy didn't move. She wasn't obeying his orders, and her heart was beating strongly in her chest. Would he reject her? Would he force her to move back to his boots, make her lick them, shine them in that degrading way?

Bitch.

She would do it, she realized. She would do it with pleasure if she could feel his desire, his... his love. But there was a shadow on Guy's heart. Jane didn't want to spare herself a humiliation, she just wanted him to be as he was a few hours ago... a few *minutes* ago, when he had looked at her sweetly in the garden.

Was it her father who had made him angry?

She kissed his fist. Guy was silent, but his eyes were on her. His body was still rigid.

She moved her mouth to his trousers, at the side of the bulge pushing against the fabric. She kissed the fly, where his arousal was evident. With her left hand, she caressed it. Her mouth became greedier; she opened it, feeling the shape of his penis under the cloth. His erection grew stronger. Her saliva was wetting his trousers, and Guy put his hand on her head. Jane felt her heart fill with happiness. He had said nothing, but he was accepting her gift... her comfort to him, for whatever had darkened his eyes and darkened his heart.

Bitch.

She unbuttoned his fly, pulling down his trousers. She didn't touch his long underpants, so he put his hand over it, to work its buttons loose.

"No," murmured Jane, stopping his hand and glancing up. "Not yet."

Guy looked at her in amazement. His little Jane had just given him an order, seriously?

Slowly, he smiled. He withdrew his hand from his underwear and put it on her cheek, stroking it with his thumb.

"You want me to beg, angel?"

Angel...

Jane swallowed, moved with joy. She didn't answer, instead tilting her head to kiss the palm of his hand. She lapped it, like a bitch, yes, *now* it was fine, now everything was fine again.

Oh, Guy, I love you so much I could die.

Slowly she returned to his huge manhood, which felt like a hot iron bar through the fabric. It strained hard against his white cotton underpants. She started at its base; cocking her head, she spread her lips wider in a side pressure. She made her way up to the head of his shaft, with soft bites.

Guy's need was growing with every kiss, and his breathing, his panting, gave her power and courage. She moistened the fabric with her eager licking, and he groaned as she took his knob in her mouth.

"Jane..." he muttered. "Jane, you're killing me..."

With one hand, she held the base of his penis, and moved her face an inch away. Sticking out her tongue, she began licking his glans through the fabric. There was no humiliation here, but power, the power of a woman who holds a man in the palm of her hand.

Guy clenched his hand in her hair. "Suck it, little one, I... I can't stand it anymore..."

Jane put her hand on the edge of his underpants, unfastening them. His cock, no longer prisoner of the fabric, stood out proudly in front of her.

"Take it in your mouth, my angel..."

She shook her head. She dragged her tongue down the underside of his penis and licked his balls, savoring every inch. She went farther behind, between his scrotum and anus. Guy let out an excited obscenity through his teeth.

She opened her mouth to take his testicles inside. Her tongue moved around his sensitive skin, it was sweet and hot. Pre-seminal liquid began to ooze from the tip of his cock.

"Oh yes... your mouth feels so... so good..."

She pulled away from his testicles, and a string of saliva linked her lips to his balls. She bathed his scrotum with her tongue, enjoying his groans of delight, she lapped her way back from the base of his penis to its tip. She licked it all around, while Guy kept his hand on her head. He was watching her fascinated, and the thought contracted her lower abdomen. Having him in her power excited her, and, in her nether parts, it was so delightful it almost hurt. She toyed with his foreskin, and then closed her lips around his glans, going back and forth, receiving it into her throat.

"That's beautiful, keep... keep sucking like this... good girl..."

His penis throbbed... Guy was about to come. Jane took the base of his shaft with her hand, and moved her mouth faster, her tongue savoring him with greediness.

"Do you like it in your mouth, don't you... oh yes, like this, like... oh God..."

He let go, throwing out dense streams of sperm. Jane greedily swallowed his load. A little of it dripped down the sides of her mouth as she accompanied his orgasm until the end with her lips and hand. Only at the end did she stop teasing him, and pulled her mouth away from his cock.

He leaned with his back to the wall, with no strength left.

Jane rubbed her head against his leg. With a finger, she wiped the seed around her mouth. Satisfying him made her happy, while she was supposed to hate it. But then, she was his slave, and God, she didn't wish to be anything else; might heaven have pity on her and her soul. She squeezed his right leg with her hand.

Guy put his hand on hers. "That was very... very bad of you, angel."

She raised her head as she heard the raucous amusement in his voice. Guy's eyes were misted with pleasure, he was smiling.

"You didn't obey, girl... you didn't finish shining my boots."

Jane licked her lips, his taste in her mouth so right and perfect. The idea of herself climaxing on his boots, while he was smiling like that, now seemed like paradise to her. "Do you want me to do it now?"

"No, it's too late... you disobeyed me and... and you're going to pay for this." He put a hand on her cheek. "You know that, don't you?"

Jane nodded, enjoying his palm on her face. He put his thumb into her mouth, and she meekly began to suck it, moving her head back and forth.

"God, you do *really* like it..."

Guy's words were slow, filled with languor. He was in a privileged position. He had already come, so he was taking his sweet time. Jane might beg for the need she had of him.

"And you *did* disobey," he went on, relaxed. "So I'm going to punish you."

He pulled his finger out of her mouth. He was not angry; he was not angry at all. Therefore, Jane doubted that he would hurt her... but then, she had actually disobeyed him.

Around the table were some padded chairs, and Guy, going in that direction, seized two of them by their backs. His movements were sluggish, softened with pleasure.

From her subordinate position, Jane looked at him impatiently. Her craving for him was strong, and his preparations were a torture to her. Maybe Guy wanted to make her beg for release, as he had just begged her?

The memory flushed her cheeks. Sucking him so eagerly, without even being asked! She had behaved wantonly. But Guy's groans when he had reached his peak... his taste, his pleasure... it had been worth it. And the power she had discovered she had, now that, for the first time, she had been in charge.

Guy dragged the chairs in front of her, placing them opposite each other, their backs touching at their tops. He patted the cushion of the chair closer to her.

"Get up here on your knees, you shameless little minx."

Jane moved awkwardly, the dress keeping her from being agile. She was well aware of her wet pussy, of her quivering belly. Trembling with anticipation and fear, she climbed on the chair like her master had ordered her to, with her knees on the cushion, placing her hands on the top of its backrest.

Guy moved behind her, brushing aside the locks of hair escaped from her bun, then leaned over her and put his mouth on her ear. "Naughty, naughty Jane," he whispered, filling her with shivers at his warm breath, fragrant of mint. "You wanted badly to suck my cock, didn't you?"

"Yes..."

Guy slid his hand over her butt, and she stifled a sigh of desire.

"That's a prize that must be earned, angel. Did you earn it?" He reached out and caught the hem of her skirt, starting to lift it. "Did I give you my permission to suck me?"

"N... no."

Jane helped him to uncover her buttocks, raising first one knee, then the other. Her solicitude was embarrassing, and she would have been ashamed, thinking about it with a cool head. But certainly not right now. She needed him to touch her, or just to look at her, with her skirt lifted, showing him the wet longing that shivered between her legs.

Guy's hands rested on the underwear that covered her round bottom. "Then I have to punish you, don't I?"

"Yes..."

With one hand, Guy slid her long underpants down, then lightly touched her sex lips. He chuckled. "God, you're sopping wet..."

Jane moaned. He was just brushing her pussy with the tips of his fingers, sharpening her desire.

"Please," she begged, pushing her groin towards his hand. "Please, Guy..."

"Oh no." Guy laughed softly. "You must show me how contrite you are. Lean forward and place your hands on the cushion of the other chair, Jane."

She swallowed. Leaning forward, she positioned herself on all fours between the two chairs, with her navel touching the tops of the backrests in the middle. Her knees were on one chair, her palms on the other one—and her bare bottom at the level of his penis. What she wanted most was him inside her... even that way, if she couldn't push him to make love to her at last.

"When I come in your mouth, Jane..." Guy whispered. "Good girls don't do that, you know?"

He lightly placed one hand on her right buttock, moving it up and down, between the crack of her ass, teasing her—*torturing* her. Then he raised his arm, and her punishment began.

The first spank startled her, pushing her forward. And immediately afterward, a slight, sweet touch rubbed over her sore skin. It was an insinuating, moist caress.

"Do you regret the way you misbehaved, angel?"

No. Not at all. "Yes, I... I do..."

He raised his hand and brought it down hard on her bottom again. "What are you going to do to make up for it?"

"Everything you want me to do... everything..."

Another spank fell, on her left cheek, and then that caress again—that stopped too soon, retreating from her. Making fun of her.

"Please, Guy... oh please, I can't wait anymore..."

But he had no pity. He continued to torture her in that way, by slapping her ass and caressing her skin. Her bottom burned and stung from his hard spanking. Between her legs, her soft curls were wet, her *legs* were wet—and she moaned, begging for release.

"Your little ass is all red..." muttered Guy with a strange tenderness, stroking gently her sore buttocks. "But not enough. Open your legs, Jane. Open your pretty ass for me."

Jane obeyed as much as the position allowed her to, and she arched shamelessly, pressing her belly on the backs of the chairs to spread her buttocks apart in an obscene invitation. Invitation that Guy caught, by inserting a wet finger into her anus and beginning to move it inside her. He prepared her for a few moments, then he pressed his penis to her forbidden little butthole, penetrating it slowly.

He was ready again, ready for her... his arousal filled her with absurd happiness.

He didn't push himself all the way in. He was always very gentle when he sodomized her, but the first few times having him there had seemed strange to her, not entirely pleasant. Now it was different. She loved to have Guy inside her, although by the wrong entrance. He kept his hands on her buttocks, squeezing them and giving her a slight tingling sensation due to the spanking, spreading them wide open and moving faster.

She moaned with pleasure, her body rocking back and forth with his thrusts.

"You like this, Jane... you like your punishment..."

"Yes... oh, yes..."

He brought a hand to her vulva, touching her firmly. He moved his middle finger up and down, reaching her pleasure's little pearl, that tiny, sensitive knob of flesh at the center of her womanhood, while pushing his cock to the hilt, slamming his balls against her butt.

"Oh Guy, yes... oh, yes, my love!"

Guy pulled her hips to him as the violent contractions of orgasm shook her. He was about to climax too, but with a groan he pulled his swollen cock out of her, and, moving in front of her, stood with his rock hard erection level with her face. Jane kept her head bowed, everything forgotten in ecstasy; Guy grabbed her hair and lifted her face.

Jane half-opened her eyes.

"You've earned it now," Guy murmured.

It took just one movement of his hand over his cock, and his seed covered her lips, eyelids, and hair, while Guy came all over her face.

45.

Stephen Weymouth was sitting with his feet on the desk and his chair balanced on its back legs. He was in his office, the one Guy had reserved for him at Ashbourne House.

What the fuck? he wondered as he studied some figures in a black hardcover ledger.

Some money was missing.

Stephen had never known exactly how much cash Guy withdrew from his bank accounts every month. From time to time, his friend asked him to make withdrawals for him, but, as Stephen had found out this afternoon, Guy withdrew a sum of *five thousand pounds* monthly.

Holy *fucking* shit. It was a fortune. And... how the hell did Guy spend it?

Not in investments. Investments were Stephen's job.

There were no noises in the house, for it was late at night. Stephen's office was a ground-floor room, large and airy, near the main entrance of the palace. Guy's study was on the first floor. His friend had moved up there when Jane had arrived at Ashbourne House. Probably he didn't want anyone to find out about, or hear by accident, their sexual encounters.

Except, of course, that a big peeping Tom had *seen* one of their encounters two months ago, because of the damn Macaulay's whiskey...

Stephen straightened his chair and put his feet on the ground. With a sigh, he tilted his head and studied the ledger again. Five thousand pounds. Now, that was a crazy high sum. Guy's budget was around six hundred thousand, but his financial liquidity was another matter altogether; it was based on interest and investments in stocks. And *why* did Guy spend so much money? *How* could he leave no trace behind? Stephen had tried to ask about that at White's, the club where Guy occasionally went. Stephen had pretended he was interested in investing but, given that no one would believe he had money to invest, he had said he was acting on behalf of his brother, the future Baron Weymouth.

This subterfuge had proven to be useless anyway. Nobody has told him anything he didn't already know. He had discovered nothing. Guy's money simply seemed to disappear.

It was past midnight. Jane, Charles, and Guy had taken their leave a few hours ago. Before going upstairs, Susan had thrown Stephen an eloquent look: *What have you done to solve Jane's situation?*

Nothing. He had done a shitty nothing. He had promised Susan he would fix "the Jane Hartwell problem," but the fact was, he had no idea how to do it. He didn't have a starting point. He had nothing he could use against Guy.

He felt like crap.

He felt guilty toward Jane to the point he wasn't able to speak to her anymore. When their eyes met, Stephen flushed and looked away. Not because of the situation he had put her into, supporting Guy in ruining the Hartwells. He wasn't really to blame for that. He had been unaware of his friend's diabolical plan. No, what kept him from meeting her eyes was the way he had behaved in March, when he was witness to what happened between her and Guy in his friend's study. He couldn't forget how Guy had *punished* her, and how he had been spying on them. Damn, he should have closed his eyes and covered his ears.

Was he so different from Guy? In a way, he had violated Jane Hartwell too. His friend, at least, didn't talk grandly about hypocritical moralizing bullshit, while Stephen, God forgive him, criticized Jane's situation with words, but he often thought back of her *castigation* when he jerked off. Ashamed of himself, cursing himself, but his willpower wasn't enough to keep him from thinking back to what he had witnessed in March.

God, he hated himself.

He looked back at the ledger, shaking his head. He was angry with Guy. And even more furious with himself. He needed to find something to, say, *influence* Guy. He wanted his friend to leave Jane Hartwell alone. He wanted to blackmail Guy, yes. Shamelessly. But then again, he had the best teacher for that sort of stuff: Guy Spencer, the 4th Earl of Ashbourne.

He heard some footsteps in the hallway. Someone was going towards the entrance-door. Stephen stood up. Yesterday, and the day before yesterday, his stakeout hadn't worked, but tonight seemed to be his lucky night. He took his black cloak and wrapped it around himself as he approached the window.

Sometimes Guy went out at night. He didn't follow a regular pattern; maybe he got out a couple of nights in a row, then he stayed at home for ten nights, and so on. This was another mystery about his friend Stephen needed to solve. Guy didn't go to taverns or brothels. He didn't invite Stephen to go with him. And of course, he didn't cheat on Jane Hartwell. Stephen wasn't foolish enough to hope for it.

What the hell, then, kept Guy away from Jane?

From the window, he saw his friend walk toward the iron gate. Stephen opened the shutters. Like a thief, he slipped out and followed him.

* * *

"Ashbourne," a voice called from among the trees. In the night illuminated by the three-quarters moon, Stephen recognized the voice. It was Fitzwilliam Cunning's. The grandson of the Viscount Cunning. He was one of the most debauched aristocrats in London.

Stephen had managed to follow Guy. His friend's destination was close to Ashbourne House: Cunning's garden, behind Cunning's palace. A few minutes ago, Stuart Cavendish, the 6th Duke of St. Court, had welcomed Guy out of the palace, giving him a sober nod. It had looked like the nod of an old friend; and Stephen, hiding around the corner of a house, had felt the desire to get away. Turn his back and go away. Did he need to find out why Guy was a friend of St. Court's, and why the two of them had gone to visit Cunning?

Did he really?

He hadn't gone away. The truth could be frightening, but doubt was worse. It gave Stephen constant anxiety, and he couldn't take it anymore.

Concealed by an oak tree, he saw Guy and St. Court stop near Cunning in the darkest area of the garden. They had moved into the shadows; Stephen had given them a head start before following them. Now, at a distance of about thirty feet, he could barely hear their voices.

The late hour made the garden silent and creepy. There were just occasional creaking noises in the shadows. Cunning had a lantern with him, and it illuminated the three men's distant profiles.

Why was Guy with those scumbags?

"Good to see you, Cunning," Guy said.

A burst of laughter echoed among the trees. This garden differed from the well-lit garden of Ashbourne House. In all likelihood, Cunning preferred a gloomy area like this behind his house in order not to attract attention.

"I couldn't possibly decline one of your invitations, Ashbourne," Cunning said. "They seem to be very rare."

"Yes, I like to work alone. But sometimes some friends of mine have interesting things to show. Like the instrument I told you about. The one St. Court built."

Cunning chuckled. "I wouldn't have missed it for the world, it sounds like fun. St. Court, Ashbourne told me what you did to that whore. He said he felt sick—" he grinned, making a fat noise with his mouth "—I mean, *Ashbourne!* I thought nothing could upset him. You skinned her alive, right? Oh God, I can't wait to see it myself. She must have screamed like crazy."

"Oh, yes," said St. Court's languid voice. "I love it when they scream."

Stephen felt like throwing up. Guy? Guy... doing something like that?

No, no, no.

Deny the obvious.

Believe in the impossible.

"I asked you to dress anonymously, Cunning," Guy scolded him good-naturedly. "But you shine like a whore in a brothel. That perfume you've put on... don't you know it's dangerous to walk the streets of London at night? There's that miserable gang of rebels, you know, the Gang of Knives... they are on the loose yet. And their targets seem to be us, I mean... us *aristocrats.*"

"The Gang of Knives, sure. Of course I've heard about them. Why, they even sent me an anonymous letter! And get this: they left Hawkins's corpse in front of my house. It was an eloquent warning, don't you think? Not to mention that I was a friend of half their victims... an unfortunate percentage, I dare say."

"Oh, the word 'unfortunate' has little to do with it. I'm afraid the Gang has targeted you, Cunning. They sent me a warning too. Tindale's corpse. Remember? It was found in Cleveland Row two months ago. But it was in the garden of *Ashbourne House* before I had it moved by a trusted servant."

Stephen leaned forward. What bullshit was this? When could Guy possibly have moved Tindale's body? With all the people in Ashbourne House, something like that couldn't have happened.

Or maybe Stephen didn't want to believe what he was hearing. He didn't want to believe it for anything in the world.

"You had it moved away, good for you. I wasn't so lucky. Hawkins was on the public street, and the milkman's screams woke me. Horrible, isn't it?"

"Indeed."

"Has it ever happened to you, St. Court? Have you seen how they rip their victims' guts out?"

"No, not yet." The Duke's voice sounded calm and relaxed. "Unfortunately, I might add. I feel undervalued. I could derive some inspiration from them."

Cunning laughed in his disgustingly creaky way. "Oh, yes, you're not wrong. The body of that son of a bitch Hawkins was lying naked, belly up. Without eyes, hands, and feet. And he had his cock cut off: the bastards had put it in his mouth, can you imagine? Holy balls! It even seemed Hawkins was eating it with pleasure."

"You're making fun of him," said Guy. "And here I thought he was a friend of yours."

"Let's say I'll miss him, that son of a bitch. We used to have fun together. He had a certain flair for choosing the best cuts, if you know what I mean."

"Oh, yes. I know exactly what you mean."

"But," St. Court said, "you looked calm despite witnessing such a show. Do you think it is sensible to be dressed in this flashy manner? You can change your clothes if you like. Ashbourne and I will wait for you here. As I told you, it is better to be as discreet as possible."

"No, I won't change my clothes. Disguise yourself if you want. I won't dress down because of some pathetic anarchists. Besides, I am well protected."

"Protected?" Guy asked. Stephen, who had known him for years, caught a tinge of worry in his voice. Everything was clear, was it not? He was witnessing a meeting of sadists. It was an atrocious thing, but easy to understand. Yet, some details didn't add up. And inside Stephen, there was still the stupid hope for a different explanation, along with the physical pain he felt at his heart.

Guy, you can't be like this. Not you. I can't believe it. I won't believe it.
It's not possible.

Behind Cunning, five imposing shadows appeared suddenly. Five tall, massive men. They were soldiers, probably. Stephen's breath choked; if—let's say hypothetically, just hypothetically—if they saw him...

Fuck, fuck, fuck, *fuck.*

"I thought I made it clear," said Guy coldly. "We need discretion."

"Oh, my guards are discreet," Cunning chuckled. "I assure you. Now, would you mind if they frisk you both?"

"Are you kidding us? The Duke and I are the ones who risk more from the Gang of Knives."

"I know. But even if it's silly, I don't trust anyone. You don't mind, do you? You know what they say: better safe than sorry."

He gestured to the bodyguards, and two of them advanced toward Guy and the Duke. And then it happened. Both Guy and St. Court raised their arms at once. Everything was so quick, Stephen couldn't quite understand. A flash of blades appeared in the dim light of the lantern. Four knives flew through the air at the same time.

What the fuck?

Four shadows—Cunning's guards—fell down with the gurgle of their own blood. Had they been hit? Where, in the throat? The body? If so, by what, how... what the hell?

Cunning looked so shocked he couldn't move. He opened and closed his lips like a fish. "God..." he stammered, "so are you... the *Gang?*" This seemed to shake him—the sound of his own voice. He turned and fled in Stephen's direction, screaming like a madman.

"Murder! Murder!"

"Get him, Third!" St. Court ordered, and then turned to Cunning's last bodyguard, who, left alone, stepped back. St. Court threw a knife at the man—where the fuck was he hiding all those knives?—and the soldier flung himself down on the grass. St. Court was on him with unexpected agility, as if fighting and killing, to him, were normal things; the Duke of St.

Court, no less. The *Duke,* who usually moved with lazy motions and imperturbable calm!

Guy chased Cunning. While running, he threw a knife at him, hitting him in the right shoulder. The man fell on his belly, still screaming. Guy jumped on his back, pinning him down with his knees. He pulled the knife out of Cunning's shoulder. He was about fifteen feet away from Stephen, who, shocked, saw his friend, his best friend, bring the blade under Fitzwilliam Cunning's chin and slit his throat open without hesitation.

The blood came gushing out in a violent, almost black jet in the night.

A man appeared behind Guy. One of Cunning's bodyguards. He must have got up from the ground, or maybe he was hiding somewhere. In his hands he held a knife, but Guy hadn't noticed the silent and deadly danger moving forward on the grass.

Stephen had only a moment to decide: Guy was a killer, the entire scene was sickening, he felt dizzy, as if someone had kicked him in the face over and over again. Yet he knew immediately what to do.

"Watch out, Guy! Behind you!"

He came out from behind the tree and threw himself on the soldier who was about to stab Guy in the back. Stephen managed to deflect the blow, which took Guy in the shoulder instead of the throat. Stephen clung to the man, knowing he had no chance of getting out of this alive. His heart slammed in his chest; inside his head, he heard a deafening din, it was like cracking glass, two, ten, a thousand bottles crashing together.

Was this the sound of death?

He didn't want to die.

Do you hear me, God? I. Don't. Want. To. Die!

He pushed the man aside, causing him to fall; but the soldier stood up and shrugged him off. Stephen lost his grip and fell to the ground. He saw blood flowing from Guy's body, then hit his head and saw nothing else.

46.

Guy was floating... where? He didn't know. He felt weak and buffeted. His eyes were closed. His head was heavy and kept him from thinking. Mud, there was mud in his brain. Blood was soaking his shirt. Had he heard Stephen's voice, just a few moments ago? And now... was he hearing Jane's voice?

Jane, Jane.

"Guy!"

Was it Jane? Was it her voice he was hearing from afar, from this place where cold didn't exist—where hunger didn't exist?

"Guy, if you die, I'll die too!"

He had never made love to her. As he felt his mind turn off, sinking down just as he had sunk into the Mole River years ago, this was his only regret.

* * *

"Time to rise and shine, Weymouth," said a voice coming from about six or seven feet away from him. "And in order to eliminate any pleasantries, I'll have you know that you are a prisoner of the Gang of Knives. That means you are in deep trouble, in case you're wondering."

At hearing these words, Stephen stopped breathing. He saw nothing. He had some kind of hood covering his face. There weren't holes in the burlap fabric, neither for the eyes nor for the nose. The air could barely get through the cloth, and the hood smelled of flour and apples: maybe it was once used for such innocent purposes as containing food. Now, it prevented a prisoner from seeing the place where he was held captive.

Stephen was sitting on the ground, on a hard-stone floor, it seemed. His hands were tied behind his back. His shoulders rested against a bumpy wall. In total darkness, he could rely only on the surrounding noises. Just a few minutes ago, as he had opened his eyes, the dark had terrified him. He had cried out and called for help. Now his efforts had been rewarded by his captor's arrival, and he cursed himself.

The Gang of Knives.

The murdering Gang of fucking *Knives*.

328

Oh, fuck—fuck, fuck, FUCK!

His legs were as stiff as iron bars, his hands cold, his breath held.

A lock clicked.

Stephen's hair stood on end. He focused on the sound of a rusty steel door. He was... where? In some kind of a cell?

With firm fast steps, his jailer approached him.

"Please don't kill me," he pleaded, on the verge of tears. His head was bursting from the blow he had received... when? Where? He remembered little about what had happened.

The man laughed, and his laughter sounded cold, emotionless. The man was standing before him; the sound of his laughing came from above Stephen's head.

"Are you already begging?" the man said. "Oh, it will be a breeze dealing with you."

The man's voice was like metal, just the voice a suit of speaking armor would have.

"I haven't any money of my own," Stephen whispered, "but if you want a ransom, the Earl of Ashbourne..."

He paused. Guy. Guy had been in a garden; it had been night, and...

Some images ran through his mind. Guy was in Cunning's garden, it was dark, and...

He couldn't remember... had Guy killed Cunning? What the hell?

His heart stopped. The last scene appeared before his eyes—it was as if someone slashed a whip across his face.

Guy. Stephen had seen Guy falling down. An assassin's knife had wounded Guy.

"Guy... Ashbourne, I mean... is he..." He couldn't let the question come out. He feared the answer; but he had to know. "Is he... dead?"

"Unfortunately no," said the voice above him. "That pig managed to get away."

The tears Stephen was holding back fell on his cheeks in a sudden, heavy burst. Oh thank goodness, thank goodness... "Are you one of the guards hired by Cunning?" he asked in a broken voice. "Did Cunning belong to your... *Gang?*"

"No, he didn't, but yes, I am. He hired me and other members of the Gang of Knives to *protect* himself. Have you ever heard anything stupider? Hiring his own murderers, that's hilarious."

Stephen didn't find it hilarious. His brain was exploding. He couldn't follow the logic of his captor. "Did you set a trap for Cunning and St. Court?" he asked. In his head, it felt like hammered anvils; into his eyes, a thousand needles. The air was thin and unbreathable under the hood.

"Yes, we did. A trap for them... and for Ashbourne."

Guy? But Guy... Stephen had thought... "No," he said in a whisper, "that's not possible. I saw him killing Cunning... I... I thought..." He swallowed hard. "I thought he belonged to your... Gang."

"And would he hold you prisoner here?" The man laughed; being hit by his laughter was like standing in the midst of a violent storm, with hailstones as big as rocks crashing down on you. "You really have a high opinion of your friend. No, he's not one of us. That bastard has just thought, like you, that Cunning was a Knife, and had killed him. You must have noticed that he hurt others among us. Soon, very soon, he's going to pay for it." These words should have sounded disappointed, but the cold man's voice gave nothing away.

"And St. Court? Did he survive too?"

"No." The man made a sound... a sneer, probably. "I myself had the pleasure of cutting his throat."

The place where Stephen was being held had to be isolated. He couldn't hear any noise from outside, not even the wind. Or maybe it was the deafening roar in his ears—his own heart, slamming like crazy—that was preventing him from hearing any other sound.

The smell of flour and apples filled Stephen's lungs as he sucked in all the air he could get. He had to ask his captor a question. He could no longer procrastinate.

"Will you kill me?" he whispered.

Was it cold or hot in his cell? Stephen couldn't tell; only silence filled the room—and his world. It was a long moment of fear, an endless moment in which, perhaps, Stephen's pathetic life should have flashed before his eyes, with all the useless dreams he had never realized.

But Stephen's mind was blank.

Hanging on the answer that wasn't coming.

Was it yes?

Was it no?

"That's up to you."

Stephen let go of the breath he was holding. His captor's answer wasn't quite an answer, but he clung to it anyway.

"Do you want money?" he asked. "Ashbourne will pay you, I'm sure."

"Haven't you understood yet, Weymouth? We don't want money. We don't kill for money."

His head, God... his head was bursting. "Why do you do it, then?"

"Don't you get it?"

Stephen swallowed. He couldn't even follow his own train of thought. The migraine would kill him, if his jailer didn't do it first. "Some say you're anarchists," he managed to spit out. "You target aristocrats and rich men."

"Neither aristocrats nor rich men," was the man's reply. "Haven't you noticed how disgusting the victims of the Gang of Knives are, Weymouth? They're rotten to the core. They're putridity on two legs who don't deserve to be called human."

What the hell was his captor saying? The Gang of Knives's targets were... evil people? It didn't make any sense. More than that: it was a blatant lie! "Some of your victims were respectable... decent people," Stephen objected weakly.

"Oh, *really*. Who was respectable among them, in your opinion?"

"Edmund Millfort," he murmured; he remembered his consternation when reading of that famous philanthropist's dreadful assassination. "And... Sir Geoffrey Ross. He was a magistrate everyone held in high regard."

The man laughed. "Regard? Well, if you think a man full of shit is worthy of regard, then yeah, he was."

Stephen heard an unmistakable sound; the man had spat contemptuously on the floor.

"The list of Ross's crimes," the man went on, "was longer than Priapus's cock. Ross took advantage of his position to make money. If you couldn't pay him, he picked on your kids. He would have your sons arrested, and even sent to the gallows. Your daughters, if young and beautiful, would be brought to prison and forced to entertain... friends of his, as respectable as he was."

"And... Millfort?"

"Oh, he was a true jewel of society. He went to orphanages for the express purpose of charity. The truth was, he used to choose the prettiest kids to have fun with. I think you—" his tone of voice changed, lowering in complicity "—know what I mean."

A shudder shook Stephen. Yes, he did know what the man meant.

"Millfort," continued his captor, "killed a little girl, while having a bit too much *fun* with her. Do you still consider him 'respectable'?"

"But... no one ever spoke ill of him," Stephen murmured. "Are you sure of what you're saying? What if... you made a mistake? Maybe you believed in false pieces of information."

"We don't make mistakes."

Who did he think he was, God Almighty? "Why do you do it?"

"Why do we kill sons of bitches, you mean?" The man's voice hadn't come from above him this time. It had come down to Stephen's level. It seemed his captor had leaned down, maybe on one knee, three or four feet away from Stephen. "Any of us Knives has their own reasons. Some do it for justice, others for revenge. Why would you do it?"

"I'd never do it." The answer came out easily and, obviously, it was wrong. Logic was deserting Stephen. He was just hot breath in the darkness under his hood, and a pounding heart, and a rigid body. "I could never decide whether or not one deserves to die," he continued with difficulty. "I would never be sure to know them enough to judge them fairly."

"That's bullshit. You can judge anyone fairly if you want. All you need to do is investigate them."

"No, you're wrong." There was something else in Stephen, apart from his terror. He was angry, and anger is a very vulnerable emotion—it was prompting him to speak, even though he was at the mercy of this bastard. Even though he should have just begged for his mercy. "You wanted to kill Ashbourne, didn't you? But he's not a rotten man. Whatever you think, you are wrong."

"Seriously? Weymouth, you saw him kill at least three men last night. You saw him with that son of a bitch St. Court. What more evidence do you need?"

"It was your men who attacked him."

"And he ran away. Tell me, doesn't that make you shudder? He left you in our hands and saved his own ass."

What aim did his captor think to achieve by saying these words? Did he think he could convince Stephen that Guy was a piece of shit? If that was the case, he was doing it wrong. In a minute, Stephen's doubts vanished: the man before him was telling him a steaming pile of lies. "No," he said, "Ash would never quit on me."

"Wouldn't he? Yet you're here, aren't you—and he's *not.*"

Good objection. The tears Stephen had let fall a few minutes ago had wet his neck and tie. The moist air warmed up his difficult breathing. He swallowed, trying to think. Think, goddammit, *think.* His head hurt, but... but he remembered that things had *not* gone as his captor was telling him. "I..." he murmured, trying to follow his own thoughts. Jesus, he needed to make this absurd situation logical. "I remember I fell, and... and a man hit me. St. Court..."

"St. Court's dead, as I said." The man's voice sounded cheerful. "And thank goodness, I might add. He was a lousy dog. You have no doubt about that, I hope?"

"And me, then?" Stephen snapped. "What horrible things do you think I did, to have me here?" Thick fury swelled against his chest. He was about to *die* because of some bastards with delusions of grandeur. Holy Jesus Christ, these men positively thought they were the Four Horsemen of the Apocalypse. "Tell me, I'm curious! Since the worst thing I've ever done was to steal my brother's lemon pudding when I was seven years old!"

"No, this is not correct," the man replied calmly. "The worst thing you've ever done was to cover for Guy Spencer, the 4th Earl of Ashbourne, when he beat your uncle to death in Summer 1846."

The answer shocked Stephen. He didn't reply.

"A few minutes ago, you called Ross and Millfort 'respectable men,'" said his captor. "Even Ashbourne is, in your opinion. So, why do you think he killed your uncle? Do you think he did it because of what your uncle did to that maid's son? Or because of what your uncle did to *you?*"

Stephen closed his eyes. A buzzing sound filled his head. For a long, terrible moment, he was afraid of losing consciousness.

For two reasons.

In Summer 1846, Guy was in Derbyshire visiting the Weymouths. One afternoon, he and Stephen had heard a sobbing coming from the barn.

They had entered it.

There was a child among the hay. A thin child, with dark hair. His pants were down to his knees, his anus was bleeding. He was nine or ten years old. He was crying, and Stephen... he had begun to cry too.

The child had run away without revealing the name of the man who had abused him. But Stephen had guessed. He had told Guy it must have been his uncle, who was visiting his older brother.

Guy hadn't asked Stephen why he was sure his uncle was the one to blame. He hadn't asked why Stephen was crying. And Stephen had been grateful to him for this—for not having forced him to explain. He had already been dangerously close to revealing the secret he was so ashamed of. A secret he had told no one. Even when drunk he had never spoken about it. Even opium had never opened his lips. It was his personal abyss, nobody should ever know what his uncle had done to him. But that afternoon, when he had seen that kid in the barn... something had just snapped inside him.

Guy had looked at Stephen and his face had hardened with restrained ire. And on that very night, Hugo Robert Weymouth, the younger brother of Baron Eugene Carl Weymouth, had died. Some servants had found his body in the middle of a muddy street. They had thought he must have fallen from his horse. And the horse, they had said, must have trampled him badly, for his face was smashed and his ribs broken.

"I don't know what you're talking about," Stephen replied as the pain from these memories exploded inside him. The absurd thing was, he was the prisoner of the most ferocious assassins in London, he was facing the deadliest danger of his life—but at this very moment, his guts weren't torn because of any of this. He felt like dying inside because his captor, a crazy man not even worthy to lick his boots, knew his secret. This man here, this crazy man—he knew what Stephen's uncle had done to him. He knew what his uncle had forced Stephen to do.

Nausea rose to his throat. Guy suspected it, yet Stephen could tolerate it. Yes, Guy had surely figured out what had happened to Stephen as a child, and that was indeed painful—but bearable, for Guy was, well, *Guy*. But as for the others... God, he could not stand the shame; his cheeks burned hot and tears filled his eyes; he bowed his head.

"No?" his captor replied. "Come on, man. He beat him to death. He split his head open with a stone and then made it look like an accident. You and I both know your uncle isn't dead because of a fall from a horse.

Maybe you think your uncle deserved to die. Maybe you think Ashbourne killed him for this reason. But honestly, haven't you realized Ashbourne murdered him just for fun? Haven't you realized Ashbourne *enjoys* murdering people?"

Stephen swallowed his tears and mustered enough pride to reply. "No. He's not like that. You are wrong."

"I already told you, I'm never wrong. Ashbourne is a sadist, as his father was before him. He's a murderer."

"You can't be sure! You're not infallible, you're just a worthless man with an abnormally large ego. You can't read people's hearts and you have *no* right to make yourself judge and jury. In fact, tell me," he said, smiling desperately under the hood, "tell me why I should die, according to your Gang!"

"But you don't have to die," his captor said with a matter-of-fact tone. "Excess of stupidity isn't a valid reason to deserve a Level One. Not yet, at least."

As he said so, his hands touched the hood over Stephen's head. Stephen instinctively drew back and slammed his nape against the wall.

The man grabbed the hood, pulling it away.

Stephen blinked at the sudden light. It was day; through a barred window, about six feet up from the floor, came the sunlight. It had to be protected by very thick glass: silence reigned in the room.

Stephen's eyes adjusted to the light. His head was throbbing with pain from the slam against the wall, not to mention his migraine. He was in a cell, about seven feet by nine. There was no bed or basin; three sides of rough stone, and in front of him, thick steel bars.

His captor stood up. Maybe he wanted to intimidate Stephen with his considerable height. He was an athletic man; he was wearing a black cloak, and a hood of the same color covered his face, except for two slits for the eyes.

He had chilly, light-gray eyes.

"So?" asked Stephen, and he couldn't even hear himself because of his pounding heart throbbing with fear. "Why am I here, then?"

"Haven't you got it yet?" The man stared at him coldly. "We want Ashbourne. You must help us kill him."

* * *

Hell. This had to be hell. It hurt so fucking *bad*.

"He's waking up. Doctor!"

The broken voice wasn't a devil's, but an angel's.

Guy tried to open his eyes. Too much light. He closed them.

"Earl? Lord Ashbourne?"

It was a male voice this time. An annoying voice.

Where is my angel?

"I'm here."

Had he spoken out loud? He didn't know. He felt cool hands on his forehead and fell back to sleep.

* * *

The cell door opened, and Stephen pissed on himself. Again. Footsteps, the ones he had come to recognize and fear more than anything else in the world, came toward him.

Stephen was sitting on the ground, with a burlap hood over his face and his arms tied behind his back. His legs were free and stretched in front of him. He didn't use them to kick his captor. He had already tried that move, a few hours ago, and his captor's reaction had been terrible. That son of a bitch had pulled out a knife, torn Stephen's shirt and wounded him. Two deep, scorching cuts on his right shoulder. Laughing, that bastard had sprinkled his bleeding flesh with salt. It had been like a fire burning his arm. Stephen had screamed, kicking in the air. His captor had let him suffer for long, and finally, immobilizing him, had washed his wounds with whiskey.

It still hurt like hell.

A fist suddenly hit his face and made him turn his head. His left temple slammed against the wall. Tears pushed into his eyes, and he let them fall down his face.

"Please, let me go," he sobbed.

A cold sound of laughter came from above him. "But of course, you sissy. Of course I'll let you go. You just have to do this little thing for me."

His tormentor's hands lifted the hood from his face. Stephen squinted, blinded by the light of the flaming torches into the cell. It was nighttime... but of what day?

How long had he been there?

Before him, his captor's silver eyes scanned him. Stephen had started to think of him as "the Iceman," for he showed no emotions at all. Just like now. He was standing in silence, and behind the hood his eyes gave nothing away.

Stephen had learned from the two previous sessions with him that he wasn't supposed to speak without the Iceman's permission.

He remained silent.

His trousers were stuck to him with his own pee. Blood clots on his right eyelid prevented him from opening the eye. His mouth was swollen from the punches he had received. He still had all his teeth; but how long would they last? God, he didn't want his teeth knocked out. This thought was silly, since he was going to lose not only his teeth, but probably his *life;* yet, if his eyes filled with new, hot tears, it was for this stupid reason.

Not my teeth... please, not my teeth, not my teeth...

"Come on, man. He's just a scumbag, you know it, and I know it," said the Iceman, waving a white sheet of paper before his eyes. "Write him this letter. You just have to tell him you're waiting for him at 31 Bolton Street. The Gang of Knives will take care of the rest."

Stephen knew what his words would cause. Sniffling, he said them anyway. "N... no."

"Am I to assume you're a bastard like him?"

"Ashbourne is not... he's not a bastard!"

"Fuck yes, he is. And we'll kill him. I like you, Weymouth, I know you're going to do the right thing. I'm asking you again. Will you write this fucking letter?"

"No," Stephen repeated. He would have liked to use a booming voice, devoid of fear. He sobbed, like the sissy he was.

The Iceman dropped the sheet of paper to the ground. "Then I must persuade you," he said.

A blade appeared from under his black cloak. As he brought it to the wound on the prisoner's right shoulder, Stephen noticed for the first time that two fingers were missing from his hand. For some absurd reason, even more panic exploded within him.

"Now I'll reopen this wound of yours," the Iceman said quietly. "Then, to disinfect it—" his eyes sparkled cruelly "—I'll sprinkle it with another bit of salt."

* * *

"Guy, please, eat something."

Semi-reclining in bed, he grunted. His ribs hurt like a son of a bitch. "Still no word from Weymouth?" he asked weakly.

Jane shook her head. "If you let Papa send for the police..."

"Nonsense."

"It's *not* nonsense. The police could catch the criminals who attacked you and Mr. Weymouth."

"They were just two miserable thieves. And I didn't see their faces, anyway. Reporting the incident to the police would be useless."

"But Mr. Weymouth... the police could find out where he is. Maybe he's in some hospital... maybe he needs some help."

"If he's in the hospital, your father will find him." He shrugged, and the gesture hurt him like a knife. "As soon as I came to my senses, your father promised me he would go all around looking for him."

Guy had come to his senses four hours ago. He had been sleeping, drugged with some narcotic, for two whole days. Two whole *fucking* days. He had lost a lot of blood. He still felt damn weak, but he could think clearly at least. His mind was no longer confused. The fever had gone down and he could even sit up. He threw his head back.

Stephen.

What had happened to him? It was his voice. It surely was. Two days ago, it was Stephen's voice that had shouted: *Watch out, Guy, behind you!*

336

Stephen had saved his life.

What the fuck had happened after that? The Gang of Knives...

He swallowed hard. The Gang of Knives would inform him about what had happened that cursed night. They had to tell him what had happened. Charles's search among the hospitals of London was just to distract him and Jane. Wherever Stephen was, in whatever condition he was, the Gang of Knives would surely tell Guy soon.

He half-opened his eyes and looked with a grimace at the spoon Jane was holding out to him. He had no intention of eating. The thought sickened him. He felt awful. A few minutes ago, he had tried to move a leg to get up and go to St. Court's, but he had managed to lift his foot only a few inches before letting it fall back, exhausted by the effort, in a lake of sweat.

Please, God, tell me what happened to him.

Two nights ago, it had been a mess. Cunning, that bastard Cunning. He had hired soldiers to defend himself. Guy and Stuart had reacted quickly, but not quickly enough. And Stephen...

Guy closed his eyes.

And Stephen had saved his life... but had his act of friendship killed him? God, Guy couldn't even think of the possibility.

"Guy?" Jane said.

He opened his eyes, and Jane held the spoon filled with soup to his lips. She was sitting in a chair beside his bed. Judging by the deep dark circles under her eyes, she hadn't slept since he had been brought home injured.

Guy turned his head away. "I don't want to vomit on you," he explained before she could protest.

Jane didn't drop the spoon. "It doesn't matter if you vomit on me."

"Well, but it would be painful in my condition. Come on, angel, I promise you I'll eat something later. All right?"

Jane shook her head stubbornly. "Even not eating is not good for you. Please, Guy, just one spoonful."

Please, just one spoonful. In a flash, he thought back of her as a child: how much she tormented him when he was ill. "You were a pain in the neck even as a child," he murmured.

Jane's mouth twisted downward, saddened by his words. And Guy gave way, as usual. He opened his mouth. The chicken soup was delicate and light: it wouldn't nourish him, he thought, it would just make him throw up. But Jane brightened up, and that was enough.

"You always tried to drive me away," she said, scraping his chin with the spoon, where a drop of soup had dribbled down. She was treating him like a child, even if he was this big, tough guy; and since he hadn't shaved for two days, he was also as dark and prickly as a hedgehog.

"No, my mother tried to drive you away," he whispered. "But you always came back."

Jane gave him another spoonful of soup. She smiled as he swallowed it. "I didn't let anyone else in your room. I wanted to take care of you all by myself. Except a little girl wasn't of great help to you, I guess."

"No one would have come in my room anyway." Guy swallowed the soup, but there was some sort of cork in his throat. Nothing could go down it.

"Don't say that. Of course someone would have."

Jane slipped the spoon into his mouth. This was the girl he had enslaved for more than four months, humiliated, used in every way. He had made her climax so hard she had wept with pleasure—and now she was treating him like a baby. Somewhat inexplicably, it didn't bother him.

"Even as a child you were a liar," he murmured.

She picked up the spoon and carried it to his lips. "Hmm?"

He breathed slowly and, with an effort, swallowed the damn soup. God, it hurt like hell, was it really necessary? "You used to tell me that my mother knew you were with me. In my room."

"That was true. Open your mouth... good boy."

Guy smiled. *Jane, as soon as I pull myself together, I'll make you swallow that "good boy" of yours.* "My mother would never have let you set foot in my room, Jane. But since she herself never came to visit me, you could pester..." A spoonful of the damned soup interrupted him. He swallowed hard and concluded, "...pester me with total impunity."

Jane chuckled. "You always tried to send me away. Once you told me, get out or I'll decapitate all your dolls. But you were too weak to get up and throw me out, so—" she gave him another spoonful of soup, with no warning "—I simply remained there." She gave a sly smile. "Like now."

Just like now. Jane, sitting at his side acting as a nurse, and Guy, letting her take care of him. His pestiferous little angel. "Had I really wanted to send you away," he heard himself say, "I would have done so, angel."

Jane's hand froze in mid-air and started to tremble. She dropped the spoon into the bowl, her eyes veiled with emotion. "Didn't you want me to get out?" she murmured, her voice shaking. "And... not even now?"

Guy realized his misstep. "Jane..."

She leaned forward and kissed him. He had to drive her away, he was giving her unrealistic hope for a future together, but he was too debilitated to raise his arm, turn his head... and it would take too much willpower to tell her to get out. Jane's mouth pressed on his, and burned just a little because of a cut on his lower lip. She was so tender, his angel, his little witch. Guy closed his eyes, touching her tongue with his own. Here it was, her candy taste, and...

Someone knocked on the door. Jane startled and, parting quickly from him, she stood up.

"Come in," she said, burning with an emotion between happiness and agitation.

The door opened. It was a maid with dark-brown hair.

"Your father is looking for you, Miss Hartwell," the maid said, making a little bow.

"Is he already home?" Jane asked, puzzled. "Why didn't he come up here directly?" She turned to Guy biting her lip, troubled. "Perhaps he's too tired to climb two flights of stairs. I'll go see what he wants, do you mind? Maybe he found out something about Mr. Weymouth."

"Yes, of course, angel," Guy replied distractedly, looking at the maid who was keeping her face lowered. Despite the almost perfectly counterfeit voice, Guy had recognized her.

She was Isabelle Smith, the Fourth Knife.

As Isabelle raised her face, her cat's irises gleamed. "Please leave the tray, Miss Hartwell," she said, behaving very properly. "I'll handle that."

Jane smiled with her usual kindness and hurried out of the room. Isabelle narrowed her eyes, watching her leave with a mocking smile.

"What a fairy," she murmured. "I'd enjoy having her chained to my table, some time or other."

Guy clutched the sheet between his fingers. "Four."

Isabelle giggled. "Oh, my God... you're just crazy about her, aren't you? That's *so* romantic. It was moving, you know, two nights ago... when we brought you here. You were delirious and kept calling, 'Jane... Jane.' And besides, I knew you must have been in love with her to want her so badly," she added, approaching the bedside table and fiddling with the tray. "But ruining her father's business wasn't nice of you, naughty boy. She doesn't have a clue about that, I guess."

"Four, where is Weymouth? It was him, wasn't it, the one who saved my life two nights ago? I couldn't fucking remember, is he..." Dead? He couldn't ask. The word just didn't come out. "Is he fine?"

Isabelle hesitated. "Yes," she finally said. "But..." She glanced at him and paused.

Guy's hair stood on end at the nape of his neck. "The Knives are questioning him," he finished for her. He threw his head back against the pillow, closing his eyes. His forehead, already hot with fever, seemed on fire. "Jesus Christ."

"I'm sorry, Number Three. The First Knife has deemed it necessary. Your friend saw too much."

"Is he at the shack?"

Guy moved his legs sideways. He was weak; but he had to get up, he had to go save Stephen.

"No," Isabelle said, stopping him, "he's not there. Before you ask, the First Knife didn't tell me where he would take him."

Fuck. Fuck, fuck. This meant that, even if Guy had been strong enough to look for him, he would never find him in time. "Tell the First Knife that if he kills Stephen—" he swallowed; he wanted to shout, but his voice came out faint, his head was spinning. "Tell him that if he kills Stephen, I'll kill him."

"Do you believe your friend will betray you?"

Guy's chest rose in heavy breaths. "Am I the jackpot in this shit? What the fuck did they tell him, he has to betray me to save himself?" His voice swelled with furious distress. "God, First is a bastard. He really is. And who is questioning him? Five. Tell me it's Five."

Isabelle shook her head.

Guy's heart slammed against his ribs. Second was torturing Stephen. At this very moment, Second was torturing Stephen.

"What happened after I blacked out?" he asked, putting his head back on the pillow. Nausea pushed its way up his throat, but he endeavored to give a firm tone to his voice.

Isabelle brushed back a curl from her forehead. "The First Knife saved your friend's life, so you see, if he is indeed a bastard, he is not a *total* bastard. He cut the throat of a soldier who was about to kill your friend. Weymouth fell unconscious. He didn't understand who was with whom. The Second Knife told him a crazy story, and looks like he bought it. More or less."

"And now Second is trying to persuade him that he has to betray me to save himself." Persuade him... Guy knew what methods the Knives would use, and his chest couldn't expand enough to get the air inside of him. Holy shit, he just couldn't make his bloody lungs inflate. "Tell One not to kill him, I... I'll prevent him from damaging the Gang. Please tell him that, whatever Stephen does, he must not kill him. He's not as strong as us, but he's a good fellow, he is, and I... I don't want him to die."

"I'll tell him," promised Isabelle; she gave him a sorry, sympathetic look. The look that perhaps, years ago, she had had for her daughter.

But what good would that do? Stuart had his inflexible rules; he wouldn't change them for Stephen.

Don't kill W. God, I care for that fellow.

Isabelle put her hand on his shoulder. She squeezed it gently. "I'm sorry, Third. But you know what? The First Knife said your friend's doing well so far. I think he'll make it."

Guy clenched his hand on the sheet. His knuckles turned white, and the effort made his shoulder flare with pain. He spread his fingers. The bloody soup came up his throat.

Don't. Vomit. Right. Now.

He managed to wait for Isabelle to leave his room. Then, leaning sideways over the edge of the bed, he regurgitated to the last drop. Partly on the floor. Partly on the sheets.

Partly on himself.

* * *

"Please... please don't."

Humiliating tears flowed down Stephen's face. Fear made his breathing difficult and shallow.

He just had to betray Guy. He had to get his best friend killed.

"I want you to write that you're at your old apartment in Bolton Street. Write that you're waiting for Ashbourne there. Then you'll be free to go."

Guy was a scumbag, the Iceman had said.

The Gang of Knives killed only people who deserved it, and Stephen could see this now.

"Kill me," he answered between sobs. "Because I won't write your bloody letter. Never. I don't believe this shit you're saying... I won't believe it unless Guy confirms it himself!"

The Iceman made a noise that sounded like a laugh. "Whatever you want, man. I'll kill you. But—" he pulled out a knife "—not right now."

After a moment, Stephen began to scream.

* * *

"Oh, Guy, you shouldn't get up... please, go back to bed."

"In a moment, Jane. I just need a moment." He looked out the window of his bedroom, waiting for a sign from the K-Gang. For a message. For Stephen's return.

Outside the sky was agonizingly clear and blue. He still felt like shit; he had to clench the curtains to stand.

"Guy..."

"Jane, could you please leave me alone, angel?"

"Are you worried about Mr. Weymouth?"

He closed his eyes and dropped in a chair next to the window, resting his forehead in his hand.

"Can I do something for you?" Jane asked with a desolate voice.

"No, little one," he said softly, "this time you can't."

* * *

"I could keep torturing you," the Iceman said, his voice muffled by the hood pulled down over his face.

Stephen was lying on one side, semi-reclining on the ground. His own feces soiled his clothes. His eyes were half-closed from the blows he had received. His hands were tied behind him, and his right shoulder throbbed with pain from the knife wound on it. Two crossed cuts, opened and opened again, several times, by his tormentor.

He hadn't eaten for a time that seemed very long. He had drunk something, though. The Iceman himself had forced him to drink, ramming a bottle into his mouth and pouring water of rancid taste down his throat.

341

"But it would be useless, wouldn't it?" his captor went on, watching the flame of a candle placed on the ground next to them. "So, that's it. I give up on you, Weymouth. That means, I'm afraid, that I have to kill you."

Stephen's heart began to beat wildly, thudding into his throat. Into his ears. *Tum tum tum.* He had come to hope to die soon, during these long hours of anguish; however, the air was going down inside his chest, the pain from his wounded shoulder was better than nothing.

But it was too late to love his life. He was about to die.

Why?

Why, my God, why?

Just because of Guy Spencer.

Just because of a bastard, a scumbag, a murderer.

Tum tum tum.

"You think you are God Almighty, don't you?" Stephen hissed between cracked lips. "You fucking know what, Mr. Gang of Knives? You're just a sorry coward."

The Iceman shrugged, totally indifferent to his words. "I'm going to ignore your insult," he said. "In fact, I'll grant your last wish, as it is customary. No." He made a motion with his hand before Stephen could speak. "You don't need to tell me what you want. I already know it. Wait here."

As if Stephen could go elsewhere.

Tum tum tum.

The Iceman walked out of the cell, and his footsteps stopped behind the wall. Stephen could not see him, but as he heard a slight gurgle, and a sweet, unmistakable scent, his breath stopped.

God, it couldn't be—

The Iceman reappeared behind the iron bars. In his hands, he held a ceramic pipe-bowl with a long stem. Stephen immediately recognized the shape.

"I know you like opium," the Iceman said, coming closer to him.

The son of a bitch. The Iceman hadn't prepared just any opium. It was top-quality opium, perhaps Turkish, judging by its intense musky perfume. Oh, that scent from the treasure-laden Orient was a promise of heaven. The color of the poppy flower filled Stephen's mind, like a flash of longing through his body. He could almost see it, its light-purple, delicate, provocative petals. It was an image of sensual beauty and, at the same time, of innocence. Maybe Guy would bring poppies to his grave. Stephen deeply hoped so. It would be nice, for once, being free to enjoy their scent without feeling weak-willed and worthless.

One of the indisputable advantages of being dead.

The Iceman leaned toward him, so close their heads almost touched. "So, would you like one last shot?"

Yes... oh God, yes. "No," he said with a strangled voice. "I'd rather have... clean water to drink." Meanwhile, he was thinking: *Curse you, Guy Spencer, you bloody Earl of Ashbourne. I can't even enjoy my last dose of opium because of you, damn you.*

Because opium would break his resistance. Not immediately, maybe, but eventually, when the effect would disappear. And then, he would ask for more; he would beg, he would cry... and perhaps he would write a letter to his best friend, condemning him to death.

He couldn't.

He wouldn't.

"Not only will you die for him," the Iceman said, lifting the hood up to his nose and uncovering lips too sensual for his cold voice, "but you're also giving up this last pleasure for him. That's remarkable. Or remarkably stupid, anyway."

Stephen raised his left shoulder. It was the only movement he could make without too much pain. "The fact is..." he said, more to himself than to his jailer. "The fact is, Ash would do the same for me. See, you said you know him, but..." He closed his eyes, filling his nose with the opium scent, without, alas, enjoying the vaporizing peace it could carry with it, renouncing to the calm and the serenity it could offer. "But you don't know shit about him."

Yes, that was so. The tremor caused by his wet clothes stopped. Saying these words aloud had helped him to stay strong; he hung onto this as if it were a physical foothold for his willpower. Guy would die for him, yes, Stephen knew he would. What did it matter what the Iceman said? What did that asshole know? Nothing. He knew so fucking nothing.

The Iceman held the pipe-bowl to the lamp, setting the pipe-stem to his lips. Half smiling, he sucked on it with a gurgling noise. "Wonderful," he said, gesturing with the pipe toward Stephen's face.

"Go fuck yourself."

"Fuck myself?" The Iceman laughed, revealing white and regular teeth. "Oh come on, you don't mean that, do you? Why, I think you're hoping I'll fuck *you*. Would you like that?"

"All right, that's enough, Second." The voice came from outside the cell, around the corner between the wall and the narrow corridor. The voice was slow, drawling.

Unmistakable.

Stephen's eyes widened as the man who had spoken appeared behind the iron bars.

"St. Court?" Stephen said, totally bewildered. "But you... you're alive?"

Pretty damn alive. He wore a black cloak, and his unmasked face was perfectly shaved. He had his usual, incongruous look of a diligent student.

"What a keen observer you are, Mr. Weymouth." Calmly, His Grace pushed the cell door open and came in.

"But... but this man told me..." Stephen swallowed hard. "He told me you were dead."

The Duke lifted an eyebrow. "Since I'm standing before you, I'm inclined to believe he lied to you. We can make other hypotheses, of course. For example, maybe you're having some sort of hallucination. Or maybe I'm a ghost. Or maybe we are all dead and, to make matters worse, we are sentenced to the same circle of hell."

Absurdly, Stephen felt like laughing. Since he was about to die, perhaps it was the most logical thing to do. "Well, I guess you'll kill me now," he said, trying to figure out what the fuck was going on. "That... crap about you being the Gang of Knives," he muttered wearily, "was... what was it, precisely, St. Court?"

"Ashbourne will explain everything to you."

This struck him. He straightened up and, defying the pain from his injuries, he sat with his back against the wall. "What did you just say?"

"We won't kill you, Mr. Weymouth. This was a test and, I am pleased to say, you successfully passed it."

"Test?" Stephen, who had his trousers soiled with urine and feces, realized that the words *successfully passed* would sound different to him from now on.

"Try to focus, will you?" the Duke said with restrained impatience. "Second, please, clean him up and give him new clothes, then put him into a carriage. At my expense, of course," he added with a polite nod to Stephen, as if to say, "hey, am I or am I not a gentleman?"

"That's really, uh... generous of you," said Stephen, with all the sarcasm he could muster. In fact, he felt his head going thick with dizziness. What the devil was going on?

"You're welcome," said His Grace. "Anytime you want to do it again, just give me a holler."

The Iceman—or Second, as St. Court had called him—lowered the hood over his lips and threw the pipe down on the floor. It broke into pieces, and Stephen looked at the porcelain fragments with regret. Refusing to smoke opium was one thing. His longing for it, alas, was another.

"What a pity, letting him go," said the Iceman. "I grew fond of him. Do you think I could take him to my house and keep him as a pet? Ashbourne has trained him perfectly. He would jump through flaming hoops if he asked him to."

"Second."

"All right, all right. But don't say I am the one in the Gang with no sense of humor." The Iceman shrugged, approaching Stephen. He put a knife behind his back and, with one clean cut, freed Stephen's wrists, then stepped away.

Stephen felt debilitated and hungry, but he wouldn't stay on the ground while these sons of bitches laughed at him from above. He stood up uncertainly, his legs as stiff as sticks. The wall behind him was indispensable support to him. He did not try to lash out at them. He did not have enough strength, and besides, he had seen St. Court in action: certainly the man had several knives hidden under his sleeve.

He swallowed. "How do you know," he said with a lump in his throat— hold on, wasn't he about to die, then? He wouldn't die, seriously? "How do you know I will go to Ashbourne and not, say, to the police?"

"I would like to answer we are not worried about that, given the loyalty you have shown your friend," St. Court replied. "Alas, the truth is more prosaic. Some men will follow you at a distance, Mr. Weymouth, ready to intervene if it becomes apparent that your destination is not Ashbourne House."

Stephen raised his hand to his forehead, rubbing it across his temple. Hunger, weariness... confusion mixed in his dazed mind. "St. Court, I... the rumors people say about you... are they based on true events? Or is your reputation just a facade, like—" He stopped abruptly. Was St. Court's reputation as fake as Guy's? Yes, probably—yes, that must be the case. Stephen did not say it aloud. He did not trust St. Court. Maybe this bullshit the Duke was telling him was a trap to push Stephen into betraying his friend after all.

Stephen hoped it wasn't a trap. He could earnestly say he would be quite pleased to get out of here alive. Aside from the obvious reason—that was, well, staying actually *alive*—he couldn't wait to see Guy and ask him for an explanation.

And wring his neck, too.

St. Court gave a slight smile and turned around, going to the door. His cloak spread behind him. "Truth can be easily manipulated, Mr. Weymouth, don't you think?"

He left without waiting for an answer. The Iceman followed him, maybe to gather the necessary things to prepare a bath for Stephen. The man locked the cell door, and his footsteps echoed down the corridor.

With weak legs, Stephen dropped back on the floor again. He put a hand over his eyes and burst into tears. He didn't want to cry, he *didn't* want to, but God, God—it seemed that, after all, today was not his day to die.

47.

"Damn, I said I'm fine! I want to get up, by God, you can't stop me!"

Sitting on the bed, with his trousers still unbuttoned and only one boot on, Guy reached out to grab the doctor's neck. The sudden movement didn't prove to be a remarkably good idea. The white bandage wrapping his chest, underneath his open shirt, strained and seemed to be about to tear.

Dr. Kenneth stepped back before Guy could grasp his stethoscope. Medical instruments were in danger with this patient. Yesterday, the Earl had grabbed his syringe, breaking it, and Kenneth did not intend to repeat the experience.

"You're not well enough to... for heaven's sake, just stay still, your lordship!"

The Hippocratic Oath defeated the doctor's instinct of getting away and leaving this stupid man alone. Or maybe, it wasn't just the Hippocratic Oath, it was because of Jane Hartwell's wonderful eyes. She had asked him to take care of her stepbrother. Her *exasperating* stepbrother. John Kenneth had been dreaming of seeing her again—how much he had missed her, after she had stopped going to the Christian hospital! And he had finally got to see her again. The negative aspect of this was, of course, that he had to deal with this... this stupid... arrogant—

He placed his hands on Ashbourne's shoulders and held him down, stopping him from standing up. The patient was strong and troublingly massive, but he was also weakened. It was a good thing, from a certain point a view. Kenneth was athletic, but under normal circumstances, he could never manage to impose upon Ashbourne.

"You need to rest," he said, ignoring the alarming manner in which the Earl's eyebrows had furrowed above his nose. "I promised your stepsister I'd take care of you, and you know what, your stubborn lordship? I will do it!"

Ashbourne swore fiercely. "Why the hell did Jane ask *you* to check on me? Why didn't she call Wilson, for fuck's—"

Ashbourne went on and on, and the words he used to express his point of view enriched, in a not exactly pleasant way, Kenneth's vocabulary.

New and unexpected words indeed.

All right, the Earl wasn't happy with his presence. Jane had called Kenneth yesterday, worried about her stepbrother's convalescence, and the doctor had rushed to her.

Obviously he had.

"Wilson would say what you want to hear," he snapped. "But I am here to heal you, not to get rich."

"I'm not going—" The Earl grabbed Kenneth's hand, the one pinning down his right shoulder, and squeezed it with considerable force, frowning as only a damn nobleman can do. "I'm not going to stay in this fucking bed one more minute, is that clear? Now take your hands..."

The door swung open behind them. Kenneth couldn't turn to look at the door but was grateful for the unexpected help.

"Give me a hand with him, quickly!" he called out. "This..." idiot "...bloody stubborn—"

He stopped speaking, for the Earl had dropped his hand and his expression had changed.

Ashbourne was looking at the door, and a slight smile had transformed his face, turning a waste-of-air earl into a man who had just witnessed an apparition.

Kenneth turned to the door. It wasn't exactly an *apparition*. On the doorstep was a young man, about twenty-five years old. He was elegantly dressed, and that was weird, because his clothes formed a singular contrast with his bruised face and his bent, suffering posture.

More worryingly, the young man was pointing his index finger at Ashbourne with murderous ferocity.

"You bastard," the young man growled. "Now I'll rip your guts out and strangle you with them."

Kenneth sighed, spreading his arms wide open, like a wall between the killer in the doorway and his patient. Oh, damn it. Sometimes he heartily hated the Hippocratic Oath.

* * *

"You are a son of a bitch." Stephen sat down on a chair next to Guy's bed. "I'm going to kill you, of course. But I want to hear a fucking explanation first."

"I'm glad to see you too," Guy murmured.

The door was closed. Dr. Kenneth wasn't in the room anymore. He had left after they had assured him that no more ribs would crack inside his patient. He had appeared to be overly anxious about some damn Hippocratic Oath. He had promised them he would "stick around," just to check on them from time to time. And so, now that Stephen could finally face Guy, he had to whisper in order not to be overheard from behind the door. Shit. He wanted to scream, and punch his friend, and... and...

Oh, he was just kidding himself.

Guy was sitting sideways in his bed, with his feet on the floor. He had just one boot on. He was pale and pasty. But he was smiling. And Stephen foolishly wanted to smile in response.

He stopped himself from doing it.

For God's sake, he did not even know who the man on the bed was. Not to mention that, because of him, he had lived three days of hell.

His... test, did he have to call it so?... well, whatever; his test had finished last night, but the Knives had released him only this morning. After St. Court had gone away, the Iceman, with his face still covered, had given Stephen clean clothes, a tub, and two buckets of hot water. He had ordered him to take a bath. Stephen had obeyed, but moving had been painful, and he had poured almost all the water on the ground.

Eventually, his jailer had brought him food and drink. There must have been some narcotics in the food: Stephen had fallen asleep like a stone. It was late morning when he had woken up. He was still in the bloody cell, lying on a clean mattress, under a warm blanket. Yet, the good night's sleep had done him good, and he could see it now with the benefit of hindsight. The tremors had almost left his body, and the memory of what had happened seemed less scary in the daylight. His nightmare had ended half an hour ago, when the Iceman had put him into a carriage. Before slamming the carriage door in his face, his captor had told him something that had turned out to be right. "Don't worry, Weymouth." These had been the Iceman's goodbye words, his voice emotionless even in the last minutes. "When a memory is too hard for us to bear, our mind buries it somewhere, and we forget about it soon. Someday you'll wake up, and this fear will be gone. Just like that."

Stephen's eyes, swollen and rimmed in black and blue by the Iceman's punches, threw a heavy look at Guy. "Don't you have anything to say to me, man?"

"Actually, yes: you look like shit."

Guy was in pretty bad shape too, the large bandage under his unbuttoned shirt revealing how serious his wounds were. It was strange to see him like this. Guy always looked as strong as a bull.

"Well, old bean, I can say the same about you."

Talking was causing Stephen pain. During the three days of his captivity, the Iceman had done no heavy damage to his body: he hadn't broken his bones or his teeth; maybe a couple of Stephen's ribs had cracked, all right, but nothing more than in an angry fight against Guy. At some point, the Iceman had stuck a needle under the nail of his index finger, and Stephen had fainted with pain, but not even that had had consequences. His fingernail hadn't even fallen off. Only the wound on his right shoulder, the knife wound the Iceman had opened and opened again, would leave a scar.

That scar would never fade.

He blinked himself out of these thoughts. The last three days had been a horror, but around him there was daylight. He was at Ashbourne House, in Guy's bedroom; and Guy was alive, sitting on the unmade bed, with his hair uncombed.

Stephen was *here*.

"I'm sorry, Steve."

Guy's voice sounded soft and gentle. It was no longer ironic; it was husky with emotion. Stephen's lower lip shook, but dammit, he had been crying like a baby all the time of his captivity, and probably Guy knew it. He could weep a little more. His embarrassment could not grow bigger than this, that was for sure.

"Oh. So you're sorry."

"Hey, I didn't know where the Knives brought you. I woke up yesterday, and let me say it wasn't the best day of my life. In the evening I was informed that you... well. They informed me you did just fine. And speaking of which—" he looked up at him and gave his usual smile, the sideways one, but his eyes were dancing with warmth "—thank you, my friend." He closed his fist, stretched out his arm toward Stephen and rubbed his friend's head with his knuckles. It was similar to a manly pat on the back, or a sort of a hug, maybe. Besides, both of them were way too weak to do complicated things like hugs.

Stephen's heart, as stupid as it was, swelled with emotion. Spending three days locked in a cell while a sadistic, frightening bastard tortured him had been not so high a price to pay.

He cleared his throat, blushing like a girl. "Not the best day of your life, you say?" he murmured, taking refuge in sarcasm.

"You make it sound insensitive of me. But I know what you went through." A cheerful light shone in Guy's eyes. "I went through it too, over three years ago."

Astonished, Stephen could only stare at him for long moments. "W-what?"

"They tortured me, W." Guy rested his right elbow on his knee, looking down at the tip of the only boot he was wearing. "They submitted me to a... what does Stu call it? A... test."

Stu. Was this what he called that son of a bitch St. Court?

Stephen rubbed his forehead with his hand. "Why did they test you?"

"They wanted to make sure I was the right person for their Gang. I mean, before admitting me among them. You know that scar I have on my shoulder? It was a gift from them."

Sudden understanding hit Stephen hard.

I have it too.

The scar.

The thought gave him sudden vertigo. He tightened his fingers around the arms of the blue chair. He cleared his throat to ease the stiff dryness in it, but it did not work. On his lips, he could still taste the water the Iceman had made him drink during his "test." It tasted like rotten eggs and dirty socks. That son of a bitch. It was part of his torture. Stephen had not dared to ask him what he had used to dirty the water and give it such color and flavor. Probably the Iceman had put something harmless in it, but that bastard had the sense of humor of a vulture. Had Stephen asked him, he would have told him a lie, just to have fun at his expense.

"They tortured you to test you too," whispered Stephen. He wasn't able to put two of his own words together, he could just repeat his friend's words. He gave him a look. Guy was strong. He looked impressive even like this, sitting on his bed, debilitated by his injuries. "But you didn't cry, right, Ash?" he heard himself ask. "You didn't beg as I did. And you didn't even..." Stephen bowed his head down, blushing with humiliation, "...piss yourself in terror."

Guy raised his head. His eyebrows furrowed over the bridge of his nose. "What was that supposed to mean? Apart from the fact that what you say is bullshit, of course." Guy's voice was annoyed; he was giving him the "Soon a Punch Will Knock Your Teeth Out" look. "You have a lower pain threshold than me, so what?" he continued with an exasperated voice. "If anything, it makes what you did more valuable."

Valuable? I cried, man.

I begged.

I'm ashamed of myself. I'd just like to be like you.

Is that so terrible a thing to wish?

"Well," he finally said, smiling with an effort. "You make it sound like I'm a fearless hero. By the way, you can go on if you want. I sort of like it."

He had so much to ask, so much to say. But in his throat, foolishly, tears were pushing; tears of happiness, even more embarrassing than his tears of panic.

He swallowed several times, to keep them away.

Guy didn't rush him; he held his head down to look at his unmatched feet. On the nightstand, next to the bed, there was a pitcher of water and a half-full glass. Stephen was not sure he could lift the pitcher up. He took the glass and its poor contents. With unsteady hands, he brought it to his lips.

It was fresh.

It was clean.

He drank it all. He felt stronger; he opened his mouth, and the words came out without hesitation. "Who were you supposed to betray to save your life, Ash?" Carefully, he forced himself to put the glass on the bedside table without breaking it.

Without breaking it, Stephen, for God's sake.

He succeeded and looked back at Guy with a certain anxiety. The question he had asked was necessary, and he hoped that the answer would be, "It was you, Steve. That person was you." Holy shit, he had every right to hear that. "They asked me to lure you into a trap, in case you didn't know," he pointed out emphatically.

Guy chuckled, and a tuft of hair stood out, very dark, over his forehead. "I know. And I'm afraid you won't allow me to forget this, right?"

"You can bet your ass on it."

Sitting that way, leaning forward without his usual arrogance, Guy looked very young, and Stephen had this weird feeling, as if he were looking at the schoolboy he had met at Eton thirteen years ago. "So, what was at stake for you?" he asked again.

"Oh, no big deal," Guy said. "There was this table—" he moved his hand in front of his chest "—and on it, there was a plump baby about one or two months. I don't know who Stu borrowed this baby from, but that's not the important part. The important part is that, next to the baby, there was a butcher knife. And next to the knife, there was a hooded man. He was the same man who tortured you, by the bye, you'll be pleased to know. Well, listen to this. This man looks at me and he says very plainly: either you kill this baby, or I kill you."

Stephen's eyes widened. "Holy Jesus Christ. Are you kidding me?"

"No, I wish I were. Anyway," Guy said with a shrug, "they made things easier for me. I mean, I had to choose between my life and a baby's life. He was an innocent little thing, while I, well... I've never been innocent in my entire life. So yes, I decided to save him—but then again, it was an easy choice. Not like yours." His voice became gruff, and he gave Stephen a strange smile. "You had to choose whether to save yourself or a sadistic bastard. Yes—your test was way more complicated than mine, W."

Stephen's heart began to beat hard against his rib cage. Never, in all these years, had Guy looked at him with so much overt affection. "You are not a sadistic bastard," he protested.

"But I'm a murderer," Guy replied simply. He had mentioned the real, fundamental point, and Stephen was grateful to him for that. "You can't have any doubt about it."

No. He couldn't. "You and... St. Court," he murmured. "This, uh... this thing you do..."

"Don't you approve of it?"

Silence.

"I don't know," he finally said. "These people are... I mean, your victims, they deserve it, or so I was told by... by that son of a bitch who tortured me. But some would say the same about you. The problem is... your Gang takes God's place, man. You judge these people in His place, and that's... damn. That's impossible. That's wrong."

"God's place? Actually, we Knives are *better* than God. God creates bastards—we correct His mistakes."

Guy's blasphemy made everything seem normal, even Stephen's last three days of hell. And the light coming through the large windows seemed to say, "It's all right, Steve, really," and the gentle air of May came in through the half-closed shutters, and it was warm and smelled of flowers and spring.

"Is this why you withdraw all that money from the bank?" Stephen asked, finally linking all the pieces together. "Do you need it to research to find scumbags—and kill them?"

"I do. I need it also for helping abused women, or pregnant ones, and the children who, you know... need to forget bad experiences."

Stephen rubbed his forehead. "God, Guy."

"I know."

"The man who tortured me," he muttered, and the words were like thorns in his throat, "he said you killed my uncle. Is that true?" Speaking of his uncle was difficult to him but, six years after his uncle's death, it was time to.

Guy glanced at him sideways. "What do you think?"

"I think... yes. Yes, I think you killed him."

Guy squared his shoulders. "Would you hand me my other boot? It's behind your chair. There, to the left. I feel like a moron with just one boot on."

Stephen bent and, even if it hurt him, grabbed the boot and handed it to Guy. His friend put it on without a groan. He just clenched his jaw.

He put his foot back on the floor and, straightening, looked into Stephen's eyes. "It was an accident," he revealed with no emphasis. "I didn't mean to kill him, not really. I just wanted to teach him a lesson. I hit him a bit too hard, and he fell and his head smashed into a rock. It happened like that, it took just a moment. And the rest, as they say, is history."

"Did you... was it the first time you killed someone?"

"It was. But you know what?" He rubbed his forehead, eyes half-closed, absorbed in his thoughts. "Killing him gave me no emotion. I felt no guilt. I thought what I had done would haunt me. I thought I would have trouble sleeping. Except no—I didn't. That was when I realized I had this... *talent*. I've inherited it from my father, I guess."

"That's bullshit. Your father *loved* to kill. He enjoyed seeing people's agony. You don't. You killed because your victims deserve to die, that's it." *Putridity on two legs who don't deserve to be called human*, the Iceman's mocking voice rang in his mind. *That's it, just like I told you.*

"That's a simple way to put it, isn't it?" said Guy with a gentle, somewhat melancholy sarcasm. "Everything's clear and acceptable to you. You won't even ask me the question, will you, my friend? You fear my answer."

I want to hear one answer and one answer only. "Sometimes justice can't be done in legal ways," Stephen muttered between his teeth. "You patch over these situations, and that's all."

"That's all." Guy laughed. "Of course, I kill for 'justice.' But you believe in justice too, don't you, W.? God, you're the most pathetic moralist in the world. Yet, you'll never kill anyone, and we both know it. No, don't look away. Look at me, W. Accept what I'm saying. I take the bastards, I tie them down on the floor—and I feel nothing. Their blood spills out, their agony is terrible, but I feel *nothing*. Neither pleasure nor pain. It's something I do because I'm good at it. Because it's in my blood." He turned up his forearm and showed Stephen the veins at his own wrist. "Because something's wrong with me, W., and I have accepted this about myself. I try to take the good from it. I look on the fucking bright side of my being a murderer."

"There's nothing wrong with you."

"Thank you for your loyalty, my friend, but I torture and kill people. Maybe you're not getting the point."

"They're just villains. My uncle... Jesus Christ!" Stephen jumped up from the chair, forgetting his cracked ribs in the moment's turmoil. A sudden pain made him double over. He put his hands on the back of the chair for support, his breath taken away. "Jesus Christ," he repeated, hiding his face the best he could. "My uncle deserved it."

He took some slow breaths, his fingers clutching the backrest of the chair. He sat down again, carefully. He had to restrain his rage, and fuck if it wasn't frustrating!

"You said you joined the Gang of Knives over three years ago," he murmured when he managed to repress the excruciating emotion from his old memories. "But you killed my uncle in 1846. What did you do in the meantime?"

Guy cleared his throat. "Until twenty-one, I was a good, very useless boy, who studied and spent Christmas with family. When I came of age, I realized that I had the strength and means to fix what bothered me."

Thank Heavens, Stephen was sitting. "You mean..." He stopped, unable to continue.

"Yes, I *mean*," Guy said, answering Stephen's unspoken question. "And no longer by chance, W.," he added with an explanatory glance.

Accept it, Guy's dark eyes told him. *Just accept it.*

God, it was hard. "How many, Ash?"

"Uh..." Guy shook his head thoughtfully. "Not enough, I guess. If you want, I'll make you a list later. I assure you one thing though. They were lousy bastards, not even worth the air we're wasting talking about them. You need not worry about them."

"I suspected nothing."

"You would have. I wasn't any good at handling the situation. I used to threaten people personally. I beat them up, as I did with Susan's husband... Lady Susan Emerson," he clarified, throwing a glance at him. "Did she tell you?"

Stephen shook his head. He felt dizzy. His reactions were slow. Suddenly, many details of Guy's behavior made sense.

Was the doctor still outside the door? Yes? No? It didn't matter, for Stephen kind of liked that their dialogue was taking place in low tones. These whispers were helping him to listen to the truth with less angst. As if the words *murder, torture, death* were less frightening if spoken in a quiet manner.

"Well," Guy shrugged and went on, "a lot of people noticed my, say, flair for self-made justice. Or for revenge, if you will. Police would have linked my name to some unsolved murder, it was inevitable. My luck was that St. Court recruited me into his Gang. He'd been observing me for a while." Guy smiled as if the thought amused him. "And he did not doubt that, after telling me for the purpose his organization existed for, I would like to be part of it."

Stephen rubbed his forehead. "So, let me get this straight. St. Court first tortured you, and then he said, 'Let's kill some people together, shall we?' "

Guy grinned. "Yes, more or less. He said he liked my style. To tell the whole truth, he thought I was a bit rough. He was sure they could make me more refined, anyway."

Stephen found himself chuckling, half-hysterical, half-stunned. "I can just picture him saying this pile of crap with his fine-student voice."

Guy nodded, amused. "After a while you get used to him," he said. "He's smart, you know. It was he who taught me to bring out something good from this... *thing* of mine. From him, I learned to use a cover. And to use a throwing knife."

"So, your bad reputation..."

"It keeps the suspicion away. And it also allows me to set some traps."

"As you did with Cunning."

"As I did with Cunning."

"It's fucking dangerous, Ash. You nearly died three days ago." He shuddered as he said it. If every time Guy went out during the night, from now on, Stephen had to be afraid that he would die...

God.

"Don't look so troubled, it's not always like that. Cunning caught us off guard, that's all. A quite unique event."

"Ash..."

"Hey, don't start preaching at me, all right? Sometimes I will face some risks, it's true, but—" he looked at him intently: it was important, this thing was damn important to Guy "—W., I am what I am, and I can't change it. I'm sorry."

Stephen swallowed hard, with the anguish that, from now on, would be with him during the nights of the Gang of Knives.

"Steve," added Guy, very seriously, "don't you ever try to follow me again. It would be dangerous for you and us."

Stephen clenched his jaws. He gave no answer. Of course he would follow him. To save his life a thousand times, if necessary.

"W., you're not completely stupid," Guy said as if reading his mind. "Try and follow my line of reasoning, if you apply yourself you can do it. You've got no training, you don't know our methods: you'd be a loose cannon. You understand that? I want your word. It must not happen again."

Silence.

"All right, I was wrong. You are *quite* stupid. Then I'll lock you up in a cell on every K-Night."

"Guy—"

"No, W. You'd get killed, and we'd get killed. Don't you ever follow me again. How would you feel if I died because of your good intentions?"

Stephen swallowed. Fuck, fuck, fuck. Guy always found the words to convince him. He was right. Damn it, he was right. Stephen had insufficient training to save him. His inexperience would endanger them all. He would die or, worse, Guy would die. "All right," he murmured, discouraged. "All right, I give you my word. But... be more careful, will you?"

Guy relaxed. "I will," he promised, his voice tinged with comprehension. Heartfelt understanding of Stephen's state of mind, even.

For the moment, Stephen could do no more. He looked down at his feet. The carpet was decorated with intricate gold-and-white patterns, like thorny brambles. Scratchy brambles, similar to the fears he felt in his heart. "St. Court..." he muttered, after a pause to calm his tension. "Why has he founded this... *organization?*"

"I don't know. His life, from the outside, looks perfect. He had a loving father, his mother was a famous benefactress. Before discovering his bad reputation was a cover, I wondered how he could be such a scumbag, coming from such a decent family."

Stephen put his elbow on the arm of the chair and rested his forehead on his palm. "And... what about the other man?" he asked, trying to maintain his voice even. Talking about the Iceman was hard. His silver eyes still haunted him. He couldn't even say his name, Second, as if he were a demon you could summon by calling him. Stephen had been afraid of him even after St. Court had said the Knives would let him go. When the Duke had left Stephen's cell, the Iceman hadn't tortured him anymore; in fact, Stephen hadn't seen him more than three times—when the Iceman had given him the water for his bath, some food, and, in the morning, when he had brought him, blindfolded, to the carriage. But Stephen couldn't stop being afraid of him. He hadn't been able to believe he was safe until the carriage with tinted windows, after a bumpy ride, had finally stopped in front of Ashbourne House, and the coachman had opened the door, and Stephen, breathing heavily, had got out, facing Guy's imposing palace.

"Second, you mean?" Guy asked. His expression hardened. A few minutes ago, when he had been talking about St. Court, a bright gleam of respect had shined in his eyes; now the respect was gone. "He's good with the knife. And at hand-to-hand combat."

"But you don't like him," exclaimed Stephen, very relieved to know that.

Guy shrugged. "Stu vouches for him."

"I'd like to see his face, Ash. You know, maybe..." he swallowed. "I don't know. Maybe somehow it'd make me less scared of him."

"I'm sorry, W., that's not possible. You already know about me and St. Court, and that's too fucking much, really."

"How many are you in this... gang of yours? Can you at least tell me this much?"

"It's just me, St. Court and Second, whom you saw at his best. And, W.... you must never betray us, or talk about us."

Stephen raised his head suddenly, incredulity lighting his eyes. He felt angry, and this was a good thing. At least, his fear gave way to other emotions. "You don't say!" he snapped. "And here I thought I could tell all my friends, tonight at White's."

"No, you didn't understand the implications of my words. Let me be clear. It means that from now on you can't go near drugs ever again."

Stephen stared at him in silence for a few moments. "So, you've finally managed to set me up."

Guy's eyes twinkled with affectionate fun. "I think so."

"Ash, you don't know how much I'd enjoy kicking your ass, but—" he glanced at his friend's open shirt, where the bandage wrapped his chest "—I'll wait for you to get better."

"Says the man who looks like shit."

"These, then, were the 'secrets that can save lives,' as a very pompous man once told me."

"These very ones. You know, you're smart, kid. The Gang of Knives could use someone like you."

Stephen grinned, then realized Guy was serious. Deadly serious. So serious that Stephen's buttocks shriveled in fear, like two dried plums inside the elegant trousers St. Court had chosen for him. "You want me to kill someone?" he asked, panicking.

"Hey, hello there? Were you even listening when I told you about predestination and all the other shit about being a natural-born killer?" Guy shook his head, stunned by his friend's slowness. "Yours is such a stupid question, on another occasion I would have punched you in the nose. But under the circumstances..."

"Circumstances that include the fact that I saved your life, maybe?"

Guy rolled his eyes, but there was cheerfulness in his sarcastic half-smile. "Circumstances that include the fact that I feel like shit. The punch in your nose is only delayed. No, I don't want you to kill anyone. Of course I don't. I was thinking about enlisting you as an accountant. The Gang of Knives's money management is complex and, for obvious reasons, we keep it secret. If you helped us, that would be extremely useful."

"I see." Stephen rubbed his forehead. "Well, I have the scar already after all, don't I?"

"What?"

"Your friend, the one who tortured me—" he touched his own right shoulder "—cut me here. Two crossed cuts. Just like that scar of yours."

Guy stared at him for a long time. There was a light in his eyes that seemed—no, it didn't just seem, it really was—a deep emotion. "What a romantic fellow he is," he muttered hoarsely.

"He is indeed." Stephen cleared his throat, moved with emotion. His head was confused, but no longer hurt. "I... I'd like to take a look at your accounting records, and... and think about your offer. I'd like a little time if it's fine with you."

"Sure it is."

"And, Ash..."

Two heavy knocks at the door interrupted Stephen, and Guy glared toward the door. "Who is there?"

"It's me, Kenneth. Is everything all right in there? I can't hear you. Have you two killed each other?"

Guy snorted. "Please, W., throw him out of my house."

"Everything's all right, Doc," shouted Stephen. "Just ten more minutes and I'll leave. Meanwhile, please, could you prepare one of your biggest syringes? For my friend here. And, uh—he also says he urgently needs a purge. I strongly hope you have one with you." He looked at Guy with a smile on his bruised face. "I can't wait to let him in, but first I'd like to talk to you about one last thing."

"Why, everything's so simple and clear. We take them. We kill them. What more is there to add?"

It sounded like a normal thing when he said it like that. *Dear God, I thank you for this man, just the way he is,* Stephen thought while looking at Guy, his strange soul... his strange heart. "It's not about the Gang of Knives," he replied softly.

Guy squared his shoulders suspiciously. As if he were ready to flee.

And that was an inevitable reaction, was it not?

"I have a fucking wound on my shoulder," Stephen reminded him, anticipating his objections. "I was willing to *die* for you. This gives me a bit of power over you, don't you think?"

"Actually it robs you of all the power you had. Now I know you can threaten me, you can scream at me... but in the end, you'd never do anything to harm me."

Stephen hadn't thought of that. "What a scam life is."

"Fuck yeah, it is."

Stephen took a deep breath. "At least tell me why you hate her, Guy. Just this. It would make me feel better."

"It wouldn't make you feel any better." Guy stood up, and the movement caused him to grimace in pain. "W., you know how families are," he murmured, taking a tentative step toward the foot of the bed. "They're just the worst places to live. Family members always end up hating each other. It's inevitable."

And this answer was kind of good—so why wasn't Stephen satisfied with it? "You were in love with her, weren't you? When you were a boy."

Guy's legs were weak. He stopped, supporting himself with one hand against the bedpost. "I *hated* her. She was an unbearable spoiled brat. Do you have any idea how many times I got punished because of her?"

"Guy, cut the crap. I'm not *that* stupid, you know. I remember the look on your face, at Eton, when her letters came. It wasn't the look of one who hates 'a spoiled brat.' "

From the window came the sounds of the garden: a slight rustle of leaves and wind, singing birds, the sound of full spring. Guy looked out between the open curtains, out at the arrogant sky with its riot of dazzling blue.

"Something happened, didn't it?" Stephen asked when Guy did not answer. "Something that changed things between you and her. What happened, Guy?"

Guy's hand tightened on the bedpost. "Well, I must have done something awful to her, mustn't I?" he asked with bitter sarcasm. He turned toward him. "Look at me, Steve. I am a..." he lifted his hand in front of his face, waving his fingers up and down and making his voice hollow, "terrrrible monsterrr."

Stephen felt like throwing something at him. The glass, maybe. "You did nothing awful to her."

"How can you be sure?"

"Old bean, I feel obliged to remind you that I was willing to *die* for you. That's how much I'm sure."

"How many times a day will you tell me that, from now on?"

But Stephen wouldn't let him change the subject. "She hurt you, Ash. It must be so. That's why you wanted to take this cruel revenge on her, am I right?"

"Come on, W., what does it matter anyway?" Guy couldn't conceal his bitterness. "In a month and a half everything will be over, and she'll be free again." He shrugged, then turned to the closed door. His eyes flickered, and "Kenneth!" he shouted out a moment later. "You can come in now, you damn sawbones. And bring that purge with you!"

The door opened after one second flat.

"You'd do anything to avoid the subject, wouldn't you, Ashbourne?" Stephen snapped, exasperated.

Guy raised an eyebrow. "Actually, the purge is for you, W."

48.

Well, I must have done something awful to her, mustn't I? Look at me, Steve. I am
a terrible monster.

7 Courtnell Street, 10th April 1844. Morning.

Guy was in front of a hired carriage. The coachman was loading Guy's
luggage on the roof of the vehicle; the carriage was glossy black. Its door
was wide open and Guy could see the red interior. The moisture of drizzle
was coming inside, yet Guy remained outside, with no umbrella, while the
man tied his suitcase with a rope. There were drops of rain so light Guy
could hardly feel them.

No one was with him on the muddy sidewalk. His mother had wished
him a safe journey in the living room, without holding out her hand or
kissing him. Charles Hartwell had done the same, but afterward, he had
ruffled Guy's hair, laughing and moving away as Guy balled up his hands
into tight fists. Charles hadn't tried to accompany him to the carriage; Guy
had shown his distaste for such a sappy habit in the past by pushing his
stepfather away, cursing, and telling him to leave him alone.

Very explicit signals, Guy believed.

Guy looked up at the gray sky. *Spring.* Someone called it *spring.* It was not
cold, but the street lacked colors. Everything was black and white; the
drizzle moistened his skin and coat.

Jane had not shown up.

Was it possible that Rona had not let her?

But Jane would never listen to Rona about that. Was it possible that...
but no, it wasn't; a kiss—come on, it had been only a tiny kiss. She always
asked Guy to marry her, didn't she? Yes... or at least, she had done so until
a few years ago. Now she was shier, her demands for his affection had
become... not less insistent, but more embarrassed; she always found silly
excuses to be in the same place with him. She had grown up, she had

learned to be proud... but she was still the same little girl.

She loved him, as always.

A carriage passed at full speed, splashing water and mud on the sidewalk. One of the two horses of his hired vehicle neighed. The coachman finished tying Guy's luggage and gave him a look. Guy had gone out of the house before the carriage was ready; with a little time more, Jane could find a way to slip out to talk with him.

But she had *not* shown up.

He hadn't seen her since yesterday. Since their kiss. Rona had kept her away from him quite effectively: she and Jane hadn't even come downstairs for dinner. Guy had eaten in silence with his stepfather, his head turned toward the fireplace to his left. The fire was out; not even the flames, with their red, yellow, ungovernable motion, had been his companions on his last night of vacation. But his heart was not tight with anxiety. Restless, yes; he needed to talk to Jane as soon as possible. He needed to explain himself. Not to reassure her; there was no need for that. Not for her. Not with her.

"You can get in now, your lordship."

Your lordship. Guy almost forgot to be an earl, when he was in Courtnell Street. At Eton he was "Ashbourne"; for the coachman, he was your lordship.

For Jane, he was Guy.

He sucked a breath in. All right, no problem. He would write to her. It was clear that Rona must have told her something that had scared her. Or maybe his mother had blackmailed her in some way. Maybe she had pretended to be ill to touch Jane's tender heart.

Yes, it was certainly so.

In a grim mood, with his skin and hair wet, Guy placed his boot on the footplate. And at that very moment, he heard the door of 7 Courtnell Street opening and some light steps coming closer. His heart leaped, and he realized how painful it would have been if he hadn't heard these little steps.

He turned. He didn't have the time to open his mouth. Jane, without a coat or umbrella, threw something at him, maybe a pebble, which hit him in the chest and bounced to the ground with a metallic clang.

"Jane, is that because of the kiss?" he asked, puzzled, raising his hands as he approached her. Jane stepped back. With her pink cotton dress, her neck uncovered, her hair plaited in two braids—she stepped back on the sidewalk full of mud.

"I... I'm sorry, little one, I didn't mean to scare you," he tried again, although she was looking at him wide-eyed, horrified—a look she had never given him before. "I don't know what my mother told you, but I..."

Jane shook her head. "You disgust me, Guy Spencer!" she cried, bursting into tears. "I don't want you to kiss me or talk to me, I don't even want to see you ever again!" She turned away and ran into the house, slamming the door behind her.

For a few moments, he just stood there, staring at the red door and its carved rectangles and decorations. The coachman called him; the horses whinnied. His eye was attracted by the golden little object Jane had thrown at him, and he stooped to pick it up. It was his Eton lapel pin, the keepsake Jane had taken from him.

She didn't want it anymore.

49.

Guy sank into the tub. Well, what was wrong, what the fuck was wrong? He took the towel placed behind his neck and threw it away. He was taking a bath, and damn it, wasn't that supposed to *relax* him?

Except no, it hadn't relaxed him at all.

Holy shit. This morning Jane had done everything to provoke him—to push him to make love to her. She had asked him directly. She had begged him. How sweet she had been, and wet and excited, while spreading her thighs wide open in an explicit invitation...

Do it, a little devil had whispered in Guy's ear. *Make love to her.*

He had resisted, yes, but fuck if this situation wasn't driving him mad. Good grief, he couldn't go on like this.

And the third week of May was already over.

Panic ran through his body, chilly panic inside the warm water of the tub. His time with her—his heaven with her—was about to end soon.

He jumped out of the tub. The sun outside was blinding. It had rained yesterday, but now the trees outside the window, heavy with green, stood out against the blue sky. And Jane, soon, would leave. There was a little more than a month left.

Guy shuddered. *Let's pretend it's because of your wet skin. Let's pretend that everything's fine. Everything is going according to plan, isn't it?*

He reached out to the towel placed on a bronze bar to the side. Even that gesture weighed on him. It was the residual weakness because of the stab wound of ten days ago, he said to himself.

It was not because of Jane. It was not because of the words she had whispered to him.

I love you, Guy.

Cursing, he ran the towel over his body. Since when had he become this stupid? Jesus, his wound had healed, he had even taken part at yesterday's Night of Knives—all right, it was just a Level Three; but still, he had done pretty good—so why did this weariness anchor him to the ground when the morning was beautiful, the sky was blinding blue?

Guy, my love... my love.

He wrapped the towel around his waist. To the devil with it.

He stretched out his hands to his shirt as the door flew open. Guy turned to the intruder. It was a woman.

Lady Susan Emerson.

"Lord Ashbourne."

The woman came in and pulled the door behind her. She didn't close it completely, and this was a good sign. Their discussion would be brief. For she was there to *discuss* with him... wasn't she?

Hmmm. No, maybe not. She approached him with a kittenish smile, and a smile like that usually means there would be very few words and a lot of... actions.

She was dressed in a dark-gray dress, and gray was a color suited to a good widow... well, if you didn't consider her deep neckline, that was almost completely exposing her breast.

"Do you need help with your bath, your lordship?"

"Have you tried to ask Charles Hartwell?"

She twisted her mouth into a grimace of capricious displeasure. She was over thirty-five, but Guy had to give her that, she could simper better than a twenty-year-old courtesan.

"He doesn't seem interested in me," she purred in response, looking at him from below her eyelashes. "And I was just wondering if maybe..." She shrugged. "If maybe I lack the necessary appeal. What do you think?" She undid the buttons over her bosom: she wasn't wearing any corset, and her white, generous breasts offered themselves to his eyes without warning.

So, this was a premeditated attack.

"Would you help me understand if I am still charming, Lord Ashbourne?"

Susan's breasts were firm and very pretty for a woman her age... for a woman any age, but Guy ignored the open flaps of her dress.

"Do you think I can still please a man?" she insisted.

All right, the woman was incomprehensible. She was no longer talking to him about Jane. In fact, she had become friendly with him, giving him a thousand smiles when all the inhabitants of Ashbourne House gathered in the living room in the evening, to read or play cards. Was it the fear of being sacked that was pushing her to offer herself to him? She had entered his bathroom and now was showing him her breasts, and if mathematics was not an opinion... not even prostitution was.

"I'm not going to fire you," he said, annoyed, while the last drops of water slipped down his skin in a faint tickling sensation. "There's no need for you to lift up your skirt for me, milady."

Susan laughed. "No one is as blunt as you, Earl. What if I told you I would *love* to remember what it is like to have my skirt lifted by you?"

"Three weeks ago, you seemed disgusted by me."

"Three weeks ago it was not the right time of the month."

This time it was Guy the one who laughed. He'd never heard of an attempted seduction based on a woman's menstrual cycle.

"Now, Lady Susan, you and I are adults. Tell me, does all of this have something to do with Jane?"

Susan came up to him. She had put on makeup with accuracy and was wearing an intense fragrance. She smelled of daffodils and roses. "Jane?" She brought a hand to Guy's chest and touched it with her fingertips. "I'm not thinking about Jane now."

Guy grabbed her wrist. "Susan. I don't like to repeat myself. Why are you doing this?"

Susan looked at her wrist, tightly clutched by Guy's hand. "You're hurting me."

Guy let her go abruptly and turned away. "Get out. Right now."

"You asked me what Jane has to do with this."

He looked back at her. She was beautiful and, even though a dozen years older than him, her sensual body could satisfy any man. So why wasn't he interested in fucking her? With her, sex had been fun. Susan was generous and attentive, and Guy wasn't particularly demanding. He had given her some jewels when their affair had ended. He had had no long-term relationships. After a while, women had the annoying tendency to expect something from him, so he always respected one rule with his mistresses: fuck them three times at most—and then get rid of them.

Guy sighed. Here's a new rule: never hire ex-mistresses in your house. "So?"

"Rumor has it that you're no longer going to Madame Catherine's brothel."

"Do you wish me to put in a good word for you?"

Susan's eyes narrowed for a moment, then a mask of sensuality veiled them again. "What I meant is that, in all likelihood, you aren't... adequately satisfying your needs, my lord. Needs that, if I remember right—" she smiled as she moved a step closer to him "—are many and very, very..." she touched the towel over his penis, "huge."

"And you're afraid I might satisfy them in the wrong place? Between my stepsister's legs, maybe?"

Holy shit, it always came back to that, didn't it? Back to his "needs." But he was not an animal, by God. He could control himself. He could avoid hurting Jane, he just fucking could...

He just fucking couldn't, bloody hell.

He hadn't made love to her. He hadn't fucked pussy for five months. Well, that was largely compensated by the hours he spent having sex with Jane—three hours a day, more or less, compared with the three hours a week before Jane. And of course, it was completely different. Sex with Jane was, quite simply, the best sex he'd ever had.

Jane was a sensual girl, a strange and wonderful combination of shyness and passion.

And his harsh, aching need to sink into her grew stronger day after day. And that was the real problem, wasn't it? He feared he couldn't restrain himself for much longer—not now that he was about to lose her for good.

Do you want to ruin her life this way?

"A man like you should have a regular sex life," Susan murmured in a husky, sensual voice. "It's difficult to believe you haven't had a lover in *months.*"

"I'm getting old."

"You are still a boy, Earl. It's impossible that..." she moved closer, touching him lightly "...you didn't want to be caught between warm, cozy thighs."

He wanted to. Very much. Not with the woman in front of him, not with her. But Jane couldn't help him satisfy this need. Jane thought she could, but what did she even know about him? Nothing. She didn't know what he did when he went out at night. She didn't know that having her in his bed was the first joy Guy had felt at Ashbourne House since he had been living there.

Jane didn't fucking know.

She said she loved him, but Guy was the one who filled his lungs with her presence as if she were the air he breathed. He was the one who needed her as he needed the water. And in just over a month, he would also be the one who...

The one who what?

Thinking of it gave him a kind of dizzy sensation, and he clung to what was closest to him.

Susan.

He put a hand on her shoulder.

He couldn't even imagine himself in a month, without Jane. Without Jane, and a wave of sudden anger flooded over him. Rage *against* Jane. She would forget him so easily, while he would have to learn to live again in his old, monochrome world. He needed to learn that again, he needed to get used to this idea.

He looked at Susan.

Never more than three times with the same woman.

Never with a woman working in his house.

Steam was rising from the tub, the bathroom was damn hot.

Never with a virgin.

Never with *Jane.*

They were simple rules.

Susan took his hand and ran it over her breasts. "You see, Lord

Ashbourne... if you want, we can find a way to get along."

* * *

Jane read the note on the desk in her room. It read only: *In my bathroom, at a quarter past eight.* It was written in capital letters, and signed *Guy.* She was surprised—and happy: did he need her again? Did he miss her already?

She was puzzled too. Maybe he wanted her to help him bathe. It had happened several times... but never in the morning, when Jane was always in a terrible hurry. She blushed at the memory of a few evenings ago, when Guy had made her wash him not only with a sponge, soap, and water. And afterward, he had washed *her.*

Her neck warmed with a flush of embarrassment and desire.

But now they did not have enough time. It was eight twenty, for one thing, and *her* children were waiting for her. And even though the prospect of seeing Guy—and *touching* Guy—was appealing, she had already put on the dress to go out. She had come back to her room just to get her hat and coat.

She sighed. It was odd, really. It was the first time Guy had given her an order in writing. Besides, it wasn't safe, it wasn't safe at all. She smiled. Maybe he wanted her so badly he hadn't thought of the danger. This idea was pleasant, and she couldn't help but smile.

Placing the note in her pocket, with some apprehension mixed with unforgivable excitement, Jane left her room and walked to the wing of Ashbourne House where the Earl's rooms were.

* * *

Susan was really good with her hands.

Guy closed his eyes as she, after taking the towel off him, masturbated him vigorously. What a difference from his sweet, shy Jane. His angel touched him as if he were made of porcelain; yet, the erections she provoked were bigger than this.

But then again, this was what waited for him in a month. This mechanical love... this mechanical emptiness.

"Let's make love, Earl," Susan whispered in his ear. She had slipped the dress off; she was naked underneath. "Don't you want to?" she asked, kissing his cheek.

That kiss bothered Guy. His body responded to her, but Susan's scent—a fashionable French scent—pushed him away. Jane... his little girl... she smelled like candies and soap.

"I want you inside me..." Susan said again. "Don't you want that too?"

Make love? Yes, he wanted to. That very morning, he had thought he would explode with frustration when he had touched Jane's opening with the tip of his penis.

He closed his eyes. He could *not* have Jane that way. Maybe sinking himself inside Susan could mitigate his dissatisfaction, at least for a few days. Maybe it could mitigate his increasing panic at the thought of the upcoming June 30th. But also, and above all, it would make him less dangerous to Jane.

The solution was here—the same, sleazy solution he had found in the past.

Except it felt more like a punishment than a pleasure. And if so... against whom?

Against himself... or against Jane?

"Turn around," he told Susan dryly. "And lean over the tub."

* * *

Before walking down the corridor, Jane made sure that there were no servants around. Then she moved quickly toward Guy's bathroom. As soon as she was in front of the open door, she heard whispering sounds— moaning sounds, like the ones cubs in a den would make. She had heard sounds like these many years ago, while standing outside of a pantry room, in the house on Courtnell Street Number 7.

The hair on her head stood on end, and her heart told her to run away.

Don't look inside.

Oh no please, please don't look; this time, don't look!

But she pushed open the door, as she had done in the past. And this time, she couldn't suppress a desperate cry.

"Guy!"

* * *

In the middle of a vigorous thrust, Guy froze inside Susan. He took a deep breath before turning around.

Oh, Jesus.

He looked toward the door. Pale and shocked, Jane was there.

He swallowed and straightened up, stark naked. "Jane..."

She opened her mouth. Then she closed it. She put a hand to her lips, turned her back, and ran away. Guy stared at the open, empty door.

Susan picked up her dress from the floor. "She was not exactly the person you wanted to be caught by, I guess."

Guy turned toward her, without really seeing her. All he could think about was the shocked look on Jane's face.

Susan quickly slipped the dress on. He had been inside her until just a moment before, yet she didn't look sorry for the interruption. A fit of dull fury grew in Guy as understanding took root into him.

"Tell me, Lady Susan," he said stiffly, retrieving his shirt and putting it on with livid movements. "Why did you come in here?"

"I told you."

"Tell me again."

Susan lifted her chin. "To save Jane's innocence."

"Did you tell her to come here?"

"Why, don't you think it was a coincidence?" Susan smiled. Her eyes sparkled with flashes of mocking satisfaction. "You know, things like these happen, your lordship. Just by chance. Besides, the fact that I left a note on her desk might have helped fate along a little."

"Why the hell did you do this to her?" Guy reached out and grabbed Susan's arm—strongly, to frighten her, to vent his anger, but Susan held her breath, swallowing the pain, and didn't do any resistance or complain.

"I didn't do her any harm." Susan looked at him straight in the eye, and she didn't stop speaking even as Guy tightened his grip on her arm. "At all. Now she knows who you are. So you can't hurt her anymore. It's only the people we respect who can hurt us."

Guy let go of her abruptly. God, he felt like wringing her neck. "I warned you not to mess with me," he said, his voice low and fierce. "And you're going to regret it. I'll burn every bridge you have, I won't let anyone give you financial aid. Except for your brother-in-law. Yes, the old Emerson can have you if he wants. I can easily imagine you with your head buried between his legs, and that makes me feel a lot better. That's all a whore like you deserves in this life."

"Please tell me, Lord Ashbourne. Are you using such crude language to hurt my feelings? If this is the case, don't waste your breath. As I said, only the people we respect can hurt us. And these insults of yours, rather than offending me, make me happy."

"Good for you, for you will realize soon enough what a mistake you made using your whoring skills with me and not with Charles Hartwell."

"Charles Hartwell," Susan said, pursing her lips with contempt, "is a man willing to sell his daughter to a sorry bastard like you. No thanks. I much prefer my decrepit Lord Emerson." She raised her chin and headed for the door. "Goodbye, Lord Ashbourne."

50.

Jane would have never believed one could suffer so much twice in just one lifetime. She had thought one would die of pain first.

Lying on the bed in her room, Jane was not breathing; she didn't move. She didn't cry.

Lord, how much longer was she supposed to stay at Ashbourne House? Five weeks?

This thought was more painful than the first. What would become of her, after leaving this place? She had been happy here. With Guy.

She had never had him, never. She had had his kisses; she had deluded herself, just as she had done as a child. She had thought he loved her. Oh, God—God. And yet, she was supposed to be grown up now. Tomorrow she would turn twenty-one, and all she had learned was... nothing. She had lied to herself; she had wanted to believe that he loved her.

As a child, she had suffered so much, oh so much, after losing him. She had cried a river of tears... she had cried for *years*. She had never been able to forget him, never been able to move on. And now... would she die of pain?

Guy was... was—he was making love to Susan. Sometimes he had made Jane bend over the bathtub; but on those occasions, he hadn't made love to *her*.

Probably, he had been with many women during these months: when he hadn't returned home at night, Jane had told herself that no, he was out just to play cards in some club, or to fight in a boxing ring, or, or, or. She had never told herself the truth: she was just a plaything for him, and, without the hatred he felt for her, he would have let her go long ago.

Without the hatred he felt for her, he would never have returned in her life.

In these last few months, while he humiliated her day after day, hour after hour... he was cheating on her.

Cheating?...

A slave girl who thinks she owns her master, whoever heard of anything so ridiculous?

The door opened and Jane held her breath. He had come to her... but to tell her what, her heart asked?

Was she ready to say goodbye to him for good, was she ready for that?

* * *

Guy entered Jane's room from the front door, slamming it behind him. To hell with caution. The room was divided into two by an arch. Guy walked quickly and, beyond the arch, saw Jane on the bed. The parted curtains let in the morning light; she was lying on the right side of the bed, the side farthest from the door.

She had not moved at his entrance.

Guy went to the left side of the bed. Jane had her back turned, and he sat down, then laid next to her. He moved closer, touching her body with his own, and reached out to her left hip. She remained motionless under his fingers; the slight rise and fall of her breathing was almost imperceptible.

Guy squeezed her arm and kissed her hair.

Nothing.

He had expected tears, recriminations. He had expected he should justify himself.

There were no tears, no words. This silence was worse. Come on, why did he feel so guilty? He owed her nothing—nothing.

And yet, he had run behind her. He was here, now.

"What do you want me to do, Guy? Do you want me to undress for you?" Jane's voice sounded low and... empty, as if all her emotions had been erased. "Or to put myself on all fours?"

"Jane," he murmured into her hair, gently stroking her, "I didn't take everything from you. You know that, don't you? I didn't take... your virginity."

"You've taken..." Her voice trembled; the pain was back and filled it, a bitter start, but still a start nonetheless. Jane took a deep breath. "You've taken *everything* from me," she finished in a whisper. "Everything. And now I have nothing left. I... I was aware that you were humiliating me, and that..." Her voice became acute. Jane paused to regain control. "And that it was just a game for you, but... God. I am like any other woman to you, perhaps even worse... How many like her do you have around? No, not like her... like *me*?"

"Jane..."

"I can't do this anymore, Guy... I just can't..." she sobbed, beginning to cry. "Please, let me go. Set me free. You have your women, and I... I'm just the revenge you were seeking, and... and you got it, don't you see? You have made me an empty shell, happy just to lick your boots... to do everything for you. Let me go now... please, let me go far from you!"

Guy's arm contracted around her waist. Setting her free; now or in one month, what was the difference anyway? Sooner or later it would come to that. He had destroyed Jane. It was just like she had said: he had finally realized his glorious revenge.

Set her free.

And here his chest tightened. He gasped for breath, he gasped as he had done many years before, on a sunny day, with his face pressed against the bowels of a little fawn.

He could not let her go. Not now. Not in a month.

Not ever.

His heart beat violently against his breastbone. The truth hit him hard.

Jane swallowed several times, her body shook in silence, racked with unstoppable sobs. "I," she began, her voice low and filled with a kind of sad amazement, "I never thought you really hated me, you know, I... I never believed what you said, your cruel words... even if you never answered my letters, I... I never... oh, God, what a fool I was. I truly thought you loved me, that... that we would be together forever."

His never answering her what? Her *letters?* What the hell was Jane talking about? About the past? Guy's hair rose on the back of his neck, as a vague understanding dawned on him. Those words of hers made no sense, no fucking sense: and what about their kiss, then, what about the absolute refusal she had given him, years before?

"I was so silly... and I loved you so much," murmured Jane. "As only a little girl can love. You were my everything, Guy, God... how much I believed in you. You were invincible, and strong, and... and..."

"Jane, what..."

"I thought... I dreamed..." she whispered, "that, despite everything, you loved me. For you were always there for me, when I called you, when I was afraid of something, or maybe just when I wanted to see you, you were there, but then..." It took a while before she could continue. She shook her head on the pillow, giving up trying to explain herself. "And now it's happening again... and it hurts... it hurts so much!"

"Jane," said Guy, with all the passion and anger built up inside of him over the years, "why did that little kiss disgust you so much, years ago? Did my mother frighten you in some way? Jesus Christ, you began avoiding me as if I were..." *As if I were a damn monster.* And he was; he was. But not for Jane, not in her eyes. He had never felt like a monster with her. Then there had been that kiss, and she suddenly had looked at him with different eyes. Eyes filled with hatred, disillusionment, revulsion. Her eyes—the only ones important to him, the ones that had deceived him, that had made him feel loved just to make him more miserable.

What happened that day, Jane? Did you finally see the horror buried inside me?

"That kiss..." she murmured, then cleared her throat, her voice low and broken. "Oh, yes, you kissed me, did you not? And... and you kissed *Sophie White,* too, in the pantry room of Courtnell Street."

"Sophie... *who?*" His heart began to pound in his chest, painfully. That day in the pantry, among dried sausages and bags of flour... yes, he could still see himself—with his pants down, between the open legs of Sophie, his mother's maid. The maid who had offered herself to him many times, the one Guy had given five pounds in order to lose, finally, his virginity.

"You don't even remember her, Guy?" Jane asked softly. "No, of course you don't. She was just a thing to be used by you... just like me."

He barely heard her words. He closed his eyes, breathing heavily. Jane had seen him with Sophie, perhaps through the crack of the door. She must have heard some noise, or, more likely, she had followed him. As always.

Guy's chest swelled, he tightened his hand on her waist.

So it had been for *that* reason, just for that reason. Knowing it now didn't make him feel any better, didn't make him feel good. All he felt was anger, anger that exploded inside him.

He closed his hand into a fist, and for a moment he couldn't see anything but red.

"So," he said slowly, "that's why you stopped speaking to me." *And looking at me. And needing me.* He grabbed her shoulders and turned her abruptly toward himself. "You were so ready to think the worst of me, weren't you, Jane? You immediately decided I was shit. Without a second thought, did you? Without any regret."

"You are... the *worst!* You..."

And this was just too much. Guy's emotions took over him and he covered her body with his own, gripping her hair in his hand. Jane's golden eyes, filled with tears, widened in panic.

"I did it for *you,* just for *you,* because I was *protecting* you! Goddamn it, Jane! I was *always* protecting you!"

He bent his head and kissed her violently. Jane kept her lips shut tight and tried to pull away, raising her hands in defense.

"Don't you... don't you dare touch me! You... smell of her!"

"Do you want me to smell of you? Is that what you want?" He clenched her hair tightly, making her sob. "Do you have a clue how damn hard it has been for me to leave you intact, Jane? Do you have a fucking clue?"

He reached out and clasped her dress beneath the throat. He didn't bother to slip it off or lift it. He ripped it open to the waist.

"No, Guy!"

Her voice was terrified. She had any reason to be.

Set me free, she told him.

No.

He covered her mouth with an aggressive kiss, while his left hand squeezed her breast with no tenderness. He hooked an arm under her right knee, lifting it. "You damn, damn fool! Why didn't you ask me? How could you throw me away so *easily?* I never hurt you, Jane—never!"

On top of her, he was yelling at her, feeling her wet cheek under his mouth. He felt no pity; the image of Jane surrounded by blond children, with the same golden eyes as hers, faded in his mind, along with any other scruple.

You've taken everything from me.

Not yet.

Let me go.

No.

"You ran out on me years ago, do you think I'll let you run out on me *now?*"

Was it hate? Was it love? Fear of losing her forever, above all else, prevented him from thinking rationally. He didn't even want to think rationally. He couldn't lose her again, he just couldn't. She was air to him, he needed her. He had *always* needed her. He had hidden his pain after her refusal, he had hoped for years, for fucking *years,* that it would be just a matter of time—that eventually Jane would come back to him. He had been watching her from afar. He had been hating her. He had been *wanting* her so badly. But she was an angel, he was a devil: she had deceived and rejected him. Thrown him away like a damaged toy.

He hated her. He hated her so much.

He hated her, because even though she hadn't been with him all those years, she *had been* with him. She had always been with him. Not only during the hours Guy had spent spying on her, hidden inside a carriage, looking at her as she came out of the orphanage. Always. In his mind, in his dreams. He'd give up everything to have her. Jane was the dream of his life, his body—his soul—he had always longed for her. And now what would be left of him, if he let her go?

* * *

When Guy moved on top of her, Jane realized what he wanted to do to her. Panic caught her breath and stopped her tears. Guy grabbed her skirt, lifting it, moving his hand to the edge of her underpants. He pulled them down without unfastening them, with a loud noise of tearing fabric.

"Guy, no!"

Her heart was pounding with fear.

She put her hand on his, stopping him.

Guy looked up at her. His face was livid, his jaws were clenched. His stormy eyes shone with fierce, unfair anger. "Now I'm going to hurt you," he said with a growl that made her shake with fear. "And you'll have to accept it... you'll have to be *grateful* for it!"

"No! You were doing it with her... a moment ago!"

Guy grabbed her wrist and pulled her hand away, tearing another piece of cloth. He slipped his fingers under her ripped underwear.

"You're not done with Susan... so you want to do it with *me?*"

Guy fisted one hand tightly in her hair, hurting her. "That's what you wanted." He lowered his face over her and said in a brutal whisper, "That's what you begged me for, and that's what you'll get, by God! Spread your legs," he ordered as he pressed his hand against the folds of her vulva, to better slide into her, "for I'll never let you go, do you hear me? I'll *never* let you go... ever again!"

One of his fingers slipped into her sex, all the way in. Guy rubbed her inside, ferociously, painfully.

"No," Jane sighed, "if you really want me, swear... I'll be the only one for you, swear it, Guy... I need you to swear it!"

"No, I won't, God damn you!" His finger pushed inside her, intrusive. It seemed more like violence than the intoxicating sex he had got her used to. "What value could you place on my word anyway, tell me Jane... I mean nothing to you!"

He meant *nothing* to her? "I *love* you, Guy! I'd do *anything* for you! But please don't cheat on me, I..."

"You'd do everything for me," repeated Guy, biting her cheek angrily, interrupting her words and her tears, "oh yes, you'll do..."

He placed his hands inside of her thighs and spread them apart. Jane stiffened and resisted, terrified, when he unfastened his trousers and freed his penis. The tip of his index finger pushed into her opening again.

Guy put his other hand under her head, and pulled her mouth against his in a fierce kiss. Between her legs, his finger sank into her all the way to the palm of his hand; no, there were two fingers—his middle finger had slipped inside her too, and rubbed between the tight walls of her vagina, wetting her, hurting her, in a harsh, desperate way.

"Tell me you'll be faithful to me..." cried Jane, clutching to the man who was giving her so much pain, pain to her body, to her soul; "even if it's a lie, please tell me..."

Guy spread her legs wide, lifting her knees high, and placed his penis on her vagina. "May you be damned with me, then," he whispered in her ear in a voice filled with dark emotion, "that's what you'll get."

He pushed himself inside her in one, abrupt stroke, and Jane cried. The invasion was total and painful. His penis rubbed her vaginal walls, too huge and brutal, and broke her hymen violently, sinking into her. A burning ache grew unbearable in her belly, the world began to spin around her. She struggled and Guy held her by the wrists, keeping her shoulders pinned with his own; he froze into her, he was deep, so deep inside her, and so big!

"Does it hurt, Jane..." he murmured lowering his face into the crook of her neck, "that's what you deserve, you... you, stupid..." His words were ruthless, but his voice was shaky as if he were about to cry as well.

"Hate me, then..." Jane stopped resisting, sobbing; his words hurt her as much as his penis, which was inside her with no kindness. She raised her hips, allowing him to go deeper, fully accepting the pain. "Hurt me all you want, because I love you—" his presence was so overwhelming, too much, burning, and almost prevented her from breathing "—do you understand?... I love you..."

"Say it again," he hissed, biting her neck, her earlobe, tightening and squeezing her hair... adding pain to pain.

"I love you," she cried. "I love you, I love you..."

Guy released her wrists and raised his head, kissing her with cruel passion. Her face, her puffy eyelids, her neck. "I smell of you..." he murmured. "Only of you, can you feel it? Damn me, Jane... you're mine at last."

His voice was thick with emotion, the voice of a man who, while confessing the crime that will lead him to the gallows, finally feels relieved from an intolerable burden.

She caressed his shoulders, stroked his hair with painful, deep love; kissed his cheeks, lost in him. His manhood was like a dagger into her bowels, it sank deeper in her blood, and Guy was on her. Guy, who had betrayed her, who had deflowered her with no tenderness. Who was hurting her so badly.

"Forever, Guy?"

"Forever, angel."

Supporting himself on one elbow, Guy began to move his pelvis. His hard penis made its way deep inside her tight vagina, up and down. There was no gradual movement, no attentive thrust, as if he was running to escape guilt. He moved back and forth, and the burning ache inside her returned, along with the feeling of being completely filled by him.

"My little Jane," he murmured. "My sweet angel."

He held her tight, increasing the pace of his thrusts, and closed his eyes. Jane's pain eased gradually into mild discomfort, and the intimate massage became more sensual as her body got used to his size. Guy was already the master of her soul, they were one flesh now, and she whispered words of love while Guy kissed her passionately. A sort of heat, which she already knew, grew from between her legs and invaded the rest of her body. The juices of her excitement, along with the blood of her lost virginity, began to make her feel good, finally good; but Guy did not think of her pleasure, maybe he couldn't; he suddenly pulled out of her, letting out an animal cry, as if shocked by himself.

A moment later, he ejaculated on the sheets, collapsing on her with all his weight.

51.

Guy opened his eyes after a few minutes. Jane was beneath him, her hands clutching his shoulders. She didn't complain of his weight, just as before she had not complained of the violence he had deflowered her with.

He rolled away, relieving her of his not so light fourteen stone. After an orgasm—*this* orgasm in particular—thinking wasn't easy. He closed his eyes, forgetting the world. Minutes passed, how many Guy had no idea.

He felt Jane move on the bed beside him—maybe she wanted to sit up, maybe she wanted to clean up her blood—and reached for her, without opening his eyes. He took her wrist, pulling her against his body.

"Come here."

She rested her head on his chest, and Guy began to come to his senses. He stroked her golden curls. She hadn't reached her climax; what a ruthless first time she had had.

A deflowered angel.

He held her in his arms. He hadn't been gentle. He hoped at least that an embrace would somehow comfort her.

Jane said nothing. It had been such a strange birthday present for her.

"I'm sorry," Guy finally muttered. "The, uh... first time... is not very good for women, but... it won't be that painful in the future." He cleared his throat, embarrassed. "It won't be painful at all," he corrected himself. He didn't acknowledge aloud that it had been his fault, and his alone, if her first time had been such a disaster. Jane certainly knew that had he wanted, he could have made it more enjoyable for her, with kisses, and caresses, and sweet words. He hadn't wanted to slow down, this was the truth. He hadn't given her the time to get used to him. He had hurt her, beside himself to the point of almost coming inside her.

He had rushed everything with fury, just to prevent himself from thinking.

Just to stop his conscience from speaking.

And now it was too late. Under his hypocritical and inevitable shame, he was also feeling the fierce joy of having done the most selfish and wrong thing.

Jane put her hand on his chest, clenching his white shirt. She said nothing.

"Angel, do you happen to remember what I told you some time ago?" Guy asked her, stroking her hair. "When you asked me to keep you with me forever?"

Jane moved her head up and down.

Do you regret it now, my angel?

He didn't dare to ask her. He was a coward, he really was. Jane's blood shone vermilion against the white blanket, and he brought his hand to her cheek, lifting her face.

Jane opened her golden eyes, still moistened with tears. Her lips were red, swollen from the violent kisses she had just received.

Guy put his index finger to her lower lip, touching it with painful guilt. "This wasn't what an angel deserved, was it?"

"But that's what I wanted, Guy." Her voice was a whisper. She kissed his fingertips with tender devotion, even now, even after his brutal behavior. "I need you, I... how can I make you understand? These last five months have been the most beautiful ever since... ever since I was a child, Guy... when you were everything to me."

The words were a balm for him—and yet, stupid pain, and stupid thoughts, were still there, inside him. Everything to her, had he been? And yet, she had given him up so quickly back then. He tightened his hand on her shoulder. Her rejection had broken him. Without her, he had finally resigned to accepting his nature. He had accepted to be this killer.

To be this monster.

With her, he had hoped he could be different; he had even hoped he could be... what, *loved?* It didn't really matter, after all. He had just hoped a lot of stupid things.

"Why didn't you just tell me?" he heard himself ask. "About Sophie. Why didn't you ask me for an explanation?"

Why didn't you fight to get me back?

"I..."

Jane swallowed. Gentle tears wet his chest, but Guy couldn't forgive her. He didn't hold her tighter.

Why did you give up on me that easily, Jane?

"When I saw you with Sophie," she whispered, "my whole world fell apart. You were the only one I trusted, and you betrayed me." Jane's breath was warm over Guy's shirt; she didn't lift her eyes to meet his. "I had been foolish enough to think you loved me, but that day, I finally realized something. I could never have made you love me back, no matter how much I wanted to. Because... I wasn't worth that much to you." She paused, taking a deep breath. "*I'm* not worth that much."

"Jane, angel..."

"No, you need not lie about this." She swallowed many times before continuing. "Just look at me, Guy. I'm in this bed with you after I've seen you with another woman." Her voice shook. She cleared it and went on with effort. "But the truth is, I can't even think to live without you again. It was too painful to live without you. Feeling alone all the time. How can I make you understand what you mean to me? When I was a child, before meeting you, I could trust no one. I... you know, I..." She stopped, overwhelmed. "When I lived with the Gardiners..." she tried, but then she stopped again, shaking her head.

Words were failing her, yet Guy had understood what she was thinking about. And he hated her, he couldn't forgive her, but he wrapped her in his arms as she began to sob silently. "Shhh, my angel," he said. "Everything's all right. You don't have to speak about them if you don't want."

"But I need you to understand," Jane whispered. "It wasn't just the Gardiners. My father is a very special person, but... I know this is unfair of me, but I've never been capable of trusting him."

No, of course not. As Guy rocked her sweetly, he couldn't help but think: *that bastard Hartwell.* After the death of his first, beloved wife, Charles had left Jane in the care of some unaffectionate maternal relatives of hers—the Gardiners. The loss of Jane's mother had broken Charles's heart. He hadn't been able to take care of his daughter for a long time.

And Guy could never forgive him for that.

He checked his tongue and didn't say it aloud. He didn't intend to hurt Jane more. But inside him, he couldn't help but curse Charles, especially now, with Jane weeping quietly over his chest, sweet and tender and helpless. It didn't matter if Charles still regretted the way he had behaved back then. It didn't matter if he was only human. It didn't even matter how hard he had tried to atone for this mistake.

He had abandoned Jane for the first five years of life.

Fucking *five* years.

That bastard Hartwell.

Jane cleared her throat. "And Rona..." she continued in an unsteady murmur. "I loved her deeply, and I miss her every day. And yet, I never felt at ease with her. She... she used to think of me like an innocent, sweet child. Except I'm not that innocent, Guy. I don't think she'd have liked me if she had gotten to know the *real* me."

"Jane, you're the most innocent person in the world."

"But you know what I mean." She stopped him from denying it further, putting her index finger on his lips. "I think you *do* understand what I mean."

He kissed her finger, pondering her words. Then he slowly nodded. "Yes. I think I do."

Oh, Jane. She was innocent, of course she was. But she was right, her innocence wasn't the type Rona could have approved of. Rona had never understood her stepdaughter. The flames of passion had died inside Rona after her marriage with Guy's father. She could never have understood the sensual, stubborn, lovely girl Jane was.

This little after-sex chat of theirs was whispered. It was as if the pain Jane had just suffered had broken down some barrier inside her. Lifting her head, she looked at him with red, loving eyes. That look... how could he have believed he could live without it?

"You... you were the only one I really trusted." Her words sounded like a pained, inevitable confession. "You were the only one who knew me *for real*. And the strange thing was, you didn't care if I wasn't perfect. You didn't care if I was spiteful, or silly, or selfish. You accepted me just the way I was."

She was perfection, just the way she was.

"Well, I had to, didn't I? You'd have burned all my books otherwise."

She giggled between her sobs. "Oh, yes. I would."

The fresh air of May filled the room with its aroma. The sounds outside were birds, gentle wind, swaying grass. London and its grayness seemed so far from here.

Maybe Ashbourne House had been hell for some people. Sure it had.

To Guy, it was heaven.

Now, it was heaven.

"Do you know when I realized I could trust you?" Jane asked.

Guy had never questioned himself about it. To him, Jane had been part of himself since forever. "When I saved you from the Mole River?" he tried.

"No." Her hair brushed his chin with a gentle tickle as she shook her head. "I was already addicted to you on that wretched day. In fact, the picnic at the Mole River turned into such a disaster because I was trying to get your attention as usual. What I'm speaking about happened almost as soon as you and I met for the first time." She caressed him over the shirt he was still wearing. "It was because of that boy... the Smithers boy. Do you happen to remember him? He was the son of a businessman who came to Courtnell Street to meet my father. Your mother had married Papa only three days before, and we had moved to Courtnell Street to live together like a real family."

My goodness, the Smithers boy—of *course*, of course Guy remembered him, and involuntarily clenched his fist as he heard his name again. "Smithers, you say? I always called him *Shitface.*"

Jane gave a little punch over his shoulder. "Oh, but Guy!" she scolded him for the name-calling. But then she giggled. "You beat him to a pulp, remember?"

He nodded. A pulp—to put it mildly. He could still see the boy before his eyes. He could feel the fury he had felt back then. And there was also something else stamped in his mind.

"I remember you weren't calling for help," he murmured, feeling as bewildered as he had been when he had found Jane and the Smithers boy on the first-floor corridor. Guy was passing there by chance, because Jane wasn't screaming: that *shitface* was thirteen, she was five; the boy had cornered her against a wall, and he was a giant to her—but she *wasn't* calling for any help.

"No, I wasn't." Jane lowered her face over his chest, hiding her eyes from him. "When I lived with the Gardiners, they taught me not to bother them. So, you know, I... I believed that, had I been too much trouble to my father and Rona, they maybe... they..."

She shrugged and didn't end the sentence. It wasn't necessary. Guy had understood.

That *bastard* Hartwell.

"I don't know why that boy picked on me." Jane's looked away, remembering that day long ago. "Maybe he was just bored to wait for his father's meeting to end. Maybe he just wanted to have a bit of fun."

And she had been easy prey—a stammering, tiny, lovely little girl.

Guy didn't interrupt her to comfort her with a gentle word. He sensed she needed to talk after her violent defloration, his aggressive behavior. He stroked her head to console her with his touch.

Jane took his hand in hers and brought it to her mouth, kissing it tenderly. "That boy..." she murmured. "He grabbed a handful of my hair to hold me still. He had... he had this worm in his hand." Jane shivered with disgust. "He was bringing it near my face. I don't know, maybe he wanted to put it in my hair or maybe he just wanted to scare me. It was alive, I mean, the worm... it was long and was wiggling frantically in his hand."

And the helpless look Jane had had in her eyes—it had been the same look a fawn in the wood had had once. A look Guy could never forget.

Without releasing his hand, she lifted her head to look at him. "You overreacted *a little* that day." A mischievous smile appeared on her face. "Don't you think?"

"On the contrary. Shitface got *exactly* what he deserved."

"Oh, the poor boy." Jane's voice was compassionate, except she couldn't help but giggle again, both shocked and horrified. "I mean, Guy—you forced him to *eat* that worm in the end."

Guy chuckled. The memory was still *so* good. He was ten back then, Shitface was thirteen—but he was *Guy Spencer*. He was afraid of no one. And he had beat the shit out of the boy, while Jane looked at them with wide eyes a few steps away. He had beat him until that bully had begged for mercy. And then yes, Guy had made him open his lips, and had put the worm in his mouth, and had obliged him to *chew* it—and *swallow* it.

"Well, he was the one who said it was nice in the first place, wasn't he?" Guy replied in a very reasonable voice.

"He actually did," Jane agreed, and then laughed again.

Oh God, how he loved hearing her laugh.

"When Rona and the others saw him," Jane continued, "oh, dear! He was crying so hard. And his nose was bleeding to the point he left a trail all over the carpets. But of course, he didn't say it was him who started it. He said you attacked him for no reason." She became serious, and her hand clutched his shirt. "And I was scared, Guy. What if your mother found out you had beat him because of me? We'd lived together for only three days, and I was already causing trouble. What if she decided I had to go back to the Gardiners? So I... I asked you not to tell her."

And incredibly, he had understood her strange, babbling words.

Plllls... ainn't... s... ssay... Rona...

"And you didn't tell her." She lifted her eyes, and his heart skipped a beat. "She punished you severely. You couldn't leave your room for an entire month. She even confiscated your books and toys. But you did *not* tell her. And *that* was the moment—that was the moment when I found out I was no longer alone."

Her voice shook, and she leaned her forehead over his chest. Guy placed his hand on her soft hair. He could die for this girl, he realized. He would die for her right now, if she asked him to.

She breathed in and out, slowly, to regain control of her emotions. And then, suddenly, a little, shaky giggle escaped from her mouth again. "From that day on," she said, her voice trembling and laughing at the same time, "I began to pester you."

He remained silent a few moments before answering. God, it was difficult to swallow the stupid lump in his throat. "Are you admitting, by any chance," he muttered at last, "that it was you the one who pestered me and not vice versa?"

"And proud of it." She lifted her head and her eyes met his again. Hers were reddened by tears and dancing with joy, and trying to understand why such a contradiction was even possible would be enough to drive anyone crazy. "I always called you for help, only *you*. Sometimes I just pretended to be in danger, just to see if you'd come and rescue me. And you... always did."

He always had. He always would. And something grew inside Guy, something that was sweet, something that made him want to cry. A blessed moment in which his fears, for once, remained silent.

The smile on Jane's face slowly faded. Her hands tightened his shirt. "So maybe you can understand me now? Maybe you can understand why seeing you with Sophie nearly destroyed me. And today, seeing you with—" she swallowed hard before saying the name "—with Susan, it... it was..."

"Jane, angel..."

"No, please, please, Guy," she interrupted, whispering. "I know what happened can't be undone. I know it. It pains me, but I cannot do other than accept it. Because I can't live without you—it's terrible, and it makes me want to scream, but that's how it is. Just swear to me this: there will never again be another woman for you. Please... it would kill me if you cheated on me again. It really would."

Begging for the fidelity of a bastard like him. The world didn't turn in the right direction, that was obvious, and Guy found himself smiling tenderly. "Why on earth should I cheat on you, my angel?" he said, brushing her cheek with his fingers. "I need nothing else. In fact, I'm completely—" he put a hand over her beautiful ass, massaging it eloquently "—pleased with you."

"Then swear it," she whispered, "I'll do everything you want, but you must not cheat on me... ever again. Swear it!"

"Everything, you said?"

Jane blushed when she met his eyes, where passion was burning hot again.

"Everything."

He touched her lips with his thumb, then pushed it inside her mouth. Jane sucked it softly, pleasing him with love. Guy exhaled through his teeth. "All right," he muttered hoarsely, as she moved her head back and forth on his finger and licked it all around, "I swear it. I'll... oh, God, you're so beautiful, Jane... on our honeymoon, we'll have sex for days, I can swear *this* too... I'll fuck you *nonstop* for weeks."

Jane widened her eyes and threw her head back. "On our... honeymoon? Do you want me to... marry you?"

Guy laughed. Laughed at Jane's incredulous expression, at the tears of joy filling her eyes, at his own joy, and at every other fucking reason that made him the devil that, inevitably, he was. "Of course, my little countess. You don't really think I could continue to sneak out of your room at seven in the morning, every morning?"

"Will you marry me just for that?"

"*Just* for that? It's the best motivation I've ever heard for a marriage."

Jane looked down; she didn't seem at all amused.

"Are you already sad, little one?" Guy traced the contour of her face with his index finger, realizing once again how beautiful she was, how perfect... and his, God—she was his, and this time, it would be forever. "Don't be. You'll have plenty of occasions to be sorry for having married me in the future."

"So... you don't love me, Guy? Not even one bit?"

Love? Only love? To him, Jane was the air he breathed, the water he needed to quench his thirst.

He swallowed.

But she was the girl who had doubted him so easily. She was the one who would doubt him many times to come. He needed to keep her on a leash; it was the only way he had to be sure she would never get away from him. She said she loved him—but he couldn't rely on this. He had made this error once; he wouldn't repeat it.

"I'm going to marry you, aren't I?" he said. "Isn't that good enough for you, my angel?"

"But Guy, I..."

"Hey, you know what?" He moved her beside him, then rolled on top of her, sliding his hand down between her legs. "This little, sweet pussy has been treated harshly," he whispered in her ear, beginning to brush the soft curls between her thighs. "I think I should make up for it. Don't you agree?"

And he *did* make up for it, with his hands, with his kisses, with his tongue. He savored her flavor mixed with the blood of her defloration, until Jane climaxed in his mouth. And there she was—a beautiful young woman, soon to be a countess, having an orgasm on a bed stained with her blood, in the scandalous light of full morning.

52.

It was lunchtime at Ashbourne House, and as usual, the menu consisted of a succession of colorful, gourmet dishes. Four people approached the table, called by the sound of the bell.

Jane, with her face flushed and her head down. The bright color in her cheeks was proof of what had happened a few hours ago. There was a bittersweet joy in the twitch of her lips, a kind of shadow in her happy smile. The shadow of an unsaid "I love you," maybe, while looking at Guy from time to time, both glad and uncertain.

Stephen walked into the dining room talking about the weather with Charles, and furtively he scanned Guy's face, looking for new wounds or signs of pain from his friend's night's activities.

Charles moved his chair to sit down, then stopped. He nodded to the empty seat beside him. "Lady Susan isn't here," he murmured with a wry smile. "If we start lunch without her, she will bring the house down with her complaints."

Guy sat down. "She's not coming, I'm afraid, Mr. Hartwell."

The smile disappeared from Charles's face. "Oh. May I ask you why?"

"She doesn't work here anymore."

Jane clenched her hands on the back of her chair. After a moment, she sat down, careful not to show her face. *Poor little angel,* Guy thought. The wound Susan had done to her wouldn't heal anytime soon.

The wound *Susan* had done. It sure was a convenient way to think of it.

Charles did not sit down. In fact, he straightened his shoulders. "So, she left... and this suddenly, without saying goodbye to anybody?"

"She said goodbye to me," Guy told him with a cold smile. "A very *intense* goodbye."

"Did the two of you have an argument?"

Guy noticed, much to his surprise, that his stepfather was not indifferent to the whore he had hired for him. "Since when are you interested in her, sir?" he provoked him, pressing his shoulders against the back of his seat. "For five months, you barely exchanged two words with her."

Between the two men passed a look of understanding.

"I hope that's not why you sacked her."

Charles was finally speaking of what they had avoided talking about since Susan had started working at Ashbourne House. Narrowing his eyes, Guy decided to make a little fun of his stepfather.

"Let's just say she hasn't properly done the job I hired her for."

Hartwell's face went white with rage. Oh, that was so typical of him—to feel guilty for *not* having fucked a woman.

"You're not serious."

"Why do you care anyway, Mr. Hartwell? Lady Susan is very... *resourceful*, I daresay. She'll find a way to make her living."

Charles stepped back, away from his chair. His movements were much improved, and the stiffness he was showing, Guy suspected, wasn't due to physical pain.

"Come with me, you rascal," Charles said, turning away from the table without waiting for his answer.

Guy shrugged and stood up. He had to talk to him anyway. He might as well get it over with immediately. He glanced at Jane. They both knew what he would say to her father.

Stephen opened his mouth to say something. He had a puzzled look on his face. He seemed disappointed: he probably thought Guy had fired Susan over an argument about Jane, and considered that unfair. Guy raised his hand to stop his friend from speaking.

I'll explain everything to you later, he told him with his eyes. *Don't be upset, you pain in the ass.*

Stephen closed his mouth. Guy followed Charles down the hallway.

* * *

Charles moved decisively. He was using his cane, but perhaps he could have done without it. He opened the door of the study Guy had reserved for him at Ashbourne House and motioned for his stepson to enter.

Guy smiled at being treated like a child.

"I didn't fire her because she didn't seduce you," he said, anticipating his stepfather's question. He went to sit on a chair in front of Charles's desk. They were acting the roles of the naughty child facing a stern father, and Guy had enough sense of humor to play his part perfectly. "I sacked her because she seduced *me*, Mr. Hartwell."

Charles was moving to the chair behind his desk, but these words froze him like a statue of marble. "Oh."

"I see the news bother you, sir. To be honest, I'm happy to see that. I didn't think you were still functioning down there." He motioned with his chin toward Charles's pelvis.

"Have a little respect, kid." Charles remained standing, confused by the events. "I don't mind if you had sex with her. That's hardly any of my business, isn't it? What I don't understand is why you sacked her. Does it have anything to do with me?"

"It doesn't bother you *at all,* are you sure? And yet, your face is strangely green, Mr. Hartwell. Anyway, I'm sorry to inform you that, even though you admire her, the feeling was far from mutual. Susan had nothing good to say about you. If you really want to know, she deeply despises you."

His stepfather took a deep breath. Guy loved to see him lose his cool. He liked to find flaws in his damn patronizing condescension.

"You know what I like about you, Guy? You have this special tact when it comes to saying something unpleasant." Charles put his hand on the back of his chair, tapping his index finger up and down. "Anyway, you aren't telling me anything new, so stop gloating, big boy. Lady Susan thinks I'm here with the hidden agenda of becoming your father-in-law—as if anybody in their right mind would find something desirable about it. But if you've sacked her for this reason," Charles's eyes flashed with a green, angry light, "I'll make you swallow this inkwell." He actually lifted up the inkwell from his desk. "Pen included," he added.

"It would be fun to see you try to, but alas no, that's not the reason. I threw her out because she tricked me into... well. Let's say into having an *intercourse* with her."

"Oh, am I to understand she forced you into having sex with her? That's *so* believable."

Guy stroked an eyebrow with his finger, looking down. "Well, uh... no. Not exactly."

"Son, explain yourself. You hired the lady for me." Charles looked sideways at him., "And we both know it. I want to know why you sacked her."

"Very well, then. The thing is, Susan didn't want to have sex with me any more than she did with you. I'd have preferred not to have you know this, for I'm enjoying very much to see you jealous, but it's the truth."

"She never put a gun to my head to make me lower my trousers."

"I don't have any trouble believing it." Guy grinned, although his predominant feeling wasn't exactly joy. He didn't know how he felt. He was feeling too strong an emotion to be able to name it. Jane was his, now and forever—and this was ecstasy. But if Susan "The Whore" Emerson hadn't tricked him into this, maybe he'd have let Jane marry someone else. Someone better than him, someone who could have made her a *mother.* Jane said she couldn't live without him, and he, stupidly, couldn't help but hope it was true. But love is just a word, isn't it? And if Susan hadn't been the whore she was, maybe Guy wouldn't have condemned Jane to stay with him. Maybe he'd have found the strength to do the right thing—giving her up. He could have at least tried to drive her to hate him.

Or maybe not, and he was just kidding himself. Because to him, love was *not* just a word. Jane was an illness too rooted in his soul to ever be healed.

Anyway, now it was too late. There was no way back.

And that was scary... and wonderful.

He cleared his throat, uncomfortable with what he was about to say. "She was pretty convincing to me. Susan, I mean." The whore, he added to himself. He clenched his fist, still angry about the scene Jane had had to witness. Poor sweet, wounded angel. "But she didn't do it for me, Mr. Hartwell. She did it for your daughter."

These words ripped the look of faked indifference off Charles's face. This conversation was no longer about his barely concealed sexual desire for Susan Emerson. His stepson wasn't mocking him anymore.

"She did it... for *Jane?*"

"Please sit down, Mr. Hartwell. I need to tell you something." When the man just looked at him, motionless, Guy nodded more explicitly toward the chair. "I will not utter a word until you get your ass on that seat."

His stepfather clamped his jaw tight. He moved to the chair and sat down. "She did it for Jane, you said?"

"She did. You see, Susan wanted to prove a point to her. More specifically, she wanted to show her what a filthy libertine I am." Guy drummed his fingers on the desk, clearing his throat. "So this morning she entered my bathroom. I was without clothes, and, after a few minutes, she was in the same... situation. Do I need to be more explicit, sir? Do you still remember what happens between a man and a woman when they're both naked?"

"Guy."

"You really liked her, didn't you?"

"Don't push me too far, big boy. We're talking about my daughter here. What does Jane have to do with all of this?"

"Haven't you figured it out yet? Jane came into my bathroom while I was... well. Having that *intercourse* I told you about." God, the look on Jane's face at that moment... the distraught pain she had felt. Guy thought he could have strangled Susan. "It didn't happen by chance," he murmured with his gaze down. "Jane wouldn't have come to my bathroom, of course, if your adorable milady hadn't written her a note, asking her to come there."

"Oh Jesus," Charles exclaimed, distressed. "It must have killed Jane to see that."

"Kind of." Guy cleared his throat. "Actually, more than you can imagine."

Charles did not speak for a few minutes, with an anxious expression on his face. "I see," he murmured finally. "That's why you sacked Susan then. She dared to show Jane what a libertine you are. But she didn't actually do anything wrong, Guy. You know that, don't you? My daughter had a right to know. That sure was a... a somewhat rude way of opening her eyes, I'll give you that. It was cruel. But perhaps it was the only way to convince her you'll never marry her."

Guy laughed. He couldn't help it. "No, Hartwell? Jesus Christ, haven't you got it yet? Of course I'm going to marry her."

His stepfather's mouth dropped open. He stayed like that for a few moments, then stammered: "W-what?"

"Jane and I have to get married, Mr. Hartwell. When she saw me with Susan, she was... let's say upset, all right? Damn it. Distraught. She was distraught. I... I followed her to... oh, by God. I've made a mess, all right?"

"A... mess?"

"Yes, well, I... I mean," he rubbed his forehead with his fingers, nervously, "really, I don't know how to tell you this, Mr. Hartwell. Let's just say I have to marry Jane. I leave you to guess the reason. But please, don't look at me like that. It wasn't my fault. It happened because of that whore... I mean, Susan. The only thing that makes me happy is that the damned woman will go back to be the mistress of her stinky brother-in-law, as she used to do before coming here."

Charles looked dumbfounded. "Guy, let me get this straight," he managed to say. "You've just told me this morning you had sex with Susan, and now you're saying that you're going to marry my daughter. Did I get it right?"

"What part of 'I have dishonored Jane' didn't you understand?"

"She was upset and you wanted to console her?"

"What I wanted..." He stopped. "Hartwell, for your peace of mind, please don't make me answer more questions. Listen," he said to try to calm his stepfather down, "Jane is not mad at me. Not anymore, anyway. You shouldn't be either."

"Shouldn't I? Are you kidding me? Jane saw you having sex with Susan, you ran after her and had sex with *her!* With my *daughter!*"

"It wasn't quite like that." It was exactly like that. "For Christ's sake, Hartwell," Guy snapped, "what else was I supposed to do?"

"Certainly not that!"

"Well, it's done now. I can't change it."

"So the two of you will get married just because you have messed everything up?"

"Well... yes. I couldn't have said it better, sir, your sense of romance is overwhelming." He exhaled slowly. "Anyway, what about putting an end to this conversation?"

"Guy, I haven't—"

"Mr. Hartwell," Guy interrupted him, "do you happen to remember what I told you when we talked about a... a possible marriage between me and Jane?"

"Hell yes, I remember well enough."

Guy pretended not to notice the anger of his future father-in-law. He stood up. "I don't see, then, what else we have to discuss. Truly, I think we are done here, Mr. Hartwell." *And may God forgive me,* he added to himself. "I think it's best to plan the wedding as soon as possible. I'll ask Weymouth to handle the details. He's good at this stuff. You may discuss the marriage contract with him anytime. I guess you want to see Jane, now," he said, going to the door in an attempt to end the conversation. "I'll tell her you're waiting for her."

"Oh, you're *not* getting out of this that easily! I need to talk to you, come back here, Guy Spencer, Earl of Ashbourne! This morning you were having sex with another woman, by God. That's what you're used to? Fucking women in bathrooms? I'm warning you, you'd better behave yourself once you're married, or else you'll have to deal with me."

Guy had stopped, but he hadn't come back to sit down again in his chair. "I was fucking Susan, yes," he snapped, exasperated at this accusation. It always came back to this, didn't it? To this same, bloody, *false* accusation. "I couldn't do it with your daughter, but, you know, maybe you're forgetting this detail."

"You *did* it with Jane, are we or are we not talking about that?"

"I'm going to *marry* her, Mr. Hartwell. This usually solves this kind of problem, so please, just out of curiosity, tell me: are you really upset, or is all this fuss just a pro-forma thing you are supposed to do as a father? Dammit, I honestly thought you would be happy about the way things have turned out."

"I don't know," Charles said, his voice low and tired. "Jane is so in love with you, Guy. Oh, damn. Now she's over the moon, I guess. I just didn't expect it to be like this. I mean, you jumping from one bed to another with such ease."

"I don't jump from one bed to another, but you know what? You want to think so, be my guest. I'm not going to waste another breath on this crap."

"Guy, don't go. Wait."

Charles's voice was quieter, and stopped Guy when he had already turned toward the door. He looked back at him. Charles was just a father who cared about his daughter; and, after all, Guy had to admit he wasn't quite the ideal son-in-law.

"Do you love her, Guy?" Charles asked softly. "Or are you vaguely aware of your feelings toward her, anyway?"

"If you think of any legal detail related to the marriage settlement," Guy said, putting his hand on the door handle, "let me know within a week."

"Guy..."

"No, that's enough, sir. Some time ago, I explained to you my doubts about marrying Jane, and you said I should ignore them. Now you can't blame *me* for what happened."

Why, wasn't it wonderful the way he was passing the blame? Guy had two scapegoats, not just one, for what had happened this morning. Susan "The Whore" Emerson and Charles "The Annoying Stepfather" Hartwell.

Just perfect.

Charles took a slow breath. "All right, then. But you said we can talk about the marriage contract."

"Actually, I'd prefer you to talk to Weymouth about it."

"Guy, I need to talk to *you*. I want you to give Jane an allowance. She needs to have some economic independence as your wife. Some *personal* independence."

Guy smiled dryly and stepped outside the door. "Don't worry. In case of my death, she'll find provision made for her in my will."

"No, that's not what I..."

"In case of my death, Mr. Hartwell."

"Why do you still feel the need to have her under your control, big boy? You've finally found the unconditional love you've always been searching for. What are you still afraid of?"

Guy walked out of the room making no answer.

Watching him leave, Charles realized something. In the marriage between Guy and his daughter, the most insecure of the two wouldn't be Jane.

53.

An elegant, beautiful lady stopped on the sidewalk opposite the orphanage. A man was watching her from around the corner of a house. He knew that the woman would remain motionless for a few minutes. Just enough time to have a quick look at the orphanage kids playing in the garden, then she'd go away. Just as she had done yesterday, and the day before.

He gathered his courage and approached her.

"Why don't you go in?" he asked when he was still behind her.

This startled the woman, causing her to jump a little. She didn't turn toward him immediately. It was typical of her: before turning, she wanted to plaster a mask of impassivity on her face.

"Mr. Hartwell," she finally said, turning slowly around. "What a *wonderful* surprise."

Charles grinned at her sarcasm. "I knew you would be pleased with it, Lady Susan."

She smiled coldly. Charles didn't remember her being so beautiful. No, that was bullshit. He remembered *exactly* how beautiful she was.

"I got things to do." Susan began to walk away. "And since I don't consider your presence a good enough reason to stay... goodbye, Mr. Hartwell."

She raised her chin smugly. Charles reached out and grabbed her arm.

The woman stopped and coldly looked at the hand that held her, then looked at him, making him feel terribly rude.

Charles released her. "Please, just give me two minutes of your time."

"You're not worth two minutes of my time."

"Why? Because I was right and you were wrong?"

Susan raised her eyebrows. "Your daughter is betrothed to the Earl, yes—I read about it. The newspapers write about nothing else, actually. So, you got Ashbourne's money and status, did you not? It's not so important that he'll make Jane unhappy, I guess."

"He won't make her unhappy."

"Oh, come now, you seriously..." She stopped and shook her head. "Mr. Hartwell," she began again, "I don't understand why you're trying to convince me. It's a waste of time—my time, for frankly I don't care about yours."

Charles rolled his eyes. God, she was so annoying! "Guy loves Jane just as much as she loves him," he snapped. "Don't you see it?"

"That man is incapable of loving."

"How do you know?"

Something—a feeling Charles wouldn't name—stabbed him in his stomach.

"Because he's a sadistic bastard. He's a villain. He'll make your precious Jane miserable. But you don't care, do you?"

"A sadistic bastard, is he? Just out of curiosity, where did you get this piece of information from? I'd like to know. From the rumors in some clubs, from the veiled accusations you can read in the press?"

"I wouldn't have believed those sources. My information is first-hand. The Earl himself told me so."

Charles laughed.

"I'm glad you're having fun," said Susan, puzzled. "And since cruelty seems to amuse you, if you like I can pick up a newspaper and read to you about the ongoing wars, or about the horrible murders perpetrated by the Gang of Knives, or about any of the thousand atrocities which happen daily."

"No, cruelty does *not* amuse me. I'm laughing because... come on, haven't I already told you that what Guy *thinks* and what Guy *says* are two different things altogether? You should learn to doubt yourself a little, madam. You said he would never marry my daughter, and you were wrong. You are not infallible, you have to admit this much at least."

"Why?"

"Why what?"

"Why do you want me to admit that, Mr. Hartwell? To feel at peace with your conscience?"

"I am at peace with my darn conscience! I..." Charles blushed and hoped that the slight tan he had gained during the hours spent in the garden of Ashbourne House would cover his emotion. "I feel indebted to you," he murmured, lowering his voice to a more civil tone and taking refuge in a half-truth. "I know what you did was intended to protect my daughter. That... 'trap' you set for my stepson, ten days ago. I know, I know—I'm not supposed to talk about it. Politeness would require me to feign ignorance. But you had lost your position because of that, and I feel compelled to thank you. Given your uncertain financial situation, it was no small sacrifice on your part."

"You need not thank me at all, Mr. Hartwell. I wouldn't have remained at Ashbourne House for much longer anyway. You know—" she looked down upon him with contempt "—there were people there who made the air unbreathable."

"So, what are you going to do now? You didn't go back to your brother-in-law's."

Charles felt his cheeks grow hot as he revealed how hard he had looked for her since the day she left Ashbourne House. It had been very difficult to find her, damn the woman. Charles had started searching for her at Viscount Emerson's palace, but the unbearable milady wasn't there. So he had asked Weymouth to help him, but Guy's friend had lost track of her. Close to despair, he had almost resolved to seek help from Guy, even at the inevitable cost of having his stepson make fun of him. Fortunately, that had not been necessary: the coachman, Lewin, had unexpectedly given him the information he needed. One afternoon, as Charles was climbing into the carriage to go to his doctor for a check-up, Lewin had mentioned Susan, much to Charles's amazement. The coachman had said that, while waiting for Jane outside the orphanage to bring her home, he had happened to see Lady Susan walking on Moorhouse Road three or four times. On these occasions, she had stopped in front of the orphanage and had just stood there, for about ten minutes, watching the children play outdoors. Then she had walked away. Lewin had told Charles he didn't quite understand why she behaved like that.

Charles did.

He did understand Susan and her thorny heart. With annoying surprise, he had realized a truth about himself. He wanted to see her again not just to thank her. He wanted to see her because he was smitten with her.

Susan's eyes flashed with understanding. A smile appeared on her face. "Don't worry," she said with heavy irony, "your stepson paid me well, and I put a little away. So you see, for now I can stay away from my brother-in-law. In any case, whatever I do—" her smile intensified, her purple-blue eyes shone with the confidence of having the power to hurt him "—it's none of your concern."

Charles took a breath. It couldn't get any worse—he might as well risk everything. "Maybe yes."

"Beg your pardon?"

"I'm offering you a job, Lady Susan."

"A job, no less." She shook her head, a mocking smile on her beautiful face. "Let me guess which one."

"Oh, just stop it!" he blurted out—and again he cursed himself. "You know I'd never ask you... for heaven's sake, you are exasperating, milady!"

"I'm not holding you here, you know. If you want to go... just go."

"No, damn it, first I want to finish what I started. I'm here to tell you that I... I'd like to hire you as my assistant. In my perfume shop, I mean.

You have pretty good taste, you're classy, in short... you'd be very useful to me."

"You really want me to work for you?" Susan raised her eyebrows, disbelief written all over her features. "I'm the worst person for this kind of job."

"No, you're mistaken." With his hand shaking slightly, he took a small glass bottle from the inside pocket of his coat and handed it to her. A golden liquid filled the bottle. No label was on it. "I'd like you to smell this, before you say no."

Susan rolled her eyes. "You're trying to convince me with your perfumes? I have smelled them before, and no offense, but I don't think they could convince me."

"This is... a new one." He didn't know where he had found the courage to say it—say it to *her*, no less. Susan, who wished nothing but to hurt him! Probably she would say his perfume positively stank.

It didn't matter anyway. She was the one who had to smell it first.

"Very well, then," she replied with an emphatic sigh. "If that's what it takes to make you go away."

Charles's heart began to race in his chest. Susan took the cork off the bottle and lifted it to her nostrils.

Four years had passed since Charles had tried to create a perfume. Now it was here: an aroma with the harshness of blackcurrant and the sweetness of iris flowers. He had made the first attempt a few days ago; a strong emotion had sprung up within him and he hadn't been able to recognize it. He had had only one choice: express himself with his only talent. A new perfume. He hadn't realized he was thinking of a particular person while creating the fragrance. He had realized it only when he had chosen the name for his creation.

Lady Susan's Heart.

Susan sniffed, once, twice. Finally, she put the cork back on the bottle and handed it to him. "It was not as bad as I expected," she said noncommittally, but when she met his eyes, hers widened with involuntary emotion.

"It's as thorny as you," murmured Charles, "but has a tender heart. May I?" He took the bottle and pointed to her hand. "Could you take your glove off and show me your wrist?"

He was almost exceeding the limits of propriety. It was full morning, and around them people came and went, glancing curiously at them. Susan bit her lip, hesitant. She stood perfectly still, then, with her handbag on her arm, turned her wrist up and pulled her glove an inch or two down, showing him her bare skin. It was a gesture Charles found agonizingly sensual.

Across the street, in the little garden before the orphanage, the children were singing a cheerful song. Their voices could be heard from where Susan and Charles were; gentle notes mixed with the scented air of the last day of May.

Charles removed the cork, wet with perfume. He rubbed it on Susan's wrist. He held his breath as he touched her skin. It wasn't anything scandalous... from the outside; fortunately, Charles's thoughts were hidden within him. He took her hand and gently lifted it, looking into her eyes. He held her wrist close to his nose. He inhaled the warm fragrance of her skin and his chest swelled with emotion. It was a wonderful fragrance, it really was. And Susan had added the missing element.

"Perfect," he whispered hoarsely.

Susan blinked. It was hard to tell if she was blushing or not, because of the rouge on her cheeks; but her eyes—peculiar eyes, of a blue so intense that it seemed somewhat violet—widened, shining with something that looked like pleasure, fear... and confusion. As Charles breathed in her skin again, she cleared her throat.

"This is the worst seduction attempt I've ever seen, Mr. Hartwell."

Oh, what a pathetic try to fake indifference.

"Really?" Charles smiled, pressing his thumb against the skin of her wrist. "Then why is your pulse beating so fast?"

With a sudden, almost scared gesture, Susan withdrew her hand. "Because I dislike you, that's why."

"So... you're refusing my job offer?"

Susan brought her wrist up to her nose and inhaled. After a moment she dropped her hand. "No," she replied, with an acid voice that couldn't quite conceal her embarrassed expression. "No, I accept, Mr. Hartwell. It's an excellent opportunity to make your life impossible. But if you're hoping I'll sleep with you—" she gave him a wry look "—you're going to be sadly disappointed."

Moorhouse Road was bright in the sun, even its stone pavement seemed to glow, and people were already wearing the warm colors of summer. A few white clouds emphasized the blue of the sky; and Susan, with her mauve hat, her elegant figure, the beauty of her heart, was just a step away from him. After more than a year of grief, regret, and guilt, Charles could finally taste happiness again. He held out his arm to her with foolish pride, and Susan took it with the haughtiness of a duchess.

"I'll be disappointed, will I?" he asked, beginning to walk with her at his side. "I wouldn't be so sure if I were you, Lady Susan. As I had the pleasure of telling you, you are not infallible in your predictions."

54.

Stephen was sitting behind the desk in Guy's study. He had turned his chair toward the open window. The curtains were pulled back, framing the view of the garden and, beyond it, Green Park. It almost didn't look like London, with all that green and blue, and clouds as white as sugar.

Sitting slouched with his legs straight out in front of him, Stephen was clutching a bottle of whiskey to his chest with his right arm. It was Macaulay's whiskey, of course; the new supply Macaulay had sent Guy. His friend kept hiding it in the same place.

Stephen hugged the bottle like it was a newborn baby. When the door opened, he closed his eyes and took a breath. And he prayed to God that he could finish his speech without crying.

* * *

Guy saw his friend sitting at his desk, sunk in his chair.

"Well, look who's back," he muttered, approaching him. During the last month, they had seen each other very little. Stephen was busy on the one hand with the Gang of Knives's accounting, and on the other with Hartwell and the wedding preparations. Basically, Stephen was never home; he came back to Ashbourne House late at night and communicated with Guy through notes.

Guy reached his side and stiffened. Because of the bottle his friend was hugging, and because of his appearance. Stephen had lost weight and was thin and pale.

Guy clenched his fist and wondered if he should punch him in the face.

Stephen stopped him by speaking softly. "No, I drank nothing but water. This whiskey?" he asked, raising the bottle. "I just enjoy holding it tightly. As an arrogant man once told me, now I know secrets that save lives." He grinned without humor. "And I don't drink or do drugs anymore."

"So what's wrong with you? Are you mad at me because you're not going to be my groomsman?"

Stephen's answer should have been amused. It was just tired. "I was the one who first suggested St. Court as your groomsman."

"Bullshit. I know you'd want to do it. But I'm sorry, man. Marrying a bourgeois girl like Jane could definitely make me an outcast. The Gang can't allow this to happen, so I need the Duke to get me back into the good graces of my peers. Just deal with it."

In response to that chatter, intended just to fill the silence—and to avoid the lecture that Guy sensed as imminent—Stephen merely shrugged.

"Well, then, what's your fucking problem?" Guy finally snapped. "For fuck's sake, for a month now you've been looking at me like I'm Bluebeard. Tell me then. That's why you're here, right? You want to tell me I'm a pig, a crappy son of a bitch. You want to tell me I should not marry her."

Stephen's chest rose and fell quickly under the horrible brown coat he was wearing. It was the kind of clothing his friend loved. Guy, of course, found it pathetic.

"You knew from the beginning it would end like this, didn't you, Ash?" asked Stephen, waving the bottle and gazing at the liquid in it. "You knew from the beginning that you'd marry her."

"No. Of course I didn't." He turned and walked to the window, placing a hand on one side of the casement. "I just wanted to take revenge on her, for everything she put me through when we were kids."

"Yeah, sure. Do you really believe that?"

"Why not? It wasn't such a crazy plan. I just wanted to have a little fun with her until I got tired of her. But..." *But you don't tire of breathing.* "But everything went wrong," he finished softly. "All because of Susan and her fucking good intentions."

"Revenge, seriously? Guy, please, stop this bullshit. We both know that's a lie. You never hated Jane Hartwell; admit it for once. Admit it *today*, the day before your wedding."

"I *did* hate her, W. Deeply. I still hate her." He watched outside. The park, the gushing fountain, the bright greens of new life everywhere. He thought about Jane, about her words. Now he knew what had happened after their first kiss, many years ago. Now he could understand how much she had suffered from his unknowing betrayal. He could even understand her broken heart. He just could never—*never*—forgive her for not having *fought* for him. For having given him up—while he had never given *her* up.

He never would. He never could.

"Above all, I hate the fact I need her so badly," he admitted in a low whisper. "I can't stand it. It makes me weak, it makes me do stupid, wrong things. Like..." He paused, then confessed his mortal sin. "Like marrying her."

"That usually is not called 'hate,' old bean. That's why you'd never let her go, whether or not dishonored."

"I... I don't know, all right? I just don't know. I want to believe so." He gave a bitter smile. "I want to believe I'd have let her marry a man worthy of her. A man who... who would have given her children. I... W., look at me. I'm a murderer. I will always keep secrets from her. I'll never tell her I was the one who put her father's company out of business. She'll never know what I do when I go out at night, when I play the vigilante hero on missions from God."

Or from the devil.

Up in the sky, swallows were darting backward and forward, a few white clouds dotted the deep-blue vault, and Guy thought back to two nights ago, when Jane had cried in bed because he had been out until dawn; his angel had smelled the scent of soap on his skin as he had come near her, and she had thought he had been with another woman. Guy had mumbled about card games, and then had made love to her, with sweetness and passion, the only way he had to show her his desire for her, just for *her*. But the doubt, inside Jane, would continue to gnaw like a worm throughout the years to come: on all the nights when he would not come home, whenever his explanations would sound like pathetic lies.

"She deserves better, I know that," he said softly. "So you see, there's no need for you to go around with that hangdog look on your face. You want to convince me I'm full of shit, but see, I already know that." He leaned forward, resting his hands on the base of the open window, breathing the June air. "It's just that... fuck it all, Steve. Have you ever wanted something you couldn't have? Have you ever wanted at least a little taste of it?"

Stephen's voice, behind him, sounded slow and full of a strange tenderness. "Oh, yes. I have, old bean. Every day."

Guy straightened and turned to face him. "And yet you're blaming me. Jesus Christ. If even you, who were ready to *die* for me, think I'll make a bad husband to her, I have no chance to make her happy."

"I don't think you'll make a bad husband to her."

"So... why do you look this down? Are you maybe... in love with her?"

"Oh by God, you just don't understand, do you?"

Stephen put the bottle on the desk with a slow movement. He stood up and moved toward him. He walked firmly yet languidly, as if there was no need to rush because, sooner or later, he would reach Guy anyway. He stopped before him, he smiled. He put a hand on the back of Guy's neck and pulled him close, and it was so shocking that Guy couldn't think how to react; he felt his friend's lips on his own, his taste of tobacco and musk; it lasted just a moment, a barely damp, soft touch, and the next second Stephen released him and took one step back.

"Is it now clearer to you what we're talking about here?"

Guy blinked and put his hand to his own lips.

"I just came here to tell you I'm leaving, Ash. I think you can understand why, now. But if you feel sick—" he took a slow breath in "—

please tell me, and I'll leave right now."

Guy couldn't answer. In fact, he couldn't even think. But... Stephen was...? He was... oh, for Christ's sake!

"I see," muttered Stephen. "Then there's nothing more to add, I guess." He turned away and walked toward the door.

Guy shook himself from his shock. "No, wait. Wait a minute, for fuck's sake!" He reached out and grabbed the sleeve of his friend's coat. Stephen stood still, and Guy understood at once many, oh so many things. He abruptly let go of his sleeve. "Let me fucking think," he said, feeling as if his world had turned upside down. "What do you mean, you're leaving?" he asked, starting the conversation with practical matters; he loved pragmatism, especially now that the whole world seemed to have gone mad all around him. "Leaving for where?"

"For my brother's estate, in Derbyshire. He needs some help with the management of Bevelstoke Grange, and I believe it's time to prove to my family that I'm worth something. So you see, Ash. From now on you won't have to worry about me."

Behind Guy was a chair. He dropped onto it, bewildered by the revelation.

"Must I bring you a chamber pot?"

Stephen spoke lightly, but his eyes were bright with unshed tears, his face was tense with the need to control his emotions.

Guy tried to put his thoughts in order. He couldn't even look Stephen in the face; he looked down at the floor. "But you... God, W. We shared women together. Betsy..."

Stephen chuckled, a bittersweet laugh. "Maybe it's time for me to confess that it wasn't Betsy I was so attracted to, during our, uh... threesomes."

Guy put his hand on his neck, unable to lift his eyes. All right, that was embarrassing. "Oh."

"Do I disgust you so much you can't even look at me, Ash?"

Guy raised his head. Steve. He was Steve, just the same as ever. His brown hair in a ponytail, his horrible coat. His best friend.

"I saw you lying in your own piss," Guy said, and the words came out just like that, without thinking, "I saw you crying like a baby, drugged to the point of not finding your own ass. You didn't disgust me then, and you certainly can't do it now, just because of a peck on the lips."

"It's not just a peck on the lips."

"I know what the fuck it is," he snapped. "Don't... damn it! I'd just like to pretend that I don't know. Why did you tell me? I would have much preferred not to know!"

"I told you because..." Stephen paused and swallowed. "Guy," he started again, "I told you because tomorrow will be your wedding day, and...

and call me a selfish, ungrateful bastard, but the thing is—I can't bear to see you married. I just can't. I'm not perfect, Ash. I can't witness your joy and pretend to be happy myself. I have to leave, you understand that, don't you? Not because I think you'll make Jane unhappy. Come on, I think she is the luckiest woman in the world. At first, I was angry at how you were treating her, but then... then I just got jealous. What a hypocrite, huh? But I am the man I am, Guy Christian Spencer, 4th Earl of Ashbourne. Or maybe you don't even consider me a man anymore, after, you know... *this.*"

Guy rubbed his forehead with his hand. "Can't we just pretend this conversation never happened?" he murmured finally. "Come on, W. I've been with hundreds of women. Why should things change between us now?"

"Because you *love* Jane. Do you understand the difference? Could you ever bear seeing Jane in love with another man?"

No. Never. The answer shot through his mind, despite all the lies he had always told himself. Oh, God—it would kill Guy to see Jane in love with another man. "That's bullshit, Stephen," he replied dryly. "You're not going anywhere, you can't even wipe your nose by yourself."

"I won't be by myself. My brother will be with me. He's not bad, after all."

"Your brother can't count to three. He finds it hard even to count to two."

"That's why he could use my help. I'd feel useful to someone at last."

"You are useful *here.*"

"Guy," Stephen said with a kind of desolate patience; "I can't stay here. I love you, man—not just as a friend."

"Could you please not say that?"

"See? And you expect me to stay here?"

"You don't want to stay in this house, fine. You don't have to. You can stay away from me for as long as you want. One month, two months. Take all the time you need to... damn it. To move on."

"One month, Guy? It's going to take more than my fucking *lifetime* to 'move on.' "

"Take all the time you need, all right? But I want to make one thing perfectly clear. I won't let you go where I wouldn't know what's going on with you. If left to yourself, you are like a three-year-old child."

"It's you who makes me so weak, bloody hell! You manage my life, you treat me like a child. It's time for me to learn to walk on my own legs."

"That's just a big steaming pile of bullshit. You're not going anywhere, and that's all. End of discussion."

Just like that. End of discussion. Guy Spencer had already decided everything; and Stephen felt astonishment at his friend's inability to understand him, frustration at his insensitivity... until, finally, he was overtaken by a wave of rage at his arrogance.

"You just want to control me, Ash!" he snapped. "You're so full of shit, you don't even know it. You want Jane, you want me, you can't give up anything because you're a selfish bastard!"

"I never said I was a nice person, did I?"

"You are... you... oh, the devil with you, Guy Spencer! Why am I still wasting my breath on you anyway? You can't do anything to stop me!"

He turned and took a step. A moment later, he was slammed against the wall, Guy's hand tight around his neck, and his friend screaming into his face.

"I can stop you all right, you bloody idiot! The Gang needs you, and you know a lot of our fucking secrets! Just imagine what would happen if I told St. Court you were a threat to the Gang. He'd lock you in a dungeon somewhere without a second thought, is that what you want me to do?"

Stephen's eyes widened. He didn't defend himself. "You would never tell him something like that."

"Of course I would. You said you're not perfect, well, you know what, you fucking scumbag? I'm not perfect either. And I will never wash my hands of you, you hear me, Steve? I... I care for you, you asshole son of a bitch." He suddenly let him go and turned away, with a frustrated exhale. "You're like a brother to me."

"Like a brother..." Stephen repeated with a slight, bitter smile. "That's not enough for me, Guy." He spoke gently, as if trying to make him understand how he felt. "Shall I tell you the things I dream of doing to *you,* when I'm in my bed at night? Guy, turn around and look at me: shall I tell you the things I dream you doing to *me?*"

Guy turned and pointed his finger at him. "No, I don't want to hear another word about this. You know what? This conversation never took place. That's it. I'm sorry, W. I don't see why your being a poof should change things between us. You like taking it up your ass, so what? I want to take care of you just the same. Just deal with it."

Stephen smiled, partly exasperated, partly touched. "You have a special talent for saying things. God, you're such an asshole." He leaned his back against the wall, pressing his hand to his eyes. "Do you have any idea how hard it's going to be for me, Guy?"

"You'll get through this. You'll move on."

"As you moved on from Jane Hartwell?" He laughed bitterly. "You'd never ask St. Court to imprison me," he murmured softly. "I know you wouldn't, Ash."

Guy just looked at him. Actually, he *might* ask St. Court to lock Stephen somewhere... for a few days. Just for a few days. Stephen was right. His threat was a bluff.

Stephen paused, rubbing his eyes. "So, you care for me, huh?" he asked, lowering his hand and shooting him a sideways look, with a slight smile on his lips. A smile he had given him so many times, a smile whose meaning had always escaped Guy.

God, life was a bitch. It really was.

"Yeah," Guy replied softly. "But don't tell anyone."

Stephen smiled, but his eyes filled with tears. "Ash, I need to stay away from you for a while. I can't stay here with you and Jane. I... I can't even look at you."

His voice trembled, and a stupid, sad emotion pushed against Guy's chest too. They were getting as sentimental as two little girls, God damn it all to hell. "Fine," he said softly. "I'll be here when you're ready to see me again. I want to make one thing very clear, though. It doesn't matter where you are, if you do something stupid, I will know... and I'll come and break your knees. Got it?"

"You're a bully," Stephen sighed. "By the way, I suppose you've already decided where I'm going to live. And what I'm going to do. In Bolton Street again, spending my hours staring at the ceiling?"

Guy cleared his throat. Pragmatism again, thank God. He loved it when he could finally talk about practical things. Everything seemed easier when he thought about what to do, and not about stupid, irrational, uncontrollable stuff like feelings.

"What about... working for Hartwell?" he mused aloud. "You'd be very useful to him. He's pretty pathetic at his business. I went to his factory a few times, and you wouldn't believe what a mess it is in there."

Stephen shook his head. "Actually, he doesn't need my help at all. Susan is helping him enough—more than enough."

"Susan? The Susan who used to work here? Lady Susan *Whore* Emerson?"

"That very Susan." Stephen smiled without looking at him, still embarrassed. "You know, it looks like your plan worked in the end, Ash. At least judging from all the little digs Susan and Charles throw at each other. I've been spending a lot of time with him, for we needed to discuss Jane's marriage settlement." He took a breath, pausing for just a moment. "And he and Susan coo like pigeons. They're hardly bearable. It wouldn't surprise me if they got married in a month or so. And get this: one day I happened to knock at Hartwell's office door. He made me wait ten minutes before opening it, and when he finally did, he was rather disheveled, if you know what I mean. His hair was a mess, his shirt sticking out of his trousers..."

"...and let me guess," Guy interrupted him, "Susan was in the room with him, and she was disheveled too." He and Stephen shared a look of total understanding, like the thousands they had shared over the years. "She really is a whore, admit it now, W. Hell, when *I* asked her to seduce him, she did not even try."

"Susan is lovely. And you know it, even if you try and deny it."

Guy shrugged. "And St. Court?" he asked, changing the subject. He had given up seeking revenge on Susan Emerson, but he wasn't ready to forgive her. Susan was the one he would blame for all the tears Jane would shed about him in the years to come. He fucking needed to be angry at Susan. It didn't matter that, as Stephen had pointed out, he would have found a way to marry Jane anyway, dishonored or not.

"I beg your pardon?" asked Stephen, puzzled.

"I said, what about St. Court? You could move in with him and work full time for the Gang."

"Hmm." Stephen frowned in concentration as he thought about it. "I don't know, Ash. Does he like being fucked in the ass?"

"Steve."

"Hey, I've been holding this in for a really long time. Let me at least have a laugh about it." Stephen grinned, and a sense of vertigo washed over Guy as he realized that this was the last time they would laugh together like this. It was the last time they would look at each other with such complicity. The thought froze the hilarity in Guy's throat, and he doubled over slowly, like a convalescent.

Stephen... he had always been there for him.

Losing him, God—it hurt like hell.

55.

Guy was wearing an elegant dark suit. Just his tie was white. The church was filled with noblemen, commoners, reporters. There were so many people there. St. George's, Hanover Square, was the most fashionable church for a wedding, and only the richest, noblest people of the *ton* were allowed to marry there.

Like Guy Spencer, the 4th Earl of Ashbourne.

The most prominent aristocrats of England were about to attend his wedding, despite the ceremony taking place on very short notice. Just one month's notice, in fact. But the presence of Guy's groomsman, the Duke of St. Court, made this bourgeois marriage acceptable by his peers. It was a well-known fact that it wasn't wise to mess with the Earl of Ashbourne. And mess with both *him* and the *Duke* would definitely be a suicidal choice.

Guy looked down the aisle of the church. It was kind of strange to have Stuart standing by his side, instead of Stephen. It was even stranger that his friend wasn't there at all. He would spend today alone, in a room of St. Court's palace, smoking tobacco and crying his eyes out. God, what an idiot he was.

An idiot Guy would miss every day.

Bejeweled ladies, sitting on the wooden benches, made the place as colorful as a garden with their large flowered hats. There was a lot of pink, white, green. There were many monocles and lorgnettes over important noses. Everyone was whispering and pointing at the Earl of Ashbourne, who, against all odds, had decided to marry young; not even twenty-six. The press had indulged in the most fantastic speculations on his bride's past. The favorite hypothesis was that the Earl, by choosing his stepsister (a middle-class girl, no less!) as a wife, had wanted to fulfill his mother's last wish. This conjecture was so wrong, Guy couldn't help but smile at the absurd irony of it.

Behind Guy, near the altar of the church, was a boy appointed to light the candles. Maybe the boy's hands were shaking with emotion, for he dropped the long candlesnuffer he was holding. It fell to the ground with a heavy echoing thud. Guy turned to him. The boy was thin, tall, and there was a big smile on his face. Guy sighed and gave him a small nod of recognition. Paul Bailey, chuckling softly, picked up the candlesnuffer from the floor and moved to the right wall, where the shadows would hide him.

What a reckless boy. Paul wasn't supposed to be there. The Five Knives should never be seen all together all at once.

Yet, he *was* there. And he wasn't the only one so reckless, in the Gang. A little earlier, while passing through the crowd, Guy had spotted a woman with unusual red hair. One of Isabelle Smith's wigs. Isabelle was sitting on the far corner of the third bench on the left, wearing on her face the pious and innocent look of a schoolgirl.

James Sutherland was the only member of the K-Gang missing at Guy's wedding. He was the least sentimental among the Knives, the most rational and professional one. He would never risk his cover by attending the wedding of a Knife. He wasn't a fool—not like Paul or Isabelle. But Guy had a weakness for fools, and, although he would never confess it—and although Four and Five would make fun of him in the next few days, laughing at him for being such a nervous groom—he was happy to have them at his wedding ceremony.

There was a low, continuous chatter in the church. Everybody was waiting for the bride. Guy looked toward the main door, motionless.

It was dark at the other end of the aisle. When the main door opened, light filled the church. For a moment, the figure standing in the doorway was just a silhouette against the light. Guy narrowed his eyes, and saw a white dress, a slender body—a beautiful face, covered by a transparent veil.

The eyes under the veil were pure gold. Guy, even at this distance, could recognize their shape, their color... their stunning beauty and sweetness.

* * *

Jane, on the arm of her father, stood at the entrance of St. George's, blinking as she went from light to shadow.

All eyes were on her. She didn't realize it. Her heart was slamming in her chest, her head throbbing, emotion made her almost dizzy. Her gaze ran down the aisle. At the altar, among the shades of the walls and the light coming from the colored skylights, a man was waiting for her. He was tall and imposing, dressed in black; sharp rays of sun hit him, casting bars of light and shadow across his face. He had ebony hair, his nose was slightly crooked, his eyes flashed with fierce heat. As his gaze met Jane's, he bared his teeth in a white smile, and it looked like a wolf's smile.

Jane lifted her chin up, took a trembling step, and began to walk toward her future husband.

His name was Guy Spencer. He was the man she loved, the man who owned her body and soul.

He was her beautiful monster, the monster that had always been waiting for her in the dark, around the corner of the attic. Now he had caught her, and might God forgive her, Jane was happy, oh so happy, to be finally in his arms.

The End

Printed in Great Britain
by Amazon

41141588R10235